Michael Jecks began his series of medieval West Country mysteries after thirteen 'interesting' years in the computer industry. He finds writing just as insecure at times but much more fun! He and his wife live in northern Dartmoor.

His seven previous novels featuring Sir Baldwin Furnshill and Bailiff Simon Puttock, most recently THE LEPER'S RETURN and SQUIRE THROWLEIGH'S HEIR, are all available from Headline.

Acclaim for Michael Jecks' previous mysteries:

'Jecks has a real knack of bringing to life the medieval era of the West Country . . . SQUIRE THROWLEIGH'S HEIR has enough twists and turns to satisfy everybody . . . An excellent addition to the series'   *Shots*

'A gem of historical storytelling . . . authentic recreation of the modes and manners, superstitions and primitive fears that made up the colourful but brutal tableau of the Middle Ages'
Northern Echo

'Girt about with a goodly helping of period authenticity . . . ends up with a thrilling cop and robber chase on horseback'
Oxford Times

'Jecks' knowledge of medieval history is impressive and is used here to good effect'   *Crime Time*

'A goodly tale in the vein of Cadfael, and equally enjoyable'
Coventry Evening Telegraph

'Combines the whodunnit format with a loving attention to detail, with lively, intriguing descriptions. It . . . will help you turn back the pages of history and enjoy the depth and texture of a long-vanished England'   *Croydon Advertiser*

'A medieval mystery to rank with the best'   *Northern Echo*

Belladonna At Belstone

Michael Jecks

headline

First published in hardback in 1999
by HEADLINE BOOK PUBLISHING

First published in paperback in 2000
by HEADLINE BOOK PUBLISHING

11

ISBN 0 7472 6361 2

Printed and bound in Great Britain by
Clays Ltd, St Ives plc

HEADLINE BOOK PUBLISHING
A division of the Hodder Headline Group
338 Euston Road
London NW1 3BH
www.headline.co.uk
www.hodderheadline.com

For Donald and Mercia
with much love

Glossary

Calefactory
Every monastery or nunnery would have had a calefactory or 'warming room', in which a good, blazing fire would be kept going through the colder months or when the days were chill.

Chapterhouse
This was the chamber in which the nuns would meet to discuss important business. Elections for new leaders could take place here, as could discussions of any issue which might affect the smooth running of the community.

Choir (also **quire**)
In a religious institution, this was the name given both to the clergy involved in performing the services and to the part of the church where they did so.

Cloister
This could refer to the whole religious precinct or an enclosed area set apart from the rest of the world; in this story the cloister mainly refers to the specific area in which nuns or monks would work, read, or merely walk. At the centre (see **Garth** below) was often a good-sized, square lawned area, around which all the other buildings were ranged.

Dorter
This was the dormitory block in which the nuns would have slept.

Familia
In the slacker convents, groups would tend to eat together regularly. While their Rule said all should dine together in common, often nuns chose

	to eat at slightly different times with their own *familia*.
Frater (also **refectory**)	The name given to the hall in which the nuns would eat.
Garth (cloister-garth)	This is the name given to the small yard, usually grassed, which was situated at the middle of the cloister.
Horarium	This was the timetable by which monks and nuns regulated their day, beginning with *Nocturns*, the first service, usually held at about 2.30 a.m., and ending with *Compline*, the final service. For the full sequence, please see over.
Laver	The room in which nuns or monks would wash. In many convents the laver would have had fresh water piped from a spring or river, sometimes brought a great distance in lead pipes.
Rere-dorter	This was the toilet block, often, like at Castle Acre, out at the rear of the dorter itself. It would lie over the top of a large channel so that running water could wash it clean. Wastes were sometimes allowed to build up and the water blocked off by means of a wooden sluice so that the deposits could be collected for fertiliser. Similarly urinals were used less for convenience and more because urine was used to manufacture vellum, or to bleach linens.
Suffragan	When a bishop was forced to spend time away from his diocese he would install a suffragan to act as his deputy and to see to the cure of the souls.

A Winter Horarium

Programme of offices to be held during winter months taken from Archbishop Lanfranc's schedule for the Benedictines of Canterbury. The times given are estimates only, for a small convent like St Mary's would have had no accurate clocks.

At about 2.30 a.m. the nuns would all be roused from sleep and called to attend the choir of the church. Here they would sing psalms and offer prayers until the first of the services, the *Nocturns*, after which the nuns would continue with *Matins*, which would be followed by *Prime* at dawn.

Once Prime was over the nuns would go out and sit in the cloister, reading until about 8.00 a.m. when they would all return to their dorter, or bedchamber. Here they would change their shoes, then go to the laver, where they would wash in preparation for the next service.

Terce was followed by *Morrow Mass*, after which the nuns would all go to their chapterhouse for their daily meeting. At this any admissions of failings or accusations of lapses could be brought up, and apologies or penances offered or imposed.

Once the daily chapter had concluded, the nuns would spend their time either working or reading until noon. Then they would all go back to the church.

Sext, *High Mass* and *None* were all celebrated, and at last the nuns could go to the frater for their only full meal of the day. This was followed by more work or studying until about 5 p.m., at which they would return for *Vespers* in the church.

Vespers was the last ceremony of the active day, and afterwards the choir would change into their night slippers and go to the frater to drink. In the medieval age people depended upon a diet which included much ale or wine, because the solid diet did not provide enough essential vitamins or protein.

Finally the nuns would troop back to church to listen to a

reading, and then would hear the last service: *Compline*.

After this, at between 6.30 and 7 p.m., the nuns should have gone to the dorter to sleep.

From the records, it seems clear that many did not.

Cast of Characters

The Inhabitants of St Mary's

Lady Elizabeth Prioress of St Mary's, a regal figure, born to a great family, and somewhat daunting for that reason. She's getting quite elderly now, being in her fifty-first year.

Margherita The treasurer is a deeply religious woman, the illegitimate daughter of another nun, Sister Bridget, who ran from the convent many years ago. Margherita is younger at only thirty-nine years, and wants to take over complete control of the convent, convinced that she would be better able to maintain discipline.

Constance At thirty-one, Constance is one of the younger nuns, and is committed to helping those who are weaker. She is the infirmarer, the woman who looks after the ill.

Joan Once the cellarer, now Joan is too old, at well over sixty, to continue with her work and is semi-retired. Unfortunately a chill has forced her to rest in the infirmary where the fires should warm her frail old body.

Denise The sacrist is dedicated to serving the church itself, ensuring that it is clean and ready for any of the services.

Ela This woman is the kitcheness, responsible for cooking and preparing all the meals for the nuns.

Emma Heavy-set and strong, Emma is the new cellaress, responsible for seeing to the storage of food and drink in the buttery and undercrofts.

Anne The refectory, or frater, is her domain, and she has the duty of ensuring that the hall has clean tablecloths, enough chairs and benches, that the floor is kept clean and that knives and spoons are provided.

Cecily An unfortunate lay sister who has managed to break her arm in the laundry. She is resting in the infirmary.

Katerine A young novice of some twenty-one years who is keen to see herself promoted. She is convinced that she will hold a position of authority.

Agnes	This novice is one of Sir Rodney's conditions; he asked that she be accepted as a novice.
Godfrey	An older man, at fifty-five, Godfrey is a canon in the male part of the church, known as a good surgeon when needed.
Luke	Younger, the handsome Luke is the priest in the nuns' church, for women, of course, may not hold a religious service.
Jonathan	Another older canon, Jonathan is the doorkeeper, making sure that no dangerous strangers can gain access to the precinct.
Paul	A young canon, Paul is deeply religious, which has led him to doubt the sanctity of Lady Elizabeth's leadership.
Elias	This lay brother works in the smithy, but now desires to escape.
Rose	Almost twenty-one, Rose was once a novice, but now has run away, and makes a living as best she can.
Moll	This young novice, pious and keen, is the girl whose death causes the investigation by the suffragan, Bailiff Puttock and Sir Baldwin Furnshill.

Author's Note

The village of Belstone sits high on the moors overlooking the deep valley that separates it from Cosdon, the massive hill that is visible from almost anywhere in northern Devon. I have known the area for years, for my brother and I visit it each New Year's Day, and walk with wives and families down south to the moors.

It was this year, 1999, that we went to walk down towards the stream, and while strolling among a heavy clitter, I mused it was much like so many spots where monks and nuns chose to site their convents, an idle thought that eventually gave rise to this story. I invented St Mary's.

Nowadays we think of abbeys and priories being set in delightful places, almost invariably among trees, with lush vegetation and parkland all around. That's because since the Dissolution, many have been converted into houses and gardens, their lands cultivated over centuries. Beforehand they were often wild, remote, cold and bleak. It's true that in sunshine they are beautifully romantic ruins, but that is because we visit them on holidays when the summer sun warms us and the ancient nature of the wrecks can give us a comfortable sense of the passing of the years. Yet for all the delights of the larger ecclesiastical holdings at Rievaulx, Westminster, York, Fountains and Whitby, many others sprang up and disappeared, unable to support their communities with their poor and scrubby land. The two years of famine (1315–17) speeded the end of some of these, as did the two murrains or plagues, first of sheep (1313–17) and then of cattle (1319–21), which devastated the English economy. Smaller, less financially viable convents were swallowed up by wealthier ones. Some of these monastic buildings can be traced on the ground, but their walls have been ravaged by time and their stones removed by farmers who wouldn't pay for dressed stone when it was lying nearby. Many have simply vanished without trace.

When you look back, you find that the *obedientiaries* – the

nuns or monks – had a miserable time of it. Woken for the first
service at some time between midnight and 2.30 a.m., they had to
go to their church in their rough woollen clothing and stand for an
hour or more in the freezing cold, trying to sound musical as they
went through the psalms and prayers. There was no fire nor any
other means of heating, and in the winter it must have been sheer
hell. Not all convents could afford glass in their windows, either.

That was part of the trouble: money. In the late 1200s there was
a rapid increase in the number of men and women taking up the
religious life, and many convents started to accumulate money
from patrons so that they could expand, but many simply couldn't:
they didn't have the finance behind them. That was why in the
early 1300s many places, as I have outlined in this book, went to
great lengths to acquire parish churches so that they could use the
revenues. Some, like the convent at Polsloe, greatly increased in
size, but others failed to win the money and faded away long
before the Dissolution.

Nuns found it particularly difficult to support themselves. The
reason was simple: when a rich man died he wanted to ensure that
his soul had as smooth a passage into heaven as possible, and to
this end, he would set up a *chantry*. This was a chapel which was
dedicated to honouring the dead man, holding services and praying
for him every day. Depending on how wealthy the man was, the
more prayers he could buy; the more prayers said for him, so the
logic went, the faster he'd be let in through the Pearly Gates.

But there were problems for nuns: first, nunneries tended to
depend upon the goodwill of their strong neighbours, and so they
would sometimes agree to take in their neighbours' daughters in
exchange for benefits, such as money, which inevitably led to
many of the convents having too many inmates for their means.
The risk of over-filling nunneries was recognised at all levels
within the Church, and not only bishops but popes too sent letters
to convents forbidding them to take on any more nuns.

The second issue was still more difficult to resolve. A man
wishing to set up a chantry wanted services held in his memory,
but this was a time when no woman could hold a religious service,
so nuns had to acquire their own priests, and what would be the
point of endowing a religious Order which couldn't even hold its
own ceremonies? Men were more happy leaving their charities to

male institutions: the force of monkish prayers was bound to have a greater impact than those of a bunch of women!

Some readers may be surprised to see that I have created a priory with men and women, but this was more or less the norm. As I mentioned above, there had to be priests to conduct services, but also, although nuns were supposed to be completely hidden from the outside world and although they did have lay sisters to do the more mundane work like washing and ironing, they generally had to have men about the place. Men farmed; men tended the buildings; men saw to the religious services; men guarded the gates to the precincts. It was true that most of the nuns were segregated and should never have been tempted by a male form, but that did not work for them all. For one thing, the priory's bailiffs, reeves, receivers and other senior officials would have been men, and all had to report to the prioress. That was why it was not uncommon to hear rumours of impropriety between prioress and her chief steward. They got to meet.

Tales of nuns misbehaving are not new, and many such stories are no doubt apocryphal, but it has to be accepted that some were true.

Young girls were thrown into their nunneries without any thought for them or their needs. No doubt some would have learned obedience, and in an age when women were possessions to be used as their menfolk saw fit, perhaps some were content. Yet this does not mean that all of them would have been happy with their lot, and records prove that many nuns were not chaste and a large number ran away. The nun of Watton was not unique, and no, I didn't make up her story. Likewise the collapsing of roofs was not unknown – at Morton the abbess allowed the church roof and the roof of the dorter to fall in. Funds which should have been used to repair them were squandered instead on Master Bryce, the vicar.

When nuns did run away, they were often sought. If found, errant nuns were sometimes treated with respect and sympathy, but once back in their convents, they would be forced to undergo a penance before being set back to work. And all too often these desperate, sad women would try to escape again. Several have been recorded as having thrown off their religious robes, committing the act of apostasy which so horrified their sisters, rejecting all the vows which made sense of their secluded lives.

And yet their lives weren't unremittingly miserable. For those who lived in a great convent, they might have been chilly, but so they would have been in any great hall; they almost certainly lived a great deal longer than their counterparts outside the nunnery; and if the quantity of food wasn't always enough, a nun would have access to ale or wine, there would always be a good fire roaring in the calefactory, and at least there would be no fear of rape or murder by a drunk at the roadside, nor an early death from childbirth.

If any readers wish to find out more about the lives of medieval nuns, I can heartily recommend Colin Platt's *The Abbeys and Priories of Medieval England* and his *Medieval England – A Social History and Archaeology from the Conquest to 1600 AD.*

It is always difficult to recreate life as it might have been, and any errors in this novel are entirely my own. All I can do is claim the best of intentions.

Michael Jecks
Dartmoor
March 1999

Preface

She was lucky not to have died.

It was a glorious day in late winter, almost early spring. The sun beamed down on the lay sisters as they hung out the washing, larking and joking. In this weather the land took on a more cheerful aspect; the moors glowed with a salmon freshness in the morning and even the drab grey of the moorstone was touched with a pink glow.

They were in the yard where the lines were strung. To get there they had to step carefully round the muddy pools with their wicker baskets on their hips, avoiding the cowpats which led to the dairy, stepping delicately over the small round pebbles of sheep excrement and the tiny deposits left by the prioress's terrier. There were many hazards in a busy priory's yard.

Agnes didn't hear them at first. The novice was too busy thinking about her meeting later with the priest. It was only a short while since she had seen him with another novice, Katerine, and Agnes still wondered whether she ought to forgive him, or whether she should refuse to speak to him ever again – but that would mean cutting off her nose to spite her face, not an attractive prospect. Brightening, she reflected that Katerine would find it intolerable, should Agnes win him back; it would mean he preferred her to Kate. Agnes was persuaded. She'd go to see him as he'd begged, and provided he showed true remorse, she would forgive him. Pleased with her decision, and feeling the thrill of anticipation, she hastened her steps as she rounded the corner of the rere-dorter to come to the yard north of the cloister.

Seeing the lay sisters and their antics, she stood watching them wistfully. Lay sisters weren't full nuns, they were women who were prepared to take their own vows, but lacked the education or intelligence to give spiritual service. Instead they offered their labour to the glory of God. As such they weren't political or ambitious – unlike nuns – and at times like this Agnes could feel a twinge of jealousy for the simplicity of their lives.

Agnes had enough troubles with Kate, but Kate wasn't her only problem. There was that miserable God-botherer Moll as well. The young novice was so full of cant, she wouldn't be truly happy until she'd died; Moll's sole pleasure appeared to be watching over the other nuns and pointing out their failings. She liked making other people miserable. No one was safe while she wandered about the place.

Katerine wasn't much better, of course. She liked uncovering other people's secrets too, but at least she strayed from the straight and narrow often enough herself. Agnes knew Kate was capable of blackmailing for her own benefit, but while Agnes knew so much about her, Agnes felt safe enough.

A sudden gust whisked about her. It whipped on, tearing at the clothes hanging on the lines, snatching at the linen in the lay sisters' hands. They squealed and giggled, and Agnes grinned. It was good to see them enjoying their work. They had so much to do, it was a miracle that they found any pleasure; but some of them were simple and others were mere serfs, peasants, and Agnes was sure *they* wouldn't need much to make them happy.

Then Agnes had to give a deep belly laugh. One of the girls, a tall, rather vapid creature called Cecily, missed her step while rescuing a white cloth. Trying to avoid stepping in her basket, she stumbled, and her foot landed on the rim. While she watched in horror, it flipped up. Another breeze blew past just at the moment as if maliciously determined to complete her ruin; it caught the basket and swiftly up-ended it.

Cecily raised her fists to her cheeks, wailing with dismay, while her friends roared their delight. Then Cecily let her arms fall and stamped with impotent rage. She stared heavenwards, screaming, 'God's bollocks! Damn and bugger!' as the contents of her basket soaked up the mire from the track.

* * *

She had to do the whole lot again, of course. Cecily thought it was unfair: anyone could have been unlucky and seen their basket tip, but the laundress was insistent. Cecily had let all her washing fall in the dirt, so Cecily could clean it again.

She rubbed her back, then put a pot of water over the fire. When it was boiling, she wrapped a cloth about the handle and carried it to her barrel, poured it in then dropped her linen in and began the laborious work of pounding it with the wooden club. When the worst of the muck was off, she wrung out the clothes and put them into fresh water, scrubbing the material up and down on a roughened board.

This laundry was a ground-floor room to the north of the cloister. Once it would have been too large for a priory this size, but now it was too small, for the northernmost wall had collapsed, and part couldn't be used. A temporary wooden partition had been erected to keep the worst of the wind and rain from the girls inside, but Cecily hoped they could get enough money to put up another wall. Breezes got in and froze the lay sisters as they worked.

The whole place was falling apart, but Cecily tended not to think about it. She was content while she had food in her belly and a gallon of ale to drink each day. Matters of finance were for those who were educated enough to comprehend them, not for the likes of her. She was only a servant for the nuns.

It was a position that satisfied her. She didn't seek higher responsibility. There would be no point, for she would never be able to understand the duties of a nun. All the same, sometimes, when she glanced about her, she wondered whether the prioress was protecting the place as well as she should. Flagstones in the yard were coming loose, there were holes in the roofs, and not only the laundry's wall had fallen. Others were weakened and looked dangerous.

Still, it was none of Cecily's concern.

The basketful took her another hour. By the time she had finished, her arms and chest muscles ached. Sitting back, she closed her eyes and yawned luxuriously. Slowly she clambered to her feet and picked up the damp washing. From here she had to walk down a wooden staircase to get to the yard, which was lower than the cloister itself. She picked up the basket and rested it upon her hip, walking quickly to the door.

At the top step she glanced down to make sure where to put her feet. Then, with the speed of assurance, she carried on down.

But after two steps she felt someone grab her ankle. Her eyes widened. She had no time to make a sound, it was so unexpected. The basket flew from her hand and she pitched headlong, falling the six steps to the ground. It was flagged in stone here, and she caught a glimpse of the moorstone rushing to meet her. In a reflex she brought her arms up to protect her face just in time.

She was so jarred that at first she couldn't believe what had happened. Then she heard the voice: 'Never blaspheme again.'

As the steps faded, the pain began to stab at her. Looking down, she wondered what the thing before her was. Then she recognised it was her arm's bone, red and bloody as a raw oxen's rib, shoved through the flesh of her arm like a dagger through parchment.

She managed to shriek just once before fainting.

Chapter One

From Moll's perspective, being taken to the place where she would soon be murdered was merely an irritation. She knew she was well and didn't feel the need for segregation in the infirmary, especially since it was impossible to get any sleep there, what with Joan snoring and Cecily moaning to herself on the bed beyond.

There were compensations. The fire made it almost as cosy as the calefactory, the hall between the dorter and the frater where nuns could warm themselves. Here, though, there were no nuns except the infirmarer; and although the room glowed with a cheery red light, and for the first time since the onset of winter Moll was neither cold nor hungry, still she could not relax. Her arm itched where Brother Godfrey had bled it.

In the pitch dark she stretched out under the sheets, wondering what could have woken her. There were no strange sounds in the room; mercifully even Joan was breathing quietly like a drowsy hog, and further on Cecily whimpered softly. Both women had been drugged. Before long she expected to hear the bell for Nocturns, the signal for the convent to wake to life, and Moll was aware of a guilty but luxurious delight, knowing she was free of her usual duties and could remain here in bed.

Moll was young to be a novice, but she had gained her place as a result of her father's string-pulling. He was, if not a great banneret, at least a well-known knight in Exeter, a man of some influence, and although he had not wanted her to take the veil, she had insisted. Ever since she could remember, Moll had felt the lure of conventual life: as a child she had thrilled to the stories told by the mendicant friars; as a teenager she had been keener to attend daily Mass than go riding with her friends. She had learned to read with the help of her priest, and was soon proficient at writing and arithmetic. It was this which had served to persuade her father, for a woman who could both read and write was potentially an uncommonly useful wife to a wealthy lord, able to administer his estates during his inevitable absences, but the sort of husband to whom Moll could aspire would be of a lower order – a squire or knight. To such a man, a wife with Moll's skills could be threatening. It was better that she should be safely lodged in the cloister.

Closing her eyes, Moll offered a prayer to God, thanking Him for her many blessings. There was much to thank Him for. He had allowed her to take up the challenge of a life of obedience, and had installed her here, where there was so much to be done – for the little priory out on the windy, rain-swept northern fringe of the chase of Dartmoor was, to Moll's eye, a pit of corruption. She intended to change all that and see that the nuns turned from their loose living to the ideal of the contemplative life.

Arriving at the section of her prayer where she thanked God for her health, she hesitated, unsure whether it would be right to thank Him for what she had suffered. She was not, if she was honest, grateful for the headache or for being bled again, and being a conscientious young woman she felt it would be wrong to say that she was. Moll didn't want to be hypocritical; perhaps, she thought, she should ask the priest when she next had an opportunity ... No, not the priest, she amended quickly. She couldn't trust Brother Luke, not since the time he had tried to molest her. A quick frown passed over her brow and she moved to a more wholesome topic.

She didn't feel ill any more; the migraine had gone even before the bleeding. When it struck she had thought she would faint; the mistress of the novices had released her from her duties and sent her here to the infirmary, where she had been told to fill a flask with urine so her condition could be assessed. It was in vain for her to explain that the headache had quite disappeared, for Constance, the infirmarer, refused to listen until she had received her instructions. In the meantime, Moll was filled with red meat and a thick broth, the best food she had eaten since her arrival.

It was all quite normal, of course, and Moll herself was ready when the phlebotomist, Godfrey, had arrived, a smiling cleric of fifty or more, short in the body, with a good paunch and an almost circular face. He had kept up a constant chatter while he tied a cord about her upper arm and passed her the bowl to hold while he stropped his razor on the leather, explaining that her body had accumulated noxious humours in her liver, and possibly her spleen. She must have them evacuated by letting blood flow from the basilic vein, near the elbow.

He paused a moment, knife in hand, a twinkle in his eye, then winked before making a careful cut, drawing the bowl in her hand underneath to catch the drips. 'That was easy, now, wasn't it?'

She nodded, watching her blood. Her father had been a firm believer in the prophylactic benefits of purging the system regularly, and Moll had been bled at least twice a year. There was no pleasure in seeing the wound, but there was nothing to fear about it either. As for the pain – well, that was only a faint tingle from so sharp a blade. The irritation would come later, when the scab formed and the skin puckered.

When he considered that enough had been taken, the physician anointed the wound with a styptic and wrapped it up in bandages. 'There! That should be enough for now. Now you stay here for three days, and when that time is done, you may go back to the cloister.'

Godfrey had tiptoed from the room as if she had already been asleep, still smiling, and she'd not realised he had left one of his knives and a small parcel behind until he had gone. Constance came in a little later, pouring out measures of her narcotic drink, ready mixed with strong red wine. Moll told her about the priest's parcel, but the nun was indifferent: his memory always was dreadful, but he would soon be back for another novice's vein, and he could collect the knife then.

Remembering him, Moll recalled his insistence that she should drink wine to cleanse her system. She licked her lips. It was warm, and she was thirsty. At the table by her side was the cup measured out by Constance. Moll had tasted it when Constance had served them all. Now Moll tried it again. The first sip made her wince: it was hideously bitter. She was about to set the cup back down again, but there was nothing else to drink, and Constance must have left it there to help her sleep. With a resolute air Moll upended the cup and emptied it, setting it down on the table before falling back and smacking her lips in disgust.

Later, Moll woke with a start. There was a curious clenching sensation in her belly, as if someone had grasped her stomach and was regularly tightening their grip; a hollowness at her throat made her feel as if she was going to be sick.

She opened her eyes. There was no light, apart from a dull glow in the hearth. Joan wasn't snoring for once and Cecily was whistling heavily as she exhaled in a deep sleep. All Moll could hear over Cecily's breathing was a light step. She heard the door open then close, and the creaking of the stairs, the murmur of voices. It hardly seemed important.

Soon she would be well again, Moll thought dreamily, and would be released from this room to undertake her mission. That was how she looked upon it: a sacred mission to cleanse the priory. God had sent her here to show the women how they were failing Him: Agnes by her lewd behaviour with the priest, Katerine with her greed, Denise with her gluttony and drunkenness, and the treasurer with her avarice. All were guilty – not least the prioress herself.

But thought was becoming difficult. Moll was befuddled, found it hard to concentrate. The wine mixed with her medicine must be very strong, she thought. The room seemed to be whirling, and she still had that feeling of nausea.

God was pleased. As she drifted off to sleep, that reflection soothed her. She had begun to show each of her sisters the error of their ways, and she was convinced that her words would soon begin to bear fruit, no matter how much they disliked it – or *her*.

Lady Elizabeth of Topsham, prioress of St Mary's in Belstone, jerked awake, her eyes opening wide in an instant.

She hardly dared move. Something must have caused her to waken, and in the dark of her curtained bed her imagination took flight: a draw-latch had broken in and was even now preparing to attack her; a serf, bitter at the priory's taxes, had decided to take revenge on the woman responsible – herself; or maybe it was a felon desperate for sex, full of lusty dreams of young, nubile nuns. Her heart thumped; she was almost sure she could hear the rasping breath of a broken-down villein, hear his shuffling footsteps approach, his hand gripping a dagger. Cowering back, she glanced about her for a weapon, but there was nothing – what would there be on a bed?

Shrinking back, covered in a cold sweat, she prepared for the inevitable, determined to behave with dignity. But suddenly she realised her dog was silent. The intruder must have silenced Princess! With a courage born of the desire to protect her dog, Lady Elizabeth resolved to look her attacker in the face. She reached out and jerked the bed's curtains aside.

Her fire crackled in the hearth, its glow giving off enough light to see that she was safe: the chest at the foot of her bed was unopened, as was the small cupboard at its side; her door was still shut, the window shuttered, although the movement of the tapestry showed breezes were gaining entry through the broken panes.

Princess, who slept on her own cushion near Elizabeth's bed, gazed up at her with bleared eyes. The terrier yawned, stretched and shook herself, before slowly making her way to the bedside and gazing up. Lady Elizabeth reached down and lifted her onto the bed. Princess nuzzled affectionately at her chin before curling up. Smiling, the prioress scratched at the terrier's head, glad that the dog appeared well again. Earlier Elizabeth had thought Princess might die. The dog had been taken with another severe bout of vomiting.

Elizabeth wondered what could have woken her. It wasn't Princess, for she had been asleep, so who – or what – had? Her heart was still beating with almost painful intensity; her waking terror had not left her. She hardly thought it could be a dream, yet there was nothing to concern her.

It was a huge relief to hear footsteps. Crisp, echoing, in the chill air of the cloister, they were proof that her world was unchanged. It was the nun going to the bell to call everyone to prayer.

She pulled her miniver counterpane up to her chin, snuggling down beneath her blankets, squirming. Princess grumbled to herself at being disturbed.

It was impossible to ignore the dog. Princess had been the prioress's companion for seven years, and over that time had taken a firm hold on the woman's heart. That was why Princess's repeated seizures were becoming so alarming. First the dog whined, then began panting, before vomiting and emptying her bowels. Last evening Elizabeth had been worried lest the terrier wouldn't see the dawn, but after an hour or two Princess had lapped thirstily at her bowl of water, into which Elizabeth had put a little wine for strength, and fallen into a deep sleep.

It was a relief that Princess had recovered so speedily. Elizabeth was sure it was only something the bitch had stolen to eat. She often ate carrion when she went out over the moors. There were always dead sheep and ponies to chew.

The bell pealed and Elizabeth heard her obedientiaries groan and murmur as they got up and prepared to make their way to the church. As always, most went quietly in the freezing corridor, huddling their arms about them, walking with their heads down, chins resting on their breasts, trying to conserve the warmth of their bodies by leaving as little of themselves as possible exposed to the bitter draughts that gusted about the dorter and church. None of the women had the energy even to bicker, not at this time of night; all Elizabeth could hear was the soft slapping of their night-slippers on the flags.

Moll stirred again before the bell, lying in a relaxed haze, her eyes scarcely open, absorbing the atmosphere with near-ecstatic yet languorous delight.

She felt as if she was in a glorious dream, aware only of a

sensuous ease in the comfort of her bed. In the hearth the logs glowed, then flamed spontaneously as the wind outside sucked at the chimney; the candles in their great holders spat and sizzled, dripping thick gobbets of wax with each fresh gust – but to Moll the room appeared suffused in a soft golden light which enclosed her within its soothing embrace.

She heard footsteps hurrying, a man's voice, speaking low and urgently, then the hasty shutting of the door. Moll knew that something strange and wonderful was happening to her. She was safely wrapped in her sheets, and somehow she was also floating inches above the bed, protected by the warmth of the room. Her body was fluffy, as light as a feather, and all sensations were dulled other than one: that of love. Although she was only a novice, she felt the certainty of God's love for her, and she closed her eyes and smiled. It felt as if He was smiling back at her, and she was convinced that here and now she had been transported from the infirmary and was somewhere else with Him, standing in the bright sunlight. Her very soul tingled with voluptuous excitement.

With a thrill of euphoria, she was aware of being touched, and although she felt a reverential trepidation, she wanted to cry from sheer bliss, convinced she was about to be granted a vision of heaven. She tried to open her mouth, but it was stopped, covered, and she smiled, thinking God was granting her the kiss of peace.

The pressure grew; she tried to return the kiss, but her lips met something else – cloth? – and it was being shoved upon her heavily, not gently. It threatened to stifle her. Moll tried to speak, to explain that His love was too strong for her, but could say nothing. The force over her mouth and nose was not that of a sweet kiss, it was the smothering of suffocation. She opened her eyes, but all was dark, and suddenly she was scared, all pleasure gone. Something was being held over her face; a pillow. It was impossible to breathe, and in that instant she knew that she was being murdered.

That awareness lent her a desperate urge to defend herself. She flung her arms out to punch, but missed; she caught hold of a tunic and pulled, trying to haul whoever it was away from her, but asphyxia made her attempt feeble; the effort exhausted her, and soon she was spent, her panic depleting what energy remained in her frail body. She knew she was about to die.

In a final burst of terror she thrashed with both fists, but a hand caught her wrist, and she felt someone sit astride her chest, thrusting her forearms under her assailant's knees. She was impotent, utterly defenceless, as the pillow was squeezed against her face and her chest was slowly crushed under the weight of her killer.

Even as she slipped away, she felt the stinging slash at her arm as the knife opened her artery.

Chapter Two

Wandering to the front of his house, Sir Baldwin de Furnshill whistled as he drew to a halt at his door and gazed out over the meadow towards Dartmoor, reflecting happily that he had much to be cheerful about.

It was only a matter of weeks since his marriage to Lady Jeanne de Liddinstone, a union formed from love and not with a view to political or financial gain. Jeanne, a tall, slender woman with red-gold hair and the clearest blue eyes he had ever seen, was to him the very picture of perfection. Her face was regular, if a little round; her nose short and too small; her mouth over-wide, with a full upper lip that made her appear stubborn; her forehead was perhaps too broad – and yet to Baldwin she was beautiful.

At first he had been prey to guilt over his affection for her. It had felt wrong, because he had taken the threefold vows: obedience, poverty and *chastity*. He had been a Poor Fellow Soldier of Christ and the Temple of Solomon – a Knight Templar – and although his Order had been destroyed by an avaricious French King and his willing lackey the Pope, both trying to grab as much of the Templars' wealth as they could, Sir Baldwin had been confused, knowing that his desire for Jeanne was most unchaste.

In the early days of their marriage he had felt as though he was denying his faith by making love with his wife; it was as if each occasion was a renewal of his act of apostasy. His vows had been made to the Pope, God's own vicar on earth, and thus were as holy as any oath could be – but gradually Sir Baldwin came to believe that his honour was not tainted. It was the Pope who had resiled, for he had not protected those who had sworn loyalty to him, and instead threw them to their enemies for money. And that surely meant that all Baldwin's vows were retracted: he was not guilty of rejecting God, he was the victim of persecution, and that reflection gave him great comfort.

He had kept his previous life as a warrior monk secret from Jeanne less as a conscious act of concealment, more as an extension of his cautious nature. Over the years since that appalling day, Friday, 13 October 1307, fourteen years ago, when the Templars had been rounded up and shackled together within their own halls or thrown into gaols, Baldwin had been forced to keep his service hidden. The Order was illegal, and any confession of his place within it could have resulted in his arrest. Some day, he swore, he would tell Jeanne. He trusted her, and it was mean-minded of him not to share his past with her, but there had not as yet been an opportunity.

At the back of his mind was the vague fear that she might not understand how he and his comrades had been betrayed, that she might believe her husband was a devil-worshipper, as the Templars had been described, but he shook off this possibility with contempt. He must trust to her commonsense. Jeanne was no flibbertigibbet, flighty and frivolous, but a mature and intelligent woman, one in whom he could trust. It was largely due to her that he felt so secure now, so habituated to his life.

The sun was high in the sky, concealed by clouds, but as Baldwin hooked his thumbs into his belt and surveyed the land, it broke through a gap. All at once the scene took on a brighter, livelier aspect. The trees which lined the meadow were touched with a faint gold, the shadows stretched stark against the bright green of the grass, while the sheep meandering about suddenly looked fresher and cleaner. On the lawn, where the sunlight had not yet reached because of the shadows of the trees, each blade of grass was rimed, while in the middle where the previous night's frost had melted, beads of moisture shone like jewels in the low light.

Baldwin sighed contentedly and watched the long feather of his breath gradually fade away in the chill morning air. It was a constant source of surprise to him how the weather could be so irregular: three weeks ago at his wedding it had been warm springtime, with fresh green colours licking at the trees and shoots thrusting upwards from the soil at the base of the trees and in the fields; now, so short a time later, the land was frozen once more, and frost had blackened young flowers and leaves. It was worrying that his villeins had sown their seeds. Sir Baldwin was no agricultural expert but he was concerned that young shoots might be harmed by the severe cold.

His view was uninterrupted from here, right down as far south as Dartmoor, the sight of which made him stop whistling, his lips still puckered, as he warily studied the grey hills, outlined with white where the snow had fallen.

Try as he might, he could not like the moors. Dartmoor was as bleak and untameable as the deserts he had seen in his youth as a Templar, when he had travelled as far as Acre in defence of the Christian kingdom of Jerusalem. To Baldwin's mind it was uninviting; threatening, almost.

But he would not allow it to affect his mood. He had enjoyed a fast ride to Cadbury and back, hurtling along on his new courser, a strong beast with powerful shoulders and haunches which had cost him thirty marks, money he counted as well spent. There was no doubt that the stallion was more than capable of carrying him swiftly over great distances, and could serve as his destrier if need be; although at this moment Baldwin was more interested in the animal's ability to cover his mares. His stock was low; a murrain had reduced his stables and he must breed more.

Hearing light steps behind him, he turned to see his wife, and felt once again the pride and longing which always seemed to accompany her appearance.

'My Lord,' Jeanne greeted him, signalling to the boy behind her. 'I expected you in your hall, but if you would stand out here, would you care for warmed wine?'

She watched hawk-like as the boy, Wat, the cattleman's son, carefully brought the jug to his master and filled a pot, passing it to Sir Baldwin. Only when her husband had taken the pot from the lad did Jeanne relax. Wat was far too interested in the manor's ales for his own good. As a servant he had come to enjoy tasting all the barrels in the buttery, and from his appearance that morning, he had tried much of the strong ale the previous night. Jeanne had been sure he would spill Baldwin's drink, but thankfully he didn't. Blissfully unaware of his pale-faced servant, Baldwin stood at the side of the doorway, his pot steaming and filling the air with the good, wholesome scent of cloves and nutmeg, cinnamon and lemon, while he gazed proudly over his demesne.

Jeanne was content. Here, with this husband who valued peace, who detested animosity and arguments, she could live restfully. Her duties were hardly onerous: she scarcely had enough to fill her day in this well-organised estate. The manor had a fund of stolid, hardworking serfs, and in the house were servants to take charge of almost any aspect of life. Jeanne saw her responsibility as maintaining the calm efficiency of the place so as to ensure the continued tranquillity of the knight, her husband.

From the look of him, she had so far succeeded. At his wedding, Sir Baldwin had been slim-waisted, a tall man in his middle forties. He had carried himself like a swordsman, broad-shouldered and with a heavily muscled right arm, but now his form was subtly altering as Lady Jeanne regulated his kitchen and forced the cook to learn new dishes. Baldwin's belly was thickening, his chin growing beneath the neatly trimmed, dark beard. Even the lines of suffering which had marked his forehead and had lain at either side of his mouth were fading, and the scar which ran from temple to jaw seemed less prominent.

His clothing too had undergone a transformation. Baldwin was not vain, as some of his older and threadbare tunics could testify. Most of them had been mended several times, making him look as tatty as an impoverished mercenary without a lord. These days, Jeanne was delighted to see her husband displaying the trappings of wealth. Today, for instance, his robe was fur-lined, his hat's liripipe trailed to his shoulder, his tunic was a gorgeous blue. It was only right. Jeanne, as proud of her husband as any young wife, felt that a man with such authority should dress himself accordingly. Beforehand, few who met Baldwin would have guessed that he was the Keeper of the King's Peace for Crediton, a man whose sway might technically have stopped short of the death penalty without a coroner's formal approval, but who was still one of the King's most important local representatives.

It wasn't the power which had attracted Jeanne to him. She had been unfortunate in childhood: a gang of trailbastons had murdered her father and mother, and she had been sent to relatives in Bordeaux as an orphan. Her uncle had married her off as soon as she was old enough to a Devon knight, Sir Ralph of Liddinstone, a brutal man who had blamed her when she was unable to conceive the children he craved, and took to beating her. It had been a great relief when he caught a fever and died.

She had been anxious lest all husbands would behave in the same way. At first, when Ralph died, she was keen never to tie herself to another man – but then she met Sir Baldwin, and something about him made her review that decision.

Sir Baldwin had an essential gentleness which she found reassuring, and his actions demonstrated a respect for her and her sex which was novel; whereas most men professed a chivalrous civility towards women, Sir Baldwin was one of the few she had ever known who took pains to behave respectfully, rather than simply using expressions of admiration and courtly love to obscure some very earthy intentions.

Yet there was more to his attraction than mere politeness and kindness. He intrigued her, for in his eyes she could sometimes see a melancholy, as if a memory had triggered a sad reflection. At those times she loved him more than at any other, and had a strong maternal urge to defend him.

'How was the horse, my love?'

Baldwin finished his pot, tossed it to Wat, and caught hold of his wife, kissing her. 'Magnificent! As fast as I could have wished, and steady, too.'

Jeanne pulled back from his encircling arms and peered up into his face, ignoring the sound of the pot smashing on the cobbles as Wat fumbled the catch. Baldwin's eyes shone with an honest brilliance, and she made a *moue*. 'I wish you would be more cautious when the tracks are iced, husband. What if you were to fall far from here, and no one knew where you were?'

'Do not fear for me, my Lady,' he grinned. 'With a horse such as him I would find it difficult to lose my seat. And the important thing is, he should sire a whole generation of foals before the end of the year.'

He stooped to kiss her, and she responded, but as he embraced her, he felt her stiffen at the sound of hoofbeats. Turning, he saw a messenger riding fast towards them.

The sun shone brightly on the convent too. Lady Elizabeth could see that the night's snow had mostly melted as she sat in the cloisters with the account rolls spread before her. She hated them. Not only was she unable to add and subtract, she found her treasurer's scrawl difficult to decipher. Most of the time she reluctantly accepted what Margherita had written – not an ideal state of affairs, for she instinctively mistrusted the other woman.

Lady Elizabeth was seated in her favourite spot. Here, she could keep an eye on her obedientiaries and now, as the women returned from the frater and their main meal of the day, was the best time of day for her to observe her nuns and assess their mood.

Giggles and laughter were quickly stilled as they approached the cloister and saw their prioress sitting there. She noted that Moll's death had not affected the novices much. They were young and were bound to recover more quickly; they wouldn't appreciate the impact this death could have on the priory. Elizabeth gave a grim smile as she caught sight of Katerine: some of them wouldn't be particularly upset to see Moll go, the prioress thought.

Katerine was a shrewd little thing. Only one-and-twenty, she was dark-haired, with pale skin, a wide mouth and tip-tilted nose that gave her an earnest, cheerful aspect – but the impression was betrayed by the eyes. Brown with green flecks, they were – a pretty combination – but there was nothing pretty about the calculation in them.

Agnes hadn't liked Moll either. This girl was quiet and self-contained, only seventeen years old, with thick red-gold hair and green eyes. Her face was heavily freckled, which added to her attractiveness, although Elizabeth felt inwardly that there was something wrong about her looks: a certain sharpness of feature that boded an unkind nature.

The prioress saw Agnes glance in her direction before walking to the door that led up to the dorter and infirmary with that sedate, gliding motion of hers. She stood taller than Katerine by at least half a head, and her body was already more full. Her hips were broad, her breasts large, while Katerine had the figure of a boy, much as poor Moll had had.

Agnes was no threat to the smooth running of the convent. She had her faults, but Lady Elizabeth was not of a mind to confront her with them. The priests were often talking about taking splinters out of a man's eye while a plank remained in your own, and she was uncomfortably aware of her own failings. Either the girl would grow out of her sins or she would leave before taking her vows.

The other nuns returned from the frater. Margherita came out with Joan, talking conspiratorially. They looked odd, Margherita large and square, almost masculine, Joan short and wiry, slim and with the compact frame of an older woman, although whiplash strong. Elizabeth felt a shiver run through her body. Unconsciously she pulled her robes tighter about her, tugging the woollen cloak more firmly over her shoulders. Something didn't feel right. There was a tension in the air. She could feel their baleful stare even when she turned away.

Constance, the infirmarer, had obviously not got over the death of her charge. Elizabeth regarded her doubtfully. She appeared to be drunk, was red-featured – somewhat sullen, or perhaps nervous? Her shoes dragged and she stumbled every so often, as did Denise, the sacrist. The two seemed to have formed some kind of unholy alliance against the world.

Elizabeth bent her head as if to study the papers before her, but kept her attention fixed on Constance and Denise. They made for Margherita and paused to whisper a moment at her side, their backs turned to the prioress, before walking on.

Last through the door was Emma, the cellaress. Tall, slim,

sharp-faced, with a cold and humourless demeanour, she glanced at the prioress only briefly. Seeing Elizabeth's eye upon her, she gave a dry, unfriendly smile, then walked over to Margherita.

Lady Elizabeth felt ice solidify in her belly. Something was wrong, and she had no idea what it could be.

The treasurer looked across and nodded smugly at the sight of Elizabeth's pinched and anxious expression.

'I came as quickly as I could, Peter,' Sir Baldwin said, marching quickly into the hall of Peter Clifford, the Dean of Crediton's canonical church. And so he had, riding speedily over the dangerous roads, wondering all the time what Crediton's priest could want. It was rare for Peter Clifford to make such an urgent request for Baldwin's help.

The hall was modern, with a good fireplace set into the wall. Logs hissed and crackled, their flames throwing a healthy glow about the room. The *un*healthy fresh air was shuttered out, and wholesome tallow candles spat and smoked in the corners of the room. Peter Clifford's table stood at the opposite wall from the fire, but on this chilly day he had dragged chairs before the hearth. He was not alone; there was a second man at his side.

'It is good of you to come, old friend,' said Peter. 'Permit me to introduce you to Bishop Bertrand, the suffragan bishop of Exeter.'

Bowing his head while Bishop Bertrand solemnly blessed him, Baldwin had to suppress a shudder of revulsion. Bertrand's voice betrayed his French birth.

Baldwin had nothing against those with a French accent particularly, but a priest was a different matter. He distrusted French priests for the same reason Bertrand would almost certainly have retracted his blessing, had he known that Baldwin was a renegade Templar. The French clergy had joined in the condemnation of the Order almost to a man. Some were no doubt motivated by greed: they had scrambled to take over churches and lands. Others were scared of the Pope's displeasure; some believed the accusations of sacrilegious and anti-Christian worship and thought it right that they should persecute men who participated

in such obscene acts. Bertrand looked to Baldwin as if he fell into
the first category. He had the disapproving mien of the professional
churchman, as if dubious whether he could be contaminated by
being too close to a secular knight of heaven alone knew what
background.

Respectfully Baldwin stood back. He had to admit that the
man probably had good reason to look suspicious. The knights
and barons of England were taking advantage of the weakness of
King Edward II to indulge in their own petty land wars, especially
those who could rely on the favour of the King, such as the
Despenser family. Hugh the Younger, son of Hugh Despenser the
Older, seemed to have an insatiable appetite for fresh lands.
Baldwin had heard that his greed had led to an upsurge of
discontent in the Welsh March, where he was attempting to line
his pocket at the expense of his neighbours. It would be no surprise
if they should all collaborate against him; the March was ever a
source of vicious warfare and was run as a series of private
fiefdoms, each lord having his own army. Now matters had grown
so serious, Baldwin had been told, that the King himself had
travelled to Gloucester to ban any large assemblies of men, but
his command had been ignored and armies were gathering.

It was just one more proof of discontent within the kingdom,
and Baldwin was growing concerned that England could explode
into violence.

'Sir Baldwin,' Peter said, offering him a seat and motioning to
a servant to pour wine, 'I'm terribly sorry to have asked you here
at such short notice, but I wasn't sure to whom I could turn.'

Peter Clifford was a tall, thin, ascetic priest with a shock of
white hair marred by his tonsure. His complexion was pale now,
because he had forgone his usual pleasures of hunting and hawking
this winter, spending all his free hours in the church's cloisters
bent over the pages of his account books while he tried to finish
off the internal decoration of the recently built church. Today,
however, Baldwin thought he looked more tired than usual.
Underlying his pallid features was a deep anxiety, bred of fear,
and at the sight Baldwin realised the seriousness of his summons.

'I am honoured you felt you could turn to me,' he said gently. 'But how can I help you?'

Peter Clifford pulled his chair nearer to the knight's. 'Sir Baldwin, what we are about to tell you is confidential. It falls under the same secrecy as the confessional, you understand? It is the business of Holy Mother Church, and must never be divulged.'

'I shall keep secret whatever you tell me.'

Peter glanced over at Bertrand. The bishop gave an almost imperceptible nod, and Peter leaned back in his chair as the bishop rested his elbows on his knees and minutely studied Baldwin.

To Baldwin's eye the bishop himself looked as though he would have benefited from more exercise and a diet of good red meat. Bertrand was surely in his early fifties, a stooped, prim-looking fellow with a long narrow face and sharp little eyes. His mouth was small and pursed, with bloodless lips, giving his face a sour appearance. His left hand was withered, and he left it in his lap, emphasising points with his right alone.

'Sir Baldwin, I came here to ask the dean for his aid because I find myself caught in a cleft stick. I am sure you know that the good Bishop of Exeter is the Lord High Treasurer, and is with the King. In his absence he instructed me to ensure that the convents within his See are all obeying the strictures of their Rules. I am the visitor, and for the last two months I have been going to all the nunneries and monasteries in the diocese.'

'A miserable time of year for so much travelling,' Baldwin observed.

Bertrand raised his eyes to meet Baldwin's. 'Cold and wet enough, but one is kept warm when on God's work. He protects His own.'

Baldwin smiled and nodded, but could not help the mental aside that in his experience, whether God was assisting or not, the rain still fell as wet on a traveller's back. He found he instinctively disliked the bishop. The man looked and sounded like a prig. His manner was affected and prudish, and Baldwin was quite certain in his own mind that Bertrand was not the kind of man with whom he could establish a friendship.

Bertrand frowned. 'Sir Baldwin, you will recall that all I am about to tell you is confidential? I have found that there are weaknesses in most of our institutions, and lapses occur not only among novices, but in the ranks of those who have taken the oaths. Even the Abbot of Tavistock regularly eats meat!'

Baldwin recalled the ruddy-cheeked face of Abbot Champeaux. Not only did he eat meat: against all the laws he regularly and cheerfully hunted venison on Dartmoor. Abbot Champeaux was no hypocrite, Baldwin knew. He enjoyed his life to the full, it was true, but that did not affect his dedication to his abbey, nor to his monks or the secular folk of Tavistock.

'It must be difficult for those who live the monastic life,' he said. 'St Bernard designed the Rule for convents in warm, southern lands, where the sun is more conducive to study, and where the Nocturns can be attended without the risk of freezing at night.'

'The good Lord keeps warm those who truly give Him their faith and trust,' Bertrand declared sententiously. 'And I fear He will not be turning His face to some of the people I have been meeting. Sir Baldwin, I have found a convent in which the prioress is failing in her responsibilities.'

Suppressing a sigh, Baldwin tried to nod understandingly. He was not surprised. In his experience many of the inhabitants of convents took their vows too young, before they could appreciate the lifelong nature of their promises. All too often girls went to a nunnery more from the desire to avoid an unpleasant marriage than from any religious ambition; men would join the monastery after being rejected by a woman, to escape the burdensome duties imposed on serfs, or – and Baldwin had met a Cistercian who admitted this – because he had got drunk while a youth and had dreamed God had called to him. That monk was forever peering into the bottom of his cup, trying to see his vision again.

Baldwin had taken his vows gladly, offering his life to the Order which had saved him from death in the hell-hole of Acre, but he knew many who were even now incarcerated in religious Orders completely unsuited to them. This suffragan did not look like a man likely to forgive an errant nun; if anything he looked the sort who would demand the harshest penance for the slightest infraction of the Rule.

The reflection made Baldwin's tone harsh. 'Where is this: Polsloe, Canonsleigh, or Belstone?' These were the only three he was aware of.

'Belstone.'

Baldwin knew of it, although he had never been there. It was tiny, with only a few nuns, a handful of canons, some novices, and a few lay brethren to do all the hard work. Baldwin was aware that it lay in a small valley with a stream flowing nearby, but had heard that the site was dreadful. He knew the moors well enough; the wind howled over them, and would whistle around a little cloister. From what he had heard, Belstone possessed a tiny amount of land that produced little in the way of usable food. The nuns relied more on the income from their flocks of sheep and their cattle.

'It must be a terrible place for the worship of God,' he ventured.

'God exists in the wilderness as much as in the city,' Bertrand said uncompromisingly. His certainty carried the force of a death sentence. 'Nuns should be grateful to have an opportunity to praise His grace in a place where they cannot be distracted.'

'And what is the nature of the good prioress's failing?'

'I had thought that her sin was the same as that of others, merely weakness, permitting greed and unchastity to run riot unbridled through her community,' Bertrand said. 'But now I have been told that worse has happened. She is not controlling the place at all; the priory is utterly lawless.'

'What makes you say that?' asked Baldwin sceptically, picking up his drink.

Bertrand's answer almost made him drop his pot. 'Sir Baldwin, a young novice has been murdered.'

Chapter Three

Joan walked slowly from the infirmary to the rere-dorter, hitched up her tunic and eased herself onto the wooden seat over the chute. The smell was awful, and she made a mental note to ask that the faeces be cleaned out again.

So the battle had begun between the treasurer and prioress. It was about time. There was no doubt in Joan's mind which of the two women was the better: the treasurer was a woman of integrity and honour. Margherita was sincere in her love of the nunnery; *she* wouldn't have let it get so run down.

Joan cleaned herself and walked down to the frater, entering and sitting alone at a table. She was too late to join with the others, but that was a matter of policy nowadays. The younger girls all giggled and chattered so quickly Joan often couldn't hear a word. Her hearing was getting odd: if many spoke all at once, she would miss everything, no matter how hard she concentrated on the person before her. It was more relaxing to eat and drink alone.

Inevitably her mind drew her back to the coming fight. It had been precipitated by the death of that novice, Moll. Joan gazed into the distance. The child was so young, it seemed terrible that she should have had her life taken away, and yet Joan couldn't regret her passing. Moll had been viewed by many as some kind of saint – it was the image she was keen to project – yet she wasn't. She was a liar. Nor was the girl as pious as she wished the world to believe; she was both devious and malicious.

There was one good thing to come from Moll's end, and that was the election of the new prioress. Joan had little doubt about it, because Margherita had told them all earlier. They had all heard the rumours about the prioress, and with the message

Margherita had sent to the visitor, he would have to come back and replace Lady Elizabeth.

As Joan often reminded herself, she had been a nun when Lady Elizabeth was still running naked in the fields, and age hadn't improved her prioress. She couldn't control a place the size of Belstone. It needed someone with a better business brain.

She shivered and scowled. The cold ate into her bones now-adays. The weather grew more chill with each succeeding year, and it was ever more difficult to warm herself. She threw back her head and finished the last of her wine, then stood. At least her legs still worked.

At the door she eyed the women at their work. A convent was always a busy place. It was a shame, but sometimes Joan felt rather left out of things these days. Oh, she was involved in the machinations of the place by Margherita and by the youngsters, who felt the need to confide in someone older without embarrass-ment. Often their problems were simple – novices often had feminine troubles, and their shame and anxiety wouldn't allow them to speak to friends or the mistress of the novices. Instead they went to Joan, who could always be relied on to give a sympathetic ear.

Deciding to return to the fire in the infirmary, Joan almost tripped over a flagstone whose edge had lifted. She closed her eyes and patiently offered a prayer, thanking God for allowing her to see it in time.

Margherita wouldn't have let the place get into this state.

Bertrand's story took little time to tell. He had visited the priory only a few days before, on his way to Crediton from Buckland; he was methodically progressing from one institution to another, and had intended staying at Crediton for some days before returning to Exeter, when the slightly garbled story of the novice's death had reached him by letter.

'I met this Moll, Sir Baldwin,' Bertrand said, turning on the knight an intent, serious look. 'She was only a child. Scarcely old enough to realise the supreme importance of the vows she must take as a Bride of Christ, and yet now her life is ended.'

'How?' Baldwin was ready to dislike this man intensely. Although his sentiments were reasonable and justifiable, Bertrand looked as though he was almost enjoying being able to demonstrate what an upright man he was; how much integrity he held. Baldwin had no doubt that by the time Bishop Stapledon came to hear of the affair, Bishop Bertrand's part in resolving it would be greatly magnified, and Baldwin felt contempt for a man who could look to make capital out of a novice's death. His distaste was so great Baldwin found himself musing on the character of the bishop, and thus missed the beginning of Bertrand's story.

'. . . she had a severe headache, and was sent to the infirmary, there to be bled by the phlebotomist. The operation was perfectly successful and she settled quickly, soon dropping off to sleep. The next morning, when the infirmarer went to attend to her after Prime, the girl had apparently haemorrhaged from the site of the bleeding, and died.'

'These accidents will sometimes happen,' Baldwin said.

'This was no accident. I know the clerk concerned myself: Godfrey of Malmesbury. He was at Oxford with me, and his skills are beyond doubt. No, Brother Godfrey would not have slipped and slashed an artery by accident.'

'A *priest* performed the letting?' Baldwin asked with surprise. Men in major Orders had been banned from manual surgery for over a hundred years. Their skills lay in selecting the best prayers and penances to cure the ill, not in butchery. When Baldwin had been a Templar they had enlisted the services of a professional, the local barber, when they needed their veins opened.

'I understand it was considered that a canon trained in surgery would be safer than an outsider when it came to dealing with a nun. Yet it was unorthodox,' Bertrand agreed.

Baldwin sipped thoughtfully at his wine. At last he set his cup on the ground. 'You clearly have reason to believe that someone wished to kill her. Why?'

'It's not my view, Sir Baldwin – I hardly knew the child, I only saw her a couple of times.'

'Then why leap to this conclusion? Your friend the phlebotomist may well be experienced, but sometimes a sharp knife will nick a vessel, and the harm may not be apparent for a day or more. That is why phlebotomists are generally safe from accusations of murder: if they were not, the courts would be filled.'

'Ah, I misled you by my answer. *I* have no reason to think someone might have wanted to kill her – it is not *my* belief, Sir Baldwin, but the belief of the priory's treasurer. It was she who wrote to me to state her conviction that the poor girl was murdered.'

'Did she say by whom?'

Bertrand looked down at his withered hand as if wondering at the accusation he had heard. 'By the prioress herself, Sir Baldwin,' he said eventually.

Peter leaned forward. 'You see the good bishop's difficulty? Bishop Stapledon is away and cannot be consulted, and if news of this were to be rumoured about . . .'

'I cannot ignore the accusation of so senior a nun,' Bertrand murmured.

'Not that you would wish to,' Baldwin stated sharply. Now he understood Bertrand's expression. The suffragan would have preferred to burn the letter and put this novice's death down to an accident so that the Bishop of Exeter would have a shining example of a perfect deputy when he received Bertrand's report. Clearly that was impossible now the treasurer had put her suspicions in writing; but Bertrand could still win the good bishop's gratitude by clearing up the business quickly or performing some sort of cover-up. 'If this is truly an act of murder,' Baldwin growled, 'it must be investigated.'

'Quite,' said Peter. 'So could you go and look into it?'

'Me? But I have no jurisdiction,' Baldwin protested with surprise.

'Of course not! This matter falls under the Canon Law, but you have experience, and you may be able to assist the good bishop,' said Peter.

'Surely you would do better to seek the aid of a coroner.'

'Sir Baldwin, this matter is *utterly* confidential,' Peter said with emphasis.

Baldwin nodded and grinned his understanding. The King's man in Exeter was a hard-drinking, whoring fool, to Baldwin's mind. Coroners were among the most corrupt of all the King's officers, for they had much work to see to and received no pay – other than what they could extort from felons prepared to pay for their release.

'No, we need someone on whom we can rely not only to advise Bishop Stapledon's man, but who shall also be discreet,' Peter said.

'Well, the Warden's Bailiff, then. Simon Puttock does at least have some secular authority in Dartmoor.'

'I have already sent a message asking him to meet you there,' Peter smiled. 'He will be at the inn at the road to Belstone, the one at the foot of the cleave.'

Baldwin remembered it. A small tavern at the bottom of the Belstone Valley, near a mill, where the Taw River rushed constantly. The memory did nothing to allay his concerns and he considered the proposal doubtfully. Admittedly there was little enough to do at his manor; his official duties would not be seriously affected, were he to ignore them for a week or two, and this affair *had* captured his interest, but ... 'I hardly think the prioress would be happy to have a complete stranger, someone who is neither priest nor monk, arrive to perform such an enquiry, especially bearing in mind the serious nature of the accusation against her.'

'She should be glad to have anyone in whom she can place her trust,' said Bertrand shortly. 'The woman struck me as being open to accusations of almost every possible impropriety.' He mused a moment, brow wrinkled. 'Take this as an example, Sir Baldwin. I raise it only as an indication of her behaviour, you understand: this prioress has permitted the church roof and that of the dormitory to fall so far into disrepair that both have holes in them. Apparently they were leaking noticeably last autumn, and yet now, months later, the choir of the church is open to the elements and nuns can't sleep in parts of their dorter.'

'I have heard of other places where similar difficulties have arisen,' Baldwin pointed out with rising irritation. That Bertrand's words were true Baldwin did not doubt, but Baldwin wondered about his motivation. There were priests who would be pleased to harry a convent to destruction if it would enhance their political status within the Church, and this Bertrand looked very like one of that sort. After all, there were many religious establishments whose basic fabric was so ancient and worn that the obedientiaries were unable to repair them. Perhaps it was less common in Benedictine and Cistercian monasteries, for such places attracted wealth, but a poor place like Belstone wouldn't be able to seduce rich patrons so easily.

'There are some which have unfortunately suffered from damage, yes,' Bertrand allowed, but then he fixed Baldwin with a glittering eye. 'But in how many of these cases have the relevant treasurers accused their prioress of lascivious and lustful disregard, because the money she should have used to fix the roof was put to another use?'

'I assume often. There are many conflicting demands on a—'

'I know that perfectly well, Sir Baldwin,' Bertrand said sharply, 'but I saw how much wealth was being brought to the priory while I was there. I saw the money given to the treasurer by the bailiff of the priory's lands at Iddesleigh – it was a tidy sum. And the allegation is that instead of paying for a roof, the prioress had given it to her new vicar, a man whom she sees regularly, alone, and at night!'

Constance reached the infirmary where she worked and had to blink to keep the tears at bay when she saw Moll's empty bed, the palliasse rolled up neatly on top of the rope mattress, just as she had left it.

Her head hurt. She was unused to so much strong wine before Vespers, and now she felt slightly confused. It was odd to be drunk at this time of day, before Terce, but kind of Denise to take pity on her and sit for so long, listening to her tale of misery. Not that she could tell Denise all.

It was so hard. She had known that her weakness would lead to evil, but she had no idea how cruel the result could be. Yet now she was a murderer. All because of her very human frailty.

There was a faint cough from the corner of the room, and Constance forced down her guilt, crossing the floor to where Joan sat. The old nun stared at the flames, but when she heard Constance she turned to her with a smile.

'Ah, Constance – are you going to give me some more of your dwale? I think I may need some tonight. The pain is coming again.'

'Of course, if it will help you.'

'How's Cecily?'

'She'll be fine. No need to worry,' Constance said gently, pulling a woollen blanket over the older woman's lap. 'It's cold out in the cloister today, isn't it?'

'For these old bones, eh?' Joan grinned.

Constance smiled down at her. The infirmarer found it easy to like Joan. She was a permanent fixture of the convent: rather wrinkled now, and white-haired, with peering, weak blue eyes. She was the first sister whom Constance had come to meet, and had always been kind and understanding. When Constance thought about what she'd done, and what she'd *almost* done to poor Joan, she could have broken down into tears again.

Joan was speaking. 'I'll soon be gone anyway, and if the Lord decides to take me while I'm lying in my bed before I can rise for Nocturns, I'll be happy enough.'

The young infirmarer shot her a quick look. There was an understanding expression on Joan's face, and Constance felt the pit of her stomach sink as if a lead weight had fallen upon it. 'Before Nocturns?' she managed to stammer.

'Oh yes, dear. It would be such a good time to die. Why, when could be better? It's peaceful, you don't have to get up early the next morning and make the effort of going to church. No, instead you get taken up by Christ after a pleasant night's sleep. Much better.'

Constance tried to chat to her for a while longer, but all the time her mind was racing. It seemed so obvious the older woman was telling her that she knew.

She couldn't stand there with the fear filling her body, the certainty that Joan had seen what she had done. Apologising, Constance left the old woman and went to her partitioned chamber. It was sparsely furnished: only a bed and a chest, within which were her medicines. She dropped to her bed and covered her face in her hands.

Guilt tore at her, although if she was honest, it wasn't so much the guilt of the act that terrified her, it was the fear of being discovered. At least Joan could hold her tongue, Constance thought.

She forced herself to set aside her morbid torpor and lifted the lid of her chest. Carefully she measured the ingredients of her dwale into a jug of wine.

It wasn't only for Joan, but for Cecily as well. Cecily was a notorious coward, and although Constance had tried to set and splint her wrist, it had proved impossible. The girl screamed and writhed uncontrollably, swinging her good fist at the novice helping Constance and using quite the foulest language the infirmarer had ever heard. Most of the nuns showed a stoic courage: they were content with a simple charm to grip and a leather strap to chew, but neither would suffice in this case. Constance had checked the makeshift dressing, but it clearly wasn't working, and she knew she would need to reset the bones properly. For that the woman would have to be compliant, so Constance intended giving her a draught to make her peaceful.

Dwale was ideal for this. It was a mixture that Constance made up specially, of belladonna, hemlock, henbane and syrup of poppy seed. It tasted foul, very bitter, but it would certainly put the lay sister to sleep. Shaking the mixture, Constance stood near the window and gazed out.

From here she looked directly north, up towards the vill of Belstone, although it was concealed from view by a hill. Far beneath her, lay sisters worked in the dairy and out in the yard, hanging washing from lines. The wind was tearing at the clothes, pulling the lines taut as bowstrings, snatching clothes from the women's baskets and whipping them over the mud if given an opportunity.

Despite her worries, she smiled as one sister reached desperately for a shift as it was caught by a freak puff of wind and flapped dangerously near a pool of ordure. The hapless laundress tripped and pitched into the muck herself. She sat up and screamed to vent her rage and frustration, slapping at the hands of others who came, laughing, to help her up.

Constance walked slowly back to the chest, intending to go through her bottles and see which draughts needed renewing, but soon she had to set aside her vessels. She felt oh, so lonely, as she went through it all again.

Moll was dead. She was unable to spread any more of her malicious tales now. She had been a malign little person. Nasty, vicious – *cruel*. And all concealed beneath that sweet, submissive exterior. It was here, in Constance's own room, that Moll had come and spoken about the man she had seen. The one who had walked up the steps to this level, as if he was coming to visit a nun. Constance had laughed it off, saying that Moll had dreamed it all, although Moll very definitely asserted that she was awake and had seen the man very clearly. Then she had winked, saying she knew where *he* was going. And she hoped the nun involved would confess her sin in the chapterhouse, before the whole choir. It had made Constance sick to see her sitting there so smugly.

Feeling the tears rising, Constance rubbed at her face with the sleeve of her dress, and gazed up at the window once more her vision blurred as she was overcome by the enormity of what she had done.

Jeanne was supervising the cleaning of Baldwin's wardrobe when she heard her husband's horse pounding along the track towards the house. She was relieved, because it was already close to dusk, and she was anxious about him riding so far on treacherous roads.

Not that she'd had time to indulge herself in fears about her husband. Edgar was in many ways an almost perfect servant, but in some matters of hygiene she thought him hidebound. It had been quite a shock to her when, after only a short time in the hall, she had discovered the first fleas on her body. She could see that Baldwin himself was repelled by the creatures, and yet Edgar appeared to be almost untroubled by them, convinced that his traps – trenchers of bread smeared with glue, with a lighted candle sitting atop – were all that was necessary. He asserted that the fleas were attracted to the trenchers by the light, and then got stuck and died.

It was an interesting concept. On present experience, it was also utterly ineffective.

Only the previous week Jeanne had set up her own defences, just as she had learned in Bordeaux. The bedchamber had three large sheets laid on the floor which had remained there for six days, on which any fleas must fall upon leaving Baldwin's clothing, her own, or their bed. These she had today ordered to be folded and carried out to the shed where the cider was made, and here the sheets had been placed in the great press. Next she had taken out all of Baldwin's tunics and set them inside as well, with the bedlinen on top of the lot, before closing the press and ordering that it should be tightly squeezed.

The servants, especially Edgar, had all looked askance at this curious demand, but complied with gusto when bribed with the offer of ale. Jeanne, not being particularly trusting with servants whom she did not know well, stood by and ensured that the men compressed the clothes to the utmost of their strength, and while they strained and swore, she explained to Edgar that fleas needed light and space to move. After being imprisoned in this manner the fleas would die. It was obvious that Baldwin's servant thought this was all moonshine and that he was going to be hard-pressed to keep her humoured, from the condescending smile he gave her.

But Jeanne ignored his patronising attitude. It was enough for her that she knew her methods would succeed. In time Edgar would come to have faith in her. Jeanne refused to allow herself to get despondent.

Here she was, a woman of some thirty summers, already once widowed, yet with no children, and she was having to start her life again. This was her fourth beginning: first when she was born, second after her orphanage when her uncle in Bordeaux took her in, the third when she wed Ralph of Liddinstone, and last of all this new start with Baldwin. Each time she had been forced to learn new ways, submit to new rules, satisfy new needs. It was fortunate her own wants were so few. All she craved was the love of a husband who could respect her intelligence. Lady Jeanne was not a woman to be imprisoned in a manor like a feeble-minded courtesan.

And Jeanne would not bow to the will of her husband's servant. Edgar would have to learn to accede to her commands with alacrity. He would not browbeat her.

He heard Baldwin's approach at the same time as she, and was about to hurry back to the hall to welcome him when Jeanne told him to go to the buttery to fetch warmed wine and bring it to the hall. Then she walked in herself to wait for Baldwin.

When Baldwin entered, she was by the fire, and as soon as he crossed the threshold, Jeanne stepped forward to welcome him, leading him to his favourite chair by the hearth. It creaked as he sat on it. It was ancient, and the worms had got into it. She cast it a dubious look. It sounded as if it might give way at any time.

Edgar appeared and filled pots for Baldwin and his wife.

Baldwin drank slowly, deep in thought. Jeanne thought he looked like a man with an unpleasant duty to perform, and she was concerned what the priest might have said to worry him so much.

At last he held out his cup to Edgar, set it refilled on the floor by his side, and threw his wife a smile of gratitude. 'Thank you for not badgering me as soon as I arrived. You have that wonderful gift of knowing when words are unwelcome, my love, and a perfect peacefulness about you that makes it a pleasure to return. I am sorry to have been so uncommunicative, but the ride was not long enough to consider all the details.'

'There is some difficulty at Crediton?' she asked quietly.

'Not there, no. It is another ecclesiastical institution. I am afraid I shall have to leave home tomorrow for a few days.'

She looked at him enquiringly, but he only grinned. Jeanne knew that sometimes her man could be called from their home and forced to travel abroad on business, but she was surprised that he would say nothing of the nature of his mission. Still, she reflected, it would give her time to get the manor into order. Jeanne was not concerned about being left alone, although she would miss her husband.

As he stood and made to leave the hall, she asked where he must go; he said apologetically: 'I am sorry, Jeanne, but I have been sworn to secrecy.'

With that he left the room, leaving Jeanne sitting surprised, but as she stared at the doorway, a smile spread slowly over her face.

While he was gone, she could execute her own plans.

Chapter Four

Looking out through the doorway from the frater, Margherita, like Constance, saw the lay sister fall in the muck. Although she couldn't help but smile, she was shocked to hear the girl swear. There was no excuse for blasphemy. The treasurer noted which girl it was. She would be punished later.

Margherita liked the view from here. She could see the whole of the courtyard behind the cloisters looking north, and that meant she could observe almost all of the activities of the lay sisters. Her only regret was that she couldn't keep an eye on the men in the southern cloister, but that would be unthinkable, of course.

Not that all the women were so scrupulous. Margherita knew that some of the nuns were better informed about the male body than they should be. She had *heard* men here in the cloister. That was why she walked about the place at night, to find out who the men were, and who the women were who dared invite them in.

At least that slut Rose wasn't a novice any more. The girl had been a source of shame to the whole place. Good riddance to her.

Margherita recalled that it was from here that she had seen Moll walking about the garden in earnest discussion with Rose. As soon as a nun had appeared, both girls quickly separated, but Margherita saw them return to each other's side when the nun had hurried past.

A girl who was prepared to consort with Rose was not the sort to take up the veil; that was what Margherita believed, and she would defy anyone who tried to persuade her otherwise. Before that Moll had shown some promise, indeed she had given every appearance of piety; a rare attribute in most modern girls. But that was no excuse for going about with the likes of Rose. Someone like Joan was much better company for a young girl;

she had experienced all the doubts, suspicions and fears that a young nun was likely to come across. Whatever happened, Joan had to be better than a common whore.

Margherita set her pot on a table and made her way to the cloister. She herself needed no confidante. She could understand why other nuns might like sharing information, and even made use of their garrulity every now and again, but she was content with herself as sole custodian of her private thoughts. Her sisters were simply useful for disseminating the little snippets she occasionally wished to let slip. She smiled to herself as she sat at her desk, then sighed and gave the papers before her a small frown. It was hard to sit here when the sun shone, when the birds were singing in the orchard and the whole world appeared to be waking from the long, slow sleep of winter, but she must show her dedication and settle down to the accounts.

Resignedly she picked up her quill, a small reed, dipping it in her ink, staring gloomily at the long columns. Running her finger down one of them, she came to the money brought in by the beadle: only a few pennies were recorded. With secret satisfaction, she recalled the heavy leather purse which the man had given her. That was safe in her personal chest now.

It was fortunate that young Moll was no longer able to poke her nose in and ask about the financial discrepancies, she thought.

Closing her eyes, she shuddered at the recollection. The silly girl had come here and asked what had happened to the beadle's money, stating that she had seen the money brought in – and yet it wasn't listed in the accounts. Fortunately, the quick-thinking Margherita had been able to discredit her memory, saying that she was thinking of money brought in by the warrener, not the beadle. At this Moll had become confused, for she hadn't expected so confident a denial, and she didn't dare make any further comment. However the scene had scared Margherita: she hadn't realised her assistant was both lettered *and* numerate. She must be more careful in future.

She turned from the unpleasant memory. There were more important affairs for her to consider: she must decide the best means of persuading her sisters to support her and not the prioress.

Her *familia*, the women who regularly messed with her in the frater some little while after Lady Elizabeth and her own little coterie of hangers-on had left, were already for her. It was the others Margherita needed to convince. The woman curled her lip at the thought of them: mostly they were fools and incompetents, yet sprinkled among them were a few Margherita would be happy to subvert, and some of these were wavering. They might be persuaded to join her camp. She had declared that her desire to run the convent was based upon a wish to see that it survived; faced with that, what could a nun say? No one could seriously suggest that Lady Elizabeth could look after the place better than Margherita. The very idea made the treasurer give a sardonic smile.

The trouble was, Prioress Elizabeth knew her well; she was quite well aware that Margherita would be doing just this. And at the same time, Elizabeth would be wooing Margherita's friends.

The treasurer idly chewed her reed until she tasted the bitterness and spat out the ink she had inadvertently sucked. Her saliva left a black spot on the flag, and Margherita stared at it. A black spot – like the mark which would be set against the convent's record soon. She wondered idly what the visitor would do to the Lady Elizabeth. After all, Margherita was able to give the most damning evidence against her.

Especially since she could explain why the virtuous, the important 'high-born' Lady Elizabeth had good reason to want to kill Moll – and Margherita could bear witness against her before the suffragan when he arrived.

Her eyes narrowed thoughtfully, and she considered her *familia*. There was no point mentioning Lady Elizabeth's guilt to other nuns. No, it would be best to win them over by guile, but pointing out how their lives could improve with Margherita in charge, or in the case of the more religiously inclined, she could point out how much more pious she was, and how much more inspiring she would be as leader of the community.

Yes, that was the right approach: damn Lady Elizabeth before the suffragan and remind the others how miserable their lives had become because of the prioress. And make sure all the nuns got to hear about Lady Elizabeth's guilt.

Later, when she had won the most senior position, she could produce her secret funds to make good the dilapidated buildings.

Bishop Bertrand rode up the long sweeping track to Sir Baldwin's house at Furnshill with a feeling of impending doom.

The men Peter Clifford had insisted upon sending appeared dull, impassive types, better than the simple thugs who usually offered themselves for hire, but not as reassuring as men of the Bishop of Exeter's own retinue. If it had been up to him, Bertrand would have sent to Exeter for more men from the cathedral, but as Peter Clifford had pointed out, not only would that involve an unnecessary delay, it would also mean entering into negotiations with the dean and chapter as to how many men Bertrand would need and for how long. The good Bishop Stapledon had himself taken many of them to protect him while he travelled to see the King, and the dean could be expected to argue strenuously against any further depletion of the cathedral's strength. Far easier, Peter said, for him to take all the spare guards from Crediton.

Bertrand clattered up towards the stableyard. The house added to his feeling of glumness. It was a well-appointed place, obviously quite ancient, with solid cob walls to the hall at the centre, and two projecting arms at either side constructed of good timber, the plaster limewashed. The welcome sight it presented, with smoke rising from the louvre in the thatched roof and children playing with young dogs on the frosted lawn in front, only compounded his sombre spirits. It would be such a difficult place to defend, he thought, and with the news Peter had that morning received from Bristol, every man might soon be grateful for a place that was better protected.

After Prime, Katerine the novice walked out of the church with her head cast submissively downwards as she had been taught, not speaking, but moving slowly and contemplatively. Not that anyone could give a damn, not now with all the chatter. Katerine privately considered she could have run naked through the cloisters and no one would have noticed, not even the mistress of the novices. Everyone was too busy assessing Margherita's chances.

They all knew the level of the antipathy between prioress and treasurer. In a place like this even the mildest arguments soon became common knowledge, but when the cause of the quarrel was the desire of one to oust the other from her post, the affair soon became vitriolic, and involved the whole community. Especially now Margherita appeared to have the upper hand. Lady Elizabeth herself seemed to have given up: she wore a perpetual worried, hunted expression.

To Katerine their mutual dislike was amusingly intense. Like boiling poison it had bubbled away for ages, every word between them acting like additional powders tossed into the brew until the potion was complete. All it had needed was the death of Moll to bring it to boiling point, but now it was ready, and the venom was destroying the whole convent.

For someone who knew who to use information, there could be opportunities, she thought.

Katerine would never have described herself as unpleasant. She had been orphaned when young, and the lesson this had taught her was that she must look to herself for everything. She was entirely self-reliant. When she learned something that could be profitable, she used it. There was no guilt in doing so: it was simply a means of survival. Blackmail was not something she had heard of, but if it was explained to her, she would in all honesty have felt it a justifiable means of gaining wealth: no worse than owning land and forcing serfs to work it and making them pay for the privilege; no worse than a lord raping a man's wife merely because he had an urge and the power to do so.

Back in the cloister, she strode purposefully along the western corridor and up to the dorter, throwing a disgusted look up at the ceiling as she changed into her day shoes. The ragged hole allowed in so much water and wind it was a miracle none of the nuns or novices had frozen in their beds. As it was, Joan had escaped to the infirmary. The daft old sow couldn't cope with the chill at her age.

It was all right for the prioress, Katerine thought. *She* had her own area set apart from the others, divided by partitions which kept the arctic gusts from ruining her sleep. Not that she would necessarily keep it for much longer, if the rumours were true; if the visitor was about to return, surely the first thing he would demand would be that the recommendations he made at his last visit should be carried out, and one of the first was that Lady Elizabeth's partitions should come down.

Not that it would necessarily help much, Katerine considered as she walked down the stairs to the cloister again, then out to the lavatorium to wash and clean herself, going straight to the frater afterwards for a large pot of wine. There she sat at a wall, slightly huddled against the gusts that howled along the building.

No, what could the visitor be expected to do when the two women were so antagonistic? They hated each other, and never more so than now, with the competition between them for ruling the convent out in the open. That was why Margherita had sent her letter to Bertrand, after all. To show that a new prioress was needed here – one who could command the respect of the other nuns. And that was why she had told the nuns about the allegations in her letter: so that all would look askance at the prioress. By the time the visitor returned, no one would believe anything Lady Elizabeth said.

Margherita was a clever woman. Dangerous, too, Katerine considered. You had to keep on the right side of her; she might be a good ally for the future. The young novice shivered. This room with its high ceiling, benches and cold stone floor, was one of the chilliest in the place. Draining her cup she hurried to the warming room.

The calefactory was filled with a glorious orange glow from the fires. Two huge hearths lighted the place, the logs merrily crackling and hissing. Katerine got as close as she could, edging up to the hearth until her face felt deliciously scorched.

She crouched, staring raptly at the fire, but when she heard steps, rather than be commanded to leave the place, she slid herself back into the shadows. Two nuns entered, walking straight to the chairs and sitting. In their habits Katerine wasn't sure who they were, but she guessed when she heard them speak.

'Do you think Prioress Elizabeth could be removed from her post?'

'Why should she be? Who do you think's going to be able to prise my Lady Elizabeth from her prioressy? You don't honestly think *she* killed Moll, do you?' Katerine recognised that voice: it was Emma, the cellaress, a woman who had not been consecrated because she was no virgin when she entered the convent, not that it ever seemed to give her cause for gloom. She was always happiest with an ale in her hand and a friend to gossip with.

'No, of course not! Lady Elizabeth is no murderer. No, I think Moll drank too much of Constance's dwale and it made her blood overheat. You know how these things happen. It opened the wound that fool of a clerk made in her arm. But the prioress is responsible for everything in her convent, and the suffragan will want a scapegoat.'

Katerine's ears pricked. This was Anne, the fratress. She had no responsibility in the infirmary, for her job was to see to the chairs and tables in the frater, but because of that she was always about when other nuns talked, so she had access to good sources of information. If she believed Brother Godfrey had operated carelessly, that was probably the view of many others.

'I wonder if Constance realises her own danger, then.'

'*Her* danger?'

'Of course – she mixed the dwale.'

'Oh yes. I hadn't thought,' Anne said, and then chuckled quietly and cruelly. 'I remember her when she first came to the convent, you know. I said at the time that she was wrong for that job. She had no idea of the importance of getting the mixtures right. Spent most of her time daydreaming. What could you do with someone like her?'

'Would she have done it deliberately, do you think?' Emma frowned thoughtfully.

'What – get the mixture so strong?' Anne grinned nastily, and glanced about her before leaning forward conspiratorially. She murmured something so quietly Katerine couldn't hear, sitting back and nodding sagely and solemnly while Emma absorbed her words, then giggled.

'You think so? Who – Constance? I find it hard to believe.'

'You watch her, Emma. It's not only her. There's that novice, too – Sir Rodney's little miss: Agnes. Watch her in church, the way she behaves, especially when young Luke's near, the strumpet.'

Emma's eyes narrowed. 'Still, if Constance is proved to be guilty of that stupid child's death, that won't help the prioress, will it? Not on top of the visitor's report. From what Margherita told me, he uncovered so much last time that this will be bound to be the last straw.'

'So Margherita has taken you aside as well? She's certainly trying to get around all of us as quickly as possible, isn't she?'

'Do you blame her?'

'Not really . . . But Lady Elizabeth is a devious cow. I'll wait and see for a while before I commit myself.'

The bell rang out calling the nuns back to the church to prepare for Terce and the Morrow Mass. The two women stood, and Katerine remained hidden until both had swept out. Once the way was clear, she too got up and hurried to the door. Their conversation had given her much to mull over: so Anne *wasn't* convinced that the prioress would be removed. From what she said, Margherita couldn't assume she would win the post, which was quite a surprise because Anne was one of Margherita's *familia*, one of her most loyal adherents. If even Anne was wavering, then the treasurer wasn't in so commanding a position as Katerine had thought.

There was also the other matter, she remembered, trotting quickly along the corridor. It looked as though both Emma and Anne thought Moll had been killed by Constance – not that she'd heard why both thought that. And there was what they had said about Agnes.

Once inside the church, she slowed her steps, genuflecting to the altar as she passed. Her quick eye caught sight of Agnes. Katerine settled in her pew, and looked over to check her impression. Yes, Agnes was staring at the altar. Her attention was fixed upon the tall, fair-haired priest as he prepared himself to conduct the ceremony: Luke.

And Katerine felt that bitter jealousy clutching at her breast once more, just as she had when she'd known Luke was with Agnes again – just as she had when she'd seen him chatting up Moll.

Sir Baldwin was waiting at the door and introduced his wife. Bertrand politely blessed them both, and gave Jeanne his hand so she could kiss his ring, accepting with gratitude her offer of a pot of wine while his men were directed to the buttery.

'My Lord Bishop, I was not expecting you,' Baldwin said as they stood around the fire. 'I thought we agreed that I should come and meet you at Crediton. My house here is far out of your way.'

'There is more urgency now,' Bertrand explained gravely. 'Since we met at Peter's house we have had news from Bristol. The King is preparing his castles.'

Baldwin understood the meaning behind those words. 'The Despensers?'

Nodding, Bertrand took his pot from Edgar and sipped. There could be hardly anybody in the country who wasn't aware of the trouble fomented by that family. Bertrand himself had heard more about them than most from Bishop Stapledon, who had supported them when they had acted as an effective brake on the King's profligacy; but now Hugh Despenser, the son, appeared ambitious to make himself the most powerful magnate in all the King's lands. King Edward II, always vacillating and pathetic, seemed keen to let him have his way, even supporting Despenser against the Marcher Lords.

'Is there any sign he is gathering an army?' Baldwin asked.

'You mean he might simply be taking defensive measures in

case of attack? I understand that the King has demanded money from the Abbot of Gloucester. It can only mean he's looking to pay men-at-arms.'

Baldwin thought about this, glancing at his wife. If there were to be another civil war, he would not wish to leave Jeanne alone. Two factors weighed with him: his home was no castle, and he had little idea how long he would be spending at Belstone. If he should be kept there for weeks on end, it was possible that war could begin, and that the tide of battle could wash over even this tranquil part of Devonshire.

His thoughts were written on his face, and Bertrand glanced warily at the woman sitting quietly at Baldwin's side. When he had accepted the role of visitor, he had not anticipated having so much to do with women. Now, here he was, preparing to return to the convent of Belstone, a place so ill-regulated it was almost a sink of corruption, especially now there had been a murder – and this knight wanted to take his wife with him! Bertrand was about to suggest that he and Baldwin should discuss matters in secret, in order that he could firmly reject the idea that Baldwin should bring his wife, when the knight turned to his servant.

'Edgar, you will have to stay here to protect the house, and do as you see fit to keep the place secure.'

Margherita was on tenterhooks; Agnes could see that. The treasurer sat for the most part gazing out of the windows, over the cloister, without seeming to hear or comprehend what was going on about her, even when the young novice dropped a pottery inkwell, smashing it to pieces on the flags and spattering black ink all over.

'Never mind, just get a cloth to clean it up.'

Agnes stood a moment gaping, but then hurried to obey. It took little time to wipe away the worst of the mess, though she was convinced the stain would never disappear. When she'd replaced the bucket and cloth in the kitchen and returned to Margherita, it was clear the nun still wasn't concentrating on the task at hand. She stared unseeing in any direction other than at her desk.

It was intriguing. Agnes was used to Margherita snapping at her, urging novices to hurry. Margherita was known for her acerbity; finding her in this reflective mood was weird. Of course Moll's death had affected everyone, and the treasurer was probably upset at the ridiculous way that the girl had expired: surgeon's mistake, everyone said.

Agnes studied her doubtfully, then decided it was more likely that Margherita was worried about herself. Rumours abounded, and the strongest was that Margherita suspected Lady Elizabeth of murder. If that was the case, Agnes could understand her distraction.

Sometimes Agnes thought she understood Margherita better than anyone else. There was a tie that connected them: illegitimacy. That was why Sir Rodney had wanted Agnes away from his estate, because she was the constant reminder of an evening of passion – and sin. For the pious Sir Rodney, that was intolerable. Margherita didn't even know who her father was, nor where her mother had gone, and that made Agnes look on her with sympathy. She could quite comprehend the desperate desire Margherita had to prove herself by running the priory.

Not that Agnes felt committed to supporting Margherita. The prioress was a shrewd and cautious woman, and Agnes reckoned she'd never be dragged from her office without a fight. There was no way the Lady Elizabeth would allow herself to be exiled to the fringes of priory business.

For now Agnes would keep her counsel.

Chapter Five

It wasn't only Margherita who was feeling strained. Joan was in the frater when she heard a call, followed by weeping. She got to her feet just as Ela, the kitcheness, entered from the yard, desperately clinging hold of Constance, who was reeling drunk. Joan was astonished: if Constance had drunk one more pint of wine she'd have been in a stupor. Of course there was nothing scary about seeing a woman drunk. Such sights were common enough even in a nunnery, and Joan wasn't upset by it, but she was a little shocked to see Constance in such a state. The infirmarer always gave the impression of being so self-possessed.

Constance was lured to a chair. She half-fell into it, and when she was refused more wine she burst into tears, blubbering like a teenaged girl deserted by her first lover. Ela went to fetch water and bread, and Joan sat with Constance, patting her hand comfortingly until Ela returned. Joan left them chatting and sat near the door to the yard.

It was while she was there that Margherita walked in. She gave Constance a contemptuous glance, and walked past her to approach Joan. Her expression made Joan frown. Constance didn't deserve to be scorned: she was a good woman, dedicated to the convent, obeying God by helping the sick. It was understandable that she should feel guilty at what had happened to Moll while the girl had been under her charge in the infirmary.

Margherita saw her reproachful expression and had the grace to look shamefaced. 'I am sorry, Joan, but no matter how she feels, allowing herself to get into this condition is simply not acceptable. Look at her! Constance is a disgrace to her robes.'

'She has had one of her patients die in her room,' Joan remonstrated. 'Show mercy. That's what a prioress should do.'

The shot hit the mark and Margherita nodded. 'Very well, dear Joan. I shall remember. Though I still feel that being sluttish drunk is contemptible for a nun.'

'Perhaps you do, but letting people know won't help you, will it?' Joan chuckled. 'What's more, the prioress is a wily old vixen. If you give her an opportunity, she'll stab you before you see her attack forming.' She helped herself to wine from a jug. Most of her spare time for the last thirty-nine years had been taken up with teaching this woman all she knew, and she had little desire to see that investment wasted. She finished her wine, cast a glance at Constance, and murmured, 'I think I should return to the infirmary. Cecily might need something, and poor Constance is in no fit state.'

'A good idea.' Margherita watched Joan rise and walk to the door. It was hard sometimes to remember how old Joan was, she reflected, looking at the woman's solid gait. She practically marched out – stolid, dependable, and resolute as a rock.

Margherita waited. Soon more nuns would enter, coming to snatch a snack to keep them going through the morning. However, as she poured herself more wine, a shadow fell across the doorway. It was Lady Elizabeth, who walked in and, ignoring her, went straight to the infirmarer, crouching at Constance's side in the humblest manner possible, speaking gently and quietly. When Elizabeth stood, a hand resting on the young infirmarer's shoulder, she met Margherita's gaze. This time there was no fear in her eyes, only cold, naked determination.

Margherita shivered as the prioress swept from the room.

When Katerine entered the frater a little later, Constance was still sitting with Ela, her head supported on both hands as she stared blearily at the wall. Nearby Denise was in her favourite place, and as Ela returned to her kitchen, Denise passed her pot to Constance, who drank greedily.

Glancing at the drunk infirmarer, Katerine was not inclined to hang around this unsavoury scene. She was on her way to the kitchen to beg a meat pie and eat it when, to her disgust, she felt Constance grab hold of her arm.

'What'd you do, eh? How can I ever get forgiven?'

'Constance, she's only a novice,' Denise giggled, reaching over to try to prise Constance's fingers free.

'So? She can love, can't she?' the nun demanded. 'She's got a heart like you or me, hasn't she?' Her truculence spent, she snivelled to herself a moment, still keeping a firm grip on Katerine. 'It's not fair, it's *not*! *She* can have her bastard, but we're stuck in here, supposed to keep away from men, and if we happen to enjoy just a short time with one, we're forced to leave 'em. But *she's* a lady, so she can do what she wants. Where's the fairness in that, eh?'

'Run along, girl,' Denise hissed as she finally loosened Constance's grip. 'Go on, get out of here! As for *you*,' she added, grasping Katerine's robe as the novice made to escape, hauling her close so that she had to inhale Denise's foul breath, 'if I hear that there are any stories circulating among the novices suggesting that the infirmarer has been drunk, I'll flay the hide off you. Understand? Now piss off!'

Shaken despite herself, Katerine scurried away; it was only when she arrived at the door to the cloister that she realised she hadn't fetched herself the pie. Irritated, she decided to avoid the frater by taking the longer route to the kitchen, so she turned up the alley that followed the back wall of the frater to the yard and the kitchen door.

The cook grinned as Katerine scoffed a small squab pie. It was common enough for the younger novices to feel the pangs of hunger between their meals, and Ela believed in filling them up. She watched indulgently while Katerine swallowed the last mouthful, licking her fingers and wiping them dry on her tunic. Thanking the kitcheness, she made her way back to the cloister. At the rear door to the frater she paused.

Inside was Margherita, in full flow. Before her were three other nuns, all drinking from large pots of wine, while the treasurer exhorted them to consider the best interests of the nunnery, forgetting their own private ambitions. The woman was using all her powers of persuasion.

'When the visitor comes back, he'll not just be looking at the prioress,' she declared, 'he'll be watching *all* of us. He's not going to be as polite and friendly as last time. Oh no. This time he'll be asking about the death of a novice, investigating how we sisters could have allowed it to happen. It's not as if he's going to be able to hide this matter from his master, our bishop. We all know what's going on. It's Lady Elizabeth and her man . . .' Margherita caught sight of Katerine. 'You – girl! Stop listening to chapter business that doesn't concern you!'

Katerine obeyed sullenly, but as she walked to the cloister, she wondered what was happening. First there was Constance, who must have been dreadfully upset to have got so maudlin drunk; then Margherita in a high old state of anxiety.

Both were bound to be perfect sources for conjecture among the novices after Compline, when all went to their beds, and she quite looked forward to holding the younger girls spellbound while she related the curious behaviour of Constance in the kitchen.

Perhaps it was the impact of the visitor. His arrival, for the second time in so short a space, was certain to cause some concern amongst the nuns. Katerine was only young, but she wasn't blind. The nuns flagrantly ignored their Rule. Many wouldn't obey even the lightest part of their duties: they didn't get up in the middle of the night to help conduct the Nocturnes and Matins as they should. And the drinking after Compline was excessive, just as if the nuns were members of a select lord's party, and entitled to consume as much wine as any wished without a thought to the fact that they should all have gone to their beds after this last service of the day.

Not that it bothered Katerine. For her, the more drunk and incapable the nuns were, the easier her own affairs became. She could learn much more when they were in their cups, and all information was potentially profitable. Such as Constance with her man – or Agnes with Luke. Katerine's face took on a bitter aspect as she considered them. Agnes – once her friend, and Luke – once her lover.

* * *

The tavern was a ramshackle, cruck-built house with a thin, moss-covered thatch, and when Bailiff Simon Puttock rode up to the door and gave it a once-over, the whistle died on his lips. Smoke floated from the louvre in the roof, but the limewash was a mess with green lichen and moss growing thickly, and his confidence in the builder was somewhat diminished by the rubble at the side of the place where a large portion had collapsed. Still, he reflected, it should last long enough for lunch. He nodded to his companion.

'Hardly looks the sort of place Baldwin would pick. More like one of *your* grotty little alehouses, Hugh.'

Hugh, his servant, ignored the jibe. He was a wiry, short man, and wore a perpetual frown on his face, as though he knew the world was making fun of him.

Today he felt particularly disgruntled, and as he hopped from his horse he tugged his thick fustian cloak about him more tightly. 'I'd be happier staying in an alehouse than going on in this weather,' he grunted.

'Enough grumbling, Hugh. Look on the bright side – Peter's message makes it look like there'll be women enough willing to warm you up at Belstone! So long as you don't let this pisshead priest Baldwin's bringing with him find you in one of his nun's beds!'

Hugh snorted contemptuously, ignoring his master's joke. The idea that nuns would grant sexual favours wasn't new, it was the fantasy of every adolescent male – and many weak-minded adult males, too. Hugh had heard plenty of stories about such women, especially the ones who escaped from convents. They often couldn't lift their tunics fast enough, from what he'd been told. Not that they were running any great risks; for if they returned to their nunnery they would be welcomed with open arms, even if they had to accept a penance of some sort to show the Church's displeasure. But there was one aspect to all this Hugh *was* convinced of. 'They'd not look at me,' he muttered.

Simon grinned broadly. 'So that's what has got to you – you reckon you're too lowly for them.'

'Nuns are all well-born, aren't they? Daughters of nobles and lords and such. Nah, they'd not look at my sort.'

Dropping from his horse and tossing the reins to the waiting
ostler, Simon chuckled aloud. 'In that case, be happy, Hugh,
because you'll not be risking your eternal soul by fornicating with
a woman dedicated to Christ.' He caught a glimpse of his servant's
black expression. 'Hell's teeth! Try to cheer up!'

Simon Puttock, the Bailiff of Lydford under the Warden of the
Stannaries, was far too happy to tolerate his servant's dour
expression. While Hugh looked over the landscape and saw grass
smothered under a freezing white covering, skeletal trees with no
leaves, paths and tracks made treacherous with ice and no prospect
of a warm meal until they arrived at the priory, Simon saw the
world differently: to him the land was delicately rimed with frost
which served to emphasise its soft contours, the trees were full of
the promise of spring, their branches preparing to explode with
fresh green leaves, the roads on which they travelled were solid
and dry instead of spattering them with mud, and the alehouse
held the certainty of a reward after having come so far: there
would be ale heated at the side of the fire. There was good reason
for his cheerful humour, for his wife was pregnant again.

He strode over the threshold into the dim, fuggy hall. Two
candles smoked at one wall, and a cold draught came in from the
high, unglazed windows, but the fire was smouldering nicely, and
the household's iron pot hung over it, a thick soup bubbling gently.
There were only a few men inside, two near the fire watching a
third man lying atop a slatternly looking girl on a rug in a far
corner.

Simon hesitated, but seeing a man near the door to the buttery,
waved to him and ordered two ales, then took a seat. Hugh soon
joined him, and eyed the two on the floor. It wasn't the sort of
behaviour he could understand. He had made use of prostitutes
himself before – which man hadn't? – but he'd never been tempted
to couple in public like these two; it reminded him too much of
dogs in the street. Although now Hugh was almost tempted to
nudge her and ask whether he could have her later.

For Hugh was lonely. It was a novel sensation to him, because he had been a shepherd out on the moors near Drewsteignton as a lad, and most of his youth had been spent many miles from other people, especially girls; his early adult life had been one of complete self-reliance, with only his charges and a dog for company, and although Simon, his master, had rescued him from the boredom – and damp – of that existence, still the change had prevented Hugh from meeting women of his own level. Those with whom he came into contact at Lydford were mostly suspicious of someone from so far away, for Hugh's accent set him apart from the servants of the busy stannary town, and when he returned with his master to their old town of Crediton, the women were prone to see him as a feeble-witted and awkward country fellow, someone of little account and useful only as the butt of jokes.

It was now over two years since Hugh had been romantically involved with a woman. There were whores in the taverns near Lydford which lined the busy roads north and south, but that was very different. And now Simon was to be a father again, Hugh was aware of a kind of jealousy. He hated feeling that way about his master, but he couldn't help it. Especially when Simon was so tediously proud.

Hugh watched as the whore and her bawd rose, the man joining the other two by the fire, casting suspicious looks at the strangers as he retied his hose and the girl went out to the room at the back.

Simon sat with a faraway smile on his face, paying scarcely any heed to those around him. Simon Puttock was a tall man with dark hair in which the grey was rapidly becoming prominent. Usually he tended to wear a serious expression, because his position as Bailiff for the Warden of the Stannaries meant that he was one of the most senior law officers on the moors, but today Simon was beaming, and the world was pleasing to his eye, for he was quite sure that his wife would give birth to a son.

They had had a son before – Peterkin – but he had died young. Simon had been so proud to have an heir, and yet when Peterkin become fractious and petulant, crying all night, he had realised there was something seriously wrong. Peterkin had a fever. Soon the poor little lad had diarrhoea, and gradually his squalling faded. Before long it was a muted whimper, and then a pained breath, and the lad passed away quietly early one morning. It was terrible to admit it, but Simon had been almost glad when the end had come, because at least he wouldn't have to confront his inability to do anything to help his boy.

And now Margaret, his lovely Meg, had fallen pregnant again. It was wonderful to think that she would soon be growing, her belly expanding fruitfully, giving life to a new child after three years of trying to replace poor Peterkin. Grinning broadly, he slapped his servant on the shoulder. 'Come on, Hugh, you've hardly touched your drink. Hurry up, or I'll let you collect the reckoning as punishment.'

Glowering morosely, Hugh took a long pull at his quart, but his stomach was not in it. 'It's all right for them as have the money.'

'I pay you well enough, and it's not as if you have other expenses,' Simon said happily, unaware how his words affected his man. He was sincerely fond of his servant, and would not have wished to hurt his feelings. 'You're not in the same position as Edgar, Baldwin's man, are you? He's going to be married soon and has to save every farthing he can.'

'Aye, well he's welcome,' Hugh retorted, but without his usual vigour.

Simon didn't notice his remark, but waved at the young prostitute as she returned to the room. She carried a jug, and refilled their ales from it. Hugh looked up at her just as she happened to glance at him, and she smiled.

'What's your name?' she asked.

'Me?' Hugh asked, then, 'Hugh.'

'I'm Rose. Call me if you want me,' she said.

Her face was plain and round. There was little about her which would usually have attracted Hugh, but today he thought her beautiful. She was perhaps twenty or twenty-one years old, not too tall, and wore her dark hair wantonly loose over her shoulders, but what Hugh noticed most about her was her eyes. They were steady and green, and he was just considering the coins in his pocket when there was a sudden row from the road, and such thoughts were thrust from his mind.

Bishop Bertrand entered regally, pausing in the doorway and perusing the hall with his nose in the air; to Simon he looked like a bad imitation of a cleric from a morality play, but he curbed the comments which rose immediately to his lips and instead stood and bowed, then winked at his friend behind.

'Simon, it is good to see you again,' Baldwin said, crossing the floor and shaking the bailiff's hand. 'Permit me to introduce Bishop Bertrand, the suffragan of Exeter.'

Bertrand held out his hand. Simon made the usual obeisance and kissed his ring, and the bishop sat in Simon's chair, pulling his coat tight about him.

'It is very bitter out there,' he murmured.

Simon took his quart pot and drank. 'Not as bad as it can be, my Lord Bishop. In this last winter, the snow down here was yards deep, and the wind as it comes off the moors is cold enough to flay a man. You could ride out over the moors, they say, and before you'd got halfway, you'd have lost all the flesh from your face.'

Bertrand gave him a look of open disbelief. 'Here? You jest with me.'

'No, my Lord. You can stand up on top of the nearest hill here, Cosdon, and stare out over the land, and when you look to the north you can see sunshine while where you are it is all cold, wet, and miserable. These moors have their own climate.'

'Then thanks be to God that I shall soon be away from the place!' Bertrand muttered. 'It's bad enough that I should be here again already because of the disgraceful behaviour of these blasted women, without having to freeze myself into an early grave.'

Simon listened as the bishop explained why he and Baldwin had been asked to accompany Bertrand. Gradually his mouth fell open with astonishment, and he absentmindedly took his third quart of ale as the young prostitute passed by. 'So you think the prioress could have been guilty of this murder? But what of the canons in the priory? Surely murder is a man's crime?'

'Women can be evil,' Bertrand said sententiously. 'Do not forget that they are responsible for the Fall; it was Eve's crime which drove us from Eden.' As he spoke his attention wandered over the room. Catching sight of the girl, he watched as she joked and teased the other men. When one of his guards called out to ask her fee, she stood and contemplated him, hands on her hips, before laughingly asking whether she should offer to please so young a boy free of charge for the honour of being his first woman.

The guard blushed, the girl winked and served another customer with ale, and Bertrand noted the guard's name for future punishment.

Seeing the direction of his look, Simon glanced around. Bertrand reddened. Simon assumed it was because he was not very experienced in dealing with such girls: tavern whores were often more audacious than ordinary women, which was bound to make them alarming to a priest, he thought.

'If the priory is efficiently run it would be impossible for a canon to gain admission,' Baldwin pointed out. He had not been watching and had missed the bishop's embarrassment.

'There are always ways for the sinful to meet the innocent,' said Bertrand shortly. 'And this priory is the least efficiently run of all those I have seen.'

Baldwin nodded, suppressing a fond memory. Before he had gone through the full ceremony to join the Templars, he could recall nights when he had made the acquaintance of the women of Cyprus. Like all the novices he knew which areas of the precinct's walls could be most easily scaled in order to spend an evening in the fleshly delights available outside the Temple. Now he was married and could once again enjoy natural, carnal pleasures, it astonished him that he had remained celibate for so long.

Simon waved the girl over again and had his pot refilled. The ale tasted stronger than when he had first arrived, and he assumed that she had fetched the house's best in deference to the bishop. He was aware of a growing somnolence. He put the pot on the table and concentrated. It was not so easy as before, and he determined to slow his consumption.

For his part, Hugh was bored. Talk of high affairs in a convent were of little interest to him. Picking up his pot, he wandered to another bench and sat down. He had no desire to stay in the bishop's company. Whatever was happening in the little priory in Belstone was nothing to do with him, and he didn't want to listen to a prelate sounding off about its apparently dishonourable occupants.

Here he was nearer the entrance, and the draught was more noticeable, blowing in through the badly fitting planks that made up the door, and he yanked his fustian cloak closer about him. The local men stood silently, eyeing Bertrand, Baldwin and Simon, while some of the bishop's guards sat nearby.

The priest was describing some of the infractions of the Rule which he had witnessed while he had stayed at the priory, then he went on to explain to Simon and Baldwin what the treasurer had told him in her letter.

'And do not tell the prioress of this,' he said, fixing Simon with a meaningful eye.

The bailiff pulled a face, scratching meditatively at his ear. 'You want us to hide the fact that her most senior deputy has accused her of murder?'

'If it is true that she is guilty of this heinous felony, I shall remove her from office.'

Simon was sceptical. 'You can do that? I thought a priory was more or less an individual lordship in its own right.'

'I can tell her that I shall report her action to the bishop . . . If she refuses to listen, I can demand to speak to the full chapter and let them know what she has done.'

'That presupposes she's guilty,' Simon said bluntly. 'And you're asking us to conceal the disloyalty of her most senior nun.'

'I see no other way of conducting this inquest.' Bertrand held out his hands, palms up in a gesture of openness. 'What would *you* do? Tell her, and then, if the treasurer is wrong and the prioress is innocent, wait to see what damage will be done?'

Baldwin stirred and shook his head. 'I see no point in this duplicity. If, as you say, the prioress is innocent, you cannot leave the treasurer under her authority after this allegation. She will need to be moved to another nunnery.'

'I am prepared to cross that bridge when I need to. For now I intend to investigate whether the prioress herself is guilty as the treasurer claims.'

Baldwin and Simon exchanged a glance and shrugged. Simon said, 'It's up to you, of course.'

'Yes, it is,' Bertrand replied firmly. His eye landed on Hugh over by the door, idly staring into his pot. The servant's relaxed pose sparked a brief sense of resentment in Bertrand. At that moment the visitor longed for the luxury of having no responsibility, of not having to worry.

Hugh, meanwhile, had noticed that his pot was empty, and he was looking about for the serving girl, Rose. She was attending the bishop, and Hugh couldn't attract her attention; she was doing her job, looking after the best customers. That realisation made Hugh feel even more alone: stuck, as he was, between the local men who wanted nothing to do with a stranger, and the bishop who was so superior to him that Hugh would be lucky to receive a 'good morning' from him. Even the tavern's girl had no interest in him. He was insignificant: a poor man with no wife, no child – nothing to give him any status.

One thing struck him after a while: the girl was hanging around near the bishop, as if listening very intently to all he was saying.

Agnes saw the prioress walking round and round the cloister garth, evidently deep in thought, and the sight made her pause.

Lady Elizabeth looked peevish. Despite the confident image she projected to the other nuns, it was noticeable that her *familia* had shrunk. There was normally a fair grouping of sycophantic nuns about her, but now they'd all faded away. Agnes was sure it must be due to something Margherita had said.

Agnes went to her desk and opened the book she was copying. The colours of the original were glorious and attracted the eye, and she sighed at the sight, knowing she'd never be able to reproduce such perfection. Resignedly she took her pumice and

began smoothing her vellum. She had just taken up her bodkin to
mark off the lines when she was aware of someone approaching.
Looking up, she saw Lady Elizabeth.

The prioress wore the same preoccupied expression. Apparently
unaware of Agnes at her table, she walked right past her and made
for the dorter's door. Agnes gazed after her; the older woman was
obviously under a great deal of pressure. It was one thing to be
threatened by someone like Margherita when supporters rallied
round, but a different matter when old friends disappeared.

That was part of the reason why Agnes had found it so difficult
when Luke had been unfaithful to her. She knew she depended
more on her friends than they did on her; that was why she could
understand the awful sense of being apart from others that Lady
Elizabeth must feel: one of a community, but isolated by her
responsibilities.

It had been terrible when she'd found him with Kate. The sight
of them lying together had appalled her. In a way she wished she'd
thrown something at the pair of them, or punched and kicked
them, but she'd had no energy, felt numb all over. Two people
she'd trusted had failed her. She could hardly comprehend Luke's
disloyalty. His treachery.

She was glad she'd got him back, though. It was a slap in the
face to Katerine: poor *Kate*, she thought sneeringly.

Like poor little Moll, always slightly behind the times! Moll
had told Agnes how she'd seen her with Luke. Oh? Where was
that, then? Agnes demanded. And why hadn't she gone to summon
the prioress or one of the other nuns? At this, Moll reddened and
began to stammer. She'd seen Agnes in the field behind the frater,
lying in the grass with Luke, she said, *and* she'd seen a man
entering the dorter at strange hours.

Agnes dared her to bring it before the prioress. When Moll said
angrily that Agnes should confess her sins in chapter, before the
whole community, the other girl just laughed.

Did Moll really think that Agnes could give a damn what *she*
thought? If the silly bitch wanted to go and blab to the prioress,
she could do so and welcome, but Moll had better remember that

Agnes was the last hope of the convent. Moll might wish to flaunt her immature piety, but if Sir Rodney got to hear the nuns weren't abiding by their oaths, his money would remain in his purse, and none would ever be showered on the chapel.

But Moll had been a threat. Especially when Agnes won Luke back, because no matter what Sir Rodney wanted, if he found that his embarrassment, his *shame*, as he called Agnes, had seduced a priest, he'd be furious, and would certainly take Agnes away from the convent.

That was the threat Moll posed. That was why Agnes was pleased Moll was dead.

Chapter Six

Rose hurried back to the tiny parlour that was her room, ripping off her dirty clothing as soon as she entered and replacing it with a clean shift and tunic.

It gave her a feeling of shame that she should have been lying there on the floor when the first two walked in. Men from the village were one thing; complete strangers were different. Still, she reflected, pulling her hood over her face and stepping outside, at least the prim little priest hadn't seen her coupling like a dog before the fire. A smile fleeted over her face: maybe he'd have liked to have seen that. The clergy often enjoyed watching others, as she knew only too well from her evenings at the priory.

Her mission nudged at her memory, and she scurried off along the track towards Belstone. After all she had heard, she must hurry to warn Lady Elizabeth about this cold-hearted bishop.

After all, Rose had a debt to pay to the Lady Elizabeth.

From the tavern Baldwin and the others made a slow progress, keeping to the side of the swift-flowing stream. When the ground grew boggy, they turned right and began climbing the western side of the valley.

Usually Baldwin liked the gurgling and chuckling of water, but today he was wet and uncomfortable. If there had been some sun it would have made a difference, but the sun couldn't reach down into this cleft, and all was chill. The air had a metallic edge that hinted at snow, while all the water on the track had frozen. Although it was afternoon there was a dank, icy fog lying over the water which seemed to sink into his marrow. Baldwin knew only too well that his blood had been thinned by his life in the hotter climates of southern countries, but the knowledge was no help. It was a relief when at last they broke out into bright sunlight.

Baldwin was astonished by the view that presented itself to him as they came above the line of trees. The hill opposite was thickly wooded up to a certain level, with clear moorland above. This early in the year, the sun was still low in the sky, and its rays suffused the moors with a glow like liquid gold tinged with pink. It lifted his heart, and he could see that it had the same impact on those about him. Whereas in the valley their mounts had walked along stolidly enough, now they had more of a spring to their steps; the men themselves relaxed and looked about them with interest. Even Bertrand's mood appeared to lighten.

The road wound along, rising gently, until they came out to a wide space of moor. Their path here was mired, but fortunately it was still frozen, so they were not covered in mud, and it was only when they reached the vill of Belstone itself, a tiny hamlet clinging to the inhospitable hilltop, that they found the ground softening; a farmer had brought his cattle along the way, and their hooves had broken up the ice, but soon Bertrand's retinue were out on the moor again, once more at the side of the stream, following a winding track that led them into the sun.

Their path took them almost due south. Although they were still climbing, the hills rose high above them: on their right a clittered mess with gigantic tors at the very peak, while left the ground fell away into the river's valley. Beyond it Baldwin saw a massive round hill, which dropped to a rock-strewn jumble at the water's edge. The moors here were windswept and gave the impression at first glance of being barren, with nothing growing taller than the stunted gorse. It was this which made Baldwin think the moors were so unappealing.

Between a mile and a mile and a half from Belstone they came across signs of cultivation. The bare, stony soil had been turned, and appeared to have been ploughed, although when Baldwin looked down at it he could hardly keep from shuddering at the thought of trying to grow anything in it. His manor had gorgeous, thick red soil in which any plant thrived and on which his cattle and horses grew fat with little help; here the scrubby, dark-coloured stuff looked almost poisonous. Baldwin pitied those who tried to farm it.

The hill on their right threw out spurs around which the river curled. These outgrowths obscured their view of the land ahead, but just as Baldwin was beginning to feel certain that his feet would never thaw, that his hands would shatter like ice if struck, and was idly dreaming of spiced wine before a roaring hearth, there was a cry from the front of their party, and when he looked he saw the priory.

Here the valley was broad, and the priory huddled low among the surrounding hills, a squat little habitation skulking away from view. Baldwin thought it looked as if it was embarrassed to be seen, it was so run-down: like an ageing wench ashamed of her raddled flesh and trying to gull young churls into paying for her services while keeping always to the shadows.

'A depressing place,' commented Bishop Bertrand.

'The good nuns have little money,' Baldwin said, feeling an urge to defend the priory against the bishop's contempt.

'There's corruption at the heart of the place,' Bertrand said bitterly. The ride had done little for his temper, reminding him that he should now, if matters had gone as he had planned, be back in Exeter and writing up his report for his master, Bishop Stapledon. 'They should have got their villeins to do any work that was needed.'

Baldwin had to admit that the priory did look as though it had not been maintained for years. The gatehouse was impressive, but the gates looked poorly hung, and he wondered whether they shut properly.

Behind, the precinct was protected by a moorstone wall which stood taller than a man, grey and intimidating, but there were sections which had fallen. Its protection was symbolic. Over it Baldwin could see the buildings lying within: a convent was not only a place to praise God, it was a self-contained unit capable of providing everything needed by the people inside, and this priory looked well-equipped with buildings. Directly before him was a long block; Baldwin felt sure this must be the priory's main barn, filled with hay and straw. South of the barn's yard lay another great building, probably the grange, where sufficient grain would be stored to bake bread and brew ale for the whole population. To the east of the yard were two buildings from which clouds of smoke and steam mingled: the malthouse and a kiln, both with slated roofs to protect against sparks. From the lowing of cattle there were stables and ox-stalls mixed at the western edge of the barnyard, and grooms moved about feeding and exercising their charges. To one side was the first of several storerooms with carts unloading at its entrance, then there was a low stone block with chimneys that would be the smithy. On the bank of the fast-flowing river stood the priory mill, and nearby the brewery.

There was the constant rumble and squeak of iron-tired wheels and wooden axles, a clattering and hammering from the forge, and the noise of many tens of villeins working, of cocks crowing, lambs bleating and horses snorting and blowing. It was certainly a busy priory, from the look of it.

The church was a good stone hall, set roughly in the middle of the precinct, and the first of the two cloisters was visible. Baldwin glanced up at the sun. It was standard procedure for the canons to have their area, like monks in a monastery, at the southern side of the church, while the nuns commonly lived to the north. Obviously both communities would live utterly apart, so that there could be no tomfoolery between them, and even the church itself would have two separate sections, one for each sex: the men based in the southern side. The riders had approached from the north, so presumably the nearer cloister was that of the nuns.

It was not a prepossessing sight. Shutters hung lopsidedly from windows; broken carts, dung and other mess lay in the yards behind the gatehouse; a small house had apparently burned down years before and had been left to rot; a series of outhouses looked as if they had simply collapsed, their component beams and tiles lying all about like scattered pieces from a child's game.

The outlying lands, where sheep should have been grazing and cattle roaming, were a waste. There were sheep aplenty, further up on the moors, but down here were only a few, the halt and lame, which hobbled about the grasslands. Cattle stood hesitantly by the dairy's sheds, waiting for the lay workers to allow them inside. Behind were the orchards, which should have been full of trees about to burst into blossom ready for the bees waking from their long winter's sleep. Instead the trees stood malformed, their branches unpruned, many years of growth leaving them unbalanced. Several had fallen, and yet they had not been cut up and stored – ludicrously wasteful to Baldwin's tidy mind – while the grasses grew tall and straggling between them.

Baldwin could see no vegetable plots with their serried ranks of winter cabbages, early peas and kale. The lands about the priory showed the same depressing bleakness: there was little cultivated vegetation, only weeds and furze; the land was rock-strewn and suitable only for sheep and goats.

'God's blood, but the devil would be pleased to think he could so devastate a holy site – and here one woman has wreaked his will.'

Bertrand's scathing tone made Baldwin feel a curious sympathy for the woman who was about to suffer the lash of his tongue. This French bishop was apparently determined to persecute this priory, just as his brethren had been keen to persecute Baldwin and his friends in the Knights Templar. This reflection lent an acid tone to his voice. 'It is always a tall order for women to maintain an abbey or priory, especially since nuns cannot attract so much investment as their male brethren.'

'It matters not a jot!' Bertrand snapped. 'Look at this place; if they were to work harder they could make this a small Garden of Eden, as is their duty. Instead they squander their money on fripperies.'

Baldwin noted his words, wondering what the bishop was referring to. Had he noticed too many of the trappings of wealth: fur linings in cloaks; or squirrel edging on coats? Somehow he doubted it. The nuns in Belstone would be hard set to profit from the lands they owned.

The men set their horses down the slope towards the gate. At the gatehouse, Simon sent Hugh to knock.

By the side of the door was a large metal ring, and Hugh pulled at it, ringing a bell. Soon a small door opened behind an iron grille, and an eye peered out at them, an eye which widened noticeably with surprise as it took in the retinue.

'The Bishop of Exeter's Visitor is here to speak with the prioress,' Baldwin called.

There was a squeak as the door shut, then the squeal of unoiled metal bolts protesting at being forced open, the rumble of a wooden bar being slid back into its socket in the wall, and before long the great gate was hauled wide by an anxious, older cleric. Other canons stood gaping at the sight of Bertrand and his guards riding through. While the visitor sat rigidly in his saddle and stared straight ahead of him, Baldwin found himself looking at the faces of the working men.

A priory like this did not only contain nuns. There were canons, men who served the church and ran the daily services, for nuns couldn't perform religious services. Moreover a place such as this was forced to rely on a large number of unconsecrated folk; the men and women who had taken the vows and wore the robes of the Order, but whose service was not spiritual but manual. In place of their prayers, perhaps because of their feeble wits or poor education, they gave their physical efforts.

The lay sisters who lived in the nuns' cloister saw to the laundry and the brewing; they tended the vegetables and herbs in the little garden, and plied their needles to ensure that all had clothes to wear. Meanwhile, lay brothers tended the flocks and cattle and made good the ravages of nature, seeing to the buildings, repairing roofs and windows, painting walls and woodwork, and generally making the place look as though it was cared for.

Although from the look of this place, they had failed, Baldwin reckoned.

Paint peeled; roofs were breached and leaking; weeds had cracked pathways, pushing aside stones and pebbles; cob and plaster walls had disintegrated, and were stained with the damp that had seeped beneath; fences designed to retain pigs had failed and the occupants of sties had wandered into the fields; hives lay ruined where the wind had tossed them. Near the orchard Baldwin saw a shed. It lay fallen upon the ground, its roof slates lying about it in a mess almost like a pool of grey blood. Everywhere was disrepair and dilapidation.

It wasn't so bad – or at least, it wasn't so noticeable – from the gate itself, but as they rode to the stables Baldwin could see even the scruffier of Bertrand's guards gazing about them with near disbelief.

'You see how they have let the place fall apart?' Bertrand demanded. He waved a hand as they stopped in the stableyard. The dung was an inch deep all over. 'Look at this! It's even worse than when I was last here. Then at least some of the manure was shovelled away.'

This really was an outrage. He had mentioned it to the prioress when he was here before, but she had ignored his commands. How the woman expected her nuns to study and serve God in this midden was a wonder!

Muttering a short, 'Benedicite!' in his anger and annoyance, he hitched up his robe and dropped to the ground, then froze in horrified revulsion as his legs and robe were beslubbered with faeces. He pursed his lips angrily and threw down his robe's hem before stamping off towards the main buildings, leaving his men to collect together his trunks.

His hand had been stained and he rubbed it against his now-filthy clothing as he marched. It really was quite intolerable! The stupid bitch in charge here could at least have shown willing. But oh no, actually exercising herself to make the convent look like a real place of worship would be too much for her. Or, rather, she knew damn well there was little chance that a visitor would be here again for a while, and assumed that she'd be able to get the place organised beforehand. Not looking where he was going, he stepped in a large cowpat and the muck spattered over his tunic, forcing him to suck in his breath to hold back the profanity that struggled for release.

That obnoxious woman would suffer for this! he promised himself. She was making Bertrand look foolish in front of his master, the Bishop of Exeter, by ignoring his strict injunction to smarten up the place. He wouldn't let her get away with it, though. Oh no, he swore to himself, scowling up at the walls of the nuns' cloister.

He most certainly would not allow her to get away with it.

The room Hugh was taken to was large, with good-sized beds set against the wall. He grunted as he dropped the heavy bags to the floor. As well as beds there were two chairs, a bench, a table, and a chest.

When he opened the shutter of the unglazed window, he saw a bleak view south, with endless rolling hills, their summits whitened with frost, and threatening clouds overhead. He slammed the shutter closed and surveyed the room. It was warm enough, for there was a good fire in the room beneath, and the thick tapestries on the walls stopped the worst of the draughts while the large candles gave the feeling of heat and a false impression of comfort.

Hugh picked up a bag and set it on the bed, untying the neck and inspecting the contents, but he dropped onto the bed without removing any of the clothes, staring instead at the far wall.

Since he'd worked for Simon he'd been happy enough, it was true, but now he felt only gloom. The girl upon whom he doted, Simon and Meg's daughter Edith, was growing older and didn't want to spend her spare time with Hugh any more. He tried not to grudge her the freedom to mix with youngsters of her own age, for she was fourteen now, and old enough to be wedded. It was natural that a young woman like her should seek friends of her own age, and yet to Hugh she was still a child and he found deeply hurtful her sudden – seemingly disloyal – desire to mingle with others.

It wasn't only her, though, and he knew in his heart that it was unfair of him to put the blame for his depression on Edith. His melancholy was caused by something deeper: this new sense of loneliness.

He was not sure how old he was. When he had been born such

things weren't important – not like keeping track of the sow's age or the cow's. Hugh felt empty, as though his life was drifting past idly. All his energies were spent in looking after his master and the family, and in the meantime he never had a chance to seek his own woman. His life was being used up in serving another, and soon he would be dead, leaving nothing behind save Simon's gratitude.

Never before had Hugh been so overwhelmed with non-fulfilment. It was as if he knew he was worth something, but had never achieved his value.

He sighed, stood, and began to unpack the bag. It was rare for him to feel so strong a melancholy. He resolved to seek a pot or two of ale when he was done up here.

Sir Baldwin and Simon walked with the enraged suffragan to meet the prioress.

Simon had a compulsion to laugh out loud at Bertrand's expression, in which frustration vied with pure fury. It was plain that Bertrand had realised his relative impotence in the face of the prioress's disregard of his instructions. The bishop was controlling his temper only with extreme difficulty; his anger was so apparent Simon thought Bertrand would have been incandescent if it had been dark.

The reason for his mood was obvious. Their path led them past the nuns' cloister to the southern side of the buildings. Here, at the canon's side, they entered an unguarded doorway. Even here, within the monastic clearing, Simon was struck by how shabby and filthy the place was. The buildings were in a bad state, but the problems lay deeper than that. As they passed the square of grass in the middle of the canonical cloister, he saw that a dog had been there: excrement lay on the grass. At one point Simon clearly smelt vomit, as if a monk had drunk too much and thrown up on the grass.

There came the sound of running feet, and when Simon glanced behind them, he saw the canon from the gate running to catch up with them, a younger one trailing in his wake. The cleric called out in a voice near breaking from his exertion: 'My Lord Bishop, my Lady Elizabeth will be so pleased that you are here. Let me go and tell her . . .'

Simon saw the bishop stop dead in his tracks and turn slowly.

'*Pleased*, Jonathan?' Bertrand hissed. 'I am surprised you could think my return would be in any way pleasurable. When I see that none of my commands have been obeyed, I find it hard to anticipate any damned *pleasure*!'

Whatever his words, Jonathan himself didn't look joyful at the reunion. He was a scrawny man, perhaps fifty years old, although Simon always found it hard to guess the age of men who wore the tonsure. Anxious eyes flitted over Simon and Baldwin, as if Jonathan was trying to assess the reason for their presence.

'Bishop, I know the circumstances of your return . . .'

'You mean the death of this novice?'

'It was merely an accident, Bishop.'

'Perhaps, but nothing would surprise me here: this priory is a pit of lust and degeneration – just look at this!' He held up his tunic, showing the cow's mess. The smell was noticeable and he winced, then shook with rage. 'Just look at it! I ordered that the courtyard should be cleaned and I find it worse than when I left; I ordered that the cloisters should be kept tidy and there's dog shit all over the place! What is there in the church?' he demanded, quivering with emotion. 'The cloisters are no better than a stable – I suppose you've got the oxen stored in there! Just look at the state of the buildings! Has anything been done to repair them as I told you? Eh?'

'My Lord, I—'

'No! I will not listen. Tell Prioress Elizabeth I will see her whether it is convenient or not. Go!'

Going to the rear of the church Denise fetched rags and beeswax from her aumbry, the chest where she stored all her cleaning things. She began polishing the woodwork.

Her arms had ached awfully when she had first taken on this duty, but now she found the hard effort rewarding. It was tiring, but required little thought, and she found her mind ranging over all the priory's troubles while she rubbed, burping every so often from the wine she had drunk.

Denise wasn't happy. At forty-three she was one of the senior nuns; not that she ever got the respect she deserved. She knew *she* would not have a chance of competing for the prioressy. Not enough potential supporters. Still, that didn't mean she couldn't enjoy the machinations an election would entail.

The place seemed to be falling apart around her. The discipline that a nun should have shown, the dedication, was missing with these new girls. They seemed to look upon their life as some sort of holiday. Denise blamed the prioress: she hadn't instilled the right level of reverence. She didn't seem to care about the observances – letting nuns sleep through and even bringing her dog into church.

That was the great difference between Margherita and Lady Elizabeth. The former was sincere, upstanding, and would bring solemnity to the place. Even to those dratted novices.

Novices! Huh! If Denise could have had her way, she'd have thrown most of them out. They were no good to man nor beast. Dishonest, unchaste, and sly. Nasty little girls, all of them. Katerine, Agnes – and Moll.

'Poor Moll!' Denise sneered.

The slut had deserved her end. She was no better than the prioress, all outward piety and strict devotion, while inside she was a dirty little hussy. That was what Margherita had told her anyway, and Denise had no reason to doubt her. Not after Denise's own experience: the girl had dared to accuse her of being drunk – not only that, Moll had suggested that Denise should confess to her drinking in the chapter. As if a brat like her had any right to browbeat an older nun! If Denise had dared, she'd have demanded to have Moll beaten, but that would have meant repeating what Moll had said. And Denise couldn't do that.

She spat on a recalcitrant mark and rubbed harder, her lips a thin white line. They were all so shallow: laughing and murmuring behind her back, just because she liked her wine.

Perhaps Moll's death would teach them a lesson.

* * *

Unknown to Bertrand, not that he would have cared, his voice carried clearly in the chilly air. In the canonical frater the men stared at each other, shocked to hear such rage; the grooms and stablemen near the cloisters stopped their work and gazed towards the church; in the nuns' cloister the sisters exchanged horrified glances; up in the dormitory, the prioress recognised Bertrand's bellow and gave a cold smile.

Taking a deep breath she closed her eyes. Bertrand's voice signalled that the attack upon her was about to start. His roar was like the first shot fired by a siege engine, loud and terrifying. It demonstrated that there could be no quiet negotiation, no subtle solution to protect her. Bertrand was like the King's own artillery; ponderous and slow, but once pointed in the direction of a target, he was as resolute as a machine. And here at the nunnery, Elizabeth was confident that her treasurer Margherita would enthusiastically load him with ever heavier boulders for his assault.

She looked down at her papers and winced. Even that boorish fool Bertrand in a fighting mood was preferable to more paperwork. She stood slowly, an elderly woman with a back that ached from long hours on uncomfortable wooden chairs, but as she straightened she was already planning. The death of the novice had led directly to this confrontation, and Lady Elizabeth was determined to win it. She intended keeping her post.

The visitor was here to seek an answer to Moll's death, but he would also be sure to want to place himself in the best possible light: this was an opportunity to enhance his own status.

Lady Elizabeth was old, and people sometimes mistakenly saw in her sagging jowls and slightly weak blue eyes the proofs of feminine frailty. This very Bertrand had assumed her to be an irrational woman, a broken reed – harmless, perhaps, but vulnerable. He had thought her a titular head, someone without real power.

Yet that was to underestimate her. 'So he wishes me removed, thinking to accuse me of murder,' she hissed.

It was Rose from the tavern, sitting on a bench at her window, who had helped her come to that conclusion. From Bertrand's conversation in the tavern Lady Elizabeth was to be made a scapegoat and forced to resign. Her treasurer was behind it. Well, Lady Elizabeth was not of a mood to resign. It would take a stronger man than this French idiot to remove her.

'He will not say that I am accused of murder,' she stated, peering through the dirty panes of glass to the moors.

'No. He said that they were all to keep quiet about the treasurer's letter.'

'Well, I am warned,' Elizabeth said thoughtfully.

Rose was silent, watching her at the window. The prioress stood frowning out shortsightedly, her hands clasped before her breast, but then she whirled around and faced the girl.

'You are sure, Rose – *quite* sure – that he said he had received a letter saying that I was the girl's murderer, and that this letter came from Margherita?'

'Yes, I heard him talking to the black-bearded man, saying that the letter was why they had all had to come here in such a hurry.'

There was a gust of wind, and the papers on the table moved as the window rattled. From the far end of the dorter there came a crash as a tile fell from the roof. Elizabeth winced and turned her eyes heavenwards. 'Merciful Father!'

Hearing the footsteps rushing up the stairs, she waved a hand absently, seeing Rose make ready to flee. 'It's not the bishop, child. Stay there.'

Before Jonathan could pound on her door, Elizabeth herself opened it. 'Come inside, Jonathan.'

The pale cleric glanced at Rose. 'I have come from Bishop Bertrand, my Lady, and he demands that you attend him instantly.'

'How very rude of him,' Elizabeth said primly. 'You will tell him that I shall be pleased to see him after Vespers, but that until then I fear I have much to occupy me.'

Jonathan gaped. 'My Lady, but he said—'

'You will point out to him that a prioress has other calls upon her time, and that although I have a duty to hospitality and will be happy to lodge him and his men within the precincts of the church,

I still have other responsibilities to attend to.'

'Don't you think you should agree to see him soon?' The ageing cleric stared from her to the door as if expecting the bishop to appear at any moment. 'He might think it strange that you don't go to him to talk about the dead novice.'

'Moll is dead. Talking to him now or after Vespers will make no difference to her. In any case, I doubt not that he will be more than delighted to wander around the place and talk to the other nuns. They will feed him with rumour and allegations to their hearts' content. I have other work to do. Go along now, and tell him.'

As soon as Jonathan had disappeared, this time walking dolefully in the anticipation of more furious shouting, Lady Elizabeth turned to face Rose. 'Very well! The die is cast, and this silly man will do his worst.'

'What will you do?'

'Me? Oh, I shall allow him all the time he needs to investigate poor Moll's death, and then I shall speak to him. When *I* am ready.'

Chapter Seven

Agnes hurried along the corridor and turned into the frater. Denise was in there, sitting at a bench, blearily staring at a jug, and so was Katerine, over near the far door which gave out to the yard behind.

'Katerine?' Agnes hissed. 'Have you heard who's here?'

Katerine turned to her a face from which all emotion had gone. 'Who?' she asked flatly.

'The visitor. He's back to investigate Moll's death.'

Katerine studied her for a moment or two, absorbing this news. 'Then you should be careful, shouldn't you, Agnes? After all, Moll was happy enough to spread those stories about you.'

'Me? What are you on about?' Agnes asked, the smile fading.

'Oh, nothing.'

'You're jealous, aren't you?' Agnes couldn't stop a grin of delight from spreading over her features.

'Who, me? No, I was merely wondering what the prioress could say . . .'

'Don't even think it,' Agnes smiled, but there was steel in her eyes. 'If Luke and me get found out, I'll explain how he services all of us. What is it? Do you want Luke back?'

'What would I do with him?' Katerine demanded scathingly. 'A feeble priest!'

As she stood to leave the room, Agnes barred her way. 'Not so feeble, Kate. He's got more stamina than Sir Rodney's stallion. But if I hear you've spread tales about me, I'll see you regret it. If anyone comes asking me about Luke, I'll know who has been talking. Understand?'

The older girl curled her lip and pushed her way past to the cloister, while Agnes stared after her thoughtfully. Neither noticed how Denise had absorbed every word.

* * *

It was a while after Jonathan's departure that Bertrand realised he was still holding his robe's hem, and a whiff of the ordure clinging to it made him hurriedly drop it with a muttered 'God's cods!'

It was infuriating. Here he was, supposedly invested with the power and majesty of the Bishop of Exeter, a man whom these foolish churls should fear as their lord here on earth, a representative of the God Whom they served, and yet they ignored him. They thought that out here, far from the conventions of civilised life in Exeter, they might live as they wished.

Bertrand squared his shoulders: the prioress would not get away with it! Bertrand was convinced that there was serious corruption causing the failings of this convent, here at Belstone. The prioress, if the treasurer was to be believed, was indulging her every sinful whim, and that meant that she was leading the whole nunnery down the path to evil, not even balking at murder.

And yet even he couldn't quite swallow that. Even now, standing here with the muck and ruin about him, he found it hard to believe that the Lady Elizabeth could be responsible for Moll's death. No matter how angry he became, that central and horrific idea, that a nun in Holy Orders, a prioress, could commit such a hideous crime, was so abhorrent that it was literally unbelievable – almost. That was why, if he was honest with himself, he had asked Peter Clifford to recommend a man who was able to investigate it for him.

Bertrand had no wish to conduct such an enquiry himself. There was no point. A girl had died – but boys and girls died every day. Many others would die. The death was not important.

No, the crucial thing was the nunnery itself. It was a part of God's scheme, a place in which servants of God could pray to Him for those who had died. Moll was dead, but if she had lived a good, godly life, she would have merely been hastened on her way to heaven. Bertrand did not worry about her; his concern was directed at the others, the thousands, the tens of thousands whose souls were put in jeopardy by the cancer of disobedience and sin at the heart of St Mary's. Let the secular Keeper and Bailiff

Puttock seek their murderer. Bertrand himself had a duty to the Church, to Bishop Stapledon, to the souls of the dead – to correct the lax and permissive society within the priory.

'Come with me. Let's see what these rustic cretins have done to the church itself,' he ground out, and set off at a trot.

Hugh walked out of the guests' hall just as the sun burst free of a fast-moving grey cloud; he stood a moment drinking in the air. It was cold still, but now the low winter sun was striking the far hills with an apricot hue. Rocks and bushes cast long black shadows, and the land appeared to glow with health. Even in his glum mood the sight was soothing to his soul, reminding him of his days in Drewsteignton as a shepherd boy tending his flocks.

There was the sound of chatter from further up towards the church. Hugh felt the need of something to drink, and there was a quality to these voices that seemed to promise wine or ale. He set off towards the noise; it came from a large hall set in the southern side of the cloister, and inside he found many of the lay brothers taking their ease. They sat on long benches at trestle tables, all with quart pots of ale before them to keep them going until Vespers was rung.

As he stood in the doorway the place went silent, and fourteen pairs of eyes fixed on him. Hugh entered bravely and went over to the fire, which here, as in any old hall, lay on a hearth of packed soil in the centre of the room. He held his hands to it with an apologetic grin.

Although the conversation began to flow once more, it was muted, and many of the men studied him suspiciously as they took long pulls at their ales. Then, just as Hugh had begun to doubt whether he would ever see a drink of his own, a younger man stood and walked up to him.

'Are you thirsty?'

Hugh nodded gratefully, and his new and very welcome friend walked out through a door at the back of the hall. Apparently the hall had its own buttery, for when he returned he carried his own pot and a second for Hugh. 'Here, take this.'

'Thanks,' Hugh said, his eyes closing as he swallowed almost a third in one long draught. 'I needed that! You have good ale.'

'Some of the best in Devon, I reckon. Where are you to?'

'Me?' Hugh paused, his drink at chin level. 'Where are you to?' meant 'Where are you from?' in Devon dialect, and just now Hugh wasn't sure. It was on the tip of his tongue to say he came from Drewsteignton, but he hardly remembered the place, he had left it so long ago; then again the place he really thought of as his home, the farmhouse at Sandford near Crediton, he had left five years ago; yet in his present mood, he was sure that Lydford, where he and his master's family lived out on the western moors, wasn't his home. He stared before him at the fire. 'Where am I to?' he murmured, then drank. 'Me, I come from Drewsteignton,' he said finally.

'Thought I recognised the accent. My name is Elias. I work in the smithy.'

Hugh had already guessed that from the dirt ingrained in the other man's fingers. A smith could always be recognised by the coarse black skin of his hands.

Elias continued, 'I've lived here for over ten years now, I think, working the forge and keeping all the tools in good order, or making new tyres for the cart-wheels. Before that I was apprentice to the smith in Moretonhampstead. I was born out that way, see, but when I'd learned my trade I decided I wanted to serve a religious house.'

He fell silent, expecting a similar brief summary of Hugh's life, and under his interested gaze Hugh found himself retailing his history. By the second quart of ale his temper had improved, and by the third he and Elias were enjoying each other's company.

It was as they sat with their fourth pots that Hugh noticed two canons walking quickly from the room.

'Come on, Paul. There's no point in either of us staying here,' said one, a moderately ancient man in Hugh's eyes.

'But Godfrey, I . . .' This one was much younger, maybe only twenty or so. He caught sight of Hugh and closed his mouth sharply, hurrying from the room.

When Hugh saw what had made them both leave, the servant's mouth fell open.

Elias followed his look and gave a weary smile. 'If you like her you can hire her.'

Hugh shook his head. He liked Rose and now, after a few ales, he could feel the first amorous stirrings, but through the warm haze that blurred his thinking, he knew he must tell Simon that she was here. After all, it wasn't often that a young whore could be found consorting with canons within a priory's precinct.

Baldwin walked into the church after Bertrand and gazed about him with a feeling of sadness.

In his day, the Knights Templar had possessed hundreds of little churches, all based upon the same design as Solomon's Temple in Jerusalem: unlike parish churches they were all circular. Although they were always spartan, they were as well-maintained as human ingenuity could manage, and if they needed money spent, they got it. This poor little church seemed as dilapidated as the rest of the priory.

They had entered through the southern side, from the men's cloister, and stood in the nave where men and travellers could congregate. The northern wall of the nave was some ten feet high, designed to conceal the 'Brides of Christ' from the lascivious gaze of men.

It was poorly decorated. Baldwin saw paint on the wall over the altar, and could just make out the figure of Christ, but the colours were so faded and flaked that it was hard to see what scenes were being represented. The walls at the southern side had been painted as well, and the pillars, but these too had lost all definition, especially where the plaster had fallen away because of the damp beneath. It was in a very sorry state, and Baldwin felt almost guilty, as though the church was a living creature and he was intruding on its death.

The altar was well appointed. Baldwin particularly noticed the large silver cross studded with precious stones, but this one area of perfection could not distract from the general aura of decay, an impression reinforced by the hole in the roof over the partition wall. Seeing that void overhead was like seeing a mutilated body.

'Good God!' Bertrand cried, staring upwards with a devoutly shocked expression.

Baldwin shot him a look. He had no need to remind himself that Bertrand had spoken of the hole at Peter Clifford's house. The bishop's surprise was feigned: there was surely nothing odd in finding it unmended so short a time after his visit – especially as a novice had died since; the nuns had other things to consider

Some clerics looked upon such matters differently. The fabric of a building like this was holy: it was a demonstration of the priory's godliness, proof that the daily round of services served a purpose, protecting the souls of the living and the dead. The whole place was God's own and, if allowed to moulder, that itself could be viewed as a rejection of God. The death of the novice had merely hastened her soul on its journey to heaven, to such eyes.

But Baldwin was not of a mood to allow a murder to go unavenged. If, as the treasurer had alleged, the prioress had assisted in the death of this young girl, then he, Baldwin, would insist on seeing her charged by a correctly constituted ecclesiastical court. She should suffer her penance for so heinous a crime.

'The roof leaks,' he agreed testily. 'Now, shall we go and see this prioress and make a start on our inquest?'

Bertrand reluctantly allowed his eyes to return to earth, as if he would have liked to contemplate the seriousness of the damage to the church for a little longer – or perhaps, Baldwin wondered, he merely wanted Baldwin and Simon to add their own expressions of disgust at such a flagrant act of dereliction. Whatever the reason, Baldwin was unimpressed. He was tired, hungry and thirsty, and reasonably sure that Bertrand was motivated by his own political agenda.

A door near the altar which gave into the nuns' choir opened, and a man walked through, a youngish cleric, fair and good-looking, who bowed to Bertrand and kissed his ring before continuing on his way.

Simon jerked a thumb after him. 'Who's that?'

'The vicar,' Bertrand scowled.

Baldwin stared after the man. He felt rather than saw Simon turn to the bishop.

'So, Bertrand, this prioress. Tell us a little about her.'

Baldwin looked away to stop himself chuckling. He knew how his old friend's mind worked: Simon and he had investigated too many cases together, and the tone of bright innocence in Simon's voice told Baldwin that the bailiff had little trust in the bishop.

'She is lazy. Look about you!' Bertrand said shortly.

'Is she young and indolent?' Simon pressed.

'Or perhaps she is too flighty?' Baldwin asked.

Bertrand sniffed. 'You shall meet her,' he said and stomped away.

Simon touched Baldwin's arm. 'Bertrand wants us to think an ageing trout like Lady Elizabeth could tempt a youngster like that vicar into her bed?'

'You know the lady?' Baldwin murmured.

'I know almost everyone living on my moors,' Simon grinned.

'I question this bishop's motive in asking us here,' Baldwin said. His friend's eyes narrowed as they both watched the bishop. 'He must have known that there was little likelihood of her attracting so young a priest.'

'So he's looking to ruin her for another reason,' Simon acknowledged. 'And that is why we are here – to help him. For promotion?'

Baldwin nodded. Simon had secured his position by his own efforts and was often quick to spot another man's politicking. Baldwin spoke softly. 'He's more keen on impressing Bishop Stapledon than worrying about a young girl's death.'

Simon eased his shoulders. 'He may not find my approach to his taste,' he said happily. 'For I intend finding the murderer – whatever the impact on Bertrand's prospects!'

As the two made their way to the bishop's side, Jonathan came scurrying up.

'My Lord Bishop?' he quavered.

'Where's the prioress?' Bertrand growled.

'She . . .' Jonathan's voice rose to a nervous falsetto. 'She apologises, but pleads her heavy workload, my Lord. She begs that you will leave her until after Vespers. Um . . . Perhaps I could offer you refreshments? Or maybe you would like to speak to some of the nuns?'

Bertrand opened his mouth, but before he could speak, Baldwin interrupted him. 'I should first of all like to see the dead novice's body; then the place where she died. Only when we have done that can we sit and relax.'

'Of course, sir.'

Bertrand glanced at Baldwin, then at Simon, who maintained a diplomatic silence. 'Oh, very well! But you will inform your prioress that I am most unimpressed by her lack of attendance.' He lowered his head bullishly. 'You will say that to her: I am most unimpressed.'

Denise heard his words with a thrill of excitement. She had been about to leave the church, for her bladder was full, but when she heard the angry voice of the bishop she hurriedly threw her cloth and wax back into the aumbry and picked up a broom, posting herself near the door where she could eavesdrop better.

The door slammed and Jonathan sped past. Denise tried to smile engagingly at him, but he ignored her, and soon his hurried steps had faded in the cloister outside.

Denise sighed to herself. She would have liked the opportunity to ask him what was happening. Noticing the altar, she made an absent-minded obeisance in apology for allowing her mind to wander again, then belched.

Her thoughts gravitated to the election again. To her mind, Margherita would be the better prioress, guaranteeing that the Rule would be enforced, but she could be a bit of a tyrant, and that might not be all to the good. Many nuns had their little foibles – not necessarily vices, of course, just little lapses – like her own. Denise knew she wasn't wicked, but now she came to think about it, the treasurer might prove intolerant.

There was nothing in the Rule to say a nun shouldn't have a cup of wine or two, especially in winter to keep the chill out. Yet Margherita had presumed to try to tell her she was drunk that day; the night Moll died.

Well, it was a lie. Denise knew she could hold her drink, and for Margherita to suggest she couldn't was villainous.

Pausing and leaning on her broom she recalled the scene. She had been sitting at the far end of the frater where she often settled when she couldn't sleep. At such times she would drink a bottle or two. It was pleasant there, and when the weather was very brisk the warming room was only a short walk away, so there was always somewhere to ease her chilled limbs.

When Margherita appeared that night Denise had only had the one bottle and was considering fetching a second when she saw the shadow pass on the wall opposite. At first she was struck cold with fear. All the novices were told hideous stories of the devils who lived on the moor, and no girl who had ever lain awake in the middle of a night, cold, lonely and homesick, who had heard the breeze mournfully groaning as it circled around the cloisters, or howling down the chimneys, or shrieking as it squeezed around doors, could ever quite forget the terror.

There, sitting all alone in the frater, she had felt the force of the tales return, and as she watched the massive black shadow leap across the wall, she couldn't restrain a squeak of horror: it was coming for her!

Instantly she heard the reassuringly angry voice of Margherita. 'Denise? Is that you?' She strode closer and wrinkled her nose. 'Have you been drinking again? Yes, you're drunk, aren't you?'

'I'm not, I was just having a little wine to keep the cold out. It's so bitter in the dorter.'

'You're drunk, Denise, and you should get straight to bed. What would the novices think if they found you asleep down here snoring in your cups as they came back from Matins? No, not another word: go to your bed!'

Cowed, Denise had obeyed. After all, obedience was one of the threefold oaths, together with poverty and chastity.

Yet she couldn't quite forget the sight of that shadow, not even now in the daylight. It wasn't the petrifying, creeping movement it had seemed to make, nor the attitude, as if preparing to pounce, that got to her.

Denise shivered and began sweeping more urgently as if trying to sweep away her memory. No, it wasn't the shadowy figure itself; it was the sharp outline she had seen. The pointed outline of a long dagger in one hand.

Chapter Eight

Simon's discomfort grew as the angry bishop walked to the door dividing the nuns' cloister from the canons'. He could see that Baldwin was unaffected; the knight was perfectly used to wandering about religious grounds, and Bertrand was beyond any feelings other than his own pique at what he perceived as a slight from the prioress.

But Simon knew no such comfort. To him, walking about this place was almost sacrilegious. It was a place of worship for those who dedicated their lives to God; not somewhere for the likes of him to idle about unhindered.

It was a curious sensation for him. Usually the bailiff was hardheaded and impervious to such fine perceptions, a truly secular man. Raised and bred in Devon, living almost all his life out at Crediton, he had always prided himself on his commonsense. Not, of course, that that prevented him from a certain amount of what he thought of as sensible superstition.

But Simon knew that his place was in the towns and wastes of Dartmoor, not in a convent, and especially not one in which nuns lived. If he had any choice in the matter, he'd have left right now. He was an instrument of secular law, responsible, through his Warden, to the King himself; but if a nun had committed an offence – even murder – he had no authority.

That knowledge was frustrating in its own right. He knew, just as everyone did, that England's stability was on a knife-edge, with barons up and down the realm joining forces to get rid of the upstart Despenser family. Simon was glad that he was entitled to leave his wife and daughter within Lydford Castle if they needed the security, for otherwise, with the country in the state it was, he'd not have left Lydford, suffragan Bishop Bertrand or no. If he had to leave Lydford, there were things Simon could have been doing to help secure the kingdom, raising money and assessing men-at-arms for the war which he had little doubt was shortly to come. Yet here he was, in a place where he could achieve nothing. Nuns fell under Canon Law; they were safe from prosecution in a civil court.

What was the purpose of his presence? Simon wondered as he trailed unhappily after the bishop.

Bertrand opened the connecting door Jonathan had used up near the altar and stalked through. Simon swallowed his feelings as Baldwin disappeared, and then followed them.

For the first time in his life he was in a nunnery; the experience wouldn't fulfil the occasional erotic dreams he'd enjoyed as a youngster. There would be no pleasure for him here.

Hugh missed the table with his elbow, and carefully lifted it again, sure that no one would have noticed his slight clumsiness. It wasn't as if he was drunk, after all; he was just drowsy. He needed refreshment after a long ride like that.

Elias leaned with his back against the wall opposite. He made no sign of seeing Hugh's near tumble as Hugh rested his chin on his hand, frowning with concentration. 'So she comes up here to visit each night?'

'Not every night,' Elias laughed. 'Just now and then.'

'Wha' – sort of once a week?'

'Yes, I suppose.' The smith nodded, then belched. 'Last time I saw her was . . .' he went vacant a moment '. . . oh, when poor Moll died – yes, that was last week.'

Hugh absorbed this. 'But why doesn't the prioress stop her?'

'Prioress has better things to do,' said Elias, and tried to tap the side of his nose. His finger shot past without connecting.

'What could be more important than stopping a whore in a convent?' Hugh demanded.

'It's more important she keeps it quiet,' Elias said knowingly, and grinned at his pot as if sharing a secret with it.

'You mean she's . . .?'

Elias glanced up, and then gave Hugh a very old-fashioned look. 'I won't talk about the prioress.'

When Hugh studied him, he thought the lay brother could only be some twenty-five summers old, no more, and yet his expression was as forbidding as a moorland farmer who had lived forty years on the bleak and inhospitable land.

Elias continued, 'I'm a lay brother. I may not be a priest, but that's only because of my education. I'm not going to be disloyal to my prioress.'

'Sorry, I didn't mean anything,' Hugh said hastily. There was an edge of truculence to Elias's voice that promised violence, and Hugh had no wish to be arrested for quarrelling in a convent. He hurried on soothingly, 'Look, though – all those lads seem happy enough to take her. Are they all just unreligious or something?'

Elias glanced over Hugh's shoulder to where other brothers sat drinking. Rose had gone into the little room at the back with one of her clients, out of view of the rest so that those who wanted to stick to their vows wouldn't be quite so sorely tempted. 'They're religious enough,' he said sadly. 'But you don't realise how hard it is to obey the Rule all the time, every day. Sometimes the men who've been serving longest just have to break free. Don't condemn them for being men.' He took a gloomy sip of his drink.

'I can't blame them,' Hugh agreed. 'How could I? She's a lively little thing, that girl. She could tempt Christ Himself with those bright eyes of hers.'

Elias nodded. It was hard suffering the torments of lust, especially as a man who had sworn his life to the service of his God. Whether a man could love his Lord so perfectly when he desired a woman – well, the answer was easy, wasn't it? The Rule said that any fornication was wrong, and the lay brothers must put aside lecherous thoughts. Not that it was easy when every day they knew that just a few yards away, over the wall that ran down the centre of the church, were women: some old, some young, and surely several of them as lusty as any of the men on this side.

'You must be very God-fearing to be able to resist her charms, that's all I can say,' said Hugh affably. He rose unsteadily. 'Well,

I'd best be getting back to my master's room. Thanks for the ale.'

'You're most welcome.'

Elias watched Hugh walk slowly and cautiously to the door, and then out into the darkening yard. And as he watched the servant, Elias could feel tears prickling in his eyes.

'Who are you?' Bertrand barked.

Denise dropped her broom and fell back a step, her mouth working with alarm.

Baldwin touched Bertrand's arm and stepped around him, smiling reassuringly. 'Do not worry, Sister. This is the visitor, here to speak to your prioress about the death of the novice. My friend and I are both assisting him.'

'I am the sacrist, My Lord Bishop,' Denise said breathlessly. 'I am sure that Lady Elizabeth would . . .'

Bertrand waved his hand dismissively. 'I'll see her later. For now, tell us where the poor girl's body has been put.'

Baldwin walked at Simon's side a short way behind the visitor. Bertrand was rushing at this affair like a maddened boar, he thought. The man had no idea of subtlety. Even now he moved along at a cracking pace, hands clasped behind his back, withered left hand grasped in his right as if there was need for urgency. Baldwin was convinced that there was not. As far as he was concerned, the first thing to clear up was whether or not there had been a murder. No matter what the treasurer's letter to Bertrand had said, deaths could often look suspicious. Especially if someone wanted things to look odd, and from the allegation the treasurer had made, she clearly thought something strange was going on. No, Baldwin hoped the whole matter had come up because of an accidental death; if so, then so much the better, for then they could all return to their homes.

But if the treasurer was right and there *had* been a deliberate killing, Baldwin wasn't sure the hot-headed bishop would want to solve the crime. He felt no personal animosity towards Bertrand, other than the automatic dislike for a Frenchman of the cloth based upon his Order's destruction, but he had a wish to get back to Furnshill as quickly as possible in case war should break out. In any event, no matter what Peter Clifford had told the bishop, enquiring into a murder in a convent was work for a priest, not a Keeper.

Denise brought them to the eastern wall of the cloister, and now she hesitated at the door to a small room. Baldwin thanked her before he stepped inside. It took a moment for his eyes to adjust to the gloom, and then he saw the body lying wrapped up on a trestle at the far side beneath a window.

'Could you fetch us light?' he asked, and Denise gave him a doubtful look before she nodded and went back to the church.

'Come, Simon.'

The reluctant bailiff followed him to the body and the two men began unwrapping the linen shroud. Simon disliked this task; he always found it unpleasant but this case was particularly difficult, for the girl was only a little older than his daughter Edith, and she had a similar build. As he helped pull her yielding body over to tug the shroud from her, he found himself contemplating his feelings, were he to see a man do this to his own little Edith. His imagination took hold of him, and for a moment he almost believed that when the covering was lifted he would see Edith's sightless face looking up at him. The superstitious vision conjured in his mind almost made him stop and step away.

Moll was naked. Her tunic had been saved for another novice. It was a relief to see that the woman they were exposing was a brunette and not a blonde like Edith.

'Here's the surgeon's mark,' Baldwin said. There was a small cut in the arm, just as any blood-letter would make. 'It is hard to believe that so small a scar could cause death.'

'It's like I said, Sir Baldwin. The phlebotomist is known to me. He wouldn't make an elementary mistake like that.'

'So you say,' Baldwin agreed absently. He was pulling the linen away from the corpse's face. As the last of the covering came away, he stood a moment studying her carefully.

It was clear that she had been a pretty little thing. Here in the dimly lit chamber, she appeared to have almost a pale glow about her, and in the cool atmosphere there was none of the unpleasant stench that was the usual concomitant to death. Even Simon was little affected, Baldwin saw. Baldwin was used to Simon retreating as a corpse was revealed, his stomach rebelling. With her eyes shut, this dead novice had the appearance of a girl asleep, and as Baldwin surveyed her, he was almost persuaded that there was a smile upon her face.

'Surely this child wasn't murdered. She seems so relaxed,' he said.

Bertrand gave him a sharp glance. 'You sure?'

'No, I am only going on my first impression, but her face shows no signs of fear or pain.'

Denise returned carrying a large stand with three fat candles, only one of which was alight. 'They all blew out,' she said anxiously. 'I had to return to light one.'

Baldwin smiled his thanks, and used the one still burning to relight the others. Then he set the stand by Moll's head. 'Her features are definitely relaxed, but we have to see that there is no other wound on her body, if you want to be certain.' He looked enquiringly at the bishop, who waved his withered hand in assent.

Holding the candle high over her body, Baldwin surveyed the whole of her torso, her limbs and face. There was no obvious wound. With Denise's and Simon's help he rolled the corpse over, but her back displayed only the darkening to be expected on a dead body left to lie. Blood, as Baldwin knew, tended to drain downwards in a corpse. Then he went to her head and squatted down, carefully feeling the whole of her skull, parting the locks in his search for any sign of blood, broken bones or bruising. He had once missed a crushed skull, proof of murder, on a child, and was keen not to repeat that error.

At last he stood and peered down at her face, candle held nearby.

'Nothing, is there?' Simon said softly.

'No,' said Baldwin, but as he spoke his eye caught sight of what looked like a swelling on her lip. He leaned closer, then crouched, staring at her profile. There was no discolouration so it didn't look as if she had been punched or beaten, but her upper lip protruded too much on one side.

Baldwin held the candle to her face and lifted her lip gently. He stood peering at her teeth and the inner surface of her lip. The teeth had been mashed into the lip, puncturing it in places, and weakening the teeth themselves, as if someone had held something over her face.

'Well?' Bertrand demanded. 'Can you see something there?'

Baldwin set the candle back in its holder and stood lost in thought. Then he raised her eyelids and peered at her eyes. The irises were very small, something he had seen before in men who were drugged. Baldwin went over each of her limbs once more, but this time more slowly and methodically. When he reached her upper arms he slowed, going from one to the other, peering closely.

At the front of each of her biceps was a yellow-brown bruise. Baldwin wondered whether a cord had bound them, but rejected the idea. There would have been a circular mark all around the arm if she had been tightly bound. He stood back: bruising; swollen lips; her teeth beneath slightly loose, as if she had been stifled; the cut in her arm from the blood-letter . . .

Baldwin took the candle up again and looked carefully at the slash, pulling the edges apart gently, probing into it. A phlebotomist always made one cut, a quick slash over the vein. This girl had suffered two cuts: one over the veins, the second at a slight angle to the first, and deeper.

There could be no doubt.

'She was murdered,' he breathed.

It was twilight when Agnes left the treasurer's side and made her way out to the cloister nearest the church. Here she hesitated, agonising whether to enter or not, but her caution was over-whelmed by her recollection of Luke's face and she quietly opened the door and slipped inside.

Her heart started pounding with mixed nervousness and excitement when she saw him.

Luke knelt alone before the altar, palms joined, the fingers of both hands meeting all along their lengths, and held up high in the pose of submission, just as a knight placed his hands together before his lord and held them aloft so that his master could place his own hands outside and accept the oaths of loyalty. Luke's head was bowed, his whole posture that of a devout penitent, and the sight pulled at Agnes's heart.

Rather than interrupt, she glided softly along the wall, away from the candlelight. He looked so vulnerable, she thought; like a saint about to be martyred for his faith, offering up his last prayers before execution. It must have been like this when St Thomas à Becket was murdered: the gentle cleric at the altar, performing his duties honourably when the King's assassins got in. The thought gave Agnes a most undevout and yet pleasurable thrill. She wanted to call out, to make Luke start and turn around with that fear in his eyes, like a frightened stag held at bay by the hounds.

Luke finished his prayer and stood slowly, his eyes filled with what Agnes thought was almost a beggarly fixedness at the altar's cross. He dropped his head as he turned from the symbol of his religion, and as he did so, Agnes chuckled. Instantly his face went from one point to another, seeking the source of the sound.

She let him stew a moment or two before stepping into the light. 'I thought you'd be able to tell where I was.'

Luke gave a short grunt and rushed to her, holding her in his arms and kissing her nose, her brow, her eyes, her mouth.

The bell rang and the community stirred, all the obedientiaries leaving their work; nuns in their offices set aside herbs, food, books, inks; lay women sighed and dropped their laundry back into the water or into their baskets, others stood slowly, arching backs that ached from scrubbing floors, or reluctantly turned from the fires that promised warmth and comfort and instead made their way towards the cold church. In the men's area, canons carefully closed their books and lay brothers put their ales down or dropped their tools before heading for the church.

Denise was suddenly aware again of the pressure in her bladder.

She turned an agonised face to the visitor. 'I have to go, my Lord Bishop – that's the call to Vespers.'

'Yes, of course,' he said.

His tone of voice surprised Baldwin. There was a generous quality, like an avuncular man talking to his favourite niece, and Baldwin shot him a glance. Bertrand was standing still, apparently watching Denise as she walked away, but Baldwin was sure Bertrand's mind was elsewhere. Once again, he wondered about the bishop's motivation. Most priests would have been only too happy to discover that there had *not* been a murder, that the convent was free from that stain on its reputation – but Bertrand seemed relieved to hear the death pronounced as murder.

Baldwin covered the corpse once more, tugging the linen sheet back over Moll, gazing down at her reflectively. When he was done, he was surprised to find Bertrand had moved to his side. The visitor stood shaking his head for a while, but then went out to the cloister.

'Baldwin,' Simon said, jerking his head after Bertrand, 'if I was a cynic, I'd think that bastard was happy the girl was murdered.'

'He is,' said Baldwin. 'But forget him for a while: this girl was suffocated, I think, and then had her artery opened to make it appear an accident. Let the good bishop seek whatever he wants. We shall find this poor child's killer.'

After the service Luke watched the nuns file from the church like a line of saints. He felt the mixed calm and boredom he always experienced after a service, but today there was a particle of excitement. The visitor was here to conduct an inquest, Agnes had told him breathily, as she held him close and writhed her hips against him, grinning up at him wickedly as she felt his response.

He went from the altar to the door connecting the two churches, the two cloisters. Carefully pulling it shut behind him, he walked through the canonical church to the outer door and leaned against it a moment.

So the bishop wanted to find out what had happened to Moll, did he? He'd have to dig deep – and if he wanted any help from Luke, he'd have a long wait.

Luke was a most straightforward lover. He knew that his robes excited lust in a lot of women, and he'd always made the most of the fact. Living in a convent gave him a higher probability of success, for the women here only ever saw him, and no other men.

Not that competition would have worried him. He was content that his sharply defined features, grey eyes, red-gold hair and easy smile would win him lovers wherever he went. His experiences generally proved him right.

But for every ten who accepted him greedily, there was sometimes one who rejected him.

From the look of her, Moll was as lusty as any other novice. She seemed to know how to excite a man without even touching him; she'd managed that with Luke. He could recall the first time he'd seen her, the vixen. She'd given him a cheery smile, head back coquettishly so she was looking at him low over the top of her veil, just like so many girls he'd known, sucking her veil against her face, emphasising her lips, when she knew he was watching her. She couldn't have done all that by accident. It was obvious from the start that she wanted him. And he wanted her, too.

In some ways Luke had a blind spot: he assumed all women desired him. The idea that one might only see his cloth and wouldn't consider him in a sexual light never occurred to him.

It was Moll who taught him that some novices were truly religious. Stupid *bitch*!

Chapter Nine

Denise was one of the first to arrive in the cloister after the service, and when she saw the three men still waiting, she felt her heart flutter within her. It was such a weird sight: males, and two of them in secular clothing. Entirely out of place. She felt the need of a pint of wine to settle her nerves.

'Sister!'

Seeing the bishop beckon, Denise ducked her head obediently, and made her way along the corridor towards them. 'My Lord?' She tried not to sound curt, but her belly was complaining, and she desperately wanted that wine.

Baldwin looked her over. Above her veil she had intelligent-looking eyes, although they held a certain red-rimmed dullness which persuaded Baldwin that she habitually drank too much. 'Sister, this death is terribly sad. It is dreadful to see so young a novice destroyed for no reason. Do you have any idea who could have been responsible?'

'Me, sir?' She shook her head slowly. 'I can think of no one who could wish to harm her. Moll was very quiet . . . very devoted to the church.'

'She had no faults?' Baldwin pressed her gently. Denise opened her mouth but there was a tenseness about her. Baldwin smiled reassuringly and nodded towards Bertrand. 'The good bishop will confirm that you should tell us anything which could have led to someone wanting to harm her. We are investigating her murder, not a simple matter of taking a sister's serving of wine without permission.'

As she reddened, he cursed himself for choosing so unfortunate a simile.

'Moll was a good child, I am sure.' As she spoke two other

novices came past, one very fair and full-bodied, the other olive-skinned and with dark, flashing eyes. All three men noticed them, and Denise saw their attention waver. 'Moll was like those two,' she said. 'Young and flighty. I think she was more fervent in her prayers, but she was a novice, and girls now aren't like they were in my day. They don't show the right reverence to the church and nuns.'

'Was Moll irreverent?' Simon asked.

'She was . . . *overconfident*. She was convinced that she was superior to everyone else,' Denise said, holding Baldwin's gaze. Suddenly she found that she couldn't keep from blurting out, 'She would have been happier if she could have died with the stigmata after a life of telling others how to live.'

'Ah! She was a zealot?'

'Yes – a fanatic. She'd come and chastise us for what she saw as irreligious behaviour. As if *she* had any idea! She was too young to know anything about life or service.'

'Did she try to talk to your sisters?' Baldwin pressed mildly.

Denise stiffened. His question appeared to imply that she had simply complained because of Moll's words to *her*. 'Sir Baldwin, Moll spoke to almost all of us – novices *and* sisters – even, to my knowledge, the treasurer. I don't think she had the arrogance to try confronting the prioress, but no doubt she would have rectified that before long, had she lived.'

'The other novices, how did they react to her?' Simon asked.

'They're like girls the world over – they often have to be chastised for their indiscipline. Their behaviour leaves much to be desired.'

'They misbehave?'

'If I could have my way I'd have them *thrashed*! They bring dishonour upon the whole convent.'

'In what way? Are they impious?'

'Some have only an outward display of piety,' she agreed primly. 'Forgetting their place in the world, even forgetting their vows and—'

Bertrand cleared his throat and Denise took his warning,

snapping her mouth shut and glancing down at the ground.

'I have heard talk of disobedience,' Baldwin murmured understandingly.

'It's worse than mere disobedience, Sir Knight. Some of these young ones appear to have no belief in their calling. Take that girl, Agnes, the fair one. I see no proof that *she* has a vocation, only a lord who wishes to be shot of her . . .'

'I think we should move on,' said Bertrand quickly. He had no wish to have Sir Rodney's motives in placing Agnes at the nunnery questioned.

'Very well,' said Baldwin. 'Where were you on the night the girl died?'

'I couldn't sleep, my Lord. I went to the frater for something to drink,' she said.

There was a brittleness to her smile that persuaded Baldwin she was often to be found down there, a pot of wine before her, long after she should have been in her bed. 'Did you see anyone?' he asked. 'Was the prioress about, for example?'

Her face reddening, Denise shook her head. 'Lady Elizabeth wasn't around, no. I heard her in her chamber.' She hesitated, then continued more slowly. 'I did see *something*, though. An awful apparition. A shadow which crept along the wall as if hunting me.'

Baldwin nodded seriously. 'Show us where this was, Sister.'

Nothing loath, she took them to the frater and showed where she had been seated. It was near the farther side of the room, by the screens which gave out to the buttery. 'Here,' she said, indicating the door to the yard behind. 'That door was open, and the shadow was flung against the wall before me.'

Where she was sitting, someone walking in the yard behind the hall, outside the cloister itself, would have had their shadow thrown against the wall in front of her. The wall to the cloister. Baldwin sucked at his moustache. 'Was the shadow that of anyone you recognised?'

'It was a nun,' she admitted after a pause. When the silence which followed her words became too much, she burst out, 'Margherita, our treasurer!'

Bertrand glanced at Baldwin, and then demanded impatiently, 'What of it? Why on earth should you have been so fearful of a nun's shade?'

'Because she had a dagger in her hand!'

As she swept from the church, Margherita saw the three men standing near the frater with Denise, and she caught her breath, unsure whether to take the boar by the tusks or not. As she wavered, she saw Denise move away, and then the visitor's eye lit upon her. Stiffening her back, Margherita strode to him.

'My Lord, you have come to look into that poor child's death?'

The visitor looked less appealing now than he had when he first came, she thought to herself. Then he had been all smiles whenever he met her. Now he wore a sour expression as if he trusted no one. She felt a shiver run down her spine – she suddenly realised he might suspect even *her* of having a part in Moll's death.

He gave her a cold smile and she turned her attention on the other two men. The one with greying hair she privately noted down as being some kind of clerical assistant at first, but the other was different. She didn't like the way the bearded man surveyed her. He had keen, shrewd eyes that seemed to see through her to the political machinations within her mind.

'I returned as you asked, and we have just been studying the girl's body,' Bertrand said. He introduced her to Baldwin and Simon. 'And I have to say, as you thought, she appears to have been murdered. We must establish who killed her.'

Margherita inclined her head. 'I understand.'

Baldwin said, 'Do you know what happened on the night this novice was found dead?'

'I didn't witness her murder, if that's what you mean,' she said sharply.

'We have already heard that you were walking about that night, that you had a dagger in your hand. Why?'

Margherita reeled inwardly but managed a smile although, had there been tool and opportunity, she could easily have stabbed

Denise at that moment. Silkily she said, 'I suppose you have been talking to our sacrist. Denise drinks more than she should, my Lord, and sometimes she sees things which aren't there.'

'You weren't walking about that night?'

'I did take a stroll, but when I saw Denise in the frater I told her to leave the wine for the night and go to bed. I went up as well.'

'Why were you holding a dagger?' Baldwin demanded relentlessly.

Margherita gave a small sigh. 'If I wake in the night, I usually carry a small dagger with me: there are such awful rumours of murder and mayhem in convents these days, and the good prioress has allowed our walls to collapse in places; it would be easy for men to break in. I went down to the cloister to think, and while I was meditating there, I thought I saw a man slip from the church door and go to the dorter. Naturally I followed, and equally naturally I grabbed my knife to defend myself.'

'Denise said you were out in the yard *behind* the cloister,' Baldwin pointed out.

Margherita froze a moment. 'Ah, yes, she was quite correct. I had been here in the cloister, and saw the man there . . .' She pointed at the door to the church. 'He slipped, as I thought, along the church wall and out along that alley.' Where the nun indicated there was a narrow way leading along the church's outer wall, away from the cloister. 'It gives out to the kitchen garden behind the cloister. From there a man can walk up, past the kitchen and out to the back of the frater here. It occurred to me that he would avoid the cloister itself, where he would be more likely to be seen.' She indicated another alley between the frater and the next building. 'From there he could gain access to the dorter, where the nuns were all asleep in their beds.'

'So you tried to ambush him?' Baldwin asked.

'Yes. I went up this alley and waited at the top. When I didn't see him, I walked along the outer wall of the frater, but still saw nothing. Then I noticed that Denise was sitting alone in there again with a pot of wine. I confess I was angry to see her awake so late, and ordered her to return to her bed. Soon after I went up to the dorter myself, wondering if the man had already got there somehow. I went up, but I saw no stranger.'

'Does the door to the dorter lead to other rooms?' Simon demanded.

'Yes – to the infirmary. But I knocked there and Constance, our infirmarer, told me no one had entered before me.' Margherita glanced down at her hands. The infirmarer had been quite rude about it, forcing the treasurer back from the room and closing the door behind them, snapping that Margherita should not trespass on her domain when she had the sick to protect.

'By now Denise had gone to her bed, so I did likewise and soon I was asleep. I was very tired – I suppose it's the work I do, making sure that the account-rolls are up to date.' She was keen to appear helpful to this serious-looking knight. 'When the bell tolled, I woke and went to church.'

'And at this stage there was no hint that Moll was unwell?'

'Constance, our infirmarer, is a very diligent woman,' Margherita said in a voice that brooked no argument. 'She saw that her charges were sleeping before going to church for Nocturns. She would hardly have missed the wound inflicted upon Moll.'

'So it couldn't have been a nun,' Simon exclaimed. 'They were all at church.'

Margherita tilted her head with a grimace. 'Constance first went to the laver. She woke and realised that her hands were dirty, so between her leaving and the nocturn bell . . .'

'I see,' said Baldwin. 'Who was in the infirmary with the girl?'

'Joan, one of our oldest nuns, and a lay sister, Cecily, who fell down a rotten stair and broke her wrist. And Constance herself, of course, in her cot next to the infirmary.'

'Does she always sleep there?' Baldwin asked.

'When she has patients to look after, yes. And in a place the size of this, there is usually someone who has been bled, or a lay sister who needs to recover from her efforts, so I suppose she spends much of her time out there,' Margherita said shortly, beginning to feel a trifle acerbic at his questioning. 'When Matins were finished, she'd have gone back to her patients. That was when she saw Moll's vein had opened again.'

'Yet someone thought that there might be another explanation, rather than an accidental nick in an artery. Someone thought it was murder.'

'Well, some of us wondered,' Margherita stumbled, looking to the visitor for aid.

Bertrand tried to sound conciliatory. 'Come, Sir Baldwin. We are concerned only with the death itself.'

'Quite right, and to investigate that I need to know what suspicions people have, why they have them, and who else shares them.'

'Why?' Bertrand asked.

Baldwin turned to him, an expression of puzzled enquiry on his face. 'My Lord Bishop, I am here to assist in this matter, but I really must be permitted to conduct my questioning in my own way.'

'Oh, very well,' Bertrand agreed, and gave Margherita a smile as if in apology.

'Now,' Baldwin said. 'Why did you assume this was a case of murder?'

Margherita gave the impression of being uncertain. She dropped her eyes and muttered as if unwillingly: 'It's the money.'

The knight blinked with surprise, and she could see she had his attention. Before he could ask her any more questions, she clasped her hands before her and held his gaze, putting all the conviction she could into her face.

'You see, our buildings are all in such a state. As I said, poor Cecily fell and broke her wrist because of the condition of the stairs from the laundry; look at the roofs of the church and dorter. Both wrecked. And it's all because of the prioress.'

'Explain,' Baldwin ordered.

'We are a poor institution. Ten, maybe twenty years ago, we had some wealth, but then the rich families stopped sending their daughters to us, and how else can we get money? No patron will give us funds, for what would be the point? Any man would give his donations to the larger places, where it is obvious that there will be people for many years to come, to say prayers for his soul; and then he would only give money to male convents. Monasteries get the chantry money, not nunneries; nuns can't hold services.'

'What has this to do with the girl's death?'

'Sir Rodney of Oakhampton has seen the dire condition of the priory, and wishes to confer upon our convent the parish church of Belstone, in order that the priory can build a new Lady Chapel, providing the prioress will allow him to have his tomb erected within it, and providing that she will also pay for a priest to celebrate Mass each day within the chapel and pray for Sir Rodney and his family.'

'I presume that a parish church like Belstone would allow the convent to afford this?' Baldwin probed. In truth he had never had much understanding of finance, and had no idea how much a little church like Belstone's would generate.

'Oh, yes, Sir Baldwin. It's a generous offer. He wishes nothing that need be overly expensive to the priory. Four candles to burn each day, and the priory's own chaplain to celebrate a daily Mass for the Blessed Virgin. That was about all his demand. Oh, and he expects us to accept any young girl whom he desires us to take as a nun, or when he has died, any girl nominated by his heirs.'

'I see no reason why you should thus assume the prioress to have been involved in the novice's death.'

'Sir, as a gesture of good faith the noble knight gave the priory the first instalment to help us in the short period while the church is being made over to us. That money has gone straight to the new priest.' She held Baldwin's eye a moment, then looked at Bertrand, speaking primly. 'It was intended for the roofs. Instead it has gone to this man.'

'Who has seen her with the priest?' Simon demanded.

'Sir Bailiff, the man has been seen here before. The evening Moll died wasn't the first time. Just two nights earlier I couldn't sleep, and went to fetch water. As I returned, I saw a figure ahead of me, entering the door and climbing the stairs to our dormitory. I hurried after but lost sight of him.'

'You don't sleep very well, do you?' Simon observed.

'Is your dorter so vast a man could hide in an instant?' Baldwin asked.

'Our prioress has a partitioned room near the staircase. The man must have entered it to satisfy his lust – and hers.'

'That is a strong allegation.'

Margherita drew a deep breath. 'I am not fanciful; I saw someone. The night Moll died I was convinced I had seen a man. If he wasn't a ghost, where could he have gone? Before I went to my bed, I . . . I must confess, I allowed myself to succumb to curiosity. I listened at the wall to the prioress's chamber. That was where I heard heavy breathing – it wasn't a woman's breathing, my Lord. And—'

'Do other nuns sleep so poorly?' Simon interrupted.

Bertrand held up his hand and nodded for her to continue.

She drew herself up to her full height. 'My Lord, I also heard kissing and the prioress's voice, moaning, and calling very quietly to her "love". That was when I left and went to my bed. I couldn't listen to any more.'

'You did not actually see her with this man?' Baldwin asked.

'No, sir. But the next day I overheard Agnes, another novice, saying that she had heard odd noises. And that's a great problem: Agnes is the girl Sir Rodney wishes us to look after. If she should tell her master what has happened here, I fear his reaction. He is a godfearing man, devout and honourable. If he were to come to believe that our priory was tainted, he would refuse to give us the church, and then we would be in worse financial trouble.

'So no one has seen your prioress in flagrant or promiscuous congress with this priest?' Bertrand demanded severely.

Margherita hesitated. 'No, sir.'

'And you saw nothing to indicate that your prioress so much as visited Moll that night, let alone killed her?'

'No, sir.'

'And yet you accuse her of murdering Moll, even though you have no evidence to show that she had any motive?' Baldwin asked with disbelief. 'Sister, if this were an ordinary investigation, you could be jailed for making such a malicious accusation without evidence.'

'Moll saw him.'

Baldwin turned upon her a suspicious look. 'She saw whom – and when?'

'Moll saw a man only the night before she was sent to the infirmary. She told me so, although I confess I hardly paid any attention at the time. I don't listen to the novices' gossip.'

'I see. What exactly did the girl say?'

'That she had seen a man walking up the stairs, just as I did on the night she died. He was dressed in a priest's or canon's robes; she couldn't tell which because it was dark and the two are so similar.'

'What was *she* doing? From what you say, your entire sisterhood seems unable to sleep,' Simon commented drily. He hadn't taken to the treasurer.

It was mutual and she gave him a cold look. 'Some of us, when we are concerned for the future of our convent, will waken. I daresay Moll was of that temperament. Perhaps she went to pray for the security of our nunnery.'

'I see. So what else did she have to say?' Baldwin asked.

Margherita took a long breath as if to control her impatience. 'Sir Baldwin, she told me that she saw a man going up the stairs, and yet when she followed, there was no man in the dorter. Where else could he have gone, but into the prioress's private room?'

'I still don't understand what this has to do with the death of the girl,' Bertrand put in.

'Moll liked confronting her sisters with their failings. I think she told the prioress what she had seen, and Lady Elizabeth killed Moll to hide her guilty secret.'

Chapter Ten

Luke walked slowly across the grass of the cloister-garth, and at the middle, he turned to look back the way he had come. He always enjoyed this view. From here, within the quadrangle of the southern, canonical side, the church rose upwards majestically. It had no great tower, but it was rather wonderful in its simplicity.

He stepped sideways to avoid a pile of dog's turds on the ground – *damn* the prioress's terrier! – and surveyed the eastern side. The first little block was that of the chapterhouse, where the canons held their morning meetings; next was the calefactory, in which a fire was kept roaring all through the day; then the dorter block at the cloister's south-eastern corner, with storerooms beneath and latrines behind, their chutes dropping down into the pit which was washed by the stream flowing from the kitchen's leat.

Southwards was the frater and more storerooms; the kitchen hidden beyond, far enough away to ensure that stray sparks couldn't set light to other buildings. Last, on the western edge, was the lay brothers' dorter and storerooms.

All was enclosed and secure from the outside world, and was practically a mirror image of the nuns' precincts. It gave Luke a sense of belonging, seeing all these buildings designed simply to protect the inhabitants from the brutal realities of the world outside – not that anywhere was overly safe any more. The news of war brewing on the Welsh March had reached Belstone, and Luke knew only too well that when armies began to move, they would often invade nunneries for their pleasure – being places holding both women and stores of food; in the mind of the common man-at-arms they could hardly be surpassed.

Luke shook his head. He knew how even modern men could

become brutes when there was money or when there were women to be had, and warfare meant that all the usual rules were discarded. If that were to happen, if it looked likely that an army could come here, he would leave, he promised himself. He wasn't going to run the risk of being murdered just to protect a bunch of nuns.

But for now there was no need to worry. And his life here was supremely comfortable. He had services to hold, but they weren't a burden, and there was always the compensation of the younger nuns and novices.

He had not come to this benighted spot through choice. If he'd had *his* way, he'd have taken a position as priest in a little church somewhere, so that he could get the benefit of the annual income, and then pay a pittance to some impoverished fool to actually see to the souls within that parish while he went back to Oxford to study.

Oxford. A great city – he'd loved it there, he recalled glumly. He'd enjoyed a flirtation with a merchant's daughter, but the silly wench had allowed herself to be caught while trying to meet Luke. Her father was a patron of the college, so Luke had been thrown out. The bishop, Walter Stapledon of Exeter, was unimpressed by what he heard of Luke's behaviour, and removed him from Oxford, writing to Bertrand suggesting Luke should be sent far away.

Luke had expected to be pushed off into the wilds, and indeed that was what Stapledon had intended; but the clerk who supervised such postings was a friend of Luke's who, even if he didn't approve of Luke's whoring, was happy to alter the instructions dictated to him by Stapledon's suffragan in exchange for a small barrel of wine. There were many similar areas of confusion which the good Bishop of Exeter would have to sort out when he retired from his position as Treasurer of England; cases where the bishop's clear instructions became muddled and were interpreted wrongly.

Luke wondered how Stapledon would react when he found out that Luke had been given the position of priest in a nunnery. The thought that he, who had been driven from college for his womanising, should be placed in charge of young and impressionable girls in a convent, would make the good bishop furious. And the beauty of it was that the clerk who took dictation would blame Bertrand; it was Bertrand, he would say, who gave dictation. If the visitor had intended Luke to be sent to a small monastery on the wild, wretched coast of Cornwall, surely the name of the place would have been in the document which was sent to Luke? And because the document read 'Belstone', and the document was signed by Bertrand, Bertrand himself must surely have said that Belstone was the place to which Luke should be sent.

Luke sighed and made his way to the frater, feeling the need for a drink before he went to conduct Compline, the last service of the day.

If he was to meet Agnes as he had promised, he would need to keep his strength up, he thought, and grinned to himself.

The door lay in the eastern side of the cloister. The sleeping hall was a two-storeyed building separated from the church by a narrow alley which led to a dead end, and which had once been roofed to create a small storage area. Now the little lean-to had lost its roof, which had been deposited on the floor to form a mess of broken spars and slates.

Baldwin gazed at the dorter. The nuns slept on the first floor; the entire ground area was given over to a large storage room. Inside were barrels of wine, salted meat and fish, haunches of meat and sacks and boxes. The smell was wholesome and spiced, not at all musty, although there was a slight tang in the air – probably rats. A solitary cat stood and arched its back at him from its vantage point on a tun of wine. From the look of this place, no matter what privations the nuns suffered, with the loss of roofs, the damp and so on, at least they wouldn't starve.

Simon suppressed a grin when he saw Baldwin graciously motion the visitor towards the dorter's entrance. Bertrand glowered, but jerked the door wide and stepped inside. From his expression Simon felt sure that he was beginning to regret having asked Peter Clifford to advise him on whom he could bring to Belstone.

When Simon trailed after them, he found that just inside the doorway was a staircase, roughly formed of square-hewn blocks of wood which had been sawn on the diagonal to give a triangular section, then fitted to planks at either side to produce uneven steps. It was the sort of arrangement Simon had been thinking of putting into his home for some time – for he and his wife still depended upon a ladder to reach the bedchamber in their little house.

At the top of the stairs, Simon found Baldwin staring at a heavily built partition. Simon himself had eyes only for the ceiling and the hole in it. While outside in the cloister, Simon had thought the breezes almost unnoticeable, here within the sleeping quarters there was a constant low moaning as if the souls of the damned were filing through in an unending procession.

It was only with difficulty that he dragged his attention away and studied the room. The dorter was perhaps sixty or seventy feet long, and all along it, on either side, were wooden screens, each open to the hallway, which separated the sleeping cubicles one from the other. He took a few paces forward and peered into one. It contained a rough mattress and pillow, covered with a blanket and some sort of coverlet, and a three-legged stool at the side. By the wall stood a large chest, its lid down and apparently locked. Certainly the hasp was firmly shut.

Idly he wandered along the corridor formed by the outflung partitions. Some beds were made, but equally many were not; some had chests, and those with the more ornate ones had chairs. A few of the beds appeared not to have been slept in, and when he looked up he could see why. Directly above was the hole. Beyond, several of the partitioned areas seemed more heavily used, and Simon rightly guessed that here nuns and novices shared beds to keep away from the rain or snow that fell in.

At the far end was a billowing curtain, and he was about to haul it aside and glance behind it when Bertrand coughed. 'No! You don't want to . . . That's the rere-dorter, Bailiff!'

Simon quickly drew his hand from the curtain. Thank God Bertrand had warned him. It would have been appallingly embarrassing to have entered the nuns' toilet and encountered one of them in a – in a compromised position. He turned and made his slow and thoughtful progress back along the dorter to join the others. They were still standing at the partitioned area near the door. 'What is it?'

'You are not aware of the strictures of the Rule, of course, Bailiff,' Bertrand said stiffly. 'No nun – and that includes the prioress of a convent – should divide up the dorter so as to give herself more space than other nuns.'

'Especially,' Baldwin added, 'when that nun intends to shut herself off from her sisters. This is almost sacrilege. You see, she is not superior to her sisters, just an elected leader.'

'This is not the worst, Sir Baldwin,' Bertrand intoned 'That was *one* of the points I was forced to include in my report to the Bishop of Exeter, but so was the fact that the prioress has seen fit to permit her nuns to keep their own possessions. She allows them to keep personal items locked away in their own chests.'

Simon could see that Baldwin was surprised by these revelations, but the knight was determined not to jump to conclusions. 'Fine. Now, we were going to see whether the man Margherita saw could have gone anywhere else other than into the prioress's chamber, weren't we?'

Returning to the top of the stairs, Baldwin looked about him. There was a small landing, created by the prioress's partition and a large board which was evidently designed to limit the draught that howled through the room. Beyond the prioress's wall was a small doorway.

'The infirmary,' Bertrand confirmed.

'Margherita said that the infirmarer prevented her from entering, didn't she?' Baldwin mused. He made as if to walk towards it, but then gave the visitor a quick look. 'What else was in your report, Bishop?'

'About the prioress? Well, I had to comment that she keeps a pet dog . . .'

'That is hardly a crime.'

'. . . and takes it to Mass with her.'

'I see,' Baldwin murmured. Being fond of his own hounds, he was not prepared to condemn the woman for that, but he could see that the visitor was working himself into a fine fever. To stem the flow of outrage, Baldwin held up his hand and smiled soothingly. 'We were told that the lady would see us after Vespers, were we not? Shall we see whether she is here now?'

Bertrand shut his mouth and nodded. Half-heartedly he knocked on the door to her room but there was no response. She hadn't yet returned. 'Where can she be?' he muttered.

'Perhaps while we are here, we should take a short look at the infirmary?' Baldwin suggested.

Bertrand agreed ungraciously. There was little point, he felt, in going to take a look inside, not when the treasurer had already told them that the prioress had been making love with a man. Wasn't that enough?

A good oaken door on well-greased hinges opened silently, and they walked inside quietly. The infirmary was a small hall, but warm and comfortable. A fire burned steadily in the grate, the glowing logs throwing out a golden light that invited drowsiness after the chill, wind-swept atmosphere of the dorter. Baldwin felt as if his face was absorbing the whole of the heat from the flames.

Down the left wall three wooden partitions jutted into the room, making four units in all, each holding a large bed so that eight invalids could be accommodated with ease.

At one end was a small altar with a cross so patients could always see the symbol of their faith; at the other was a screen with a curtained doorway. The only noise was a snoring from the bed nearer the curtain.

'Is it time for Compline?'

The reedy voice came from an old nun huddled near the fire. They had not seen her at first because she was so low in her chair that her head hardly rose above the bed between her and the three men.

Bertrand made no effort to speak; he was still furious that the prioress was not attending to him, and so Baldwin answered. 'Not yet, Sister. Compline will be a while yet. What is your name?'

'Who are you?' she asked in a quavering voice. 'What are you doing here? Men aren't permitted inside the nuns' cloister.'

'It was the visitor who invited me in, Sister. I am the Keeper of the King's Peace in Crediton.'

She studied his face with frowning concentration for a while. 'If you say so. You look more like a lay brother, though. Are you sure the visitor invited you?'

Baldwin showed his teeth in a grin. 'He's here. Why don't you ask him?'

She followed his gesture and stared full at Bertrand. 'Him? A visitor? He doesn't look like he's got the bollocks for it . . . Looks more like a pox-ridden tranter.'

'Oh, *damn* this community!' Bertrand exploded. 'I will not stay to be insulted by a decayed and ancient vixen! If you wish for me, I'll be in the quadrangle.'

With a glance towards the woman in which loathing and rage were equally mixed, Bertrand stormed out of the room. Baldwin could hear his boots stomping down the stairs, and then out into the yard.

'He has a temper like a visitor,' the nun observed calmly.

'What is your name, Sister?'

'I'm Joan. I used to be the cellarer,' she grinned, 'but now I can spend my time in contemplation.'

Baldwin smiled back, sinking down to his haunches. 'I expect you have seen many changes here.'

'Things move ahead, but often too fast. It's not right that the prioress should be looking to so much building. She ought to take stock, think about what she's doing. We're not some sort of business; we're God's house, and ought to behave like it.'

'You think the prioress is failing in her duty to the convent?'

'Don't assume things like that, young man,' she said sharply. 'There are too many tales being told in this convent about people. It doesn't do the place any good, and only leads to us all looking like fools. I never said the prioress was failing. She's a good woman, in her own way, and shrewd too, which is more than you can say for some. No, I only meant that I don't agree with her way of trying to ensure the future of the place. Building another chapel won't help much.'

'But you need the money from Sir Rodney's church.'

'Oh, piffle! So what if we do? *If* the convent has need of the money, wouldn't we be better off saving it for the use of the church and protecting some of the existing buildings rather than putting up yet another?'

'That is what you would do?'

'Perhaps. Or maybe I'd prefer to spend it on ale and crumpets! There are worse things, when you pass your life sitting before a fire in the cold weather. At least you can eat crumpets without teeth.' And she opened her mouth wide to display toothless gums.

'It must have been a great shock when the novice died,' Baldwin said gently.

'At my age you're used to the sight of death,' she shrugged matter-of-factly.

'Did you know her well?'

'Young Moll? Yes. She wasn't a nice person, but then so few of them seem to be. All outward penitence and humility, but too keen on seeing what others are up to rather than making sure their own behaviour is beyond reproach.'

As concise an obituary as he had ever heard, Baldwin thought to himself. 'Did you hear anything on the night that she died?'

Joan pulled a face. 'No. Nor did the other girl.'

'The lay sister?'

'Cecily.' She nodded towards the snoring figure huddled in one of the beds. 'She's got a broken wrist. The infirmarer made us dwale to help us all sleep. Needed it with Cecily's racket.'

'Is she asleep now?'

'Listen to her!' Joan cackled. 'She couldn't be much more asleep whatever you did to her!'

Dwale, Baldwin mused. Not a flavour to be mistaken: although the precise mixture varied, it was inevitably sour and unpleasant. Dwale was another name for belladonna, deadly nightshade, but leeches used it mixed with henbane or hemlock and a soporific, usually poppy syrup, to comfort those in pain. Many patients took it – especially when their surgeon needed them quiet. 'You all slept when Moll died?'

'The infirmarer had made it a powerful dose, but even the smallest amount knocks me out at my age. I know Cecily was well gone, because she spent all her time whining with pain beforehand. After she'd drunk it, she went quiet.'

'Was Moll served first?'

'No. I asked Constance to give Cecily hers first. The poor girl was in terrible pain, and I couldn't sleep with the row. Then Constance brought me mine and Moll last.' She shifted slightly, and now her face was turned to the fire. Her features were lighted by it, and the benign flickering of the flames tended to smooth some of her wrinkles, lending her a more youthful aspect, but the sadness of old age was upon her. Although she had no apparent regret, her life was almost over, and she was contemplating the life to come. She had little interest in earthly matters.

Baldwin glanced at the beds. When he asked, Joan pointed at the bed nearest the door. 'That was hers – my bed is that one.'

There was a third bed between them, Baldwin noticed. 'Did you fall asleep soon after drinking?' he asked.

'Very soon,' Joan agreed. 'As I say, Constance had made the potion strong and I remember Constance smiling at me as I drank, then going to Moll. I saw Moll take a sip before putting the cup on her table, but then I began to feel drowsy. Soon I was asleep and I didn't wake until morning.'

Simon frowned uncomprehendingly. 'But shouldn't you have gone to Nocturns?'

Joan shrugged. 'I often miss them. So do many others. Even the prioress herself is sometimes too tired to go.'

'You usually sleep through the whole night?' Baldwin asked.

'No, Sir Knight. I am usually too wakeful. I've been living here in this convent for most of my life, and the horarium has eaten its way into my soul. When I am bored I will often walk about the cloisters, and I find my bed a tedious place at night. As

I get older I need less sleep. But Constance believes that I need to rest. That was why she made me drink her strong dwale.'

Baldwin nodded slowly and he saw her face light as if with amusement.

'Sir Knight, there's no need to look at me in that suspicious manner. If you doubt my word ask Constance, the infirmarer. She stood over me to ensure I drank her potion. She'll tell you that I was dead to the world all that night.'

Baldwin smiled and rose to his feet, knees cracking. 'Thank you for your help.'

She gave him a sharp look. 'Help? I didn't think I told you anything new. Are you as foolish as that visitor?'

'I hope not.' Baldwin beckoned Simon and the two men walked out to the small curtained chamber at the far end of the room. Inside they found another locked chest, and a shelf or two set into the wall, on which were placed bottles of powders and liquids.

None looked appetising to Simon, but he distrusted most of the potions given out by tooth-pullers and other quacks.

Baldwin pulled half-heartedly at the lid of the chest, but it was locked. 'Everything in this place is stowed away, hidden from sight,' he complained. 'They must know it's against their own ordinances, so why is it allowed?'

'Why shouldn't they be allowed to store their own goods apart from each other's?' Simon asked. 'It sounds daft to expect everyone to leave their stuff out on show.'

'Men or women joining a convent give up their worldly possessions. As soon as they enter the cloister they reject material things, taking nothing with them. All they have is owned by the institution. These chests point to the heart of whatever is wrong here.'

Simon gave him a sidelong glance. 'Really? I'd have thought that the lay sister and old Joan there being utterly intoxicated would be more to the point. If they were all so heavily drugged, is that because the murderer chose to silence them all? Which begs the question of whether the infirmarer was told to drug them.'

'Or whether the infirmarer herself was the murderer,' Baldwin mused thoughtfully, absently shaking a glass beaker with a pale white powder inside. He set it back on the shelf. 'If she was, then why should she have bothered to smother Moll? All she needed do was give the girl a stronger dose of dwale, enough to make her unconscious, and then open her vein.'

'Perhaps she got the quantity wrong,' Simon suggested. 'Anyway, why should the infirmarer wish to kill the girl?'

'An excellent question,' Baldwin said. 'And yet if Margherita is right and a man did come up these stairs, he could have gone into the infirmary. Drugging the patients would guarantee they wouldn't see him.'

Lady Elizabeth sat in the chapterhouse and watched as Simon and Baldwin left the building and strolled to meet the visitor. Bertrand was bitter at being frustrated in his wish to see her. His anger would have increased if he had known how his dramatic gestures, intended to demonstrate his irritation, only served to make her smile broaden.

Chapter Eleven

'Where on God's good earth *is* that woman?' demanded Bertrand. 'God's balls, but she'll regret this! I'm tempted to go and wait in her room; force her to see me. She's avoiding us, and that's a clear enough sign of her guilt.'

'I feel we should seek her down here rather than waiting in the nuns' dorter. Were we to be found in the nuns' sleeping area, I think it might give rise to talk,' Baldwin mentioned with a twinkle in his eye.

Bertrand was not of a mood to see the humour of the situation, but at last he gave his ungracious agreement. The last thing he needed was an accusation of impropriety against himself. Glancing about the quadrangle, he saw two novices walking to the frater.

'If I know the religious mind at all,' Baldwin said, following his gaze, 'they will be drinking until Compline.'

'Well, they can't object to our joining them,' Bertrand said with determination, and set off after the two girls.

'Baldwin,' Simon said quietly. 'The visitor has obviously made up his mind. If he could, he'd have the prioress strung up for murder.'

'Yes,' Baldwin agreed. 'And to be fair, he may well be right. But I want to give the woman the benefit of the doubt. And even if she were guilty in some way, that doesn't mean no one else helped and was not equally to blame. Is it conceivable that the prioress helped mix the dwale, or helped pass it to the invalids?'

'If the infirmarer was her accomplice, yes. You're quite convinced it was murder?'

Baldwin nodded. 'There is no doubt. Moll had something thrust over her face, and her arms kept still while her artery was opened. She died of asphyxiation, but someone wanted to cover their tracks. There was a clear second cut that went to the artery.'

They had come to the door that gave into the frater. Simon's face held a worried frown. 'Do *you* reckon the prioress could have done it?'

'Moll was a young girl, but strongly enough built,' Baldwin theorised. 'She should have been able to fight – but not while drugged.'

'Which makes the infirmarer more suspicious than the prioress.'

'I suppose so. Although I confess I am beginning to think they all are. Margherita wandered the cloisters regularly, as did Joan; Denise liked sitting up with a drink, and from the sound of it, Moll herself and this other novice, Agnes, both saw men about the place. Do any of these nuns stick to their Rule? Can we take anything for granted about their behaviour?'

And with that quiet reflection, Baldwin walked into the frater.

When the bell for Vespers tolled, Elias the smith had walked out with his companions, but then ducked back as if realising he had left something behind while the others continued on to the service. He could be punished for not attending, but that was of little concern to him now.

It was rare that he had an opportunity to rest peacefully and meditate, and he felt the need of it more than ever just now. The service wouldn't last long, and he wished to make the most of the time he had, to consider his plans and review his options.

Westwards the sun was failing, leaving the cloisters in shadow as it sank behind the tall hill, and there was an icy freshness in the air that sank through his heavy robes. He shuddered from the sudden change in temperature, pulled his coat tighter about his shoulders, and walked slowly along the side of the building.

They ran a great risk, he knew, but they had little choice. Especially now. If they were to remain living as they did they were an insult to God. He hadn't taken the full vows like her, but that was no excuse. Both of them would be committing apostasy by going. She would be sought with the utmost energy of the Church, and brought back here to continue to serve for the rest of her life. He wasn't sure what would happen to him.

Not that his mind could concentrate well. Whenever he tried to think about what they would do, a vision of Moll's face kept springing into his mind. He fetched a jug of ale and sat down.

Hearing the canons and lay brethren leave the church, he drained his pot of ale. It was the signal to end his maudlin reverie. Outside, he straightened his shoulders with resolution and strode along the canons' cloister to the dim little passageway that led out to the stables southwards.

There was a small outhouse leaning against the stables, and it was here that he had stored his bundles, hiding them under a pile of straw. One for her, one for him: two packages tightly wrapped, containing dried meat and fruit, tinder, a parcel of bread each, a pair of wineskins, and cloaks, sheepskins, furred boots, jacks, and even spare hose for them. He was leaving nothing to chance.

Well, it was a huge responsibility, knowing he was going to be a father, he thought as he carefully concealed the lot beneath the straw again, after checking it was all still there. He sprinkled spare dirt over the top, then stood back to make certain that his disruption of the cache was not visible. Satisfied, he left the room and, looking about him swiftly, walked back to the cloister. He sneaked into the church, sat in a pew and bent his head in prayer, waiting. She had said she would try to leave an hour or two after Compline, so he had a while to wait.

All because of Moll. That treacherous little snake had died, and now everyone thought Constance had done it.

Elias had to rescue his woman before she could be accused.

The smith would have been more anxious still if he had known that as soon as he had returned to the cloister, a figure had moved out from the shadow of a buttress supporting the stables and silently stepped into the lean-to. Rose soon found the hidden parcels and knelt, sniffing at them, opening them to see what was there before carefully rewrapping and hiding them again.

It was obvious that Elias was going to make a run for it. That news might well be useful to the prioress, Rose didn't know. She couldn't tell what things were useful to Lady Elizabeth, but she herself was intrigued. She knew Elias as the strong-willed brother who had always refused her charms, and here he was planning to escape. With whom? She could hazard a guess.

But she couldn't go and see Lady Elizabeth about it, not now. The prioress had enough to worry her with the suffragan bishop. Rose eyed the spot where the bags were hidden. What if Elias returned in the meanwhile and fled the convent?

Behind her was the doorway to the great smithy. The forge was still alight, filling the place with a warm glow. She dragged a bench to the door. From here she could keep watch and make sure Elias didn't run. Tomorrow she would seek out Brother Godfrey and ask him for his advice: should she tell Lady Elizabeth about this, or could Godfrey speak to Elias and prevent his running away?

She nodded happily. She trusted Godfrey.

When the three men entered, there was a sudden horrified silence. Too late Baldwin reflected that these women were unused to the sight of men. Soon the shocked glances were cooled as Bertrand was recognised, but everyone felt awkward with the three men standing in the doorway staring about them. The conversation faltered and died.

Frowning, Bertrand finally called to Margherita, who sat at the far wall: 'Treasurer, where is the prioress?'

'Alas, visitor, I have not seen her since leaving the church. She was there for Vespers, but when I left the choir I met you, and I don't know where she went while I spoke to you.'

Bertrand stood quivering with emotion, and was about to explode when Baldwin interposed.

'Do you think you could let her know that we have been seeking her? Tell her the novice *was* murdered, and not by dwale – she was suffocated and then stabbed. For now we shall return to the canonical cloister, but please inform the prioress that we shall return tomorrow and would be grateful for a moment with her.'

Margherita nodded, and Baldwin walked from the room.

Twilight had fallen, and the air was bitterly cold. He could taste a metallic tang in the air. In these parts, that could only mean severe weather.

He had never stayed on the moors during the winter, but Simon had told him how foul the weather could become; earlier in the year, Baldwin had experienced the misery of riding through what had appeared to be only a slight drizzle: it had left him soaked to the skin in no time at all. That escapade had convinced him that moorland weather could be more inclement than that which he was used to.

And he had no wish to be stuck here, in the middle of nowhere, when war could threaten his home at any time.

Had Jeanne known the turn his thoughts were taking, she would have been gratified to learn that her husband, while incarcerated in a nunnery, was thinking only of her.

In truth, she had no thoughts for him; she had been too busy since his departure. All the servants had been mobilised. First the exterior of the house had been cleared of its covering of ivy and other vegetation, and tomorrow it was to be attacked in force by all those men who could wield a brush or carry a pail of limewash. Any spare souls would be marched to the woodwork and ordered to smother that in new paint.

Indoors she had already finished the removal of fleas, other than those living on Baldwin's mastiff, who now, after Edgar's constant tuition, only answered to the name 'Chops'. He still occasionally displayed signs of itching, but Jeanne had no idea how to remove his infestation.

Now, late in the evening, as dark fell over the house and the animals were all settled for the night, she sat before the fire in the hall, Edgar beside her. Wat the cattleman's boy sprawled on the floor, pulling a thick lump of rope in a ferocious-sounding game of tug-of-war with Chops.

'Wat! The dog is growling enough, there's no need for you to as well,' Jeanne called sharply.

Wat threw her a look over his shoulder, and was quieter,

murmuring snarls as the mastiff tugged and jerked his toy.

'So, Edgar, with the old linen thrown out, we shall need plenty of new. You will have to arrange for bedclothing, a fresh mattress – that old one is awful – and buy a wall-covering. A good, thick tapestry.'

'What picture would you like on it?' he asked.

There was a particular tone to his voice. Jeanne didn't look up for a moment while she considered. Edgar had been Baldwin's sole friend and confidant as well as his servant for many years, according to the little she had heard. It must be painful for him to see all that he had grown used to being discarded on, as he would see it, the whim of a woman.

Jeanne smiled. 'What would he like best, do you think?'

Edgar, who was well used to feminine wiles having been a successful philanderer for many years, recognised the appearance of the olive branch and grinned back. 'I would think a picture of hunting, or hawking.' It was not as if he found his new mistress overbearing or difficult; she was a great deal more straightforward than he had feared, if a bit demanding. But after being first Sir Baldwin's man-at-arms and then his servant for more than thirty years, since they had met in the mess that was Acre in 1291, it was hardly surprising that Edgar found so much change over so short a period unsettling.

He left Lady Jeanne by the fire. A pot was boiling and Edgar took it to his buttery. There he drew off a quart of wine and prepared hypocras, putting broken lumps of sugar into a pan, adding boiling water and spices and leaving them to stew for a while.

He had enjoyed his time with his master, but now things were changing. Sir Baldwin was married, and didn't need Edgar's help to buy clothes or organise the estates. And Edgar was finding himself forced to look to his own future. He was handfast to Cristine from the tavern in Crediton, and she was growing impatient with Edgar for his delay in formally giving her his vows. She understood that he had been unable to do much until his master's wedding was over, but now Cristine wanted their arrangement made binding, and Edgar wasn't certain how his master would take to having yet another woman about the place – nor was he sure how Lady Jeanne would react.

It added up to a disturbing time, and one in which Edgar found himself confused. All in all, it was most unsettling.

He added the wine to the pot and carried it to the hall, pouring a large measure into a pewter jug. It was as he passed Jeanne the drink that they both heard hooves in the yard and Edgar walked to the door.

'Wat, quiet, boy!' Jeanne snapped, trying to listen. In a few minutes, Edgar came back with a grubby and dirt-stained man, who panted like a dog from exertion.

'My Lady, this man is a messenger for the suffragan bishop, on his way to find him at Peter Clifford's house. I told him that Bishop Bertrand is not there, but I think you should hear his news.'

Jeanne noted his serious expression and nodded to the man, who dropped onto a bench while Edgar fetched him a large jug of ale. The messenger took a long draught and glanced up at Edgar thankfully, but then recalled his place, and sat upright as he met Jeanne's eye.

'My Lady,' he declaimed, 'I have been sent by Bishop Stapledon of Exeter, who advised me to visit Furnshill to warn his good friend Sir Baldwin, and to inform the bishop's suffragan in Exeter, that although our King has instructed Humphrey de Bohun, the Earl of Hereford, not to discuss the affairs of the realm nor to have any assemblies of men, the Earl has ignored the King's command. He has raised his levy to form an army.'

Edgar offered the messenger more drink, but the man refused. 'A place to unroll my blanket near a fire is all I crave.'

'Then you must sleep here,' Jeanne said, rising to her feet and indicating the hearth. 'Pull a bench to the heat and rest. For my part, I am grateful to you for stopping here on your way to Crediton. When you wake, tell the servants that I expect them to feed you well to keep you going for the remainder of your journey.'

She accepted his thanks, and walked from the room out to the little solar, Edgar close behind her. He took his rest on a bench near the entrance to her private rooms, the mastiff with him. Edgar never took risks when he could avoid them, and although he had little doubt that the messenger was perfectly innocent and honourable, Edgar was not going to leave his mistress unguarded while his master was absent.

Comforted by the knowledge of his nearness, Jeanne sat in a chair in her bedchamber. There was no need to undress yet, especially with the freezing gusts wafting in from the unglazed windows, and she wanted a few moments to consider what she had heard.

No matter what the deeper political problems were, one thing was quite obvious: the country was teetering on the brink of disaster once more. The King and his friends the Despensers, father and son, were rushing towards another civil war with the barons.

Jeanne found herself praying to God that her husband would not be sent to fight. She didn't want to be widowed so soon after finding him.

Constance smiled at Joan as she sipped her dwale, pulling a face as the bitter mixture went down. After the death of Moll, Constance had been very cautious with the measures of belladonna, but tonight she had added more poppy syrup. She needed the security of knowing that she could see Elias.

Joan settled back against her pillows and closed her eyes, and soon her breath was more stertorous as she slipped into unconsciousness. With a brief sigh of relief Constance left her and went to the door, where she listened carefully. Compline was a while ago, and all the nuns should be asleep, but someone might still be up and about. Constance had little to be happy about. Her guilt felt like a heavy weight pressing upon her breast, almost stifling her, and she longed for Elias to hug her and whisper soothing promises of how their lives would change.

Elias had promised to rescue her as soon as he had heard the first gossip. Many in the convent were convinced that Constance had given Moll too much dwale. Margherita was trying to persuade everyone that the prioress was guilty, but Constance knew better. She had doubted the sense in running away, but now her misgivings were bent in the other direction. She couldn't stay here any longer.

There was no sound. She lifted the latch and walked out to the stairs. The dorter was silent apart from the snuffling and sighing of sleeping women. Reassured, Constance lifted the hem of her tunic and tiptoed down the stairs. Opening the door, she went through to the cloister. The church door was in front of her, and she pulled the dorter door shut before setting off along the corridor towards it.

It was when she reached the corner that she felt the hand on her shoulder.

'Hello, Constance. Couldn't you sleep?' Katerine said, and Constance recoiled at the cruel expression in her sharp little features.

Elias sat biting his nails. The last service had finished an age ago, and he would have expected Constance to have arrived by now. She had promised to get here after Compline, and he wanted to set off as quickly as possible, now he had their packages ready. His face was screwed up with fearful expectation. He was waiting in the church, for the prioress never saw fit to lock the dividing door, and he and Constance used to meet here often to talk when they had first confessed their affection for each other, although more recently, like the night when Moll had died, he had gone to meet her in her own chamber at the rear of the infirmary.

That night had been wonderful: she had agreed to leave the convent with him. From that day his every spare waking moment had been spent arranging their escape. And tonight they would go.

But she should have been here by now. The suspense was unbearable, and Elias stood, walking to the door. As he opened it, he saw his woman approaching hurriedly.

'Thank God, my love. I thought . . .' Although there was little light, with heavy clouds scudding across the sky and no moon, he could sense her agitation. 'Constance? What is it?'

'I can't leave with you,' she whispered brokenly.

'Why? Everything is ready.'

'Katerine knows everything. She accused me of killing Moll!'

Elias felt his heart lurch within him. 'Forget her,' he said harshly. 'It's because of the rumour that we have to go. I can protect you. Look, all the food is ready, everything's packed. If we . . .'

'No, Elias,' she said, touching his cheek. Her voice was strained as though she was close to crying. She swallowed. 'Moll saw you coming to my room one night, and told Katerine. She guessed, I suppose, or perhaps she watched herself. What does it matter? She won't let on because she wants me to give her my enamelled brooch. I have to go back now and give it to her.'

'The thieving slut!'

'It's better that I should let her have it.'

Elias was silent. His plans, their future together, everything was fallen into ruin. It was only with a struggle that he could keep his voice from breaking as he pleaded, 'Then come straight back and we'll go.'

There was a crack, as of a pebble kicked uncautiously against a wall. Constance drew in her breath sharply. 'Tomorrow – tomorrow at the grille. I'll see you there after Matins.'

Elias watched her hurry away, and as she disappeared along the cloister he saw the shadow of someone else flit past the alleyway to his side. The shadow of a nun.

Chapter Twelve

Hugh opened an eye and pulled a face. It was the darkest hour of the night. Pulling his coat up to his chin, he thrust his head beneath his pillow. Even then he couldn't keep the row from his ears.

The tolling bell was still more unwelcome because of the relative silence of the world. There was no birdsong, no barking, no crowing of cocks or clucking of hens; only a dead, dull nothing that somehow emphasised the melancholy nature of the hour. The bell itself sounded flat and doomladen, as if it heralded the Day of Judgement which the priests so enjoyed predicting.

To Hugh it was intolerable. His head ached, and although he knew he would soon have to rise to go and find a urinal-pot somewhere, he longed to put off that hideous moment when he must emerge from his blanket and coats, and expose his body to the stark gelidity of the cloister.

A groan and muffled comment of 'God's blood!' told him that his master had not managed to sleep through it either, and when Hugh opened his eye again and peered through the gloom towards the bed, he saw that Sir Baldwin had already got to his feet, and at the other side of the room the bishop was out of his bed and stood huddled, his robes pulled tight around him.

Seeing Baldwin haul Simon's bedclothes from him with a chuckle, Hugh hunched his shoulders against the horrible prospect, but soon he was exposed, and found himself glowering up at the repellently cheerful knight.

'Come on, Hugh. Even your master has managed to get up.'

It was many years since Hugh had spent the nights out with the sheep and lambs on the moors near Drewsteignton in sub-zero temperatures, and ever since he had enjoyed the sensation of snugness that a warmed hall gave him. There was no such comfort here.

Wind penetrated every corner of the room, whistling and moaning gently, and bringing with it the promise of snow, while doors rattled against their latches and shutters complained. Each breeze managed to find a fresh gap between Hugh's clothing, or perhaps it simply forced its way through, like daggers of ice. He stood, shivering, trying to pull on tunic, jack and cloak in one movement before he froze into a block.

Out of their room it was no better. Bertrand led the way, walking at a solemn pace which gave the men no opportunity to warm themselves. They went from their guestroom down a ladder to the ground floor, and from thence to the passageway that gave on to the cloister itself. Here the cold was, if anything, still more intense, for the wind eddied and blew around the buildings. It was like a mischievous animal suddenly released, enjoying the freedom of the garth by whipping around unprotected legs, delving down through the neck of shirts, or searching upwards from loose-fitting hose.

Hugh trailed miserably after the other two men to the church and waited with them in the queue at the door while the canons filed inside. Remembering what he had seen the night before, he tugged at Simon's sleeve. 'Sir?' he asked quietly.

'What is it?' Simon hissed. 'If you're going to complain, I'll give you something serious to complain about.'

Hugh knew his master was as unenthusiastic about early rising as he himself. 'Sir, it's what I saw last night in the frater while you were with the nuns.'

Quickly he told his master about the prostitute, and Simon gave a low whistle. As the queue moved into the church, Simon whispered the gist of it to Baldwin.

At last they were in, but even inside there was nothing to take the edge from the bitter weather. With no fire, many gaps between ill-fitting doors and the hole in the roof, the four walls about them might have not existed for all the use they were. And Hugh became aware of another effect: at least outside while walking his feet had remained reasonably safe; now, standing on the tiled floor, it felt as though the heat was being sucked away through the soles of his boots, leaving the rest of his body frigid.

In these circumstances, Hugh looked about him to find something – anything! – which could distract him from the misery of the hour and the temperature.

The canons appeared to be taking a great deal of time to prepare for the services. They muttered amongst themselves, occasionally throwing interested glances towards the four strangers, but no one appeared to make any effort to observe the rituals. Then he realised that they were waiting for a signal from the other side of the wall where the nuns congregated, and when a single, male voice rose from the nuns' cloister, suddenly the canons joined in.

It was all new to Hugh. He had never been in a cloister before, and the ceremony was strange and not a little threatening. He was used to the little shed-like church at Drewsteignton, and after that the chapel at Sandford, then the larger building at Lydford, but at none of them was there anything like this. Keeping his mouth tightly shut to save himself embarrassment, he looked at the others. Bertrand, he saw, sang along, his head high and a curious expression of suspicious concentration on his face. Hugh guessed that he was listening to the women, but had no idea why. Simon tried to join in at first, but then resorted to moving his mouth silently. The strange Latin words were unfamiliar, and he couldn't keep up with the others; Baldwin appeared to know the service, and sang quietly in his deep bass.

The place was odd even without the singing. As Hugh looked along from where they were standing, towards the altar, he found himself feeling strangely out of place.

It wasn't only the sense of dislocation caused by the hour. He had no idea what the time was, but he had heard that this first service of the day was held in the middle of the night because it was intended to herald the new day, which according to the priests began somehow during the night. To Hugh this was daft: he knew, like everyone, that day started at dawn, but there was no point arguing with priests. They believed what they wanted to.

No, it wasn't just the time, it was the whole atmosphere: the men facing each other in the choir forming a tunnel, the distance between them emphasised by the candles in their brackets behind, which seemed to create another tunnel, this one of light; while incense wafted, and reinforced the oddly otherworldly nature of the sight, creating a kind of fog around the men's ankles, almost as if they were floating on a whitish, yellowish smoke that rose in whisps and peaks where the gusts from outside caught it. And all the time the high voices of the nuns floated above them, reaching over the high wall which separated the cloisters.

Hugh wasn't fanciful, but as he stared along the ranks of canons, he had the impression that he was dreaming. The voices were not as smooth, refined, or pleasant upon the ear as they should have been; they didn't match with the female singing, which itself sounded harsh and unmusical; the whole appeared even to Hugh's ear to be too fast, and in some parts he thought the nuns were gabbling their words, like women keen to return to their beds.

There was none of the religious atmosphere he would have expected, and when he glanced at Baldwin and the bishop, he saw that they felt the same. Sir Baldwin stood stiffly, his eyes drifting along the lines of men in the choir, and every so often his gaze would rise to the dividing wall as if in disbelief at the racket from the other side.

The nuns' choir was a long, darkened tunnel, filled with the scent of incense; candles guttered, giving sufficient light to see the nuns' features, and the priest's up at the altar, each face flickering into clarity as a nearby candle responded to a short gust, then dimming once more. The great doors creaked and rattled. At one point there was a long slithering sound as a slate slipped free from its moorings and hurtled down the incline of the roof to shatter into fragments on the cloister, but this was too regular a noise to cause any of the freezing nuns to look up.

Lady Elizabeth winced as yet another psalm was hurried, but she was more intrigued by the gap in the ranks of her nuns.

Margherita was there, as was Denise, and most of the others, but there was a plain gap where the infirmarer should have been standing.

Presumably one of her patients was unwell, Lady Elizabeth thought. At least that overblown fool Bertrand wasn't here in the nuns' choir to see her absence. If his raised voice yesterday was anything to go by, Lady Elizabeth felt sure he would throw off his lightly worn cloak of urbanity at the faintest provocation, and rant. She found herself looking forward to the spectacle.

In the meantime she had many other considerations; the peace of the church, with its familiar psalms, prayers and rites, was the perfect setting for concentration. She allowed her mind to run over her problems while her voice joined with the others in the cadences.

First there was Princess. The poor little terrier had been unwell again during the evening, whining, then panting and lying down, eyes wide, tongue lolling, and vomiting while her bowels opened. The prioress reflected that she would have to get one of the lay sisters to clean up, but that was hardly the issue. She had never known a dog suffer from so appalling a flux before. Oh, several of her pets in the past had been sick – that was hardly surprising for a dog which scavenged, as all did – but this was worse, and Lady Elizabeth was worried.

Then there was Bertrand. The suffragan's aim was clear: he wanted to get rid of her. Moll's death had given him the ideal excuse. Allied to this was the headache posed by Margherita. The treasurer had ever been keen on taking over the leadership of the convent; she had her sights firmly fixed upon Lady Elizabeth's post, and had obviously enlisted Bertrand to help her.

As the first part of the service ended, Lady Elizabeth unconsciously glanced up towards the windows. Matins. She felt a small smile rise to her face as the first soaring notes rose to the ceiling.

Alas, her delight was shortlived. Even as she felt her spirits join with the music and climb upwards, she saw the white flakes begin to pour in through the hole above. Snow floated down, wafting as it was caught by the side-blast travelling the length of the nave.

The sight made her close her eyes, but not before she caught the treasurer's triumphant expression.

Once more, the Lady Elizabeth peered back towards the gap in the pews where Constance should have stood. She suddenly found herself hoping that the young infirmarer had not run away. Not only would that be a confession of guilt, it would also involve almost certain death if the weather were to turn, and from the look of the snow, it had.

When the last notes faded in the grey dawn light, and the canons rose, shuffling towards the door, Godfrey too got to his feet, but before he could slip through, he heard his name called out. Stifling a momentary panic, he fitted a subservient smile to his face and turned to face the bishop.

'My Lord Bertrand! I heard you were returned. I suppose it was that poor girl? Such a shame; a terrible waste.'

Bertrand introduced the two men with him, and Godfrey ducked his head quickly to each of them. 'I am delighted to meet you, gentlemen. I only hope I can be of some use.'

The bearded one called Baldwin motioned towards the door. 'Shall we find a fire and a warm drink?'

When Godfrey had made them all comfortable in the frater and had asked the lay brother for wine and ale, he sat and eyed them all benignly. 'How may I assist you?'

It was the bearded one again. Godfrey had never liked men with beards. It made them look sloppy, to his mind.

'Could you tell us what you did for the girl? I understand you bled her?'

'Yes, Sir Baldwin,' Godfrey answered. 'It was the day that she died that I was called into the infirmary. Moll was suffering from a headache – what I would call a migraine, or a hemicrania – a sick headache of the most extreme form. This kind of illness can be cured by a small cut in the basilic vein. I explained what I was about to do, then gave her the bowl to hold while I made a small incision. The blood was taken, and then I sealed the vein. That was all.'

'Why did you perform this operation?' Baldwin asked quietly. 'Surely cupping is more usual with women.'

Godfrey kept the smile on his face, but he had to take a deep breath to control his nervousness. 'Why, you are right, of course, Sir Baldwin. But after studying her urine I felt sure that releasing a little blood would be more effective. The infirmarer here tries very hard, of course, and she is absolutely devoted to her charges, but . . . Performing something like cupping on a girl of her age seemed unlikely to result in success. No, I thought that blood-letting would be better.'

'I am surprised that you were content to conduct the operation yourself.'

Godfrey was happier with that question. 'But who else would have been able to do it? I know that priests are banned from surgery, but it is better that I should become involved than that a mere barber should be permitted to enter the nuns' cloister.'

'You think so? When the Pope has said that you should effect the cure by the strength of prayer?' Baldwin murmured.

'I acted as I thought best.'

'And yet she died.' Baldwin held up his hand to halt the sudden burst of anxious self-justification. 'No, I do not say you killed her. But please confirm: how many cuts did you make in her arm?'

'How many?' Godfrey repeated, still smarting at the perceived insult to his professionalism. 'One, of course. I am a trained man, Sir Knight, not some quack-salver operating from the back of a wagon.'

Baldwin grinned inwardly at the thought of this serious-looking cleric selling mixed salves and potions from the back of a wagon like a charlatan at a market. 'No, I am sure you are not,' he said soothingly. 'But it is nevertheless a fact that the girl had *two* cuts, and the one which punctured her artery, was, I assume, the second – for it instantly allowed her life to flow away. Thus your assertion that you did not make a second incision means you cannot have been her killer.'

'I most certainly am not!' Godfrey declared hotly.

'And not only that, but there are other factors which I find most interesting. Did you, for example, need to restrain her? Her mouth is swollen, and there are bruises on her upper arms.'

'No, she was perfectly quiet and meek throughout the operation,' Godfrey said with surprise.

'Then I am sure you cannot help us further,' Baldwin said pleasantly. 'Unless . . . Could you tell us what sort of a girl she was? Do you know whether anyone bore her a grudge?'

'As to what sort of girl, I should say she was an uncommonly religious young lady. She came from a good family, I believe, the daughter of a minor knight, and I think she had always had a hankering after the religious life. Her father wasn't too keen, but agreed to allow her to follow her vocation.'

'Was she always well-behaved?'

'Yes, from what I've heard. You have to bear in mind that I only rarely go to the nuns' cloister – mainly when the infirmarer has a problem, such as young Moll's blood-letting. But as far as someone holding a grudge against her, well . . .' he smiled suddenly. 'The idea is ridiculous. Who could hold a grudge against a nun? Surely not another nun.'

Baldwin held his eye for a moment. 'I suspect you have heard of such things before. Who else could have had the opportunity to see her in the infirmary overnight? Which man could enter the convent?'

Godfrey's attention wavered and he allowed his gaze to move to Bertrand. 'Nobody that I am aware of, naturally. And yet I refuse to believe that a nun could be responsible.'

'What of the nun of Watton?'

Godfrey's expression hardened, his eyes flashing back to Baldwin's face, but before he could answer Bertrand interrupted furiously, talking in a low hiss. 'Are you mad, Sir Baldwin? Don't raise such matters! You have no right to bring up something like that.'

'I have every right. We are here in a convent, investigating a crime which only a nun could have committed – unless, like at Watton, the place has been run with such extreme laxity that any act of wickedness is possible.'

'It is! The prioress in charge is incompetent to run a pigsty, let alone a . . .' Bertrand blustered.

Godfrey gave him a startled look. 'Rubbish! This place is—'

'Quiet!' Baldwin commanded. 'Godfrey, have men regularly gained access to the nuns' cloister?'

The man shook his head. 'Oh, I'm sure not,' he declared, but even he could hear the lack of conviction in his voice.

Bertrand ignored him. 'Men are probably getting over there and committing sins with the nuns every other day. It's appalling, but it's also proof that the prioress has failed in her duty.'

'No, honestly,' Godfrey protested. 'I don't think the canons have been behaving like that.'

Now neither Bertrand nor Baldwin paid him any heed. They sat staring at each other, silently. It was left to Simon to say something. He took a deep breath.

'Perhaps the girl suffered a fit or something? Couldn't she have banged her head against the bed, and bruised her face that way, and thrown her arm about and caught it on something, ripping the flesh?'

'The skin was cut with a knife,' said Baldwin. 'No, the question is, who had the chance of getting to her? Was it only women, or were there men in there as well?'

'It's a disgrace, but I believe that some of the canons were in the habit of visiting the nuns and any one of them could be responsible for Moll's death. No doubt he shall confess and be given his penance,' Bertrand said heavily. 'In the meantime, the most important thing is to replace this foolish prioress with someone who can lead this place with piety.'

'No!' Godfrey said. 'Lady Elizabeth is honourable.'

Baldwin nodded, asking, 'And what of the girl who has died, Bishop? Shall she be left unavenged?'

Bertrand stood. 'This is not some petty bickering in a town, Sir Baldwin. This is a convent for the celebration of God's goodness.

Why should we avenge a girl who has been fortunate enough to be taken to His side?'

Baldwin was about to get to his feet, but Bertrand waved a hand patronisingly. 'Please remain here, Sir Baldwin. You have helped me greatly. I must now go and seek the prioress. There is no need for you to join me. I shall be returning to the nuns' cloister.'

'How am I to search for the killer?' Baldwin demanded. 'I have to speak to the prioress as well, and the infirmarer.'

'There's no need. You are too keen to bring up salacious events which are better left forgotten, Sir Knight. I have reached my conclusions. Now, I suggest you and the bailiff here finish your drinks, and then pack your belongings. You are no longer required, gentlemen. I am sure you would prefer to return to your wives.'

Chapter Thirteen

The woman most on Bertrand's mind was at that moment surprised, on opening her door, to find a nun, weeping piteously, waiting in her room.

'My daughter, what's the matter?' she asked solicitously, crossing the room to Constance's side. 'Come – sit here, and tell me all about it.'

Constance allowed herself to be drawn away from the window, and rested in a chair, gratefully taking the cup of wine which her prioress thrust into her hands.

It was miserable, this existence. She had only wanted to do good and look after others, but now she thought she'd have done better never to have come to Belstone. She had never wanted to join a convent, and if she'd had any say, she'd have remained outside, living in peace, but when her brother Paul had insisted that she should find a husband, one with whom he could work, her life changed for ever. The only man to suit her, in Paul's opinion, was someone who already had a good fortune or possessed a ship for trade. It was all Paul ever thought of – money and the means of securing more power for his family. There was never any consideration for his sister's feelings: Constance was only a useful pawn to be swapped in exchange for suitable concessions.

It was that which led to her incarceration here. She would not have come to Belstone, except the only man whom Paul could find for her who possessed the right attributes was Master Gerald, a burgess in Exeter: a gross, fat man, with pendulous jaws and slack mouth, piggy eyes, and perpetually sweating brow. Master Gerald was certainly rich, but he was repulsive as well. The thought of his drooling mouth approaching her in their marital bed was repellent, and Constance had instantly spoken to the local priest, declaring her intention of joining a cloister.

That was over nine years ago, when she had been already old, at almost two-and-twenty. In truth she could say that she had never had any difficulty with her vows. She had made them in good faith, and intended to stick to them. When she came to the convent, she was a virgin and believed that she could keep to the claustral life. Celibacy was a small price to pay for the escape from Master Gerald, and as for poverty and obedience – well, poverty was her lot now that she was cut off from her family, and obedience was a feature of everyone's daily existence. We all obeyed someone else, a lord, a king, an abbot – or a husband.

And then everything changed again – for she had met Elias.

Constance was tending to her tiny herb garden out at the western edge of the cloister, behind the lay sisters' dorter, and picking leaves for a poultice when she had cut her thumb on her little sharp knife. She had been down at the southernmost corner of the garden, where the wall dividing the canonical side from the nunnery was a simple metal fence with iron bars to separate men and women without leaving all the nuns' plants in the shade. As Constance stood, staring at her bloodied finger with dismay, Elias had appeared in the grille, and from that moment Constance had known love.

She felt the prioress's arm about her shoulder, and drank again. Lady Elizabeth was a kind woman, Constance knew, though sometimes her advice was not useful.

Lady Elizabeth sat at her desk and gazed sympathetically at the weeping nun.

'I wondered why you did not attend Matins,' she said softly. 'But I see you wouldn't have been able to concentrate. Well and good. It is better that you should come to sing praises to Christ with a happy heart, not one which is downcast.'

'My . . . my Lady,' Constance stammered. 'I have broken my vows.'

'You have made love with a canon?'

Constance stared up at the prioress. 'You knew?'

'My dear, I know much of what goes on here, but it did not require great intuition to guess what you meant. It was a sin, but you could hardly have broken the oath of poverty without my knowing, and as for obedience, I have always found you most straightforward. What else could it be, then? Now, you are not the first to have done this. Are you with child?'

Feeling her face redden, Constance turned away in her shame.

'That is a pity, my dear – a child can be an embarrassment, and it is difficult to conceal something that can grow so large. Still, there are ways of keeping such matters quiet.'

'But it's not the point! What of my promise to God?'

'He has many problems to look at, and I fear your lapse is only one of many, even among nuns. He has other, more serious issues to occupy Him.'

'But what about Moll? I *killed* her!'

Elias walked into the frater just as the bishop hurried out, and Elias had to stand back as Bertrand shoved past, rude in his urgency. He left Elias standing at the doorway staring after him with surprise as the suffragan darted back along the cloister towards the church. When Elias peered into the frater, he saw Baldwin and Simon, both looking bitterly angry, and Godfrey sitting opposite them with an expression of resentment marring his normally pleasant features. Hugh sat close to his master, looking sulky.

Although he had no wish to be questioned by the knight or the bailiff, Elias was thirsty, and he also wondered whether he could learn anything useful about the investigation. He walked in and collected himself a jug of ale before wandering as if idly to a bench nearby. This early in the morning the frater was nearly empty. Elias sat as close as he could without looking conspicuous; he was at the next table with Jonathan, a man whom Elias usually tried to avoid, but today he had little choice if he wished to hear what the men were saying.

At first he could hear little, and what he did hear made no sense to him.

Baldwin: 'What do you think, Godfrey?'

Godfrey, peevishly: 'Me? Why do you persist in asking *me*? The good bishop has decided upon his actions. He's wrong, though. My Lady Elizabeth is—'

Baldwin: 'You know about Watton. Almost anyone in a double convent like this will have heard of the story. Could it have happened here?'

Godfrey, dismissively: 'Oh, *rumours*! If you listen to half the gossip that circulates around a nunnery, you'll believe that the Devil invented them for his own amusement.'

Baldwin: 'Has the same crime been committed here?'

Godfrey: 'Leave me alone, Sir Knight. I don't know anything about this Watton.'

It was at this point that Jonathan nudged Elias. 'I think that knight has got a shrewd idea what's been going on here. You should watch yourself, Elias, eh?'

Elias could have hit him. The canon sat with a suggestive leer on his face, nodding knowingly when he saw his bolt strike the mark. Instead, Elias stared over the other man's shoulder and spoke softly from the corner of his mouth. 'You think so, Jonathan? If I were under any danger, it would be as nothing compared to what would happen to *you* if I were to tell our Lady the Prioress whom you have been trying to tup.'

Jonathan's face changed. 'Come, there's no need for that. I only made a comment in jest, Elias.'

'So did I. Don't make me have to repeat it in seriousness, will you?'

Jonathan gave him a fawning smile and moved further along the bench, leaving Elias fuming. He knew his behaviour was wrong, against the teachings of St Benedict, and ran utterly against the Rule designed for their convent; he was guilty of failing in two of his oaths – he had been neither obedient nor celibate – and still worse, he had tempted a nun to fail in her own oaths.

Yet that wasn't the worst of it, he reminded himself. Far worse even than that was the fact that he was planning to remove Constance from the convent, leading her into the crime of apostasy.

* * *

'Watton!' Godfrey exclaimed. 'You keep referring to it. I know nothing of the place.'

'Then allow me to inform you,' Baldwin said steadily.

Simon cast a look at Hugh. His servant was staring away, plainly bored by the conversation, and Simon could well understand why. Baldwin appeared to be talking about something that had no relevance.

'Watton,' the knight said, 'was a small convent far from here, but it was not dissimilar to St Mary's. It was Gilbertine, I think, which means it was a double convent, with the two cloisters, just like this one.'

Godfrey sipped from his pot and refilled it carelessly, Simon thought, as though slopping the drink over the table was proof that he was hardly paying heed to Baldwin's words.

'But in this little place there was a great sin committed,' Baldwin continued. 'Because in Watton it was discovered that a nun had been dallying with a monk, and the nuns were deeply shocked; more so still when they found that the girl concerned was now with child. Of course this sort of thing is common enough, isn't it, Godfrey? We know how it can happen, but at Watton, the nuns took an extreme view. They condemned the girl and the man. They forced her to cut off his . . . let's just say that he was gelded by her. And then the nuns locked her away in a cell. In chains. She was allowed to give birth to her child, I think, and the baby was brought up in the monastery, but the mother was never released.'

'An interesting story, Sir Baldwin. But hardly relevant to our—'

'What I always wondered, after I heard that tale, was how had the two managed to meet?' Baldwin said, peering into his cup. 'If they were in a double convent, then there would have been great controls over who could cross between the cloisters, wouldn't there? Like there are here.'

'Of course. No one is permitted to go to the nuns' area unless—'

Baldwin interrupted him once more. 'Unless they have a good

reason to. Like, for example, a doctor, a specialist in the arts of surgery.'

Godfrey avoided his eye. His hands were shaking slightly, like a man suffering from too much wine the night before, and his face was red. 'I don't think I understand you,' he managed after a few moments.

'I think you do, Godfrey,' Baldwin said quietly. 'I think some of your colleagues have enjoyed visits over to the nunnery. Perhaps you yourself have made the trip occasionally, eh?'

Godfrey set his cup down and made as if to rise.

Baldwin grabbed his wrist. 'Godfrey, the girl is dead.'

'May she rest in peace. I know nothing about that. I did everything in my power to save the poor child,' the brother said in a low voice.

'And what of her soul, Godfrey? Did you do all you could to save that as well?'

Suddenly exhausted, Godfrey dropped back down into his seat. 'I didn't touch her. Never! I only opened her vein that one time.'

'How is it done normally?' Baldwin said, his tone cold and relentless. 'You tell the young nun or novice that she need not fear, that making love with a priest is no rejection of her vows to God. Is that not how it's done? And then, of course, the priest gives absolution. He can confess her, so she need not even look to another man for forgiveness, which could be embarrassing. No, she can gain that from the man who serviced her.'

'It's not like that!' Godfrey said, and now at last he looked up. He held Baldwin's gaze a moment, then his eyes dropped again. 'It's not like that,' he repeated, and glanced over the room. Luckily the place was almost deserted, with most of the canons having gone about their duties, some to study, others to work. He didn't see Elias, who sat behind him. 'Sir Baldwin, I shall tell you all I know, but you must trust me when I say that I am innocent.'

'Tell us what you know.'

'I know that the connecting door between the cloisters is rarely locked. Men can cross from one to the other as often as they wish. I have to visit the infirmary regularly enough when Constance needs assistance. But I also go to talk to ladies whom I know.'

Baldwin nodded, but his face showed no compassion or sympathy. He had been a monk himself, and once he had taken the vows, he had never broken them. To him, an oath was itself sacred, and he knew perfectly well that breaking one of them meant breaking his own solemn word. If a man could do that, he was capable of anything. 'What of the dead girl?'

'Moll? She never knew of my visits.'

'How can you be so sure?'

'Easy, Sir Baldwin!' Godfrey gave a sheepish smile. 'When she knew of any such affairs, she would instantly break with the nun concerned, and try to persuade her to alter her evil ways!'

'You mean that your "friends" never had such a conversation, so Moll never saw them with you. Would you say that Moll was a very religious young woman?'

'How should I know?' Godfrey said, taking a drink from his pot. 'It's hard to tell with these young novices. Some of them look ever heavenwards, others are always concentrating on the world here, professing their purity as a means to acquire power. When they're playing that game, it's hard to see what they're really like,' he added gloomily. 'I mean, they don't react like real women. Look at that appalling woman, the treasurer. I wouldn't trust Sister Margherita further than I could throw her. She's determined to win power, and God Himself knows what she'll do with it.'

'But Moll never gave you the impression that she was not honourable and devout?'

'She never gave me cause to doubt her sincerity, no. Others, maybe, but not her.'

'Who did?'

'That little Agnes. She's been put here by Sir Rodney as the first of the women he claims the right to install here, because of his generous donation towards the Lady Chapel, but she is hardly chaste, from what I've seen. Perhaps that's why Sir Rodney decided to have her imprisoned here.'

'You have seen her misbehaving with a canon?'

Godfrey gave him a twisted grin. 'I appear to be talking more than usual, Sir Baldwin. Perhaps I have seen her, perhaps I haven't – but I seem to recall the good suffragan telling you that you should consider packing your things. So why should I tell you any more?' He stood. 'I shall leave you. If you want to know anything else, find another informer.'

Elias watched him go with waves of relief washing over him. For an instant he had thought Godfrey would give Constance away. It was fortunate that this knight was about to leave: his questions were approaching the truth. However, as a secular man, Sir Baldwin was potentially dangerous. What if he told others?

Elias chewed his lip as he considered the unpalatable results of Baldwin's letting slip rumours of what was happening within the convent.

Lady Elizabeth squatted before the weeping infirmarer and used the end of her sleeve to wipe away her tears. 'Constance, don't trouble yourself in this way. What do you mean, *you* killed her?'

'It's true, my Lady,' Constance said, and the tears flooded down her cheeks as she stared hopelessly at her prioress. 'I gave her dwale so that she wouldn't hear me or see me with my lover. I killed her as surely as if I'd stabbed her – I poisoned her.'

Lady Elizabeth opened her mouth to speak, but thought better of it. The woman before her clearly believed what she had said, and although Elizabeth herself didn't, she should give Constance an opportunity to explain why she was so convinced of her guilt. Elizabeth returned to her desk, and nodded seriously. 'Go on.'

Constance closed her eyes and allowed her head to fall at an angle. She took a shuddering breath, then, 'My Lady, I mixed dwale for Cecily, the lay sister, because she had broken her wrist and would not otherwise sleep. I gave her a strong helping. The infusion of poppy seed acts as a good soporific, and . . . and I wanted to ensure that Joan and Moll were peaceful as well.' She looked up at the silent prioress. 'I did it so that I could enjoy my lover alone, without fear of discovery by one of my patients.'

'Especially Moll, I imagine,' Elizabeth smiled tightly.

'Especially her, yes,' Constance agreed dolefully. 'She always stuck her nose . . . Well, you know. Anyway, I gave all three a generous draught. Cecily drank hers down and was soon asleep. Joan is old and reacts quickly to dwale: I saw the drug overcome her almost immediately. I watched Moll drink a little of hers and left the rest of the jug at her side. It was not long before my lover arrived and we went to my chamber.'

'I see,' said the prioress. 'And this was some time before Nocturns?'

'Yes, my Lady.'

'Would you have heard someone entering?'

'Margherita tried to,' Constance said. 'I heard her and pushed her from the room, she made so much noise.'

'She woke Joan or . . .'

Constance shook her head. 'All three were still asleep. I had given them enough dwale to sleep through anything.'

The prioress gave a fleeting frown. 'The door to the infirmary opens very quietly, doesn't it? Why should Margherita have made so much noise?'

'It was almost as if she wanted to make sure everyone could hear her.'

Now she thought about it, Lady Elizabeth herself could recall having been woken by something. At the time she had assumed it was Princess, feeling poorly and wanting to join her mistress in the bed.

Lady Elizabeth fixed Constance with a firm stare. 'And the man was?'

Constance covered her face with her hands in a moment's indecision, before meeting her prioress's stern expression. 'My Lady, I cannot tell you that. I can answer for my guilt, but I cannot take another's decision for him. How can I accuse him without redoubling my guilt? If I speak of him, I force you to judge him. Better that he should have the opportunity of admitting his guilt before his confessor. It must be enough for you to know that I was there, I committed this sin, and I am to pay the price for my stupidity and . . . and lust.'

Lady Elizabeth was about to speak when her door opened, and the red face of Bertrand, breathless after climbing the stairs two at a time, appeared. 'Lady Elizabeth, I would have a word with you,' he began.

For the second time in twenty-four hours the cloister rang to the bellow of a raised voice, but this time the astonished nuns and canons heard the distinct, precise enunciation of their own prioress.

'Who do you think you are, to thrust yourself in upon the confessional? Do you dare to assume the right to interrupt a nun in solemn declaration? Remove yourself this instant!'

Bertrand had expected an apologetic, slightly anxious woman, a prioress anticipating removal prior to the installation of her replacement. To be met with this icy blast of rage was almost physically blinding. He blinked and took a step backwards. Rallying his forces, he managed to point out, 'But you cannot take confession. You're no priest, you're a woman.'

'BE SILENT!' Lady Elizabeth stormed, rising from behind her desk. 'How dare you question my rights in my priory. Get out of here before I have the canons remove you from the whole of the precinct and bar you from ever returning. And be assured that if you force me to take this action, I will immediately write to my Lord, the Bishop of Exeter, and demand that you be advised *never* to come here again. Now be *gone!*'

The man licked his lips, glanced swiftly from the prioress to the nun then back again. Lady Elizabeth appeared to have grown to fill the room. Her unblinking stare was appallingly compelling. It was hard not to meet it. And once he had, he was mesmerised by her sheer fury. He wavered, but only for a moment, then withdrew, quietly closing the door behind him.

As soon as he had gone, Lady Elizabeth let out her breath in a long, disapproving sigh. 'Stupid little man,' she muttered under her breath. 'Now, then, Constance, where had we got to? Ah yes, you were saying that you felt the guilt of your action. You need not worry yourself about that.'

'But I killed her!' she wailed. 'My dwale overheated her and caused her artery to burst!'

'No. Did you smother her or cut open her arm?'

'Her arm?'

'She was murdered. Someone went into the room and suffocated her then opened her artery to make it look like an accident.' Lady Elizabeth was suddenly silent. 'But tell me, when you met your lover before, did you also give the inmates dwale to keep them asleep?'

'Yes.'

'So he was aware your patients would be quiet?' Lady Elizabeth asked.

'Well, yes, I suppose so.'

'Then surely you weren't responsible for her death in any way. Your lover wouldn't have killed Moll either, for her knew Moll would be asleep.'

'I *am* still guilty.'

'Why, Constance?'

'I should have been there to protect her.'

Bertrand stopped at the bottom of the stairs, trying to gain some composure. He had never been shrieked at like that before, and the shocked cleric put a hand to his breast, feeling the thundering of his heart as he took some steadying breaths.

The church door was before him. Keeping his eyes fixed on the ground in a solemn imitation of meditation, he slowly walked along the cloister and went inside. All was still and he made his way swiftly to the connecting door into the monks' section, sighing with relief when he could shut it behind him.

Lady Elizabeth was no better than a fishwife, he thought. Screeching in that manner – she was obviously brought up to behave like a villainous peasant. With such reflections to soothe his ruffled feelings, he walked to the men's cloisters, but before emerging on to the grassy quadrangle, he let his feet take him away from the gaze of all the brothers. Before he knew where he had gone, he was near the grille, where he saw Elias hanging around.

The sight made Bertrand curl his lip with contempt. That a lay brother should lurk, waiting for an opportunity to ogle the sisters was deplorable. He was tempted to shout at the man – but something made him stop. A brother so debauched was surely past redemption.

Bertrand turned on his heel and went back to the cloister. He was almost there when he heard the shouting and the loud cry.

In the guestroom, Simon dropped onto his bed and gazed speculatively at Sir Baldwin. 'So you think that this place is rife with rampant clerics, and somehow that's why young Moll got herself killed?'

Baldwin made a small, futile gesture with his hand. 'It sounds perfectly stereotypical, doesn't it? The nuns all repressed and suppressed within the cloister, a number of men living alongside; inevitably the two mix. Stereotypical, and yet so often it proves true.'

Simon knew of Baldwin's past as a Knight Templar and didn't need to ask how Baldwin knew so much about the deeds of religious people. 'You reckon Moll herself was having an affair? It was another nun, a jealous one, who killed her?'

'It could have been, certainly, but it could equally easily have been a canon. Don't forget, it was ridiculously easy to cross between the cloisters when we wanted to, wasn't it?'

'It's all very well to say that, but remember how the nuns gawped at us when we asked for a drink? It was as if they'd never seen a man before.'

'Most of them, yes, were taken aback to see us there – but that means nothing. An individual nun finding a man somewhere she expected him to be wouldn't react in the same way. Godfrey implied he could get to the infirmary whenever he wanted; others could probably do so just as easily.'

'So we're probably lucky to be told to go home,' Simon said.

'Yes,' Baldwin answered with a sigh. 'You could say so. If we were to remain, we would have to question all the nuns and all the canons – not forgetting the lay brethren.'

'Then thanks be to God that we can return home,' Simon said with feeling and allowed himself to fall back on his mattress, closing his eyes. 'I don't know about you, but I will be glad to get back to my Meg and Edith. The thought of leaving them both while the Despensers are trying to start another war is not pleasant, even with the castle for them to run to. You must be relieved, too.'

'Hmm?' Baldwin looked up, a faintly confused expression on his face.

'I said it'll be good to get home and make sure that the Despenser armies don't destroy our houses,' Simon said with his eyes closed. 'Although for now, I'll be glad to take an hour or so to snooze. Rising in the middle of the night doesn't do much for me.'

Giving a half-hearted grin, Baldwin walked to the window. The ever-glum Hugh was already lying on his bench, with every appearance of being dead to the world, and Simon was soon breathing quietly, always guaranteed to be the prelude to loud snoring.

Baldwin threw open the shutters, catching them before they could slam against the wall, and stared out. South of the cloister, the weather was gloomy and threatening. Dark, steel-grey clouds hung apparently motionless in the sky, and when Baldwin leaned out and peered at the hill to the east, the whole of its summit was hidden. The snow which had fallen overnight had melted, but the air was sharp with the promise of more to come.

He pulled the shutters to. Getting up for Nocturns and Matins had not affected him so severely, for his experience as a monk had inured him to being deprived of his sleep. He felt fine now, although he had a sneaking suspicion that he would feel worse later.

It was hard to concentrate. He was used to action, and to have come here with a specific purpose which he had now been told to leave felt oddly anticlimactic: he was at a loose end, and had no idea how to fill the time until their departure.

On a whim he pulled on a cloak and went out, walking along the cloister. The frater was on his right and he stepped into the garth, crossing the grassed quadrangle to approach the church.

Something struck his cheek and he glanced upwards. The clouds were unleashing their burden and fresh snow began to drop. It was a curiously peaceful sight. The breeze had died away and snowflakes were falling in a continual stream, not dancing or eddying, but drifting down in great numbers, like the feathers of thousands of geese. Baldwin closed his eyes and inhaled with delight. Snow meant that war was all but impossible. Armies could not fight when the clean white covering smothered the landscape.

Opening his eyes, he stared up and suddenly caught a flicker of movement on top of the church roof. It was a huddled, robed figure. He screwed up his eyes to focus better on the strange sight, but with the swift-falling snow and the distance, it was impossible to see whether it was male or female, let alone recognise who it might be.

His curiosity stirred, Baldwin wandered to the church's wall and stared upwards. He stood near the cloister's roofed corridor, trying to see who it could be. Then a huge snowflake hit his eye, and he blinked, turning away, wiping at it with his palm, bending down and inclining his head.

Thus it was that the slate did not hit his head directly, but caught him a glancing blow, a sharp edge raking along the back of his skull and slicing off a long strip of his scalp. He fell, eyes wide, his head filled with the thundering roar of his blood, and was aware of the cold white snow covering the grass beneath his face. A loud whistling in his ears seemed to be deafening him, and he blinked slowly. Then, realising he had been struck, he rolled to one side, and found himself staring up at the cloister's covered walkway.

It was at that moment that the body struck the roof of the cloister and he saw the slates shatter with the force of the blow before the figure rolled down the incline and crashed on to the grass surrounded by shards of ruined slates. Baldwin had enough energy to throw himself out of the path of the shower, but as he moved the pain in his head expanded to cover his whole body. Even as he cried out, his vision clouded and he fell unconscious.

Chapter Fourteen

Simon grinned at his wife as she shook her head at him. Meg had a way of half-raising an eyebrow, while mock-seriously admonishing him, that never failed to give him a warm erotic charge, and he was about to grab her and tease her all the way to their bed when their house began to ring with the pounding of artillery. The Despensers were attacking – war must have started without his knowledge! Meg was terrified, he could see it in her face, but before he could protect her, he heard a scream, and saw that Edith, his daughter, had been hit by a huge block of falling masonry.

He gave a great roar, for she was his only child now that his boy, Peterkin, was dead, and he ran to her side, trying to lift the lumps of moorstone from Edith's body, but no one would help him. It was impossible to shift it on his own. The rocks were too massive for him to move, and even as he stared down in disbelief, he saw the light of life fading from Edith's face.

'Bailiff, in God's name! Wake up!'

It was a man-at-arms for the Despensers. Simon grabbed the arm that shook him, reached for his sword, but the hilt was missing, so instead he grasped the bastard's throat.

'Master, no.'

Simon felt his hand prised away from the man, and opened his eyes to see Hugh staring down at him in concern. Behind him was the suffragan, who gave him a baleful look while he rubbed his neck.

'Bishop, my apologies, I never intended . . .'

'Remind me, Bailiff, never to insult you. If this is what you can do in your sleep, I hate to think what you'd be capable of in wakeful anger.'

'I dreamed someone had murdered my daughter,' Simon explained. He still felt shaken.

'It was a dream, no more,' Bertrand said. 'However, your friend *is* in danger. A novice fell from the church roof, and a dislodged tile knocked him out.'

Simon swung from his bed. 'Where is he?'

After speaking to Baldwin and Simon, Godfrey had gone to walk in the precinct, and it was here that he met Rose. Godfrey was concerned at what she had to say. There was no doubt in his mind that Rose thought she was telling the truth, but he wasn't sure she had got her story right. Elias was not the kind of man who would try to run from the convent, and he would find it hard to persuade a nun to go with him.

No, Godfrey was fairly confident that Rose had misinterpreted the whole thing. All the same, perhaps Godfrey should ensure that Elias had absolutely no opportunity of leaving, just to make sure.

'Godfrey, Godfrey!' A young canon came running breathlessly towards him.

'What is it?' he demanded testily.

'Katerine fell from the church roof and hit the knight, in the cloister, right in front of me – come quickly!'

As the two hurried to the garth, the youth told Godfrey how Baldwin had been hit, how Katerine had struck the ground moments after. Godfrey shuddered with horror and quickened his pace, but he still had to ensure that Elias's supposed plan to escape was foiled. Reluctantly he decided he must tell the prioress.

'There's something I need you to do,' he gasped. 'Tell no one except the prioress, understand? *No one!* Tell her this: that Elias is going to try to escape from the priory, and . . .'

Lady Elizabeth had been called to see to the mangled body as soon as the novice had been brought back to the nuns' cloister. Now she stood over the corpse, her soul heavy within her. To see this second young life destroyed was terrible. It was as if the convent itself was damned. Lady Elizabeth had seen enough lives ended in her time, but to have lost two promising novices over the space of a few days was awful: first poor Moll – and now Katerine.

Not that there was much similarity between the two, of course. One had been murdered, although *why* was anybody's guess, and now this child had fallen from the roof – although God only knew what she had been doing up there. Either she had slipped, or . . . But Lady Elizabeth shied away from the notion that one of her novices could have committed suicide.

Katerine's face was scratched on one side, and there was a deep, jagged cut on her cheek where a sharpened piece of slate had caught her, but neither of these injuries had ended her life. The reason for her death was obvious from the hideous, leaking wound in her head. Blood mingled with her hair to form a hardened, matted cap. Lady Elizabeth grimaced at the sight, and didn't fail to notice how the girl's head sat at an odd angle. When they had carried Katerine's body here, her head had flopped loosely. She must have fallen head first, her neck breaking instantly upon hitting the ground.

More embarrassment for the priory, Lady Elizabeth thought, turning and walking back along the cloister. She went to her desk and sat. The account books were ready for her, but she couldn't pretend to read them. Katerine's death had affected her more than she would have expected.

The child was not special. She had not possessed any particular skills, but was pleasant enough, even if she had displayed an unedifying greed, as Rose said. Katerine had been friendly with Agnes for a while; the two had been quite close when Agnes had first arrived, Lady Elizabeth recalled, but then their friendship had cooled. At the time Lady Elizabeth had thought it was girlish jealousy or pride, but now Rose had enlightened her: they had both desired the same man.

It would have been a surprise if they could have remained friends, one being the daughter of a nobleman, the other a bastard; it was much the same as she and her treasurer. Lady Elizabeth had been born to a great family and Margherita had not.

Her rivalry with Margherita had begun long before either of them had anticipated leading this community. Perhaps Elizabeth should have been more conciliatory towards the younger woman, but there was so great a chip on Margherita's shoulder that any overtures on her part caused offence and were rejected with contempt. Margherita was the one who had decided that they were enemies, not Elizabeth – and this for the simple reason that Margherita could not envisage being the friend of someone who was of noble birth.

Margherita was Sister Bridget's illegitimate daughter. Elizabeth remembered Bridget. Friendly, she was, always smiling. She had run away the last time while Elizabeth was herself a novice, little more than a child. Margherita seemed to think her mother was cause for shame and embarrassment, although Lady Elizabeth had no idea why. As far as she was concerned, the sins of Margherita's parents were not their child's responsibility, and in any case, Lady Elizabeth was the daughter of an old-fashioned nobleman. She was fortunate to have been born to his legitimate wife, and not to one of the many other women with whom he was wont to spend his leisure. Illegitimacy was no slur on the character of a good person.

Lady Elizabeth picked up her reed and idly scratched at the page before her. She had no regrets about being on adversarial terms with Margherita – although right now it would have made her life a great deal easier to have the woman as an ally.

Especially, Lady Elizabeth realised, since the local peasants were bound to start talking about the convent.

Her scalp crawled: the death of Moll was bad enough, but it would have been perfectly simple to hush it up. It was in nobody's interests to bruit knowledge of it abroad, and even the suffragan, who would have been happy to use it to his own advantage, should he manage to find the murderer, would still only have told the Bishop of Exeter. Even that idiot Bertrand could see that there was no benefit to anyone, to allow information of that kind to be spread.

But now a second death had occurred, and while one dead

novice could be put down to bad fortune, two in as many weeks was news of the most dramatic kind imaginable. Lady Elizabeth knew perfectly well how people who had nothing to do with the cloister would dream up the most incredible stories about nuns, and to add two dead novices to such gossip would have the effect of putting oil to the flames of rumour and conjecture.

It was intolerable, but it was a fact. Then another thought struck her, with sufficient force to make her drop her reed.

Sir Rodney had wanted to put his money into an institution where he thought there could be no hint of scandal. He would be able to ignore the death of one novice, but this second would lead to gossip of the most prurient kind. Lady Elizabeth had seen it all before: when an accident occurred in a nunnery, people were always prepared to put the worst possible slant on it. Hearing of two novice nuns dying, Sir Rodney would assume it was proof of the unsanctity of the place. He was a pious knight, and wanted his bones interred in a sanctified chapel where they would be protected, along with his soul, by the constant prayers of the nuns. If the site was rendered unholy in his eyes, he would withdraw his money.

Lady Elizabeth stared up at the window, searching for an answer to the perennial problem of where to find the money to maintain the convent. Without Sir Rodney's contribution, she couldn't keep the nunnery from collapse.

If Sir Rodney heard a series of suspicions and half-garbled rumours, he would feel justified taking his patronage elsewhere; the only defence for the convent was proving who had murdered Moll – and why. At least Katerine's death couldn't be murder, Lady Elizabeth thought. A doubt pricked at her mind, but she thrust it away. Katerine had fallen while . . . while playing on the roof?

As an explanation it was as good as any other, she thought.

Paul, the canon despatched by Godfrey to take his alarming message to the prioress, hesitated at the connecting door in the church. He tapped on the wood, trying to gain the attention of the

sacrist, but dared not walk straight into the nuns' cloister. It was
something he knew others occasionally did, but Paul had scruples
about obeying God's commandments, and even if Godfrey wanted
him to go straight in, Paul was quite sure where Godfrey stood
relative to God in Paul's scheme of things.

There was no answer; nobody answered his anxious rapping.
Screwing up his courage, he pressed the latch and opened the
heavy oaken door, peering round it. There was no one there.
Hurriedly he pulled the door shut and stood nervously tapping his
foot and sucking his lip. He daren't return to see Godfrey without
attempting another means of speaking to the prioress.

Not that he wanted to help her. The Lady Elizabeth had not
controlled the place as efficiently as she should have, and Paul,
who although slightly eccentric was still enthusiastically religious,
felt that her tenure had not served to honour God as it should
have. He could see the advantage of another prioress taking over.
Apart from anything else it would free him from that horrible old
man Jonathan.

Paul pulled a face as he recalled that Jonathan had asked him to
go and walk with him in the garden. The very idea made his flesh
creep, and Paul shuddered. If the prioress was doing her job, an
ageing satyr like Jonathan would be controlled. Margherita
wouldn't allow Jonathan to try to seduce other canons.

Suddenly, Paul realised there was another way to get a message
to the prioress via the grille in the herb garden. He could call
through it and ask a nun to fetch the Lady Elizabeth to come and
hear Godfrey's words.

But arriving there, he saw Elias already at the grille, eagerly
peering through it. Paul stopped and frowned. This was out-
rageous: didn't the smith have any sense of wrongdoing? It was
just one more example of the slack discipline at Belstone. The
prioress was responsible; she was in charge. It was *wrong*! She
shouldn't permit such open communication between canons and
nuns. If Elias was guilty, then so was she. It was high time the
Lady Elizabeth was removed and someone else took over.

All this passed through his head as he stood watching Elias at the grille. Paul tutted to himself. He had a message to pass on, and how could he do it now? If he was unable to speak to a nun, how could be bring the news to the attention of the prioress? Of course . . . he could tell someone else – someone who was known by all in the convent to be the implacable enemy of the prioress: Bishop Bertrand!

If Paul told the suffragan, Bertrand would be bound to take action – and it must surely help remove Lady Elizabeth. Even she would find it hard to survive an apostate canon, a nun turned apostatrice, as well as two deaths and the near death of the knight.

In confiding in Paul, Brother Godfrey had unwittingly ensured that his message went to the one man he wished to remain ignorant.

Bertrand led the way through to the cloister and in at the frater's door. Here Simon and Hugh found Baldwin unconscious lying on a trestle table. A perplexed Godfrey stood cleaning Baldwin's scalp with a cloth damped in warm water; he gave the men a cursory once-over before returning to his work, utterly absorbed.

'Baldwin? What has . . .?'

'He was walking out in the cloister, when a terrible accident happened,' Bertrand said. He stared at Baldwin's hideous wound; the sight of the long flap of flesh slashed away with such precision was horrible, but fascinating. 'A novice was up on the church roof, and slipped. The poor girl fell to her doom, but as she toppled, she dislodged slates, and one of them did this to your friend. Only God's own grace saved his life. If the slate had fallen an inch to one side, he would be dead.'

'He'll be fine, Bailiff,' Godfrey said, reaching for a pair of scissors and beginning to cut away the knight's hair. 'For so old a man, he's healthy.'

Simon nodded distractedly. To have woken from his nightmare to be presented with a real one was appalling, and for a moment he seriously wondered whether he was still dreaming. He took a step forward. 'He will live?'

'He's fit enough. Leave him to me.' Seeing the fearful

expression on Simon's face, Godfrey's voice became more kindly. 'Don't worry, Bailiff. I've seen to many similar wounds, and he'll be all right.'

'Thank you for your assistance,' Simon said, and made to walk out of the room, but then he stopped and gave a quick frown. 'Hugh, you wait here,' he said in an undertone. 'Stay with Baldwin and don't let anyone near him if you don't trust them.'

'Why? He is perfectly safe here,' Bertrand said.

Simon glanced at Godfrey. 'You say a second novice has died?'

'This has nothing to do with the death of poor Moll . . .'

'Perhaps, but seeing my friend here like this, I am not prepared to take the risk. Baldwin was certain that Moll's death was murder, and I find this "accident" to be suspicious. Now show me where this all happened.'

Bertrand agreed with a bad grace, convinced that the bailiff was allowing his imagination to run on a light rein, but Simon didn't care. He knew that accidents happened at the worst possible moments; a tile falling from a roof wasn't rare even in better maintained places. All the same, he felt deeply uneasy.

It was ironic that this should happen just as Baldwin and he had been ordered home. *Home*! With an inward groan, Simon thought of Jeanne: she must be told – but not until later. For now, Simon must concentrate on how Baldwin had been wounded.

'He was here,' Bertrand said, motioning towards a thick sprinkling of slates on the grass. Thin snow had been trampled, but two clotted spills of blood stood out distinctly.

Simon peered upwards. The cloister roof had been wrecked, but it was a good twenty or thirty feet from the church roof in a direct fall, and a body weighing some stones would have dislodged them without difficulty.

'Did anyone see what happened?' he asked.

'There was a canon here called Paul: *him*.'

Simon followed his pointing finger and saw a gawky young canon entering the cloister. Walking up to him, Simon asked, 'You saw my friend hit by the slate?'

Paul forgot Elias at once. Seeing Simon's serious expression

Paul was reminded of Katerine's body, her wide, scared eyes, the way her head rested at such an impossible angle. It was enough to make him want to weep with sadness. When that tile had fallen, he had been in the middle of copying a book, trying to ensure a perfect replica of the writing, but it was a dull treatise, and when he saw Baldwin in the cloister, Paul had been distracted and had watched him. It took little time for Paul to tell Simon what he had seen. While he spoke, Simon was aware of Bertrand joining them. Paul's attention went to the suffragan while he talked.

'So my friend was out there looking upwards?' Simon asked.

'Yes, but then he turned away, and rubbed at his eye, and a moment later the slate struck him. Then there was an awful crash, and the next thing I knew, something was rolling down the roof above me, and fell almost on top of Sir Baldwin.'

'How do I get to the roof?'

There was a stone staircase inside the church. Soon Simon was hurrying along the cloister towards it.

When he was gone, Paul turned to Bertrand. 'My Lord, may I speak to you a moment?'

It was very windy on the roof and Simon had to take a good breath before he dared approach the edge. He was afraid of heights. Looking down, he found himself staring at the upturned face of Bertrand, who remained standing in the quadrangle with Paul.

To take his mind off the suffragan, Simon peered straight down on to the roof of the cloister. Some twenty yards farther along, he could see the point where the novice's body had struck it. Not only was there a roughly circular pattern of dark, wrecked slates showing through the snow, which corresponded to the place where she had apparently fallen, there was a broad red stain. He'd heard Katerine had broken her neck. Hitting headfirst, she must have wrecked her skull.

Simon was aware of an overwhelming sense of inadequacy. Usually he could rely on his native intelligence to solve local mysteries, but today, with his best friend unconscious and unable to aid him, he felt all at sea.

From the corner of his eye he saw movement, and when he glanced down he saw the suffragan walking with Paul towards the stables. The sight of the two men drew Simon's attention back to the present, and he found he could concentrate once more.

Very well, the girl had fallen from the church roof. Either she had slipped – in which case what was she doing here? – or perhaps she had jumped and it was pure mischance that she happened to land on Baldwin, dislodging a slate on the way . . .

Simon caught his breath. The canon had said that he saw Baldwin look up, saw him turn away, saw the slate strike, and *then* heard the girl hit the roof.

His confidence returned. He marched along the roof until he was in a line with the mark on the grass and the ruined slates on the roof. Here it was maybe fifteen or twenty feet to the cloister roof, Simon guessed. A light dusting of snow clung to the vertical stonework of the church. A line showed where the snow had been swept clear as the girl fell down the wall. Simon had a vision of her toppling headfirst, her skull grating down the stone and losing the flesh.

Struck by vertigo, Simon had to close his eyes and lean away from the terrible drop. Rather than gaze down, he decided to survey the roof.

There was no lead here. The convent had not enough money to fully waterproof the place; only the greater houses could afford that sort of luxury. Instead, like the cloister roof below, this one was slated. Each slate had a pair of holes drilled through it so that oak pegs could be thrust through, hooking the tile to the lathes beneath. There were no slates missing nearby, but Simon had hardly expected to see any gone. If someone *had* done as Simon suspected and thrown one at Baldwin, it would have been an act of extreme stupidity to pull one from the roof. That would prove ill-intent.

However there *was* a pile of unfitted slates near the low parapet, as if the builders had left them for use as spares as and when needed, or perhaps the canons thought this was the best place to leave them, rather than taking up storage space in the undercrofts.

When Simon examined them, he was struck by their new appearance. All looked unused. Even the top one was perfectly cut, its surface a smooth blue-black colour.

Simon turned slowly back from the pile and stared down at the roof at his feet. The girl had obviously been up here a while, for the snow had been swept clear of much of the area, and where she had clambered over the parapet she had cleared a small space of snow.

He froze; utterly immobile for a moment, he held his breath. It was so obvious, so clear that someone had tried to murder Baldwin that Simon was unable to turn and confirm the proof for a moment, fearing to find his recollection was wrong.

Slowly he swivelled around and walked the two steps back to the pile of new slates.

The slates which had no snow upon them.

Chapter Fifteen

Constance returned to the infirmary and found Joan sitting before the fire. Pouring her a cup of spiced wine, Constance stood back to watch the older woman drink. It was peaceful now that Cecily was asleep again, this time drunk on wine rather than dwale and poppy seed, and Joan was clearly enjoying the quiet.

There was no such peace for Constance. She was confused, anxious and scared. It was while she was still talking to the prioress that the message had arrived that poor Katerine was dead, fallen from the roof, almost braining Sir Baldwin *en route*.

Everyone had heard stories of nuns who lost their faith and believed that they had the right to end their lives, denying God's own supreme responsibility for choosing how and when to call His people to Himself, but Constance would never have believed that of Katerine. Especially since she had always appeared so full of life. She was the last person to look for death. Constance privately thought the girl must have slipped – but that begged the question of what Katerine was doing on the roof in the first place. Spying on the canons?

It was a thought. The girl was always happy to use information to her own advantage, as Constance knew only too well, although what she could have hoped to have seen up on the roof was a puzzle.

Constance left the jug by the fire and walked back to the little chamber, standing in the doorway and staring about her.

Only a few nights ago, when Moll died, she had told Elias of their joint parenthood, while they lay naked in each other's arms on her mattress. At first he had not wanted to believe it, his face registering shock, but that was only for a moment. Then his expression changed. His eyes had creased, his mouth broke into a wide smile and he had pulled her towards him, embracing her fervently.

It was his idea to leave the convent. How could they stay? he had demanded, his strong, muscled arms wrapped about her, talking softly into the side of her neck while she stared up at the ceiling, tears filling her eyes.

He still wanted her to go with him, she knew; he would be waiting for her down at the iron grille that separated the nunnery from the canons. Waiting for her answer.

And she would have gone, if Katerine hadn't accosted her. That had forced her to decide: Elias or the convent. At least the prioress had been kind; understanding. There were rumours that she herself had once fallen in love, and had only come to this convent after being thrown from another in disgrace. Perhaps that was why she was less harsh with her nuns and novices: because she knew what it was to hold a man in her arms, to feel doubt and dual loyalties, one to God, and the other to a man.

Constance stared at her belly with near revulsion. It had never occurred to her that she could come to this. Elias had been a flirtation, an amusement snatched between services and the routines of claustral life. She had enjoyed flirting so much that one day she had shamefully passed near the grille, and when he made to catch at her robe, she made a show of sweeping it away, casually allowing her hand to pass so close to his that he could hardly help but catch it.

As soon as his fingers gripped hers, she felt the blood stop in her veins. She was frozen in time; her eyes transfixed by his powerful fingers; scarred, grime-ingrained fingers they were, but to her they were beautiful. She imagined how they would feel upon her body, scratching slightly as the nicks and calluses scraped over her. She pulled away, scared of her own emotions, and for the rest of that day she had lived in a dream, a wonderful dream in which Elias held her hand and smiled at her.

It had not been easy for him to get to her room. She had tutored him carefully, and had given her patients dwale to ensure their silence. The only risk had been that he might be seen entering the dorter, and then, once inside, that Princess might hear him. The little dog barked whenever she heard a man in the nuns' area. It was because of her that Constance had given Elias a bottle of poppy syrup. Princess often went to the men's cloister, and there would steal any food available. Elias lured her into eating marrow bones, and fed her small pieces of bread soaked in poppy syrup.

Each time Elias had gone to see Constance the dog had been unconscious. In fact, the poppy juice worked so well that when Elias proposed that they should leave together, Constance hadn't quibbled when he asked for a larger bottle, this time to ensure that the gatehouse was still as they passed through; they wouldn't have to concern themselves with over-inquisitive gatekeepers.

But now Constance couldn't leave. Partly it was the talk she had had with Lady Elizabeth. The prioress made her feel she was wanted. Oh, she'd made it clear enough that Constance would be committing a sin by leaving, but Constance believed that conceiving her child already put her beyond the pale. No, it was Elizabeth's understanding that had struck Constance. She truly appeared to understand Constance's confusion and fear.

There was another reason why she wasn't sure about running away. She thought Elias might be the murderer.

Simon took a pace back from the parapet. It was a hideous drop, made still more repulsive by that revolting smear. Now he knew what he was looking for, he could see the traces of red on the wall itself. Not on the roof below – that puddle was perfectly clear. No, now he could see the vertical path cleared in the snow was not merely an area remarkable by the absence of snow, but also by a smear of red.

He was as sure as he could be that Katerine had been murdered: these traces of her blood up on the roof of St Mary's meant that she had already been hurt *before* falling. Simon felt his stomach churn but not now with squeamishness. A hot, focused rage was guiding him – a rage composed of the desire for vengeance on whoever had tried to assassinate his closest friend, plus requital for the slaughter of two young women.

It was not that the two were novices, but rather that they were girls just like his own daughter Edith and the thought that someone had taken it into his or her head to kill them was so atrocious that Simon was determined to repay the debt on behalf of the two victims.

How could he prove Katerine had been murdered? Obviously if someone had heaved her over the parapet, either they had carried the dead girl up here or they had attacked her when she was already here – but if she had been conscious she would have screamed as she was pushed.

Simon was no expert, but he would have thought that carrying a girl up so many stairs would be difficult. He crouched by the door in the tower to see if there was blood on the top stairs – either drips from a bleeding wound, or smear-marks on the circular tower walls from a wounded body touching its surface as it was carried up over someone's shoulder. There was nothing in the area around the door.

He turned his attention elsewhere. The church had one shallowly pitched roof, and from the door he could see that the peak was only a short climb. Swallowing his desire to return to solid, safe ground, he gingerly stepped up and peered over the other side. There was nothing lying around that looked as though it might have been used to kill, nothing lying in plain view. Gloomily, Simon returned to the door. He had to accept that he had failed. There was no sign of someone having been attacked, and no sign of blood on the stairs.

Walking through to the top of the stairs, he turned to pull the tower door shut behind him when he noticed the smear on the door itself, and if the sight hadn't been so sombre and doleful, he would have given a whoop of joy.

Hugh sucked, but no matter what he did the small sliver of meat wouldn't budge from between his teeth. He looked around to make sure no one was watching and drew his knife. Lips pursed in a low, innocent whistle, he dragged the blade along the edge of the table to peel a long, thin splinter from it. It was the perfect size.

Sir Baldwin lay still. Godfrey had bustled about collecting a bowl and knife, and asked Hugh whether he would help bleed the knight, but Hugh refused to let him go near Baldwin with a blade until the bailiff returned and gave his permission. It wasn't that Hugh had any objection to bleeding: he was bled at least twice a year, because everyone knew it was the best way to cleanse the blood of impurities, but Hugh wasn't taking responsibility for Sir Baldwin's health – especially with the man whom Hugh suspected could have had a part in the first novice's death, and especially since Hugh couldn't know whether Godfrey could have his own reasons for killing, say, an over-inquisitive Keeper of the King's Peace.

In the end the canon had huffily stalked out; Hugh knew he had offended the man, but he wasn't sorry to be left alone with his thoughts, and he would not apologise for taking a sensible precaution, either. At least Sir Baldwin's long slash had been seen to, and the wound had been left open so that any corrupt matter within it wouldn't be forced inwards to poison the body. Even Hugh, who had never had any training in medicine, knew that. Godfrey had bound Baldwin's head with a long bandage which covered a thick poultice – designed to cultivate the pus which would hopefully cleanse the wound.

Baldwin was very pale, and with his dark beard, the contrast to his marble-white features was still more striking. His breath was shallow, as if he was in a deep sleep, but there was a rasping quality to it, as if he was in pain as well.

Hugh hitched up his tunic and rested his backside on the table at Baldwin's side, eyeing the knight contemplatively while he picked his teeth.

'Is he very bad?'

Leaping from the table, Hugh turned to find himself being studied by a short woman with shrewd green eyes set in a plain round face. Her skin had a thin, parchment-like look to it, but that was common with slightly older women, as Hugh knew. At least her wrinkled face was kindly. 'No. I mean, well, I don't know.'

Her eyes creased in amusement as she walked past him. 'Let me take a look. This man is a knight, I hear?'

'Yes . . . um . . .'

'You may call me Lady Elizabeth, young fellow. Are you trained in leechcraft?'

When he shook his head, she glanced back down at Baldwin. 'Where is Godfrey?'

'He asked me if he could open the knight's arm, and I said "No". Since then, I don't know where he's gone.'

'God rot his teeth! The damned fool; getting petulant because he's not allowed to practise his blasted surgery, I suppose,' Lady Elizabeth spat, making Hugh's eyes widen to circles. 'Right, young man, I suppose we'd better get this knight of yours to a place where he can be properly nursed – and that in safety.'

The staircase from the roof took Simon back to the nave of the canons' cloister, and all the way down, he kept his eyes fixed upon the steps and the wall, seeking any other smudges of blood. At several points he found them, and with each his conviction grew.

It was apparent that the girl had been struck and carried up the stairs. The blow had crushed her skull. Perhaps to prevent drips, a cloth had been wrapped around her head, but the blood had seeped into it, and where it touched the wall, it had smeared. That fact convinced Simon that the girl was probably already dead. If she had been hit so hard that she bled that heavily, there was little chance of her being alive. Someone had killed her, then taken her upstairs to throw her from the roof.

Standing near the altar, Simon glanced at the door communicating with the nuns' cloister. She must have come from there; she could have been discovered in the canons' area and murdered there, but Simon doubted it. He also thought she was not likely to have been carried into the church. Surely someone would have seen that. No, more likely that she had walked in and was knocked down inside. A blasphemy in its own right.

On a sudden impulse, he went to the door and entered. There was little to distinguish the nuns' side from the men's side. The choir stalls were much the same, as was the altar. There were no stains on the clean floor. At the back of the room Simon saw Denise's aumbry and opened it. Inside was a mess of brushes, rags and waxes.

Plainly the sacrist would have known where to find a cloth. And she'd have known how to clean blood from the floor of the church, too.

Safely back on terra firma, Simon saw Lady Elizabeth at the door to the frater. He knew instinctively who she was. The prioress had an aura of confidence about her, like many a great lady, and she also gave the impression of power. She nodded to him, and Simon recognised in that short beckoning movement the authority of one used to command.

'You are the bailiff brought here by that infernal fool Bertrand?' she asked calmly. 'Your friend is going to make a perfectly good recovery – so long as his jaw doesn't lock up, anyway. You never can tell with these things. But I do not think it is sensible to leave him in the frater. He will cause too much chatter in there. The church would be a good place to put him, but too cold; the calefactory would be warm, but too noisy. I think the best thing to do is remove him to the infirmary.'

'Here in the canons' cloister?' Simon asked, and when she agreed, he shook his head. 'I cannot agree. In my view Godfrey has to be a suspect in the murder of the first novice, and I have no idea whether he could have been involved in the second as well.'

She rounded on him hotly. 'Godfrey would do no such thing! It's ridiculous to suggest that he might have had a hand in this.'

'You may feel so, but I couldn't leave Baldwin in his charge without guards.'

'Where else would you have the man put?'

Simon felt indecision torturing him. All he wanted at this moment was Baldwin's servant to stand over the knight and guard him while he, Simon, went to discover who had tried to kill him, but Edgar was miles away in Cadbury. 'Where is safe if someone is prepared to kill twice?'

'Twice? Do you mean Katerine was murdered?' the prioress demanded sharply.

'My Lady, I have no doubt. There was someone up on the church roof; he or she threw a slate down to strike Baldwin, then threw the novice over the parapet.'

'How can you possibly tell that?'

Simon explained about the stack of unused slates, the topmost of which was unmarked by snow, and then the other evidence.

Lady Elizabeth walked up and down, deep in thought. 'Very well. We shall take your friend to the nuns' infirmary.'

'Where the first girl was murdered?' Simon exclaimed. 'I think not, Lady. I'd—'

'I can guarantee that the infirmarer is safe. She was not involved in the first death, and as for the second – well, she was with me.'

A canon helped Hugh carry Baldwin on a stretcher improvised from a door, while Simon and the prioress watched, calling out useful exhortations to be careful which twice almost caused an accident.

The knight was partly conscious now; blearily, he gazed about him as he was carried through the church and into the nuns' cloister. Here he was taken past a row of silent, awestruck women, all of whom stared at him: one or two, Simon noticed, with that speculative expression that denoted an interest in more than just his wound as they took in his broad shoulders, strongly muscled arms and thick neck.

Hugh also saw their covert glances, and tried to avert his gaze. It was only one day ago he had been so overcome by loneliness that he had been thinking about silken-skinned, available women, and now he was confronted by what felt like a horde of them; whereas he had expected them to look down upon him, he was now given the unsettling impression that most were mentally undressing him. It made him want to cover his groin with a hand.

He noticed one in particular. A slim young woman stood near

the angle of a wall, slightly apart from the others. Her thin linen veil appeared transparent the way the sun slanted down at her, and he was sure he could see the line of her lips beneath, soft and full. As her eyes met his, he could swear that her smile broadened, and she gave him a look he would have interpreted as inviting if he had seen it on a girl like Rose in a tavern.

He could have wept.

Baldwin felt as weak as a newborn puppy. His head was excruciating; liquid fire was running up and down the side of his scalp; his brain had expanded, or his skull contracted, he knew not which, and his eyes were apparently being forced from their sockets, like pips squeezed between finger and thumb. It made it necessary to keep his eyes closed for as long as possible.

'Can you hear me?' He heard Simon's voice from his side, but if he was to move his mouth the top of his head would surely explode. He twitched his hand, frowning with the pain.

'Baldwin, you were struck on the head. You've got a great gash in your scalp. It's not serious, but you'll have to rest.'

Vague memories came back to him now. They were in a convent, the one at Belstone, and they were helping someone . . . a bishop. Not Stapledon, though, someone else. Baldwin struggled to recall what they were doing here, but his head was hurting abominably. Every time he shifted on the bed it felt as if someone was thrusting a red-hot knife into his skull.

'Baldwin? Can you hear me?' Simon said again, and when there was no reply, he took his friend's hand, repeating his question and watching Baldwin's face anxiously until he felt the knight's hand grip his own. For Simon it was proof that his friend was not in immediate danger. Simon, like most men, had witnessed plenty of tournaments and mock battles, and had seen men in the ring fighting with clubs and swords. He knew as well as any man that, provided the injured man could hear and move after a few minutes, he was unlikely to die. The others, the ones who expired, were the men who could neither hear nor move after an hour or so. They seemed to pass from unconsciousness into catalepsy, and then died.

Simon leaned back, overcome with relief at the thought that his friend would probably recover. Not that there was any guarantee, of course. Locked-jaw always lingered after a cut no matter how small, and once that hideous disease had taken a man in its terrible grip, it would squeeze the life from him without compunction. Simon feared the locked-jaw more than the madness, the foaming at the mouth that a mad dog's bite could give a man. Locked-jaw led to a slow, agonising starvation while the mind was left free to appreciate the complete indignity and horror of the death.

And someone had tried to inflict this on his friend. Simon felt blind fury rising again, and had to force it down. Such emotions were not seemly in a nunnery.

Seeing the prioress beckon, he went to her side.

'Bailiff, this is the infirmarer, Constance. She has had some experience of wounds like your friend's.'

'The best cure for him is sleep, Bailiff,' Constance said earnestly. 'But with that horrible wound, he'll not be able to get it. I want to give him a draught that will let him rest.'

'What sort of draught?' Simon asked suspiciously.

The prioress laughed quietly. 'I know your mind, Bailiff. Trust me, and trust my infirmarer. Constance here knows what is needful for your friend.'

So she might, Simon thought to himself, but if she was the murderer, she might also know what was needful for her own protection. He watched with worried eyes while the infirmarer poured a few drops of syrup from a bottle and mixed them with wine from a jug. Then, tenderly holding Baldwin by the nape of his neck, she held the cup to his lips. As soon as he had finished the draught, Simon saw his friend's eyes wrinkle slightly at the corners as though he was smiling in gratitude. Constance carefully helped him to lie back on the pillows, his head turned sideways. Baldwin's breathing became more even and less laboured as soon as his head touched the pillow.

Simon glanced enquiringly at the prioress. She gestured towards the door, and the bailiff nodded and followed her out. Once at the landing area above the stairs, he stopped, and beckoned Hugh, grasping his servant by the shoulder.

'Hugh, don't let Baldwin out of your sight, all right? Someone might try to kill him in here, so keep your eyes open and your wits about you.'

Luke heard the canons talking about Katerine's death when he was approaching the church for Terce and the Morrow Mass. He saw Jonathan and curled his lip, hurrying past. Luke knew perfectly well about Jonathan's liking for young men and Luke had no wish to be the latest focus of his desires.

All the canons knew about Jonathan. He was a pleasant enough fellow when sober, but every now and again he would get drunk, and when he did, if a youthful or impressionable man was nearby, Jonathan could fix upon him to the embarrassment of the rest of the clergy.

Jonathan never intended to cause offence, but equally he knew that his interest in other men was viewed by most of his clerical brothers to be an abomination. He was convinced of it himself. That was why he went on his knees to pray, to try to expiate the sin of his lust.

Usually his – Luke could only think of them as infatuations – would wear out quickly, just as soon as the object of his desires became aware of the direction of his thoughts. Recently, Brother Paul had appeared to be humouring the older man, and Luke wondered whether he should bring the matter to the attention of the prioress – but only for a moment. He was too open to accusations of seducing novices himself.

When Jonathan saw Luke, he hurried over to him. Luke froze, but quickly forgot his revulsion as Jonathan told him what had happened to Sir Baldwin and the novice.

Luke raised his brows and expressed astonishment. 'But this is terrible! We'll have to pray for the knight's full and speedy recovery. Did anyone see the girl jump?'

'No one, unless the knight himself did,' Jonathan said.

'Apparently Sir Baldwin looked up just before he was struck, or so Paul says.'

'Oh?' said Luke. 'Well, no doubt Sir Baldwin will have told the suffragan.'

'No, the knight was unconscious when they took him to the frater, and now he's safe in the nuns' infirmary, but still not talking, so I hear.'

Luke carried on, but at a slower pace. Troubling thoughts occupied his mind as he slowly dressed himself for the service. It was a great shame about Kate.

Hearing the shuffling of feet in the nave, Luke fitted a contemplative expression to his face and walked slowly to the altar. There he genuflected to the cross, and began the service.

Uttering the words he knew so well, Luke found his mind wandering. It was good to be here, safe in this little convent. Agnes was a very willing companion, and there would always be other novices when she lost her charm or became too demanding. That was the good thing about being in a convent; there was no need to be tied to any one girl.

Women were confusing. Luke had been so certain that Moll was giving him the eye. But when he got her on her own and she realised what he wanted, she'd gone frigid, then pious. Worst of all, she had started preaching, urging him to give up his life of debauchery. He told her of Agnes's willingness, thinking to make her jealous, but the shot went wide of the mark. Moll said he must confess his sins, then she hinted that she would speak to Agnes.

Luke shook at the thought. Agnes was terribly jealous. If she heard that he'd tried it on with Moll, she would be furious.

Moll was not only pretty, she had the attraction of being a challenge. Agnes had the face of an angel but was a nervous type, always looking for praise. She could be boring – complaining about how others were putting her down.

In contrast Katerine had been assured and self-confident. Luke knew she was experienced with men the first time she kissed him. Like Agnes she hadn't needed much persuading. The one who was different was Moll. She believed in her vocation; wouldn't swallow his guff about a priest being able to take upon himself any sin. No, that kind of rubbish was only accepted by nuns who wanted an excuse. It wouldn't work with Moll; just as it hadn't worked with the worldly wise Katerine.

Katerine, when he had whispered to her in the few moments he had managed to snatch with her when no one – and especially not Agnes – was watching, had not reddened, but simply met his look with a measuring gaze. Luke had tried to use his arts of persuasion on her, but she had laughed, mocking his pseudo-religious arguments, saying, 'If you want to bed me, say so and have done.'

And then, as if to demonstrate that she was worth his while, she had reached up and kissed him full on the lips, with a loose, lubricious lustiness that made him squirm just to remember it.

It was a shame she was dead, he sighed. But at least Agnes was still alive.

Chapter Sixteen

Hugh watched the infirmarer warily. There was no need for her to go quite so close to the knight, nor to stop and stand near Baldwin when she was walking past on her way to the chamber. He was about to demand what she was doing when she suddenly went off behind the curtain.

'Well? Did you expect her to stab him in front of you?' Joan asked, then cackled to herself.

Hugh glowered at the floor and shrugged his shoulders, evading her sharp eye. 'I was told to keep a lookout on my master's friend.'

'Course you were, young man, but there's no need to act so oddly around Constance. She's a good lass.'

'I am, am I?' Constance said, reappearing in the doorway. 'And you're a dreadful old woman, Joan.'

'Now then, Sister. Don't forget, we nuns always maintain a polite distance in front of men,' Joan said disdainfully, and then laughed, slapping her thigh with delight at her witticism.

Joan gave Hugh a tolerant smile. It was easy to like Joan. She was known to all the nuns; for many her face was the first they would see on entering the cloister. Certainly she was fearsome, almost dragon-like to the younger entrants, but once the girls got to know her, they saw the warmth of her heart. Joan was a permanent fixture of the place, and she felt that she had the right to make jokes at the expense of any of the other sisters or of the institution itself, just as she saw fit.

Woe betide the fool who tried to join her in belittling the convent, however. That was tantamount to a felony in Joan's view. She would tolerate making fun of the other sisters, but the place itself was sacrosanct. Joan had earned the right to have digs at the priory, but only as the reward for her life of service. There was no excuse, she felt, for youngsters taking the rise out of the place, and she would be quick to snap at them.

'Why in front of men?' Hugh said, glancing doubtfully from one to the other.

'Who knows what you men would make of us if you knew what truly went on in our minds, young fellow?' Joan chuckled.

Constance felt her face redden, and she busied herself with cleaning some pots and carefully drying them.

'People think nuns are religious and spend their whole time walking about with their hands in their sleeves, heads down, daydreaming about the life to come, don't they? Or they think all women in convents are so starved of sex that any man who cuts a well-shaped thigh and ankle in hose would be exhausted after two seconds flat in a place housing so many lusty young women. That's right, isn't it?' she said, her voice suddenly louder.

Hugh was startled into a partial reply. 'I doubt it. Most men think women in the cloisters are already part of the way to heaven, so they don't figure much in our thoughts.'

'Ah, but why? Because the women are the Brides of Christ, or because it's too much bother to walk all the way to their convents, and too much like hard work to go to the effort of climbing the claustral wall to get at them, especially when the precinct might have guards to defend the women's innocence?'

Hugh was flustered by her questioning and shrugged again, his face growing darker with his suspicion that Joan's conversation had a point, and that point was to belittle Hugh.

Joan watched him like a viper staring at a mouse, bolt upright, her watery blue eyes intent, but then she suddenly sank back. 'I know what men are like, young fellow; after living here for more than fifty years, I have a good idea what goes on in the mind of the average villein or freeman, because I meet them when they come here, and always it's the same. Nuns are either mad because they can't cope with "real men" in the "real world" and run away from the smelly and rather foolish acrobatics which go hand in glove with sex – and if they don't think that, they assume that all nuns are lusty wenches who will fulfil every erotic dream of the most pox-ridden and pox-marked bastard born to a serf.'

'I'm sorry,' Hugh said, and his head was hanging now, recalling his thoughts in the tavern on his way to this place. He had been persuaded that the only reason why his hose would stay resolutely tied to his tunic was the fact that he was too low-born for a wealthy nun, he recalled, and now, listening to the bitter, tired old woman, he felt guilty.

'Don't be so silly, fellow! What sort of a churl are you?' Joan said. 'You forget that women here are the same as women outside, except we have taken the vow of chastity. We have the same dreams and desires as any woman who lives outside. Often nuns will fail in their oaths, but they can be forgiven that, because to fail is human. Such women can regain their position in God's love, because He understands our frailty, and while many will enter His kingdom after a life of unremitting effort and good works, I always like to think that He would prefer one or two darker horses up there with Him, just to protect Him from the utter tedium of dealing with the most perfect people.' She suddenly shot him a sharp glance. 'Don't you think He would soon be bored with only do-gooders to talk to?'

Hugh mumbled, but Constance gave a short laugh. 'Joan, you are cruel to tease the fellow. He knows he shouldn't answer: if he agrees with you, you'll tell him he's no better than a heathen, and if he disagrees you'll tell him he's a fool. Leave him be.'

Joan cast her a sly look, and Constance lifted an eyebrow sardonically. At the sight Joan grinned, and settled herself back in her chair.

Constance mixed spices with wine in a jug and set it near the fire. As she passed, she touched Joan's hand with gratitude, for the older woman's meaning was all too clear to her: all nuns failed occasionally, and there was always mercy and forgiveness. A moment later, Joan rose and went from the room. Constance returned to her bench; she felt little desire for forgiveness. She would trade it for an hour in Elias's arms any day, and no matter how many kindly words dear Joan gave her, she would always remember her lover's strong embrace.

Elias – whom she had told only the previous night that Katerine had threatened to expose them . . .

'I am deeply sorry that this has happened to your friend,' Lady Elizabeth said when she and Simon arrived in the cloister. 'Let me know if there is anything I can do to help you.'

'Thank you. Of course the matter is in Bishop Bertrand's hands . . .'

'Let's not try to fool each other, eh, Bailiff? The good bishop loathes me, and the feeling is mutual. If he can, he will see me thrown from here, while you have a perfectly natural desire to avenge your friend. As far as I am concerned, that makes you much more likely to catch the murderer.'

Simon grinned. 'Very well – but Bertrand carries the responsibility. Do you mind if I speak to your nuns here?'

She set her head to one side. 'No,' she said at last. 'But do treat them gently. Some of the women here are not used to meeting men at all, let alone being interrogated.'

Simon promised to be careful and left her to return to her desk while he walked to the nuns' frater. He wanted to see if he could learn anything from the women about the dead novice.

There were only two in the room: one nun and a novice, sitting on a bench up near the screens. Recognising the sacrist, Denise, he considered a moment, then approached.

'Ah, the bailiff!' Denise raised her pot in salutation. She was drunk, although not yet incapable. Wine had trailed down her chin to puddle on her breast, and her eyes were too bright. 'So you haven't been harmed yet?'

Simon stiffened, but forced his tone to remain easy. 'Denise, you know that Katerine is dead and my friend hurt. Did you see anything?'

She fixed upon him a face filled with the vacuity of drunkenness. Lifting her pot, she drank, spilling more of the drink down her tunic. At last she took the pot away and grunted with pleasure. 'Bailiff, this has been a terrible shock. I was sitting in here when

I heard someone cry out, and a few minutes later I saw poor Katerine being carried out from the church and taken to rest with Moll. Poor Katerine! Awful! I'm not used to bloodshed, you know,' she declared, peering once more into her cup and taking a deep draught.

'Was anyone here with you?'

'Oh, yes. Agnes here was with me all the time. I don't know if she noticed anything.'

'I saw nothing. I heard noises from the canons' cloister, but that's all.'

'You heard nothing apart from that?' Simon asked. 'And you were both in here?'

Agnes wouldn't meet his look, leaving it to Denise to say, 'What else could we have seen, Bailiff? We were here. It's not as if we would have had any reason to wander in the canons' side, is it?'

Jeanne was in the hall when she heard them. Immediately she dropped the tapestry she had been stitching and ran to the door.

When she was young, her parents had both been murdered by trail bastons, the foul club-men who had wandered the land in the last years of King Edward I – this king's father. These sounded like another band of men-at-arms marching. It was a distinctive noise: the tinny clattering of many pots and griddles knocking together where they were hooked on the outside of the wagons, the dull, hollow squeaking of ill-greased axles, the rattle and thump of heavy wheels striking ruts, the tramp, tramp of feet, the occasional shout and jeering laugh. All these noises could be from a large entourage, one with which the King had surrounded himself, and when she fearfully stared out, she saw a procession of men, wagons and carts, all well-covered against the cold, all faceless under their hats.

Since the visit of Stapledon's messenger, Jeanne had been worried that trail bastons could come here. Furnshill was almost on the road from Tiverton to Exeter. Seeing them now, she was suddenly convinced it was the army of the Despensers.

She was aware of a thickening sensation in her throat, and the hairs on her scalp tingled; her legs felt as if they couldn't support her. There was a growing muzziness in her head, an inability to think. She wanted to escape – but she couldn't. Her duty was to her husband's manor and house; Jeanne was the wife of a knight.

The recollection cured her. By God's good grace, she would acquit herself like the lady she was. Striding to the door she shouted, 'Edgar!' and ran to the yard behind the house. Here, normality prevailed. Men exercised horses, others idled between jobs, passing the time of day with dairymaids and house-servants.

Hearing her shout, Edgar rushed from the stables, an expression of mild surprise on his face.

'There is a force in the road. We must arm the men and—'

She was talking to the air. At her first words Edgar had bolted for the screens, and now he stood at the far side of the threshold, a stout pike hidden behind the door where he could grab it at need.

Feeling somewhat ridiculous, Jeanne trailed after him. 'Shall I call the men to arms?'

Edgar surveyed the men who now marched up the lane to the manor, then shook his head. 'They don't look like outlaws, and if they were Despensers, we'd have heard. They'd have razed the land on their way here, and we'd have seen refugees passing for hours.'

'Then who are they?' she demanded, peering over his shoulder.

As she spoke, a man riding a pony near the front rode back to a man on a tall grey destrier. While Jeanne watched, the pony's rider nodded, whirled around and set off towards the house at a canter. Soon he was at the door, a youngish man with a round face and angry features beneath a wide-brimmed felt hat. He sat hunched on his pony as if frozen.

'My Lord begs your kindness, and asks would it be possible to rest his horses and men here overnight?'

Edgar was about to answer when Jeanne spoke up, her hand on his sleeve. 'Normally I'd be glad to offer comfort to weary travellers, but my husband isn't here, and without his permission

I cannot allow strangers to enter.'

The messenger hawked and spat, then tilted his hat back on his head. 'Are you sure you couldn't allow us just a couple of hours before your fire, my Lady? We've ridden far this day already, and the air has practically frozen our innards, we've been out in it so long.'

'The Lady of the house has spoken,' Edgar said, and although there was no curtness in his voice, his tone sufficed to demonstrate that he would ensure her will was obeyed.

'Oh, very well. I don't even know why he wanted to come to such a miserable spot!' the young man said, staring at the house with evident distaste. He turned in his saddle to call back. 'My Lord, they won't let us in, not even to sit before the fire.'

'Really?'

And with that voice Jeanne felt her trepidation fall away.

'My Lord Bishop! I didn't know it was you – of course you are welcome, and your men too!' She gasped with relief and delight.

It was at the door to the infirmary and dorter that Simon saw the old woman. Joan sat contentedly on a bench sipping at a large cup of wine, her legs stretched out before her. She opened her eyes as Simon approached.

'May I sit with you?' he asked.

She shrugged. 'If by that you mean, can you ask me questions, say so!'

Simon grunted as he lowered himself, rubbing at his temples.

Joan gave him a sympathetic look. 'I'm sorry. I get so used to being the first person anyone comes to for help that sometimes I make myself sound tetchy to grab a little peace.'

'The nuns all come to you?'

'Oh, yes. I am the oldest. They think I have a monopoly on commonsense and experience.'

'Where were you today when Katerine died?'

She gave a sad smile. 'I was walking in the orchard, Bailiff. Alone. I wish I'd been here to pray for poor Katerine, falling like that.'

'She didn't fall by accident. She was murdered.'

Joan's eyes opened with horror. 'But . . . How can you be sure? I thought she had slipped or something.'

Simon didn't explain his theory. 'Were you there for long?'

'Not very. I needed to clear my head a little. I am used to work, Bailiff, and spending all my days indoors before a fire seems strangely boring. I had thought sitting at a fire would be a delightful retirement – all pleasures can pale.'

'Did you see anyone here when you came back?'

'Only Denise.' Joan wrinkled her nose. 'She was rather drunk again, I am afraid.'

'Where was she?'

'She's the sacrist. Where would she be? I saw her leaving the church after cleaning up.'

'Alone?' he asked, and Joan nodded. 'Everyone seems to have been alone,' he grumbled.

She chuckled. 'It's the duty of the contemplative life! But there is one thing in my favour.'

'And that is?'

'That I had no reason to want to hurt poor Katerine. I know not all the novices liked her – in fact, I think Agnes and she had fallen out over something – not that either confided in me.'

Simon motioned for her to continue.

'I know little about it. When Agnes first came here, she soon befriended Katerine, but more recently they have hardly spoken.'

'How did Agnes get on with Moll?'

'I think most of the women here found Moll difficult. Someone who wishes to be a saint can be tedious company, especially when she considers it her duty to report any misbehaviour. Not the best way to make friends.'

'Who else could have wanted to see Moll and Katerine dead?'

'Although the nuns and novices here often confide in me, I assure you none of them have admitted to murder,' Joan said. She shivered. 'And now I think it is time I returned to the boredom of watching a fire. Alas! Although I find sitting in front of the flames dull, I still crave the heat.'

'One last question, please. Did Denise like Moll and Katerine?'

Joan hesitated. 'Denise? What on earth makes you ask that?' she said lightly, but as she walked through the door to the infirmary, Simon saw her throw him a look over her shoulder.

Jeanne had a quick eye, and while Edgar organised the servants to see to the bishop's men, she sat him in Baldwin's own chair before the fire and served him herself, darting little glances over his embroidered robes, the heavy rings on his fingers, the weighty belt with all the enamelled metalwork, the expensive Spanish boots of such soft, supple leather and the velvet hat which must surely have come from an exotic source. It was plain to her eye that the man who had left Exeter as a well-known but honourable cleric had enhanced himself by his position as the country's Treasurer.

It wasn't only the metalwork on his fingers and hanging around his neck, it was his overall form. Bishop Stapledon, the last time Jeanne had seen him, had been quite slim in his build, but now he had grown portly. His second chin had been superseded by a third, and his belt appeared to be finding the task of encircling his girth a sore trial, from the way that it cut into his belly.

But his smile was the same. Bishop Stapledon, Jeanne knew, had already created the new Stapledon Hall at Oxford, and had founded twelve scholarships for students of grammar in Exeter, as well as granting many licences for clergy to live outside their parishes so that they could go to Oxford and improve their learning. He took his bishopric seriously, always trying to improve the men whose task it was to help the souls of the parishioners on their journey to heaven.

'My Lady, you look very well,' he sighed as he leaned back in his chair, pot of warmed wine grasped in his hand. 'Marriage must suit you.'

'It would be pleasant indeed, had I more opportunity to enjoy my husband's company,' she said lightly.

Stapledon laughed. 'There are many who think that.'

'And many who will shortly think it,' she agreed sombrely.

'You are thinking of the conflict to come?'

'What else occupies the minds of most people now, my Lord?'

Stapledon idly ran his finger around the rim of his pot. When he looked up to meet her gaze, his face was serious, his brow wrinkled with concern. 'It would be troubling indeed if it should come to war. The country doesn't need the King to fight with the barons.'

'Yet it appears that the King's friends are forced to go to war,' Jeanne said carefully. She liked the bishop and enjoyed his company, but he was Treasurer to the King, and she had heard that he had won the job from the support of the Despensers. It would be best that she didn't let him know that her own loyalties were with the Welsh March barons who were showing a united front against the Despensers. Such information could be useful to Baldwin's enemies; and one never knew when a friend like Stapledon could become a dangerous ally, or an enemy himself. It was best to be circumspect.

He spoke quietly. 'The country doesn't need to rip itself apart. God knows, we have more than enough enemies over the water keen to see us destroy ourselves. And those Scottish *bastards* are always at our back with their long knives . . .' He stared into the fire, his face drawn and serious – more so than Jeanne had ever seen before.

She poured wine. 'While you are here, let us forget your great position in the country, and talk only of local matters. You great prelates, you often forget that the most important matters are not those which are dealt with by the King's Parliament, but those which are handled by the burgesses of Crediton, or the tinners of Devon, in their little taverns. That is where the really interesting debates occur, and the issues of great moment are discussed.'

Stapledon smiled, a little sadly, she thought. 'Yes. Matters here are a great deal more entertaining. I look forward to spending more time at Exeter – I am on my way there now.'

'Truly?' Jeanne asked. 'Can you take time away from your work with the King?'

'With the King? My dear Lady, I have resigned my post. I am

no more a national figure, the hated tax-collector of England. I despise the situation we are now in, with threats of war rattling shutters up and down the land, and I am simply the Bishop of Exeter once more. Damn all politicians, say I!'

After Morrow Mass, Simon went with the canons through the church and out to the cloister. Here the canons left him to go to their chapterhouse, the little chamber where they would discuss matters relating to the church and its work. At the other side of the church Simon knew that the prioress was holding her own chapter with all her nuns, and at this moment, alone, without the advice of his friend, without even his servant, Simon suddenly felt abandoned.

He was a bailiff, and as such had hunted down gangs, escaped murderers and felons, and yet now, here in this cloister, he was more aware of his solitude than ever before. It was as if his life before was cut off from him; all the normal props and supports upon which he depended had been removed: his wife, his daughter, his servant and, of course, his friend.

It was strange how attached he had become to the tall, dark-featured, austere knight. Simon was a country fellow, a cheery, rumbustious man, enthusiastic about his sports and drinks, but cautious of new acquaintances until he had grown to know them very well. The methodical, cool-mannered Baldwin was not the sort of fellow to whom Simon would normally have warmed, yet he had become his closest friend. Perhaps it was simply that both were propelled into their respective positions with little warning, Simon to be a bailiff, Baldwin to his post as Keeper of the King's Peace, and they each had need of a friend.

Certainly they had always managed to work very well together. Baldwin's learning was extensive because of his time with the Templars. Conversely, Simon's knowledge sprang less from learning and more from his background as a steward, which was enhanced by his shrewdness in dealing with people. Simon could normally see in a man's eye whether he was lying or not. That skill had helped to catapult him to his present position under the

Warden of the Stannaries, where he regularly had to test men who
tried to get away without paying tax on the tin they had mined, or
who tried to persuade him that they had taken over a concession
when there was none.

Finding himself at the entrance to the guestroom, Simon
climbed the stairs to it, crossing the room and sitting glumly on
his bed. It was only this morning, he reminded himself, that he
and the other two had gone to attend the services in the middle of
the night. Only this morning in the dark, Hugh and Baldwin,
Bertrand and he had walked through the cloisters to the church. It
had been absolutely freezing. He had been miserable – not so
miserable as Hugh, Simon remembered, but then Hugh was always
dreadful when he hadn't had enough sleep. He'd hardly said a
word during the morning. Only that stuff about . . .

Simon's eyes narrowed as Hugh's earnest expression came to
his mind. The servant had told him about the prostitute in the
frater. After all the excitement of the morning, Simon had
completely forgotten about it. He wondered how to proceed but
then reproved himself. Baldwin would not have sat about wondering what to do, he would have tried to form an idea as to what had
happened, and then test his theory. And if he had no theory to test,
he would have gone questioning anyone who might have information until he could form one.

Rising, the bailiff walked from the room with a renewed sense
of purpose.

The frater was empty bar Jonathan, who sat before the fire, a
large pot of wine in his hand. For a moment, Simon stood just
inside the doorway, gazing about him, wondering about the
doorkeeper and what he actually did for the convent.

In his experience, most doorkeepers and masters of priories
were older fellows, men who could not be tempted by the young
women within the precinct, men who had seen much of the world
and who had chosen to retire from it into the sphere of ecclesiastical life. Their duties were simple: to protect the nuns from the
unwanted attentions of people from the outside world. In return

they had an easy life, mostly spent sitting in a warm gatehouse, granting visitors the necessary hospitality and avoiding unwanted interruptions to the daily round of services and work.

Simon reminded himself of the working of the convent as he went to the seated man. Jonathan would also be responsible for the receipt of accounts from the reeves and bailiffs, for storing all the goods produced within the priory's demesne, for maintaining all contact with the secular world outside the gates.

And yet he sat here, ignoring his responsibilities at the gate, and similarly not attending the services or the chapter meeting.

Jonathan heard him and shot a look over his shoulder, spilling a little of his wine. Seeing who it was, he returned to his solitary study of the fire.

'Is the gate unmanned?' Simon asked as he approached.

'There's a lay brother there. He doesn't need my help.'

Surprised at the dead tone of his voice, Simon hesitated.

It was Jonathan who looked up and nodded towards an empty bench. 'If you wish for ale or wine you'll have to fetch it yourself.' He watched as Simon walked out to the buttery.

Sighing, Jonathan set his pot on the ground and put his hands over his eyes. He knew he was behaving ridiculously, but couldn't stop himself. He had always been petulant, and this morning, when he had realised that his feelings for Paul weren't reciprocated, he had come in here to think and drink until he had forgotten his misery. Later he would go to the church and try to soothe his soul and cleanse his spirit with prayer. After two pints of wine, the bitterness of his frustration had worn away.

There was nothing new about this sense of desperation. He had suffered from it often enough, especially when he was younger. Somehow the desires began to fade a little as he grew older, but that simply meant that there was a poignancy to each fresh encounter. He loved, but knew that his love could never be requited. It was his unending doom – a living hell in which he was forced to deny his own emotions.

The whole world appeared to abhor his kind of lust. His father certainly did, which was why Jonathan had been

condemned to a life of prayer and service to God, in order that
he could atone for the sin of his perverted attraction, and
incidentally remain far away from his family where he could
never again embarrass them.

Yet now he had heard that he was not alone. It wasn't just he
who found the male body infinitely more attractive than the
female; rumours abounded that the King himself, Edward II,
had taken the younger Hugh Despenser to be his lover, just as he
had previously taken Piers Gaveston until that man's execution
by the King's enemies. And that was why Jonathan now needed
to sit alone before the fire, ignoring the summons to the
chapterhouse, refusing to attend the church services; he knew
his life was irrelevant. If he had been born to wealth, like the
King, maybe he could have enjoyed the love he craved, but God
had seen fit to deny him that solace; to punish him with this
fixation. If he was King he could flout the law – but he wasn't
King.

He gazed sombrely at the bailiff who came and sat at his side.
'How is your companion?' he asked.

'Sir Baldwin is resting, I thank you. He was fortunate. If he
had been standing even a short distance to one side . . .' Simon
held up his hands helplessly. 'He was lucky.'

'Some luck,' Jonathan said. He drained his pot and set it at his
side, fixing Simon with a steady eye. 'So did you come here to
comment on an ageing doorkeeper's laziness, or to chat about
your friend's near-death? Or perhaps there was some more pressing
reason for your walking in here?'

'I wanted to ask, er . . .' Simon met Jonathan's gaze, and
suddenly his resolve faded.

'Whether I was on top of the church and pushed the girl at your
friend?'

'She was murdered before she got up there.'

The canon gaped, but then blinked and gave Simon a curious
look, his head set to one side like an intrigued terrier. 'You're not
so foolish as you can appear, my friend. Let me assist you to
another pint of wine. My pot is empty.'

'Here, have some of this,' Simon said, pouring from his own jug.

Jonathan sat back and held his feet to the fire, wiggling his toes. 'I had no idea the poor little thing was murdered. She was killed and tossed over the wall like a rock hurled at a besieging army? That's disgusting.'

'Whoever it was also threw a tile at Baldwin intending to kill him. I want to know where people were when all this happened.'

'It was between Prime and Terce, wasn't it? You'll have your work cut out to discover where everyone was at that time. The canons should all sit and read in the cloister, but that only happens in the really well-regulated priories, and I am sure you will have observed that this one . . .' he waved a hand airily and belched '. . . this one is hardly on that sort of level. No, here everyone gets on and sees to themselves. Some come and chat here in the frater; others go to the cloisters, it's true, while some walk in the gardens, thinking.'

'Where were you?'

'Me?' Jonathan asked sadly. 'I was alone in the orchard, waiting for a friend to meet me, but I fear he didn't come.'

Simon saw his mood, but he had no time to worry himself about the reason's behind it. 'Did you see anyone there?'

'I did see the smith, Elias. He was hanging around by the wall to the nunnery, but I saw no one else.'

'There was a girl here last night. A whore servicing the canons – is that right?'

'Yes. So what? Even canons have desires, you know.'

'But . . . chastity?'

'God's bones! What of it? Do you think all those who live in cloisters are capable of meeting each and every strict demand of the Orders we serve? I doubt whether God could be so cruel.'

'Does the prioress know?'

Jonathan took a deep breath. 'My dear fellow, there is next to nothing ever happens in this place without her knowledge. She is the spider, sitting in the middle of her web, with strands reaching into every nook and crevice of the priory, and when a canon sneezes or coughs, she knows. Did she know that a girl was here yesterday, you ask? Well, I answer, yes. She not only knew, she probably spoke to the girl.'

'That's hard to believe.'

'Bailiff, I retract my suggestion that you are not so foolish as you look. Have you not heard of the prioress's sin? The girl is Rose – Lady Elizabeth's daughter.'

Chapter Seventeen

The hardest part for Jeanne was admitting that she had no idea why the suffragan had demanded that Simon and Baldwin should go to Belstone. As far as Bishop Stapledon was concerned, it was ridiculous that two secular men should be sent to a convent for nuns, and strange indeed that the reason for their mission should be concealed. With Jeanne's permission, he had sent one of her grooms to Crediton on a fast horse, with a request that Peter Clifford should tell him the cause.

Now he paced up and down, the reply gripped tightly in his hand, chewing at his lip and scowling. Walter Stapledon was no fool, and he could easily understand the urgent desire of Bertrand to squash any rumours – especially in a case like this, where the treasurer of the priory had alleged that the murderer was . . .

He stopped that line of thought. Lady Elizabeth was well-known to him. There was no possibility of her being guilty of this crime. Surely not. Stapledon's frown deepened; there was that story in 1300, before Stapledon became bishop, that she had given herself to a man . . . but Stapledon shook his head with decision. That a woman could lapse was not evidence that she could murder. The two crimes were utterly different. Lady Elizabeth was too urbane and refined for murder. No, it must be someone else, and Stapledon could only hope that she had not taken umbrage at Bertrand's less than subtle manners. Stapledon pursed his lips. There was little likelihood that she would have suffered Bertrand gladly. Stapledon knew both reasonably well and the thought of Bertrand standing before her pointing an accusing finger and declaring her to be a murderer – the bishop winced at the thought.

The only thing that mattered was keeping news of this away

from the general public. If it should become common knowledge, the nunnery could be closed, and that was a horrible prospect.

Very well, Stapledon thought to himself with resignation. I shall have to go and make sure that any ruffled feathers are soon smoothed.

Yet when he announced his intention, Jeanne was aghast. 'Look at the weather! You can't go out in this – think what it could be like in an hour or so! And getting to Belstone is not so straight-forward as riding to Crediton. It's much farther – you couldn't get there before nightfall even if it was summer.'

Going to the door, Stapledon was forced to agree. The snow was light, simply a thin scattering of tiny flakes so far, and the road was not hidden; the air was too warm and the snow melted as soon as it landed, forming a thin, muddy sludge, but Stapledon knew only too well how different the weather could be on Dartmoor, for he was a Devonshire man, born and bred. He gauged distances in his mind and decided. 'You're right. We'd not make it to Belstone today; we shall need to travel as far as possible, though. We should be able to reach Bow before nightfall, and it would be a short enough journey from there. Yes, that would be all right,' he said.

He turned to the buttery and ordered his men to prepare to continue. When he returned to the hall, Jeanne saw his mood had not improved.

'My Lord, please sit and finish your wine,' she said gently.

Stapledon thanked her and sat down in Baldwin's chair, but he glanced through Peter Clifford's message once more and then muttered what Jeanne thought must be a curse. 'Bertrand!' he exclaimed, and struck the arm of the chair.

As Jeanne watched in horror, the arm fell to the floor. Stapledon forgot his anger and stared at it, but even as he realised what was happening, he felt the rocking, heard the ominous creak. His eyes met Jeanne's as there was a loud report, and then the seat collapsed.

Simon Puttock sat gaping after the doorkeeper long after the man had left the room. When a lad, Simon had been taught by the canons at Crediton. It had been drummed into him that the Church had a sacred duty to save souls; for them to achieve their duty, all clerics were men of integrity, led by their most responsible and honourable representative. It had been rammed into him while he was a boy, and he had never quite lost the conviction that those who wore religious robes were somehow different from others.

It was hardly incredible that a nun should be guilty of giving birth to a child – Simon was no fool, and news of such incidents were all too common, if regrettable – but that the prioress of a convent should do so had never occurred to Simon. It disgusted him, as if she had openly offered herself to all the men of the village.

Simon took a deep gulp of his wine and then grinned to himself. What was more astonishing was his reaction, he realised, leaning back in his seat. The woman was hardly young, and yet she presumably had only been a prioress for a few years, since her lapse – if the story of her lapse were true. When she had been younger, she had taken a lover, perhaps only the once, and had fallen pregnant. To fail was human; surely since then she must have proved herself to be devout, and that was why she had been elected to lead her community.

Although whether they would do so again was a different matter, he thought, remembering the holes in the roofs of the main buildings and the freezing wind that whistled around the dorter.

He stood. The girl was not here. He would go and try to speak to the prioress. If Jonathan was right and the Lady Elizabeth *had* spoken to the girl, she herself might have heard something.

About to seek her, he hesitated, remembering Bertrand. He'd last seen the visitor hurrying towards the stables. Bertrand was supposed to be sorting out the trouble here; it was Simon's duty to tell him about Rose. Simon was torn. He didn't want to give Bertrand another excuse to proceed against the prioress, but at the same time didn't feel he had the right to warn Lady Elizabeth.

Simon fretted but his duty was clear; he walked out to find the suffragan.

* * *

Baldwin groaned as the pain shot through his skull like a red-hot bolt from a crossbow. He half-expected to smell the singed hair and cooked flesh, and cried out as he tried to move his head again, but his mouth was oddly quiescent, as though it had been bound with velvet cords.

He tried to sit up, but his arms wouldn't obey and it was only with an effort that he could force his eyelids open.

The room was red, warm, safe. He stared directly ahead of him, feeling the massive weight of his body; it felt so gross, he was sure the bed upon which he lay couldn't support him. He felt as if he was slowly falling through the mattress, and the panic rose in his breast: he would suffocate! The bedclothes would rise up on either side and swallow him, smothering him in their warm embrace.

Even as he reached this conclusion, he forced down his fear with logic: the mattress was solid. He couldn't fall through, it was impossible. His fear was the result of the drugs. Pillows and mattresses couldn't engulf men. He forced himself to breathe slowly, concentrating on the flames of the fire.

A fresh blow of pain battered at his head, and he heard a low moan issue from his lips, as though it came from another person. He was not part of his body; he was near it, but somehow dislocated, a most curious sensation. However, before he could consider his state further, a shadow approached.

Immediately he was convinced that now, while he was incapable of defending himself, he would be attacked. For some reason he was sure that a hand would soon appear above him, from the head of the bed, drifting forward slowly, fingers outspread, before falling to cover his mouth and nose, extinguishing his life.

The feeling disappeared. He saw that the figure approaching was a woman in a nun's habit. Such a person could be no threat. Dimly, he recognised Constance's anxious but comforting eyes, and he wanted to smile back, but his mouth wouldn't obey.

Elias had not joined his brethren for the service. He had sat in the small yard, waiting desperately for Constance so that they could talk; he had to explain why their escape was so essential, but she didn't appear. Instead, as the singing in the church faded, he had lifted his eyes to meet the stern gaze of the prioress.

'It won't do, young man. You cannot have her. She is already married to Christ.'

Elias fell back as if struck. Lady Elizabeth walked forward until she was at the metal screen, and Elias couldn't meet the look in her serious face.

'Nothing to say? Well, Elias, you have misbehaved with her, but now she has partially come to her senses. She is pregnant – you knew that? Ah well, of course you did,' she added almost to herself. 'That was why you wanted to take her away from here, wasn't it? So that you could look to both mother and child somewhere. And how would you have done that?'

'I can smith – I could earn enough for us in any town or village.'

'And which town or village would allow you, a wandering stranger dragging two useless mouths behind you, to stay long enough to demonstrate your skills? Don't be a fool! You would wander the streets, declaring your love for your wife, for such you would call her, and move from one small town to another, seeking work ever more desperately. And your child would die, of course: how could a baby live in the cold and damp for days without a roof overhead? Constance would have to give birth beneath a hedge, and she would be weak and fractious. You would love her and your offspring at first, but after days or weeks you would grow to hate them both; your child you would detest as a muling, squalling brat, a blob of vomit and excrement; Constance you would grow to loathe, for as you struggled to keep you and she alive, she would always demand more, saying that your baby needed warmer clothes, or a better shelter, or any one of a thousand things a mother wishes for her child.'

'I wouldn't – I *couldn't* grow to hate her!' Elias declared hotly.

'You would,' she stated quietly. 'And you would cause the death of your baby.'

'No!'

Seeing the desperate sadness in his eyes she wanted to stop in compassion, but she couldn't. The thoughts were all there from twenty-one years before when she had run through the same things with Rose's father, and it all spilled out in a torrent.

'You would refuse to stay near here; you would insist on moving further away to be free from any attempt to recapture you both, from the risk that you would be taken to another convent many miles distant to ensure that you and she never thought of escaping your vows again. While large with child, moaning and complaining that she had no energy left to run, you would force her to walk on,' Lady Elizabeth continued relentlessly. 'And even as she gave birth, you would be looking over your shoulder to see whether the Bishop of Exeter's men were following you.'

'No,' Elias said, but his voice had sunk to a despairing murmur, and his head hung down as he stared at the ground.

She gave him a faint smile. 'And when your child was dead, and you had buried it unblessed at the roadside for fear that any clergyman you begged to speak the words might tell your pursuers, then Constance would hate you as well. She would blame you for the death of her child, probably the only child she would or could ever conceive, and for the mortal sin of burying it without its soul having the benefit of a christening or priest's blessing. And you would see her expression, and if you had any manhood left, you would cringe, and in a short time, yes, you would become disgusted with her . . .'

'No!' Elias shouted, and ran forward to grip the railings, meeting her gaze at last with conviction. 'I love her, and there's nothing you can say will alter that!'

'*Love*!' she sneered. 'What do you know of love? You have sworn to love your God, yet you're prepared to forsake Him in exchange for the fleshy delights of a woman's body. How can Constance trust your promises now, eh? Not that it matters, for she will remain here. Do not bother to sit here idling, young fellow. Constance will be staying in the infirmary, for there is a badly injured man for her to look after, and she takes her work very seriously, as she should. It is a pity that you apparently do not.'

She spun on her heel and walked away, but then stopped and fixed him with a glittering look.

'But before I go, Elias, consider this: first, I shall in future ensure that all doors and grilles between the male and female convents are locked or covered over. There should be no communication between cloisters. And second, you should know that I believe Constance to be very concerned that whoever killed Moll was someone who got into the infirmary. Someone whom she feels might have had access to dwale and who also wanted to silence Moll. And now Katerine is dead, perhaps that same someone also wanted *her* made quiet?'

In the infirmary, Hugh sat on a stool by the wall, idly musing on the novice he had seen in the cloister.

She had so slim a body, Hugh could almost have believed she was a boy, but her lips and those welcoming eyes were surely those of a woman. He might have seen her again, were he to walk in the cloister. Perhaps she would speak to him. Ask him about his life. In his wildest imaginings he couldn't dream of her as a lover, she would surely scorn any such suggestion. But she had, he considered, looked quite beautiful standing there in the sunlight.

At the other side of the chamber, Constance had little time for thoughts about her lover, even after old Joan had started nodding. She had gently wiped the weeping wound at the back of Baldwin's head, then bound it up again. Now he appeared to doze.

'Don't worry, Hugh. He'll sleep well tonight.'

Hugh nodded and gave her a shy grin. She returned it more easily. It was not difficult, for Hugh was obviously overwhelmed by being inside a nunnery, and by her proximity. Constance could see his wretchedness. It made her wish to embrace him to calm his anxiety.

She pulled the counterpane up to Baldwin's chest and smiled down at him, aware of the patient's troubled sleep. Sir Baldwin was dreaming, she saw, and fleetingly wondered what avenues his mind was running along. It was obvious that he was under the influence of the poppy syrup; she had seen his pupils reduce to pinpricks, his flesh was very warm, he was sweating, and his breathing had slowed before he fell into sleep. He moaned to himself, frowned, and once sat upright, glowering around as if staring at enemies invisible to her or to Hugh. It had taken Hugh and her some time to calm him and ease him back down to the pillows.

Gently she rested a hand on his cheek, and was gratified to see his face ease a little, a smile lifting one corner of his mouth. He gave a quiet grunt, which she interpreted as one of pleasure, and then he was still. Watching her, Hugh was struck by the kind, maternal expression on her face. The servant knew he should distrust her as much as any of the other nuns, but he couldn't. Her prettiness, her gentleness, her calm dedication; all militated against her being able to murder.

Constance quietly took her hand away and went back to her chamber.

Elias stood with his back to the wall gazing heavenwards for what felt like an age. The prioress must have spoken to his Constance, but surely she wouldn't listen to the old dragon and ignore her heart? Constance *knew* she loved him, just as she must know he loved her – and how much! Elias groaned and clenched his teeth, his eyes closed as he shook his head from side to side. He couldn't leave her here: what, go away without seeing his own child brought into the world? Never see his own baby? It would be unbearable! To live without Constance was intolerable, but what had the prioress said? Hadn't she implied Constance thought he could have killed Moll?

His eyes snapped wide as he recalled her words. She had said Constance might consider that whoever had access to the dwale and had been in the infirmary . . . But Constance couldn't think that he'd hurt Moll, could she? Elias slid down the wall and gripped his thighs, resting his head on his knees. Moll was an evil little minx, but why should Constance think *him* capable of killing her? The Lady Elizabeth had said that Katerine was dead, too. Why should anyone think him capable of hurting her?

Elias felt a cold shiver flutter down his spine, and he looked about him with a sudden premonition of doom. He would be accused and condemned; sent far away, up to the Scottish Marches, to the freezing cloisters of the North, where he would live the rest of his life in awful penance, without meat or strong wines, without ale or thick soups, but living on dry bread and cold water, perhaps locked forever in manacles.

If his own lover thought him guilty of killing the girl, how could he look to anyone else to believe in his innocence?

Elias shivered again. 'Someone walking over my grave,' he said to himself automatically, and then gave a deathly grimace as he realised what he had said. It gave him an impetus. He forced himself to his feet and set off towards the stables.

'Bishop Bertrand?' Simon shouted, but he could see no one. He strolled along the path which led to the great gate, past the stables, the mill, the storerooms, garths in which cattle and sheep wandered, a great shed which held the tools and wagons, and last the smithy at the far end, far enough away for the forge to pose less of a fire risk. After this was a stable, some hundred yards away.

Simon approached the building. Peering inside, he called for the bishop again, but there was no answer, and he stood outside and kicked at pebbles while he considered what to do. Bertrand had come this way – Simon had seen him. 'Rot him,' he muttered bitterly, and began to make his way back towards the guestroom.

As he passed by the smithy, he glanced inside, and happened to see a slim figure dart behind a post at the far side of the room. Simon's feet had already taken him beyond the entrance, and he had turned his head to face the cloister when he was prompted to return and take another peep.

When the cavalcade had left, the bishop looking curiously sheepish, Jeanne and Edgar returned to the hall and stood gazing at the broken pieces of wood.

Edgar had swept all into a small pile beside the hearth, and both instinctively looked from it to the flames like a pair of conspirators.

Clearing his throat Edgar glanced at Jeanne. 'My Lady . . .'

'Yes,' she said thoughtfully. 'But first you need to send for a carpenter. The best in Crediton, mind. I want a new chair.'

As Simon disappeared, Bishop Bertrand gave his companion a sharp glance again, grumbling, 'This is mad, we've been here for ages. Are you sure he was there?'

Paul smiled gently and nodded. Again.

Shifting his weight, Bishop Bertrand grunted with dissatisfaction. This was quite ridiculous. The lad had told him about the message, and remembering the way that Elias had been waiting at the grille, Bertrand could believe the young smith was about to try to leave with his woman, a nun.

To Bertrand's mind, this was deeply suspicious behaviour. After all, two novices had been killed and the knight wounded. Even so, if Elias had nothing to do with the murders, Bertrand could understand why he might want to leave. Any canon living in a sink of corruption like this would want to get away. Although no honourable canon would subvert a nun to join him, Bertrand reminded himself.

There was no doubt that two were planning to go. Paul and Bertrand had uncovered the pair of bundles. In one Bertrand had found the little package, carefully wrapped in bits and pieces of linen. That, he knew, was incriminating and Bertrand rather looked forward to seeing how the canon tried to wriggle out of it.

Bertrand wriggled himself. His buttocks had gone to sleep. He had rested here for what felt like an age, and all they had seen so far was an apparently endless succession of dull-looking, placid horses or stolid oxen being led by equally dim-looking grooms or vapid farmworkers. The only man who looked remotely human had been the bailiff.

And it was damned uncomfortable, sitting here in the dark without a stool or even a pillow on which to rest his buttocks.

He'd tried sitting on the floor, but now he was on the packages themselves. They didn't protect him from the freezing ground and Bertrand was uncomfortably aware that his left leg, which he had once broken in a fall from a horse, would not work when he tried to stand. It had gone to sleep some while ago.

'Where is the man? I see no sign of anyone coming. How long will the fool be?'

Paul's face reflected none of his own doubts. 'He is sure to be here shortly. I cannot say how long. No, he shall find it impossible to conceal his guilt, I think.' He froze, head cocked to one side. 'Can you hear that?' he whispered.

Bertrand listened. There was the sound of hurried footsteps, ragged breathing, and a thump as someone barged the door wide open with his shoulder. Then he saw Elias dart over the floor, reach down and pull the straw aside.

'Elias?' Paul asked, standing.

'Who's there?'

Bertrand pointed a finger solemnly and intoned, 'We know what you seek, Canon. It proves your guilt that you search for it there.'

Giving a bitter laugh, Elias stood aside. 'Why, Bishop? What was I looking for? There's nothing here – see for yourself.'

'I know there isn't,' said Bertrand. 'Because we rescued it.' He tugged the bundle from beneath him and lifted it up, pulling the little flask free. 'And we rescued this, Elias: your nice little bottle of poison.'

Chapter Eighteen

After divesting himself of his robes Luke walked slowly to the door that connected the nuns' side of the church to the canons' cloister. He had enjoyed himself here so often, it was always difficult to return to the men's side.

Agnes had been an enthusiastic bedfellow for many weeks now. At first she had appeared to believe his repeated assurances that his absolution was enough to protect her, but it was obvious that her own enjoyment was the spur to her continuing assignations with him. The only time there had been any difficulties between them had been when she had seen him with Katerine.

It had not been a pleasant meeting. Katerine had taken him almost as if she was testing herself in some way, pushing herself to see how far she dared go. She had lain there with her eyes closed, silent. Not at all like Agnes. And while he was idly comparing the two, Agnes had walked in.

There had been no screaming, just an awful silence as she stood staring at them, her face working, and then she had spun on her heel and walked out. Luke was in no position to chase after her through the cloister, and Katerine showed no inclination to follow. In fact she seemed delighted that Agnes had seen them, and pulled Luke back on top of her.

Afterwards he had not seen Agnes for some days except at services, and gradually Katerine became more willing and less self-absorbed. She laughed when she talked about Agnes, saying, 'She doesn't like to share. Maybe she won't suit a communal life!'

Yet Luke found he missed the blonde novice. He gazed at her secretly when he conducted the nuns' services, and couldn't help but measure her beauty against that of Katerine. The latter was attractive, but there was an inner fire to Agnes that was more exciting. At last he managed to speak to her, and she said she would forgive him, but only if he left Katerine alone. He had made his promise, safe in the knowledge that Agnes and Kate never mentioned him in the other's presence. And he had made sure that whoever he saw, the other was busy about her duties.

His happy reflections ended when he put his hand to the door and lifted the latch. A puzzled expression came to his face when it failed to give, and he glanced at the frame to see if it had somehow jammed.

'It is locked, Luke.'

'Lady Elizabeth, I didn't see you there,' he said, turning and smiling. 'But why have you locked it?'

'Oh, I think you know the answer well enough,' she said.

Her mood hadn't improved since seeing Elias. She felt a curious guilt about hurting him so badly, and about sentencing Constance to a life of service in the priory. She might have escaped, but not now. Elias would run.

There was more than a touch of ice in her voice as she stalked towards Luke with the deliberation of a cat approaching its prey. Instinctively Luke wanted to retreat, but forced himself to keep still wearing a faintly surprised, slightly hurt expression.

'It won't do, Luke. Ah, no! You try to look offended, as if I have insulted you, yet the insult truly is offered by you to me – and to God! You've ravaged your way through my novices like a French pirate, caring nothing for them or the reputation of the convent, and it will stop.'

She jerked her head at the painting on the wall opposite the altar. 'Look at that! Christ in Judgement. He sits above Moses, who is holding the Ten Commandments; the godly soul surrounded by the seven works of mercy is being accepted into heaven by an angel; but look on the left there, Luke. There is the sinner being cast down by another angel. Can you see the roundels about that evil man? Can you see the one depicting lust?'

'My Lady, I don't know what you—'

'*Don't* think to deny it, fool!' she snapped, turning to face him.

'Do you think I'm blind? That I don't know about Agnes? Where my room is, Luke, I can hear the footsteps of the novices when they go to pee, or when they go to meet their lover, and in your interests she has been passing my chamber too often of late.'

'Surely if Agnes was, as you say, going to meet a lover,' Luke said coolly, 'then you would have followed her and accosted them both. I am afraid I have never been found with any of your novices or nuns.'

'No, you haven't. But there is no one else in the canons' cloister who would attract her. The others are too old.'

'I am afraid you should look to one of the lay brothers,' Luke said sadly, shaking his head. 'I think there is one there who has regularly enjoyed the young women in the nunnery.'

'A lay brother?'

'I fear so,' Luke said. He took a pace forward, leaned conspiratorially and whispered, 'That man in the smithy. I think he is the one.'

'Fascinating.'

Luke glanced at her. The prioress didn't seem as surprised as she should, and even as he caught sight of her expression, he saw it harden.

'Luke, you are a liar and a charlatan. I shall demand that you be removed from here. I know about the lay brother, and have already spoken to him, and I must confess I was more impressed by his attitude than I am by yours. At least he didn't attempt to put the blame upon another. You sicken me, Luke, and the sooner you are removed, the better, I feel, for the whole community.'

He allowed his face to relax slightly, just enough to permit his amusement to show. 'So you think it would be useful for someone to investigate the level of moral laxity and corruption in the convent? It would be a most interesting study, wouldn't it?'

'Your meaning?'

'No need for such asperity, my Lady. No, I was merely thinking about the young wench in the frater. Comely lass, she is. She's been seen lying with various men, mostly canons and lay brothers, but never with me, of course. No. I'm sure that if you ask her, she'd deny sleeping with me.'

There was a gleam in the prioress's eyes, but her voice showed no emotion, only ice, deadly chill, and as she spoke, Luke felt the freezing certainty sink into his bowels.

'Luke, you are a fool. The girl is my daughter, and I have received absolution for my sin in giving birth to her. As to *her* sins, they are between her and God. But since the good Bishop of Exeter confessed me when I admitted to my grievous sin, I hardly think there is anything you could report which could harm me. However, the fact you have attempted to blackmail me will be reported to the bishop, together with the news of your affairs.'

Simon slipped inside the forge and crossed the floor to the far side, which lay in comparative darkness without candles or braziers to illuminate the gloom. There was a movement ahead, and he stepped backwards so that a shaft of light lit his face, smiling to reassure his quarry.

'It's all right, I mean no harm, I just wanted to chat.'

The noise stopped – he could see no one, but was convinced that he was the subject of a detailed study. Just when he was beginning to think that he was alone and had imagined things, he heard her speak. 'What would a bailiff want to talk to me about?'

He grinned. 'The ale in your tavern, Rose? But perhaps better would be how you rate the men here: your mother wants me to find out who was the murderer of the two novices and wishes you to help.'

'Who is my mother?'

'Prioress Elizabeth. You see, I already know much and now I must find out who killed the novices.'

She stepped into a low glimmering light that came from a tiny window high in the wall, and stood still, surveying him with a serious expression. 'Why should I trust you?'

'Why should you *not* trust me?'

'Two are dead already. A third might not matter to the person who could kill twice.'

'But why should anyone hurt you?' Simon asked with genuine surprise. 'Surely the person who killed these two was someone within the cloister, and the reason for their deaths must lie within the convent itself. You aren't part of it, are you?'

'Me a part of this?' she asked, a smile pulling at her mouth. She gazed at him dubiously. 'You know who my mother is, you know what I do here. Of course I am a part of the place, and one of the worst parts to many minds. Think of it: fornicating with the canons, perverting them and making them break their vows of chastity. I am thought evil by the godly here. Don't *you* think me evil?'

As she spoke, she approached nearer Simon, head slightly to one side, arms hanging still at her sides. Her hair was long, and hung over her shoulders in a shamelessly wanton manner, but her behaviour was most decorous, and she walked so smoothly it was like watching a ghost drift over the stones. She was an odd mixture of child, whore, and lady.

Simon laughed. 'Rose, there's no need to try to tempt me. All I seek is a murderer.' He strode to a bench and motioned to his side. She gave a brief nod.

'Very well, but if you don't like what I've got to say, don't blame me.'

'The girls who died – did you know them?'

'I tend to meet all the novices,' she said. 'They come to me out of interest, I think, and from a desire to get into my mother's good books. Not that talking to me is likely to help them much!'

She chuckled then, and Simon had to grin at the sight. Rose gave herself up to the pleasure, leaning back and gazing up at the rafters as she chortled. For the rest of their conversation she often did that; breaking off in the middle to give a delighted and delightful belly laugh, her hair dancing all down her back, arms straight, elbows locked, hands resting on the bench. When she was finished, she turned to eye Simon directly, without shame or embarrassment. 'Moll wasn't a very nice girl, you know.'

'No?'

'She was very religious, I reckon, and that made her difficult to get on with. It was all right for me, but the others found her tiring. She would keep on at them.'

'You found her easier to deal with?'

'Oh yes. I found her no difficulty at all. She thought I was the lowest of the low, but as such I merited some attention, and she often tried to persuade me from my "path of dishonour" as she liked to term it.'

Simon pulled a face. 'Just what you needed to hear.'

'It was hardly novel to me,' she agreed, then chuckled. 'My mother has spoken the odd word to me on occasion.'

'With a mother like yours, a woman so steeped in the religious life, what made you choose your profession?' Simon asked.

She grinned. 'If *you* wanted to rebel, how would you go about it? I didn't know she was my mother until I was fifteen. All that time I thought I was the daughter of someone lowly – just a cottager from a local vill who had got herself impregnated and passed her illegitimate daughter – me – to the local nuns to look after. But then I discovered whose daughter I was.'

'How did you find that out?'

This time there was no mirth in the grin. 'It was dear Margherita who let it slip. Oh, I expect it was partly by accident – but not entirely. All along she wanted to get back at Mother for being elected when Margherita wanted the top job for herself. She thought I would create a scene – I don't know, maybe go to Mother and scratch her face, accuse her, scream abuse at her – anything! But I didn't. I stored it up, just like a good little nun, and thought about it until I felt I would explode.'

She was staring out over the top of the forge now, but her eyes appeared to be staring out over an unimaginable distance. 'Then one day I had to know whether it was true, and I went to see her in the cloister. I was going to speak but she started crying. Not making a noise, just weeping, with tears rolling down both cheeks. She'd guessed what I'd learned, and I didn't need to ask her then. I just told her I was leaving.'

'Up to then you were a novice?'

She gave him a sharp glance. 'Of course. But not now. And I never took even the lower vows, so I can't be forced to return against my will. Not like a real nun running from the place,' she added as an afterthought.

'Are you thinking of someone in particular?'

'You'll know who I mean soon enough.'

'Do you mean that this person could be the murderer?'

'Oh no!' she laughed again.

'How did your mother feel about Katerine?'

Rose thought. 'Katerine was enthusiastic about the place. She always kept her ear to the ground and figured out which way a vote might go, who would say what and why. Katerine would have been an invaluable assistant to my mother. Intelligent and well-informed about how the other nuns felt. And ruthless.'

Simon fell silent. 'You said that you thought you could be in danger, that the person who killed twice may not hesitate to do so again. Why should *you* be in any danger?'

'Like I said, Bailiff, some here look down on me because I bring an ill reputation to the convent. They think I'm dishonouring the place. Some might be willing to remove me and my wrong-doing.'

'Who?'

'Well, Margherita, for one.'

Elias felt his mouth fall open with dismay as the suffragan bishop inched his way to his feet with regal slowness. His finger shot out and pointed from the bottle in his claw-like left hand to the smith himself. 'You, Elias, planned to run away with these pitiful rags so that you could escape the evil of your deeds.'

'What?' Elias squeaked.

'You murdered the two girls because otherwise they would have told the prioress about your unchastity.'

'I couldn't have – I was with the infirmarer.'

'When?' Bertrand sneered. 'You dare suggest that you were with the infirmarer when these girls were killed?'

'Yes, when Moll died, at any rate.'

Bertrand was silent a moment, then his voice dropped to a hushed horror. 'At *night*? You went and ravished the poor child in her own *bed*? Is there no end to your hideous concupiscence? You dared to take a holy child, a—'

'Oh, for Christ's sake, it wasn't like that,' Elias said, holding out both hands in appeal. 'I wouldn't have touched her if she hadn't wanted—'

'*Silence!*' Bertrand roared. 'Your assertions of her unchaste behaviour are no protection to you, and your attempt to throw the blame on her shows only a contemptible cowardice on your part. What of the second murder this morning? Do you declare that you were with your lover when Katerine died?'

'No, but I was waiting for her – at the grille between the cloisters.'

Paul whispered to the bishop. 'I saw him there, my Lord.'

Bertrand ignored him, his voice hardly altering. 'Who saw you there? Who can confirm your innocence?'

'Well, the prioress – she saw me there.'

'Bishop . . .' Paul said, and Bertrand angrily motioned him to be silent. 'While the novice was being killed?'

'I don't know, I . . .'

That was better, for Elias's voice betrayed his nervousness. Although it was quite possible that the man's damned concubine would affirm his innocence of Moll's murder, and Bertrand himself knew Elias was innocent of Katerine's death, Bertrand knew he had Elias by the balls. 'So you have no witness to corroborate your stories? I congratulate you, Paul, it seems you have indeed found the murderer.'

'I'm no murderer.'

'So you say, but the evidence is overwhelming.'

'You must believe me, Bishop. I had no reason to want to harm either of those girls.'

Bertrand sneered. 'I don't presume to understand the murderous instincts of a madman.'

'How can I convince you I'm innocent?' Elias threw himself on the ground before the priest and grabbed at his feet, missing the left one, but catching hold of the right. 'I've never hurt anyone in my life!'

His voice was muffled, for his face was in the straw of the chamber's floor, but Bertrand heard his words clearly enough. He turned to Paul. 'You may leave us, my son. I wish to speak to this man alone.'

It was difficult to keep the glee from his voice. Looking down upon the bedraggled brother, Bertrand saw only the man who would destroy Lady Elizabeth.

Simon pulled a splinter from the bench, played with it, then tossed it away. Finally he faced Rose. 'What possible reason could Margherita have to want to hurt either of those girls? She seems the woman most determined to protect the name and reputation of the convent, come what may.'

'You think so?' Rose said. 'Margherita is certainly determined to have a convent to run. To make certain of it, she's prepared to do anything to harm Lady Elizabeth, my mother.'

Simon lifted his leg so that he sat straddling the bench, facing the young girl. She spoke with an easy assurance based upon certainty, and Simon was experienced enough in interrogating felons to recognise the truth in her voice. All his life he had held priests, monks, nuns, canons, canonesses and all the other confusing clerical folk in high esteem, thinking them somehow above such foolery and pettiness. Now he saw that all men and women were alike: if they wanted power, they would fight for it, and those who sought power over other people were by definition the very men and women who should never be allowed it.

Naturally he excluded himself from this calculation.

Rose added, 'Margherita has dropped poison into the ears of all the nuns at every opportunity. That my mother killed the first novice is only the latest lie.'

'How did you hear that?'

'You spoke loudly in the tavern.'

He had to grin in mute recognition of her skill as a spy while she laughed aloud once more. Then a faint creasing of her brow made him give her an enquiring look.

She glanced away, almost coquettishly. 'I just wonder whether Margherita has told any other stories,' she said.

'Forgive me, but you appear very attached to your mother for a girl who left this place to rebel.'

'Is it any surprise? I was terribly upset when I found she was my mother, and tried to hurt her as cruelly as I could. I whored for pennies, when all my mother wanted was for me to be happy and safe. She was trying to protect me from shame and save me embarrassment, but all I saw was that she had hidden herself from me – rejected me, if you like.'

'Although in reality she had managed to keep you with her all your life, instead of being sent away to another convent, and presumably she made sure you were educated.'

'Educated? Oh, yes. I could read to you from any book in the convent, or add up any of the figures on any of the account rolls. Not many here can do so well as me. I think I even made Margherita nervous.'

'Why so?'

'Oh, when I went too near, she'd cover up her accounts before she'd talk to me, as though she was hiding them in case she'd made a mistake. The last treasurer often messed things up. In fact, Margherita had to correct many of the older account rolls when she took on the job.'

'I've heard so much about money here,' Simon mused. 'It seems the most important thing in the life of this convent.'

'Of course it is. Without money the place would collapse. Haven't you heard about Polsloe? Bishop Stapledon himself has had to order them to keep better control of their accounts, keeping records of what the bailiffs and reeves bring in, and making sure that everything is noted down. That's the only way to prevent the lazy buggers thieving all the convent's money.'

'You don't have a very high regard for the men,' Simon observed with a smile.

She didn't return it. In a cold voice, she said, 'When you sell your body to a man you lose respect for him. You soon learn that one man is much like another when his tunic is lifted and his hose are down.'

Simon cleared his throat with swift embarrassment, but she grinned and widened her eyes at him. 'Mind, I'd be happy to keep an open mind with *you*, Bailiff.'

Chapter Nineteen

Outside the church, Luke stood trying to keep a calm demeanour while the painful thudding of his heart threatened to burst his chest asunder. That poisonous old *bitch*! She had no right to rail at *him* for his misbehaviour, not after giving birth to Rose. Luke knew all about Rose, oh yes. Who didn't inside this damned convent? At least he'd never fathered a child on a nun; his sins were trifling compared to hers.

But her threat had struck home with a terrifying accuracy. It had only been a short time before that he had been thinking about his good fortune in knowing the right cleric to bribe in Exeter, but if the prioress was to go over his head to Walter Stapledon, the Bishop of Exeter, then Luke could be dragged from this place in a moment. And knowing Stapledon, that was just what the pompous bastard would do. He would remember his message to Bertrand and demand that Luke be shoved away, far away.

Luke's one consolation was that the place had lost much of its attraction now. With the communicating door locked there was going to be little opportunity for meeting Agnes or any of the other girls.

Wincing, Luke pushed himself away from the church wall upon which he had been leaning and headed for the frater. From the look of the sky he had another hour before he had to preside over Sext, High Mass and None. Plenty of time for a jug of wine. He fetched a large jug and pot and sat on a bench in the doorway. The snow had all but gone in the cloister, and while the air was chilly, Luke hardly noticed it.

It was blasted irritating, he thought, throwing his head back to polish off the first cup. Sombrely he refilled it. Knowing he would be evicted from this pleasant and convenient job was almost enough to make him weep with rage. There were other novices whose virtues he had hardly had an opportunity to study. The only ones he had really got close to were Moll, Katerine, and Agnes. And only Agnes had fulfilled his needs.

No, it wasn't right that he should be thrown from the place. He would have to find a way to escape the sentence – but how?

At that moment he saw the suffragan bishop return through the alley into the cloister, accompanied by a hang-dog figure whom Luke was surprised to recognise as Elias. Paul appeared to be waiting for them, and Luke saw Bertrand beckon the canon imperiously.

Intrigued, Luke knocked back his third pot and stretched his legs out, watching the three men through narrowed eyes. Bertrand issued instructions and waved off the two others like a herder shooing his geese before turning and making his way to the frater. He wore the smile of a man who had achieved something and anticipated a reward before too long.

Luke reviewed all he had heard of the suffragan. Bertrand was vain, self-opinionated, and very ambitious. He longed for an opportunity of advancement – everyone knew that – and yet was stuck here in Stapledon's see. Given the right prompting, Luke felt sure that Bertrand could be a useful ally in his defence, and he smiled politely up at the suffragan bishop, waving at the seat next to him and filling his own cup, he offered it to Bertrand.

The bishop took it gladly. His buttocks and thighs ached after sitting so long in that cramped position, and the strong red wine smelled wonderfully good. 'It is most kind of you, my friend,' he said, dropping down on the bench. 'Ah yes, very good! I have been in need of this!'

'You've been inspecting the grounds?'

Bertrand glanced at his innocent, enquiring expression over the rim of his pot. 'I have been investigating a couple of things. Taking a careful look around.'

'Terrible about the two girls,' Luke said sorrowfully. 'One can only imagine how the good Bishop, my Lord Walter Stapledon will respond.'

'He'll respond with extreme anger, as any good priest should.'

'Why of course! And yet, he'd not want the village gossips to get wind, would he?' Luke said. 'While the prioress still holds sway she must be supported. Even if it means finding scapegoats.'

'There will be no scapegoats. Only the guilty will be punished,' Bertrand growled. 'Where did you hear such a rumour?'

'Oh, her Ladyship wouldn't confide in me, I assure you,' said Luke off-handedly.

'Why not?'

'Let's just say that she and I have often had our disagreements.'

Bertrand refilled his pot and gazed at Luke contemplatively. 'I have the impression that many wouldn't mourn her passing if she were to be moved to a new convent.'

'Here? My God, I should think not!' Luke exclaimed. 'She brings shame upon us all.'

'Shame? Because of her laxity, you mean?'

'Her moral laxity, yes.' Luke could feel Bertrand's excitement, and was delighted that he had hooked the suffragan and pulled him in so well. Although he had no idea of the notion which had formed in Bertrand's mind earlier that morning when Paul had told him of the planned escape, the eagerness in Bertrand's voice when Luke dropped comments against the prioress spoke volumes.

'You're talking in riddles, man! What moral laxity are you going on about?'

'Why I thought you knew, Bishop. Her daughter. The whore in the vill's tavern down at the bottom of the valley.'

Bertrand gaped, and only absent-mindedly muttered his thanks when Luke refreshed his pot.

'Her *daughter*; a *whore*!' he breathed.

It was perfect. Delicious. *Wonderful!*

As Bertrand stood to seek the fire in the frater, he not only grinned, but in an ebullient mood, patted Luke's shoulder as he passed and then actually paused and invited the young man to join him in another jug of wine.

Simon waved his hand towards the cloister. 'But why do you ply your trade here? Surely it can only lead to shame – especially in front of the women you used to live among.'

She shrugged unconcernedly. 'Look – it's too late to worry about that now. When I was trying to get back at my mother, I started coming here, offering myself to all the canons and lay brothers. It seemed funny at the time; there *she* was, sitting in her great chair in one side of the cloister, and here *I* was in this side.' There was no humour in Rose's voice. She had slumped, as if flaked out after a long walk. 'But this last time, the night you arrived, it was different. I had decided to help my mother.'

'Why?'

She looked at him. 'Like I said, I heard you talking about her in the tavern when you were on your way here, and listening to that priest with you, it was like listening to a man gloating over a young virgin's body. He was repulsive, and whether he believed the letter sent to him or not, he *wanted* to believe it. He really wanted Mother to be guilty. I didn't understand then, but I do now.

'My mother is not hugely religious, Bailiff. She's a good woman in her own way, but if it hadn't been for her husband dying early and her dislike of the men put forward to her as replacements, she'd have wed again, from what she said. But she does have two loves: the priory, and me. And in that order, too, I think. The priory is still her first love.'

Simon looked up at the ceiling of the smithy. For a change the roof appeared to be whole, although patched, but when he glanced about him at the walls, he saw the damp patches from which the plaster was falling.

Following his gaze, Rose giggled. 'Yeah, it hardly looks as if she cares much, does it? But she does. The place is only suffering because of lack of money; it needs a lot to stop the rot. That's what Mother is trying to do; just keep St Mary's ticking over until she can get the money she needs.'

'From Sir Rodney.'

'That's right. Sir Rodney is prepared to give her the cash.'

'In exchange for looking after his bones and one girl whom he or his family can nominate: this Agnes. What do you know of her?'

'A bit stiff. Not the sort who'd speak to *me*, although she is little better than me herself, from what I hear.'

Simon listened attentively as she spoke of Agnes and the rumours of her affair with Luke. When she had finished, he screwed up his face doubtfully. 'You think so? It's so easy for gossip to be spread about people for no reason.'

'No reason?' Rose asked, and her laughter rose to the rafters. 'Oh, Bailiff, think carefully! There's one woman here who can tell a man's proclivities – and that's *me*! I know which men need a woman, for they use my services! I know which ones desire me but daren't indulge themselves for fear of God's retribution; some are pederasts, for they watch me with faces like those of men drinking vinegar; and there are some who watch me with interest, who admire my body, but who never offer me money – those, Bailiff, are the men who already enjoy their own women and have no need of a paid substitute.'

'There is more than one, then?'

'Only two,' she said with decision. 'Luke and Elias, who is servicing Constance, the infirmarer.'

Simon blew out his cheeks. 'Constance? With Elias?'

'I only mention the pair as an example, but yes.'

'Where? Do you mean to tell me nuns and novices bring men up to the dorter?'

'Of course not!' Rose laughed. 'But all the girls know places to go. For example there's a room behind the frater: when it's dark the girls use it; it has hay for a bed, and the roof doesn't leak, which makes it unique.' She threw a glance of sneering contempt at the holes above her.

'How does all this help me?' Simon grumbled, getting up and scuffing his feet through the dirt on the floor. 'At every advance I find another block – and now Baldwin's got a broken head. I'm no use at this type of enquiry.' He slammed his fist into his open left palm. 'What can I do? The first poor girl died although no one seems to have any idea why, and now Katerine is dead as well, although she appears to have had little in common with Moll.'

'Moll was religious, and Katerine wanted power,' agreed Rose calmly. 'But let me tell you something both *did* have in common: both Moll and Katerine knew secrets. Katerine spent her time seeking out pieces of news or gossip, and was not above using it to her own advantage, dropping hints in someone's ear to make sure that she got what she wanted. Moll was not so enthusiastic about finding people's hidden stories, but she was determined when she thought something might have an impact on the convent. She would dig or spy until she found the facts, and then she was like Katerine: she went to the one she thought was responsible, and she let them know what she knew. She didn't do it for her own benefit like Katerine, she did it for the nunnery, but the people she blackmailed probably felt the same about it.'

'Whom did she threaten?'

'Apart from me, you mean?' Rose smiled sadly. 'Because both did try to threaten me. Katerine told me she'd inform my mother about my whoring, unless I paid money for her silence; only a few days later Moll took me aside and spoke to me very seriously in the gardens, trying to persuade me to leave or stop my whoring with the canons. She said that it would damage the convent and I should desist. Desist! I remember her words so well.'

'Who would have told her?'

'Moll? Well, novices chatter amongst themselves just like any other girls. I had refused to pay Katerine, so I expect she was happy to spread the story of my sins.'

'You disliked them?'

'Not really. I just thought they were fools. Neither of them realised that I had no interest in them. Their threats were meaningless. They needed someone who would be worried that their storytelling could get back to the wrong person. Maybe when you have found the man or woman who was threatened by those two girls, you'll have your killer.'

For the rest of the day Simon got nowhere. He spoke to many of the nuns and canons, but the solution to the mystery evaded him.

He strolled about the canons' cloister during Sext, High Mass, and None. Afterwards, the canons erupted from the church, chattering excitedly and speculating about the death of Katerine. Many held to the view that she had slipped, and that her fall was neither murder nor suicide, but simply an awful accident.

Simon was convinced that the girl had been struck down in the nuns' choir, her head wrapped in rags from the aumbry, before she was carried to the roof and thrown off. Yet he had no idea who had a motive to do so.

At the rear of the long line of canons, Simon saw the grimly forbidding features of Bertrand, and reminded himself that the suffragan had not been in the priory when Moll had died, so he was surely the last person to suspect. And yet Simon could not help but wonder about the man's open disgust for the prioress. It was clear that Bertrand would be delighted to see her removed from office. And he would demand that she be replaced with Margherita, naturally – Simon had no doubts on that score.

Simon knew he should tell the suffragan about Rose, but he had a strange reluctance to do so. God alone knew what Bertrand would do when he heard that the prioress's spy within the canons' cloister was her own daughter, and she a whore!

No, Simon couldn't see Bertrand yet. He turned away and walked to the church. It would be better to sit at Baldwin's side up in the infirmary and consider all he had learned for a while in peace. But when he got to the connecting door, he found it was locked, and although he called, the sacrist was apparently else-where and didn't hear his knocking. Reluctantly, Simon decided to find Bertrand after all.

As Simon retraced his steps, making for the frater, he was forced to step over a small pile of dog's excrement on the way. It appeared most odd to him that someone should have allowed a dog in here – but then he recalled mention of the prioress's terrier, and curled his lip. A convent was no place for a pet.

Only later would he realise the significance of the little pile.

* * *

Simon found the suffragan sitting at his ease in the frater, leaning back against a wall, his good hand clasping a large pot, while about him canons twittered sycophantically like a group of women. To the bailiff's embittered eye, they appeared more unmasculine than the nuns at the other side of the church. However, something in the gossiping made him hold back and stand near the door for a moment, listening.

Jonathan was shaking his head in apparent wonder. 'And you have discovered that this is true, Bishop?'

'There can be no doubt,' said Bertrand. He waved his bad hand airily. 'The prioress's management of the convent has been a disaster. You can see for yourselves how run down it is getting. We need a woman in charge who can protect the place. I think we shall need to have another election soon. The prioress must accept her fate and resign.'

'What if she refuses to?' asked Paul attentively.

Bertrand bestowed upon him a smile of such approval that Simon almost walked from the room. 'She will have no choice, not now that you have helped me so well, Paul.' He held up a hand in a declamatory fashion. 'You may as well know, Brothers, that I have more information for you all. This very morning, I was with your colleague here, young Paul, and he showed me an astonishing sight. In a stable were concealed a pair of packs for a canon and a nun in order that they might run away from the cloister and commit apostasy. I know . . .' he held up his hand for silence as the men began to ask questions, thrilled at his revelations. It gave him an immense sense of power.

Bertrand felt as though he held all the men in this room in the palm of his hand. He looked at them, all gripping their pots or jugs as they drank in his words avidly.

It gave him a faint pang to recall that the only confession he had got from Elias was false – he knew well enough that Elias had been at the grille when Katerine died, and no doubt the infirmarer would confirm that he had been with her when Moll died, but this was more important than a simple death. Bertrand was struggling to ensure the survival of the convent itself. To do that he was prepared to blackmail any of the canons in the room – aye, or see them thrashed, if it would help. Elias's admission of his sins with Constance would surely hasten Lady Elizabeth's removal.

And that was the important thing – the removal of the woman who had led the convent to this pass. The souls of thousands depended upon the convent being cleansed! The two dead girls hardly mattered, not to Bertrand. Surely they were already in heaven.

When a niggle of self-doubt caught at his conscience, he forced it from him. The fact that his actions would help his own promotion was merely a coincidence. Nothing more. He was acting selflessly for the good of St Mary's.

When the men were still, he continued. 'I know that this is not a reflection upon all of you, but it does show how poorly Lady Elizabeth has looked after St Mary's if one of your number can consider renouncing his oaths and leading a nun astray at the same time. And then there is the matter of the prioress's daughter . . .'

Aha! thought Simon. So he already knows.

'This *daughter*, this serpent in female form, has not only rejected her former life as a novice within the cloister and turned her back on the learning she was fortunate enough to be granted by the goodness of the Church, she has turned to a vile and degrading profession. Some of you may know what I mean,' he added, glancing about him shrewdly. More than one man reddened and looked away. 'Well, I do not propose to censure those who may have been tempted from the path of purity, beyond demanding that all who so forgot themselves should confess at the earliest opportunity, but this evil cancer must be rooted out. She must be ruthlessly excised from this priory; just as a man would execute an outlaw to protect society. Otherwise her malign influence could corrupt the whole place.' Bertrand ran his words through his mind again. It sounded a little flowery, but overall he was pleased – he might use the same words when he reported to Bishop Stapledon.

One man at the table wasn't impressed or pleased. Simon could see the anxiety on Godfrey's face. 'If you do that, where shall she go, Bishop? She would be ostracised and left to wander about without home – or hope. Wouldn't it be more merciful to allow her to remain and—'

'Good God, no! Do you think we should harbour this viper? What of her foul attractions? She could well tempt more of you to stray, and it would be a gross sin on my part were I to allow her the opportunity. The unwholesome bitch must leave and never return.'

Godfrey opened his mouth to speak again, but his neighbour, Jonathan, put a warning hand on his wrist and Godfrey subsided, but as he sagged back in his chair, Simon noticed how he had blanched.

One man whom Simon had not noticed among the canons was Luke. After the service, he had gone to the door as usual, to go back into the monks' side of the church, but as under the new regime he was to be locked out and excluded from the nunnery except during services, he was forced to wait for a nun to unlock the door and relock it behind him.

It was Denise the sacrist, and as she approached, he was struck by her shuffling gait. The sight made his belly churn in disgust – he had a hatred of drunken women – and yet he saw that he might be able to turn her inebriation to his advantage.

He stood patiently while she inserted the large key into the door and turned it. The lock snapped open, and she pulled the door wide, but as she did so, Luke frowned, slapping at his belt. 'My purse!'

Denise peered at him owlishly. 'What of it? You'll have to get it when you come back.'

'But you don't understand – I've lost it,' said Luke, quickly tucking it beneath a fold of his robe. 'It could be anywhere.'

'Then seek it in the canons' cloister,' said Denise unsympathetically; she was feeling more than a little sleepy and had no wish to stand here all day. Hurriedly putting her hand to her

mouth, she tried to cover up a burp, then glowered tipsily at him.
'Come along, then. Time you were gone.'

'I shan't be long,' Luke called over his shoulder, and began to
walk back to the sacristy.

'Wait! You can't stay here, you know what the prioress said –
you have to go.'

Luke stood as if undecided, but then turned and strode back to
Denise's side. 'I *can't* go back without it,' he explained quietly.
'The thing had the key to the bishop's chest in it, and the bishop
is bound to want it for his Bible after his lunch.'

'What did you have his key for?' she demanded.

'Denise,' he said seriously, 'you know that the prioress has
tried to ban me from the nunnery, but do you know why?'

'Because of your behaviour with the novices,' she giggled, and
clapped a hand over her mouth. It was wrong to laugh at such
things here, in the nave of the church.

Luke smiled sadly. 'No, Denise. That was all invented by the
prioress herself. I am to be removed because she made an advance
to me which I rejected. Now she wants a new priest, someone
whom she can mould to her will. But Bishop Bertrand has seen
this, and he is to report her behaviour to Bishop Stapledon so that
Lady Elizabeth can be forced to resign her post. Then we will
have a new leader.'

'Margherg . . . Margherita, you mean?'

'Yes . . . perhaps. Or maybe someone else. Someone in whom
the bishop can place his trust. But I must fetch his key, mustn't I?'

Denise gazed about her vacuously. 'I have to go and get my
food,' she muttered as her belly rumbled alarmingly.

'You go, then. Leave me to find the purse, and return later to
lock the door,' Luke said.

It was all too confusing. Denise could feel one of her headaches
coming on, and wished she was sitting back in the frater with a
cool pint of wine before her. She didn't need grief from this
tomfool of a priest. The prioress had ordered her to stay and lock
the door after him, but if Luke was only trying to find the key to
the bishop's chest, surely the bishop's needs would take precedence

over the prioress's order, and that would mean that Luke could stay and search if he wanted. Serve him right if there was no food left when he returned.

'Very well, you may stay a while. But I will be back to lock the door when I have eaten my lunch.'

'You were ever a kind and thoughtful woman, Denise,' Luke said, and continued on his way to the sacristy. It was not until he had heard the door to the church close that he allowed himself to chuckle.

Chapter Twenty

After her meal late in the afternoon, Agnes was sent to the prioress's chamber to fetch a cushion for Lady Elizabeth's chair. She found it as instructed, but once outside the room, standing on the small landing, she hesitated, then walked to the infirmary.

The room was dark, the interior lit only by guttering candles and the flickering flames of the fire. Clutching the cushion to her breast, she went to where Baldwin lay, breathing stertorously, his mouth open.

Agnes hadn't seen him from close to before, and she studied him with interest. He was not so good-looking as Luke, she reckoned. Luke was slender and fair, with his golden hair and bright blue eyes, while this knight had the thicker body of an older man, muscled and powerful, certainly, but too old, too worn. Knackered. She shook her head. This man wasn't someone she could fancy; she was much happier with a younger lover.

'What're you doing here?' Hugh demanded. He entered the room belligerently, his brows black.

Immediately the curtain to Constance's chamber twitched aside, and the infirmarer herself hurried into the room. 'Agnes? How long have you been in here?'

The novice retreated at the appearance of Hugh. He shoved past her rudely to stand staring at the sleeping knight, who mumbled and gave a vague groan before snuffling and settling himself once more. Sniffing suspiciously at the jug and pot at Baldwin's side, Hugh looked back at Agnes again, who stared uncomprehendingly at him.

Constance cleared her throat. 'I shall replace it with a clean one and fresh water.'

Hugh nodded, but still eyed the quailing novice with a truculent glower. 'Well? What were you doing snooping around in here?'

'I just wanted to see the knight – make sure he's all right,' she wailed. 'The prioress sent me to get a cushion, and I thought I'd look in. That's all.'

'Did you touch him?' Hugh demanded.

Agnes felt the tears spring and run down both cheeks. 'No!'

'It's true, Master Hugh. She didn't touch him. I was watching,' said a voice from behind her, and when Agnes spun around, she saw old Joan sitting near the fire.

'Nor put anything in the jug?' Hugh demanded.

'She did nothing, master. Stop scaring the girl with your fury. It won't do her any good to be weeping when she delivers the cushion to the prioress, will it? Agnes, come here, and sit for a moment. You need to calm yourself.'

Nothing loath, Agnes gratefully walked to Joan's side. The old woman patted her hand, and motioned to a seat. Sniffling, Agnes dropped upon it, wiping her eyes with her sleeve.

'He's a good-looking fellow, isn't he?' Joan said with a twinkle in her eye. 'I once came up here to see a man who had fallen from a horse. It was Sir Rodney – such a fine-looking lad. We all wanted to see what men were wearing and how they had their hair cut and so on, and my friend Bridget was here before me; we both studied him and it was a bit sad really.' Her gaze was unfocused as she reached back through her memory. 'Nothing had changed. All was the same as when I entered the convent. But then the last King, Edward the First, was a stickler. Never let his men wear beards, never let them wear any finery. Said that fashionable clothes like the French wore were for pansies or women, not for the men he commanded. He always was a stern old devil.'

'You met the King?'

Joan shook her head. 'No. Only Sir Rodney.'

'Was Bridget a nun?' Agnes asked.

'Yes. Many years before *your* time. But then she went off with Sir Rodney – to the shame of the convent. Now, wipe your face. Don't worry – we won't tell anyone, and it wouldn't matter if we did. Everyone knows what it's like to want a little taste of what the world outside is like. What did you think of the good knight?'

'I . . .' Agnes hung her head. 'He's ancient – and I don't like his beard,' she confessed.

Joan chuckled and took the novice's hand, patting it gently. 'It's all right, dear. I never liked beards either. Now help me up, and I'll come down with you. I daresay this good servant would like to be alone to protect his master's friend.'

Hugh couldn't help feeling relieved when he was alone in the infirmary once more. He glanced at the sleeping knight and muttered, 'For the love of God, get better quickly. I can't stand this dump much longer.'

After several pints of ale Bertrand was in a cheerful mood. He had demanded the convent's accounts from Jonathan, and now sat in the guestroom studying the large roll which detailed all transactions for the last two years. The accounts had not been ready when he had arrived on his official visitation earlier, and now they made interesting – and sorry reading.

The roll showed that the nuns had not enough grain or hay to feed their cattle, and the land was unfit for much other than pasture. There were foreign lands, way off towards Exford and Crediton, but these never seemed to bring in what even Bertrand, who was no expert in such matters, would have expected after viewing accounts from other priories, especially since he had seen money from Iddesleigh's bailiff passed to the treasurer while he was last here, a healthy sum.

In terms of money, it was obvious that the priory couldn't survive. The prioress had been accused of paying her vicar too much, but there were few sums going to him according to the rolls. Perhaps the place was investing too heavily in wine and other foods, Bertrand wondered, and ran his finger along some of the columns, reading off the numbers. Even this area looked no worse than he would have expected. Then he came to a point far down, near the bottom of a page. It made him stop, blink, and peer again.

'God's bollocks!' he shouted, appalled. Then clapped a hand

over his mouth and blushed deeply when he caught sight of Paul's scandalised face.

Carrying the cushion, Agnes walked down the stairs with Joan and was about to open the door to the cloister when the old nun stopped her. 'Come, child, what is it? It's clear enough that you're depressed.'

There was a tradition in the convent that novices and young nuns could confide in the very ancient ones. The latter could advise the younger ones without anything necessarily being mentioned in chapter, thus saving embarrassment, whilst ensuring that the girl made penance of some form if necessary. Agnes was wondering how to answer when Joan chuckled fruitily, giving the astonished girl a look full of kindness.

'I daresay you're going to tell me it's a man. It usually is. My friend Bridget told me about her own man many years ago. Lovely woman, Bridget was. Confident, tall and willowy. Not at all like her daughter, Margherita.'

Agnes felt the hammer blow hit her breast. She gasped. 'What happened to her?'

'My Bridget? Ah, the poor girl couldn't stay here. She was too full of life and enjoyment of the sweeter things to be able to bind herself up in here with all the dreadful, crabbed old dragons!' Joan laughed. 'She left the first time with . . . let's just say it was a young man. And later when she was caught and returned, she had a child in tow, her Margherita. But the convent couldn't hold her, and off she went. I doubt not that she's a great lady now.'

'How come she was allowed to run away? And why wasn't she punished for her misbehaviour?'

Joan gave her a very old-fashioned look. 'Dear, when you get to my age, you'll realise that most people fail at one time or another during their lives. Even the best of us. Now – is it a man?'

Agnes nodded.

'Then you have done something very wrong. But under the Church's laws you won't be hanged! And you will be here within the convent for many years. You haven't taken the threefold oaths yet, you're too young, and you will be a nun for many years. If you are not a virgin now, you never will be again.'

'I don't understand.'

'I'll try to speak more plainly,' Joan said gently. 'All I mean is, most of the nuns here who behave so reverently have also done as you have. You will have to give up the man at some point, but you might as well enjoy him while you can.'

And with that she left the astonished novice and, chuckling, went back up the stairs.

When Constance came back into the room, Hugh pointedly picked up the jug and cup. The infirmarer removed them from his grasp, taking them out to her chamber, where she poured the water away and filled the jug from a fresh stoup, adding a small amount of dwale. If Sir Baldwin should wake, it would be better for him to have a draught to help him sleep.

When she returned, Hugh was standing defensively at Sir Baldwin's side while Joan cackled hoarsely. When she saw Constance, Joan coughed, hawked, and spat a gobbet of phlegm into the fire. 'This fine fellow has no sense of humour,' she said, wheezing still with humour.

Hugh was not amused. 'I was told to stay here and protect my master's friend, and that I'll do.'

'How did Agnes get in?' Constance asked, setting the jug down with a wiped pot. 'Didn't you see her?'

Reddening, Hugh muttered, 'I had to go out.'

'He needed a piss!' Joan burst out, and then almost choked as the laughter threatened to throttle her.

'I was only gone a few minutes,' Hugh said sulkily. It was true. He had been as quick as he possibly could be, but in the nunnery he wasn't sure where he was supposed to go, and finally had slipped between two buildings at the northernmost end of the cloister, well away from the church itself. It had taken some time to find the place, and he'd felt ready to explode by the time he stood at the wall, and then the pressure was so strong, he'd found it hard to relax and empty his bladder. As if to add insult, when he'd left the little alley and returned to the cloisters, a small dog snapped at his ankles. When Hugh almost tripped, several nuns laughed. Only a moment later he heard the prioress calling to the mutt.

Lucky really, he thought. If he'd not heard Lady Elizabeth, he would have swung his foot at the little sod.

'Don't mind Princess,' she had said as the terrier trotted back to her. 'She likes people. It's just that she will have her little joke when she hears men. Never has liked them much – I suppose she hardly ever sees one in here.'

Hugh had made no comment, but slipped straight back up to the infirmary where he saw Agnes at Baldwin's side.

Constance glanced at him, and her voice was kindly. 'Hugh, if you need to leave the room again, let me know and I'll stand watch over him. And if you are nervous about me, make sure that Joan is awake, and she and I can look after Sir Baldwin together. You should feel secure knowing that there are two nuns looking after him.'

Hugh said nothing, but his scowling countenance eased a little, and then he gave a faint nod of his head.

Agnes delivered the cushion and walked to her desk near the church, but her mind wasn't in her work, and soon she slipped along the alley which led from the cloister to the garden beyond.

She'd only gone a few yards when her wrist was gripped, and the startled girl was pulled behind a tall bush. A voice whispered in her ear, 'Hello, little lady – would you take pity on a poor man with a broken heart?'

'Luke!' She turned and threw her arms around his neck, kissing him through her veil. 'Luke . . . Ah, Luke, it's so good to see you.'

'Wasn't easy.'

She pulled away. 'You'll never guess what I just learned. My sister is here!'

'Your sister?'

'Margherita! She's Sir Rodney's daughter as well. He met her mother and got her pregnant years before he met mine.' It was incredible to think that the hard-faced treasurer could be a half-sister.

Luke thought the same. 'Will you speak to her about it?'

'Margherita?' Agnes pulled a face. 'Would you? Anyway, how did you get here? I heard the prioress was going to lock you out.'

He grinned, his teeth flashing. 'I climbed over the roof of the church just to be with you,' he stated solemnly.

She pulled away, studying him with a serious expression. 'You came over the roof? That's where Katerine died ... You weren't up there with her, were you?'

He felt as if his heart had stopped. 'What, you think I could have thrown her from the roof? Little Kate? I couldn't do something like that!'

She looked up at his wide, shocked eyes, and was impressed. If she didn't know him so well, she'd have automatically and unhesitatingly believed him; but she knew that whatever else he might be, he was a good liar. She'd seen that when he'd denied sleeping with Katerine just before she'd found him in her arms.

The distrust was in her eyes, and he put his hands on her shoulders, shaking his head with apparent stupefaction. 'You couldn't believe *I'd* have chucked her off the roof, could you?'

'She was a pain, wasn't she?' Agnes pointed out sharply. 'She couldn't stand you dumping her for me. What if she'd threatened to tell the prioress about us?'

'If she had, I'd have reminded my Lady Elizabeth that her own little bastard was screwing the canons, and she'd have shut up. What sort of trouble could Katerine have given us even if she'd wanted to?' He smiled, secure in the knowledge that Agnes didn't know he had carried on with Kate even *after* Agnes had found them together. Of course, she never would find out now ...

'The prioress might've sent you away,' Agnes said quietly.

Luke gave a grimace. 'She might anyway,' he said drily, and told Agnes about his conversation with her.

Agnes's response was predictable. Her arms slipped around his neck again, and she sniffed back the tears as she held him close. Breathily she whispered into his ear while she nuzzled the angle between his neck and shoulder. 'Luke, I can't see you go without just one more time . . .'

Margherita stalked along the cloister, evading the prioress with that contemplative expression on her stupid face. There was no point in the old woman trying to gain her sympathy. Margherita knew what she had been up to, and now the ridiculous baggage wanted to try to make Margherita regret her actions. Well, she wouldn't. Prioress Elizabeth had to go, and that was that.

She couldn't help casting Elizabeth a quick look, and almost immediately she regretted it. The prioress was watching her, and as Margherita glanced up, she saw the prioress lift her chin imperiously and beckon.

Margherita had to obey. Obedience was one of the cardinal virtues of a nun. She slowly made her way along the cloister, observing Agnes appearing with a cushion, which she passed to Lady Elizabeth, before retreating. The prioress shoved it down between her and the chair's back.

'Always was a problem, my back,' she said brightly when Margherita was before her. 'My mother had the same trouble.'

It was so small a comment, and yet so perfectly selected for impact, Margherita thought. The great lady had known her mother only too well, while Margherita, born a bastard, had not known hers. She couldn't tell whether her mother had a bad back or any other ailments. Not that she cared.

They were quite alone. Elizabeth leaned forward. 'I wanted to have a chat with you, Margherita. In part about your accusation that I murdered the novice Moll, but also because I needed to warn you about the risks you are running.'

'Risks, Elizabeth? I see none.'

'Perhaps you don't. But there are so many things that could happen in the near future, and I thought you should be quite certain of the sequence.'

Margherita gave a small sigh of boredom and bent her head in vague and disrespectful assent.

Lady Elizabeth eyed her with irritation. 'Margherita, I know what you wrote to the suffragan bishop, Bishop Bertrand. I know you accused me of having an affair with the priest, that you accused me of wishing to murder Moll, and that I killed her.'

Margherita felt the first cold, clammy suspicion that something was wrong. There was a positive tone in Elizabeth's voice that struck like a dagger into Margherita's vitals.

'It's nonsense, Margherita. I've not had an affair with Luke. The idea is ludicrous in the extreme. Apart from anything else, even if I were to wish a liaison with him, I feel it hardly likely that so youthful and attractive a man would look at me.'

'I heard you.'

'Pardon?' Elizabeth enquired, momentarily off-balance.

'I heard you. With him – in your room. I heard you the night that Moll died. The man went up to your room. I saw someone while I was outside, and he darted into the dorter's stairway. He wasn't up with the nuns, so where was he if not with you?'

'Are you sure of this?' Elizabeth asked, but internally she was cursing the foolishness of men.

'You ask me whether *I* am sure?' Margherita demanded haughtily. 'Then who was it who panted and made you sigh and weep? Who was it who made you call quietly to your love? Who was it, if not Luke? If some other man was with you, I'd be content to declare *his* guilt instead of Luke's.'

Lady Elizabeth sat back in her chair dumbfounded, and Margherita allowed herself a small sneer of pleasure. Except that it was wiped away almost immediately by the prioress's bellow of laughter.

Chapter Twenty-One

Hugh finished his pot of ale and glanced thankfully at Constance, who smiled in return. Belching, Hugh leaned back against the wall, but he was aware of the pressure in his bladder, and he wondered whether he dared leave the room a second time. It was warm in the infirmary, especially since the windows were closed, and he yawned as he peered at Baldwin.

The knight was asleep, and now his rest appeared untroubled. He snored loudly, his mouth open, and although every so often he would shift restlessly, which usually caused him to grunt as the dressing rubbed against the pillow and caused a ripple of pain to echo within his wound, he looked well enough. Hugh was not worried about him yet: concern for his health would come later, when the wound had had enough time to fester, and the infirmarer could smell whether he would live or die.

At least with a head wound it was quick. Hugh had seen a few of them in his time. If a man was scratched or cut in a limb it could take an age for the poor bastard to croak. Often the surgeon would hack off more and more of the surrounding muscle and skin in a vain attempt to save the life, but commonly the cure was enough only to exacerbate the problems, and the patient would expire in agony, killed by the regular removal of mortified flesh rather than the actual sweet-smelling gangrene itself.

With a head wound, it was easier. The patient simply died.

He frowned as the pressure in his bladder increased. Joan, over by the fire, was nodding gently, close to sleep. Hugh could see shadows moving out in the chamber beyond, where Constance worked. It wouldn't be sensible to leave the room until she was back, he knew. He couldn't take the risk, not with Sir Baldwin's safety.

Suddenly he knew he was going to *have* to go. If he didn't make a swift journey down to his little alley soon, the floor would be awash. Constance was still out there, and now Hugh had no choice. He rose and dashed to the chamber, gasping, 'Please look to the knight – I have to go. Back in a minute!' before hurrying back the way he had come.

In the alley the relief was enormous as he stood leaning, one hand pressed against the wall before him, sighing with the exquisite pleasure of emptying himself. With a brief fart, he resettled his hose, then turned to return to the cloister, but stopped, hearing a noise.

Frowning, he peered up the alley. It had been a faint, hoarse, inarticulate little cry, and Hugh recognised the sound. It was impossible not to. Private chambers were rare, and most husbands and wives had to couple in alcoves in their master's hall, or if free, made love in the bed they shared with all their children. It was a woman's cry of release – a woman with her man.

Hugh had no prurient desire to see who it could be, but he knew that at a time like this, when two young women had died, he had a duty to see who was making love with a nun. Someone guilty of that might be guilty of anything.

Setting his jaw, Hugh stepped silently up the alley. At the end was an open space, a low wall, several bushes. Approaching the wall, he heard something again and he peered over it.

The couple were shielded by the wall and the straggling bushes. She was kneeling atop her man, her habit raised to her breast, her long fair hair loose and trailing down her spine as she rocked gently back and forth, biting her lip to control the urge to cry out. As he watched, she turned, her eyes closed in ecstasy, and he ducked out of sight, but not before he had recognised her. It was Agnes, the novice he had seen spying on Baldwin in the infirmary.

With a shock Hugh realised he was witnessing a novice breaking her vow, and somehow when he saw her lover was Luke, it came as no surprise. If a beautiful young girl like Agnes could behave in such a manner, there was nothing wonderful about a man taking advantage. Stealthily Hugh turned to make his way back to the infirmary.

He felt as if the sight had punctured his very soul. There had been a sense of sadness before at the thought that the women here would not look at him, but that knowledge was tempered by the certainty that they would not be tempted by another man either. Now he knew only grief and a dreadful increase of his desperate loneliness, as if Agnes was in some way betrothed to him and he had just witnessed her treachery; he felt betrayed.

As he came to the alley he saw Denise coming towards him.

She smiled and stood to one side to let him pass, but he stopped. If she continued she could hardly miss the two lovers. In a generous frame of mind, Hugh cleared his throat loudly so that Agnes and Luke should be warned before being discovered.

His kindness failed. There was a brief squeak, a tearing of cloth, then a high giggling. Denise's attention flew to the wall, and she peered keenly at it, then lifted an eyebrow to Hugh. 'I trust that they have finished now,' she said loudly and coldly, and turning, swept back the way she had come to lock the church's connecting door.

Agnes clapped a hand over her mouth to stopper the giggle that rose naturally. Luke stared up at her with a horrified gaze. She let her finger touch his mouth. 'It's only Denise, love. She won't tell. She'll only be jealous and make some carping comment later.'

But the young priest had lost his enthusiasm. She felt him wither within her, and smiled broadly. 'No more? Had enough?'

Luke squirmed away and felt his robe fall to his ankles with relief as he stood. 'What if someone should find us?'

She watched him peer fearfully over the wall. Standing, she settled her own clothing and began tying up her hair, setting it in place. 'If they find us, that's that,' she said with finality. 'But I'm no nun yet, and maybe I never will be.'

Catching sight of his expression, she let her own features soften. 'It's dangerous for us here, but no one's usually here at this time of day.'

'We were mad!'

'Then we'll have to find somewhere more secure, won't we?' she said, walking behind him and putting her arms around his waist. He was slim, and she felt her passion rising at his musky, masculine scent. 'There's a place I know,' she whispered. 'A room behind the frater, if you can get back here tonight.'

Simon was somewhat surprised to be summoned to the nuns' cloister, but he obeyed with alacrity. He found the prioress and treasurer standing well apart from all the other nuns, who nonetheless watched intently as Simon went to Lady Elizabeth's side.

'Thank you, Bailiff, for coming so promptly,' she said, and there was a happy musical tone to her voice which made Simon smile, but which he noticed gave no pleasure to Margherita.

'It's my pleasure, my Lady,' he responded. 'But what do you wish me to . . .?'

'Merely listen, please, Bailiff. Ah, here it is!'

Turning, Simon saw a young novice hurrying to them. In her hands she carried a massive book. Lady Elizabeth smiled at the girl, and then gripped the crucifix at her belt with one hand while she rested her other on the cover of the book. 'Please witness, Bailiff, that I here swear on my oath, on the Bible and on the Cross, that what I am about to say is entirely true, and I desire God to take my life this instant if I deviate from the absolute truth in any way. May I be punished for all Eternity if I lie. There, that should do it, I think. Thank you, child. Take the book back to the cupboard now, please.'

The novice dutifully left them. Meanwhile Lady Elizabeth motioned to the other two and allowed herself to sit. When they were all comfortable, she continued: 'Bailiff, I have been accused of murdering Moll: I did not and I swear that I had no part in her death. Second, I have been accused of taking the young priest Luke as my lover: I have not. Third, I am accused of entertaining Luke in my chamber on the night that Moll died . . .'

'I *heard* you,' Margherita asserted, her face red with anger and bitterness, and, yes, if she was honest with herself, with fear that Elizabeth might be able to wriggle out of this.

'You heard me, correct. But you put a dreadful interpretation on what you heard. Princess,' she called suddenly. 'Come here, Princess!'

Simon had never liked little dogs. He wasn't particularly keen on any dogs at all, although he accepted the fact that some performed a useful purpose, such as hunters, guards or fighters for the ring, but this thing was a long-haired, pampered little barrel. He smiled at it insincerely, but as it leaped onto the prioress's lap it bared its teeth.

Lady Elizabeth stroked the little monster's head. 'Bailiff, Margherita has accused me of calling to Luke while he panted and I moaned in my room. That was the drift of your accusation, wasn't it, Margherita? Well, Bailiff, I deny her charge. On the night Moll died, not only was I *not* making love to Luke, I did not entertain Luke in any way. I couldn't – for the simple reason that I thought my dog here, little Princess, was dying.' She shot a look of utter contempt at Margherita. 'While you were listening at my door, woman, I was anxiously nursing my dog.'

Hugh sat back on his bench. Constance left him and returned to her chamber, but his mind was elsewhere. Hugh was not sure whether the news about Agnes and Luke being lovers was something that Simon would be interested in. After all, it was hardly anyone else's business. God's, perhaps, he amended with a quick glance upwards, but no one else's.

It made him wonder, though. Like any man, he had heard stories about the rampant sexual desires of nuns in their convents, and still more about the nuns who willingly escaped from their convents and threw off their habits just so that they could find and marry men. Such stories abounded, but while Hugh had always considered them potentially true, he was somewhat shocked to have been given proof. Luke and Agnes were breaking their vows within a holy precinct, and that was distasteful.

Baldwin snorted and gave a loud cry as he moved. Hugh

leaped to his feet, but before he could get to the knight's side, Constance returned to the room. In her hand she carried a small bowl, and she smiled shyly at Hugh as she sat at Baldwin's side, gentling him like a mother does a child, stroking Baldwin's cheek and beard and murmuring soft words. As she spoke, she dropped a little liquid from the bowl onto his bedding and pillow.

'It is only oil of lavender, to help him sleep,' she said in answer to Hugh's silent question. She yawned, and pulled a face, rubbing at an eye. 'I don't think I shall need anything to help *me* rest tonight.'

'At least you should be able to sleep unhindered,' Joan said from her chair.

Constance didn't look at her, but Hugh could see the flush colouring her cheeks, although when he glanced at Joan, she was sitting innocently enough, smiling in a friendly manner.

'Yes, Joan, if you don't wake me with your snoring.'

'Me snore? I think not!' the old woman exclaimed. 'Hugh, you wouldn't say I snored, would you?'

Hugh maintained a careful silence, not wishing to offend either of them, and eventually Joan gave a throaty, wheezing chuckle and stood. Standing upright, she stumbled on a loose board. Hugh made a move to go to her side but she gave him a stern look. 'You stay there, young man, and protect your knight. I hardly need your help to go for a piss, do I?' And she made her way from the room.

'I was only going to help her,' Hugh grumbled.

'She's fine. The only reason she's here is because the prioress fears she will suffer from the cold in the dorter at her age,' Constance explained. 'She isn't ill, so don't worry. She hardly needs help to go to the rere-dorter.'

'I was only trying to help,' Hugh said again. A thought struck him. 'Could she have got up during the night when Moll was killed?'

Constance smiled at him. 'Not a chance, no. I gave her so much dwale to make her sleep that not even the King's artillery could have woken her.' Her gaze shot guiltily towards Cecily. 'Cecily could have kept her awake otherwise,' she added defensively.

Hearing a muffled whimper, as if on cue, Constance hurried to Cecily's side. She took a cloth from a bowl of scented water and wiped the girl's brow. The invalid's eyes opened, but they were unfocused, and stared without recognition. Constance was aware that Hugh had joined her, and the two looked down without speaking for a few moments, but then the lay sister gave a cry and made as if to pull the bedclothes from her, tossing her head from side to side.

'She's not improving,' Constance said, almost to herself. 'If her fever grows, it might burst her heart.'

'It smells, too.'

She shot Hugh a look, but saw only concern in his face; and when she sniffed, she too could smell the sweet stench of rotting flesh. She put a hand out towards the dressed arm, but the girl snatched it away, crying out as she struck a post of the bed with it. Constance was sure that Hugh was right. The girl had flushed cheeks, and her eyes looked unnaturally bright in the candlelight. Constance very gently reached out again to take hold of the arm, murmuring softly to reassure the girl, but Cecily whipped it free. Only when Hugh gripped her shoulders and held her upper arm could Constance get to the dressing, and before she removed it, she knew her efforts so far had been in vain. The smell was sickly and repellent, and as Constance took hold of the upper arm and felt the heat within the limb, she couldn't help but throw a look at Cecily's face.

Hugh, gripping the lay sister's shoulders, saw Constance's expression. It briefly reflected her sadness, her compassion – and a kind of guilt – before she set to unravelling the long strip of cloth with which the arm was bound.

Luke quietly slipped over the wall and across the yard to the western corner of the claustral buildings. From here he could look south to the church; there was no one in sight. All the nuns should by now, this late in the afternoon, be studying around the main claustral garth.

At the church, he checked along the little alley that led to the cloisters before making his way inside through the small door to the nuns' part of the church. It was surely close to time for Vespers. He walked across the nave, genuflected absentmindedly, and was about to slip through the connecting door, which Denise had left unlocked, when the door behind him opened.

He was convinced that his heart actually stopped beating for a second; certain that it was the prioress. No matter what his carefully laid plans with the bishop might be, if she should find him here, she could have him thrown bodily from the priory, and all opportunities for advancement would be gone. His career would be over, and he would be sent to some ruined abbey or parish in the worst, most rundown part of the realm.

When he saw it was Simon, Luke almost fell to his knees in thanks to God. He turned and made as if to walk to the sacristy.

'Ah, Father Luke, I'm glad to have found you. You'll be getting ready for the service, I suppose, but could I speak to you later?'

'Oh, Bailiff, I am most sorry. I was deep in thought and didn't hear you approach. You wish to make your Confession?'

'Um no. Actually I was hoping you could tell me a little about the people here. Just your general impressions of them.'

Luke reflected quickly. If anyone was to enter the church, the bailiff would be giving him the perfect alibi for being in here: a questioning. The prioress would want to know how Luke and Simon had got into the province of the females, but Luke could defend himself against any charges of impropriety easily enough.

'Ask me anything – but don't expect me to break the secrecy of the Confessional, of course.' Luke led the way to a bench at the wall and took a seat.

'I wouldn't dream of doing that,' Simon protested. 'But I am intrigued about this place and how the women all get on together.'

'It's much like anywhere else where women congregate, I imagine.'

'No. Not at all. Rarely do you find women jockeying for position in such a flagrant manner, all racing to win the prize – Lady Elizabeth's position.'

Luke forced a sad smile to his face. 'It's hardly a surprise, is it? Just look at the state of things here: two girls dead, the fabric of the buildings falling apart, the rumours . . .' he hesitated '. . . rumours of incontinence among some of the novices, and nuns too. It is said that they occasionally take men to their beds.'

What a hypocrite! Simon recalled Rose's words about Luke but held his tongue: he didn't want to lose the young vicar's assistance yet. 'And who would you think could be involved in such goings-on?'

'There are many rumours, Bailiff. One shouldn't make too much of them. I believe there have even been malicious stories spread about *me*!'

'What sort of stories?'

'Untruthful stories, Bailiff. The sort of things that girls, nuns, and even some of the old women in the canonical cloister would discuss. You can't trust such gossip, it is all too prevalent. I've heard tales of almost all the men, and according to the stories, they are constantly making love with every nun in the cloister. There is one thing common to all the men and women in this place: frustration. The men know the women are here, and vice versa. It is bound to create tension, isn't it? And when there is little else for people to talk about, it is easy to see how they turn to imagining things.'

'So you think that there hasn't been any sort of misbehaviour between the sexes?'

'If there has, I am sure that Lady Elizabeth will resign.'

'Are you?'

'Bailiff, she would have to. She is already condemned for the amount of damage done to this place – look at the roof above you! – but if any of her women were actually fornicating, that would really be the end of her.'

Simon considered. This was more complicated than he had anticipated. Every person he spoke to hinted at misdemeanours, but none was prepared to give full voice to their suspicions. 'Can you think of anyone who would have wanted to murder Moll and Katerine?'

'The very idea is ridiculous. No, in short. The pair of them were lovely things, delightful. Moll was so endearing, especially with her constant search for the holy in everything. She would ask a question, and fix those lovely eyes upon you, and you felt nearer to God by her presence. And Katerine was different, but no less wonderful. She was always trying to improve things. Often she would come to me to suggest something that others hadn't noticed. She was a sweet girl.'

Simon was unimpressed. He noted that all Luke had said so far corroborated Rose's suggestion that he could be enjoying an affair with a nun. Out of sheer malice, Simon then asked, 'And what do you think about Agnes?'

'Agnes?' Luke's voice took on a haughty distance. 'She seems to be a very serious-minded and sensible young novice. Of course, I could hardly claim to have spoken to her often, but she confesses to me regularly, and appears penitent.'

He was clearly not going to elucidate. Simon could almost hear the lock snapping shut when Luke closed his mouth. Instead the bailiff attempted a different tack. 'And what of the treasurer? She strikes me as very dedicated.'

'Dedicated?' Luke repeated with a frown. 'Yes, certainly that. Although she has her own troubles, I fear. Largely the result of her background.'

Simon listened carefully while the priest told him of Margherita's birth and the disappearance of her mother. It struck him how similar Margherita's story was to that of Rose. 'I wonder if she knows,' he muttered aloud, and when Luke glanced at him, he waved a hand dismissively. 'Nothing. Thinking out loud. But tell me, do you think Margherita could help save the convent? It seems to me that everywhere I look the place is falling apart.'

'Which I suppose reflects badly upon the prioress,' Luke said off-handedly. 'I mean, Margherita could hardly do a worse job, could she?'

'Do you think Margherita could have prevented the murders?'

Luke looked at him coldly. 'Bailiff, if those two poor girls really were murdered, surely it must be due to the innate sins of

the convent.' Luke was rather proud of his words. His pronounce-
ment sounded stern and pious, just as a cleric's statement should.
'If Margherita was in charge, I am sure many of the sins would
not have occurred, which would mean that the murders would not
have happened.'

There was the ringing of the bell calling the obedientiaries to
the next service, and Luke stood abruptly. 'I've got to prepare for
Vespers – and you will have to return to the canonical side of the
church Bailiff.'

'Thank you for your help. I am most grateful. And now I am
going to visit my friend,' Simon said, and set off towards the door.
However it opened before he arrived and the prioress walked in.
She smiled at him politely, but then she noticed the priest. Simon
saw that in her hand, Lady Elizabeth held a large key.

While he waited near the exit, she walked to the door separating
the two halves of the church and tested it. When it wouldn't open,
she stared at Luke, but the priest ignored her, and merely went to
the sacristy to prepare for the service.

Chapter Twenty-Two

Bertrand walked slowly to the church, anxiety clutching at his breast. All his plans had gone awry: he had intended Margherita to replace Lady Elizabeth and now Margherita herself appeared no better. For once he was prepared to accept his own limitations. Today he felt in desperate need of assistance from God.

There was no doubt: he had been over the figures time and again.

Only the one hand had written in the book – Margherita's – but the figures she had entered for the bailiff from Iddesleigh were wrong. Seven-eighths of it were missing. Bertrand himself had witnessed the man giving the money to her, had seen the treasurer herself scribble down the amounts. Bertrand was left with the unpleasant certainty that the woman was embezzling money.

He had backed the wrong horse. While trying to get rid of the prioress, he had hitched his cart to another just as corrupt: the whole place was tainted!

Entering the choir, he walked to a quiet stall in a dark corner and bowed his head reverently. Surely there was a way out of this mess. He had the blackmailed Elias on his side. Elias would allege that he had been going to forswear his oaths because he was so disgusted about the running of the priory. That testimony, embellished and wisely used, could spell the end of Lady Elizabeth's rule.

But if her replacement was a spendthrift or thief, things could only get worse.

If only Margherita had merely miscalculated. But she hadn't. He had been there, he had seen the money. There was no chance of Margherita making an error.

Then there were the two deaths. One from a bleeding – the sort of thing that could have happened anywhere; the second girl had been messing about on the roof, probably, and just fell. The bailiff wanted a sensational story because his friend had been hurt, but these things were almost always pretty mundane.

Once the prioress had gone, the deaths would soon be forgotten. Much more important was the future good management of the priory, and Bertrand knew that one excellent way of seeing to its protection was to ensure that there was enough money coming in to keep the place going.

A thought struck him: if no one found out about Margherita's stealing, all would be well. Lady Elizabeth could be removed, Margherita put in her place, and Bertrand could present a decisive and successful result to Bishop Stapledon – one which could only reflect well upon him and help him towards his own bishopric.

Sir Rodney would be pleased that the treasurer was in charge; Stapledon would be pleased that Bertrand had acted correctly in removing the prioress; and if any problems occurred later, Bertrand would be far away, hopefully already a bishop in his own right, with his own episcopal see. Safe.

As the service began, Bertrand allowed himself to smile.

Cecily almost leaped from the bed when the last bandage had been soaked from her arm, and then Constance set about cleaning the red, inflamed flesh with a cloth soaked in a refreshing infusion of herbs.

Hugh couldn't watch. The whole limb was swollen and discoloured, covered with blisters weeping pus. Cecily was delirious, and each time the scrap of linen touched her forearm, she screamed and thrashed about, trying to escape the pain. He glanced at the old woman at Constance's side.

While holding the basin in which Constance dipped her cloth, Joan mumbled prayers. She had taken up her place by Cecily's bed on her return from the rere-dorter; in her eyes was a concerned sympathy, the expression of one who has witnessed many deaths in her life and to whom the passing of one more soul was of scant note, although there was a kind of measuring quality to her observation, as if she was assessing how different her own end would be – an end which surely couldn't be far off.

At last the arm was bare and clean. Constance stared at it anxiously. She had no medicine adequate for a wound of this kind: the flesh was already putrefying.

'It should be cut off,' Hugh stated.

Constance looked up, startled. To her surprise Hugh was glowering down at the lay sister as if bitterly angry that Cecily had dared allow herself to grow so ill.

'It'll never get better, that arm. Can only get worse. You need a surgeon.'

'We don't have anyone near.'

'She'll die, then. Surely there's someone.'

It was Joan who answered. 'Perhaps there is one.'

Simon walked from the church into the nuns' cloister and stepped straight into a pile of faeces. He curled his lip as the smell struck his nostrils. Ugh! It was that damned bitch Princess, no doubt, crapping all over the place. Baldwin liked dogs, but as far as Simon was concerned terriers that spent their lives snapping at one's ankles and shitting all over the place were among the most useless of all creatures.

In fact, the mutt's deposits were all over the precinct, in the nunnery and the canonical half as well. There was no discrimination.

Simon wiped his boot on the grass of the garth and studied the sole. Almost clean. It would do. He set off for the door and climbed the stairs.

Since the nuns were all attending Vespers the place appeared deserted. With any luck the prioress had left the terrier in her room so it couldn't disrupt the service.

Simon reached the landing and was about to turn in to the infirmary, his footsteps echoing crisply on the bare wooden boards, when he heard the terrier begin to snarl and yap. Simon recalled being told that the dog hated men and barked at them.

'Shut your row!' he muttered, continuing on his way, but at the door to the infirmary he stopped dead. In his mind's eye he saw again the piles of dog mess in the canonical cloister and the nuns' garth; he recalled Lady Elizabeth telling him that her dog had been unwell the night that Moll had died, and that was why she had been murmuring endearments when Margherita had listened outside her door.

It wasn't unknown for a draw-latch to poison a dog in order to remove a household's most ferocious guard, but who could have got to Princess? Sadly, Simon realised that almost anyone could have. The little devil wandered between both cloisters, so Simon couldn't even reduce the potential suspects to either male or female.

But it corroborated Lady Elizabeth's story. And since the terrier only barked at men, it was a safe bet that only a man would have poisoned it.

Elias went to the church for Vespers but remained standing in his stall when the others left the choir. When all was still within he stepped forward to kneel before the altar.

He had no wish to be the agent of Lady Elizabeth's destruction, but he couldn't see how to escape. Bertrand had made the choice very clear: Elias could either refuse to implicate the prioress, in which case he would be accused of seducing a nun and attempting to persuade her to commit apostasy, or he could agree, in which case his own guilt and that of the nun herself need not come to light.

Elias covered his face with his hands. Was it so wrong to wish to see his own child? To want to honour his love as a husband should? Yet Constance had already rejected him, apparently. Lady Elizabeth had told him so.

Struck with a sudden desperation, he threw himself before the altar, arms outspread, praying to see Constance one last time.

At that moment he heard a sound. Quickly he pushed himself to his knees again, and peered about him. He saw the door to the nuns' side of the church open and Luke slip through. Luke was with a nun, and from her slurred speech Elias guessed it must be

Denise: all the canons knew her weakness for wine. Something made Elias slip backwards so that he was concealed behind a tall pillar, and there he listened as Luke negotiated.

'Look, three quarts of my best Guyenne red is almost all I have left. I'll not be getting any more from my merchant for at least five weeks. I can't offer you more.'

'I want them all,' she mumbled obdurately.

'Wouldn't two be enough?'

'Three. You want to go and exercise your filly, you'll have to pay.'

'All right, then, three.'

'And I want to see them when I let you back in,' she said greedily.

Luke gave an exasperated exclamation. 'When you let me in? You think the prioress wouldn't notice me coming into Compline with six pints of wine about me? Or perhaps you think you could hide them within your habit and drink during the service! Be sensible, woman – I shall bring them to you tomorrow once you have kept up your side of the bargain, and that is to let me in. After Compline, make a show of relocking this door, but in reality leave it open for me. Will you remember?'

Sulkily the woman repeated his instruction and when Luke nodded, satisfied, she pulled a sneering grimace and defiantly bit her thumb behind his back, making the nail crack against her upper teeth. Moving back a pace, she swung the door shut and soon after Elias heard the lock snap shut. Slowly he turned back to the altar, and wonderingly but fervently, offered his gratitude.

As night fell, Simon sat in the infirmary watching over his friend. Hugh had gone to fetch wine soon after Vespers, and since then Simon had heard the bell for Compline. The nuns had attended this last service of the day, and now all was silent in the place.

It was a relief, for Simon felt the need of time to review all he had heard. Especially since Hugh had grimly told him of Agnes and Luke.

Every now and again he glanced up as Cecily feverishly moaned and whimpered, but Constance had managed to drop a little of her magical syrup between the lay sister's lips, so at least she slept. Joan had complained that she couldn't sleep, and rather than use more of Constance's precious dwale, she had returned to her old bed in the dorter.

Constance herself was asleep on a stool at Cecily's side, her head resting on Cecily's mattress and setting her wimple awry.

She looked like an angel in the glow of the candles, Simon thought. The light gave her features a pink tint, highlighting the high cheekbones, and making her lips appear more full and rose-coloured. With the movement of her headpiece, a tress of her hair had come adrift and now it moved with her breath, near her cheek. Although she was clearly a mature woman, her face seemed so innocent and youthful that Simon felt a paternal fondness for her, just as he did when he glanced over at the truckle-bed at home and saw his own daughter asleep. There was something incredibly attractive in a sleeping girl, he thought.

The door opened quietly behind him, and he heard Constance snort slightly, then wrinkle her nose before settling once more.

'Hugh?' he asked.

'Bailiff, I wish to speak to you alone.'

'Lady Elizabeth,' he said, leaping to his feet. 'My apologies, I had no idea it was you.'

She held up her hand. 'No apology is necessary. Your man is outside for a while. I would like to speak to you alone.'

'But of course, my Lady. Please, take my chair.'

She glanced at Baldwin, remaining standing. 'How is he?'

'He moans often, and wanders a lot in his dreams, but I think – I hope – he will recover.'

'That is good.'

'The lay sister is not so well,' Simon said softly.

'I had heard,' she said, her attention moving to Cecily and the sleeping nun at her side. 'She is so young, too,' she added almost as an afterthought.

Simon didn't know what to say. In his experience most people did die while young. It was rare for a child to grow to adulthood, still rarer for one to become old like the prioress. 'She will not live with that arm,' he said.

'How can she live without it?'

Simon held his tongue. The prioress shook her head with resignation. 'You are right,' she said at last. 'But I hate having to ask a man to exercise his skills when the Pope has commanded him not to.'

'Your surgeon?'

'Godfrey, yes.' While she spoke, she woke Constance, and led her to her bed. Returning, she said, 'He's tried to stick to dressing wounds, but every now and again something like this happens.' She sighed heavily. 'I shall ask him to come and look at the girl as soon as it is light. But that is not why I am here. Sir Bailiff, you and your man are welcome to stay here for the night so that you can protect your friend, but I have to ask that you both remain within this room.'

Simon bridled. 'There's no need to suppose that Hugh or I would attempt to . . .'

'Oh, Bailiff, you shouldn't jump to conclusions!' she said, laughing silently, but with evident delight. 'I wouldn't suggest any such thing, but you can waken my nuns easily without trying by waking Princess. If she should hear you, she would bark. As you have seen, she doesn't like men.'

'That was one thing I was going to speak to you about,' Simon said. 'If someone in the canons' cloister gave a tidbit to Princess, would she eat it?'

'Oh, I expect so. She can be quite horribly greedy,' she said, but then caught sight of his expression. 'You mean – you think someone deliberately poisoned my little Princess?'

'It's possible. There seems to be enough dwale floating about this convent to sink all of you into a stupor.'

Unconsciously Lady Elizabeth gripped her prayer beads. 'Good God!'

Hugh had gone to sit out in the cloister, but even though he wrapped himself up in a rug he had removed from a chest in the frater, it was bitter cold. Although he wriggled and squirmed, although he resolutely shut his eyes and tried to imagine a roaring fire before him, the vision alone couldn't warm him. It was a relief when the door to the dorter opened. Framed in the doorway he saw the prioress, who stood peering about her shortsightedly. Hugh hastily clambered to his feet.

'Come inside and close the door behind you. Brrr! It *is* chill, isn't it? I wouldn't be at all surprised if it turned to snow again.'

Hugh entered, but as he turned to pull the door to behind him, he caught a glimpse of something. He was going to put it from his mind, but before he let the latch fall, he frowned, then opened it a fraction and peered out once more. There, darting from one pillar to another in the cloister passage by the church, he saw a figure. Hugh stood stock-still. He was not particularly afraid of any man, but there was something unwholesome and melancholy about this apparition. Raised and bred on the moors, Hugh had a healthy respect for ghouls and the devil, and in a place like this, where the religious folk all appeared to consider their vows as irrelevant, Hugh wondered now whether a devil might wander the cloisters at night. His scalp crept.

'Hurry up, man!'

At the sound of the prioress's voice, Hugh quickly pulled the door shut behind him and ascended the stairs to the infirmary. As he stole past the door to the prioress's chamber, Princess snarled, and Hugh hurried on to the security of the infirmary.

Denise snored, mouth wide, and it was only when her pot rolled from her hand and fell from the table, smashing on the floor, that she snorted, groaned, and at last blearily gazed about her. Realising she was alone in the room, she put her hands to her eyes, rubbing with the heels of her palms and yawning.

It was hard to sleep on the table-top like this. She always had a crick in her neck when she awoke, and felt unrefreshed, as though the sleep had been of no benefit whatever.

She rose, stretching, and walked out. When she had entered it had been late afternoon, and she had intended only one quick drink before returning to her duties, sweeping the floor after Compline, but now she saw it was already late, and she felt a short stab of guilt.

'The door!' she exclaimed. Luke had been there when she had gone to unlock it, without, as he had said, the wine, but he had winked at her, and she had sat moodily all through the service, knowing that what she was about to do at the end was wrong and against all her vows, taking wine for herself without sharing it among the other members of the community, allowing a man into the cloister so he could take his carnal pleasures with a nun, and the nun herself, of course, for Denise would be helping her to break her vows.

It was all very confusing, and Denise fingered the little medal of St Mary that she always wore about her neck. As usual the Virgin Mary comforted Denise, and the nun took up her jug and emptied it, smacking her lips with gusto. It was good wine, but she would prefer Luke's best Bordeaux.

Luke! The vicar should be in the cloister by now, with his little novice. If not, he was leaving it late. When he'd made her the offer, he'd said she could lock the door again once he was past, Denise remembered, chewing her lip. Was it late enough for her to go and lock up now, or should she wait a little longer? Denise wasn't prepared to leave the cloister unprotected all through the night; she wanted to make sure at least that Luke was already in the nuns' cloister.

She made her way to the church. If he was still within the cloister, all he need do was rest in the church somewhere, and first thing in the morning, when Nocturns began, he could slip on his vestments and appear just as normal, as if he had only just been allowed in.

That was what made his affair with the girl such a thrill, Denise deduced sourly. No doubt the fool found that the risk of discovery added to his pleasure; continuing his affair beneath the prioress's very nose appealed to his twisted sense of humour. And the novice was no better.

Satisfied with her logic, Denise went to the connecting door, and turned the key in the lock.

Chapter Twenty-Three

In her small chamber, Constance slept fitfully. She was absolutely exhausted, but her mind wouldn't switch off and she kept returning to thoughts of Elias. If Simon and Hugh hadn't been snoring in her infirmary, she would have stolen downstairs, as she had done so often before, and walked to the grille to gaze out at the canons' area, hoping for a glimpse of him.

Elias was in every way the sort of man she would have married, had she been able to wed, and not only because of his physical attractions. It was more because of his kindness, his gentle manners, his generosity of spirit – and the way he could make her laugh even when she was feeling low.

Knowing that she had let him down was awful. She could see with her mind's eye how his face would have fallen when the prioress spoke to him, how his soul would have been filled with misery on hearing that he could never see Constance again. There was no need for a great leap of her imagination, for it was how she herself felt about never seeing him again, and she had to cover her face with her pillow to smother the sound of her sobs.

That was why, although she was awake, she didn't hear the quiet steps going down the stairs outside.

Agnes crept past the door to the prioress's room. Fortunately, Princess remained silent. Holding her breath, Agnes tiptoed down the rest of the stairs to the cloister, then hurried along to the frater.

Denise was sitting in her favourite place, drinking from a large pot. Her eyes were dulled and bloodshot, and when she saw Agnes, she gave a leery smile. Dropping her elbows to the table-top, threatening her pot and jug with being overturned, she sniggered. 'Looking for him, dear?'

Agnes ignored her and walked on past to the buttery. As far as Agnes was concerned, there was little point in talking to Denise when she'd been enjoying a late-night vigil with a jug of wine. Besides, Agnes didn't want to give her a chance to talk about having seen her earlier – *in flagrante*.

Denise watched the novice's shadow as it followed Agnes around the wall – a fierce black symbol of evil. It reminded her of the last time she had seen a nun's shadow, and suddenly Denise was very thirsty indeed.

Agnes passed through the screens passage to the yard beyond. The shed was silent: no animals. A candle or something had been lit inside. The door was ajar, and a soft glow lit the ground in front.

Agnes grinned. Luke knew she liked romance sometimes, and he obviously wanted to make their evening good. Her mouth widening with anticipation, Agnes shoved at the door and walked in, but as she crossed the threshold her foot caught in something, and she fell headlong. Lying there, she rolled her eyes in amusement at her ridiculous entry, and clambered to all fours. Then, before she could straighten or get to her feet, she felt someone thump her back.

'Ouch! What was that for?' she said crossly. There was a curious dragging sensation on her back, and she wriggled her shoulder-blades to ease it, and only then did she feel the quick, flame-hot pain. She opened her mouth to gasp, but before she could, the figure approached again, habit flapping like the wings of a devil, the shadow thrown on to the wall behind like that of a great predatory monster. Agnes was about to scream as the fist caught her chin. She fell, agony exploding as the dagger, lodged in her back, hit the hard, unyielding ground. She felt something burst within her as the blade was driven deeper, up to the cross-guard. She rolled over, choking, and saw bright, thick liquid fall from her mouth. In the gloomy light it looked black, as black as the shadow on the wall, as black as the sins she had committed, as black as hell itself.

When the dagger was tugged from her back, Agnes was almost past caring. All she knew was that she had to confess her sins and obtain Absolution. She looked up with mute appeal in her eyes, but before she could open her mouth to beg, the blade flashed down again to her breast, and this time it found its mark. Agnes felt her heart stop within her, and in the moments left to her, she saw her killer make the sign of the cross and leave.

It was the barking rather than the scream that woke Simon from his heavy sleep. He yawned and blinked, stretching. In front of him he saw Constance appear in the doorway to her chamber, her eyes wide with fear. 'What is it?' he asked. 'Damn that bloody dog, does it always yap like this in the middle of the night?'

'That scream, didn't you hear it?'

'Scream? What, from here?' Simon demanded, staring down immediately at his friend. To his relief Baldwin appeared oblivious to the noise.

'No, outside,' Constance said. Her hand was on her breast, and she almost appeared to be panting. 'It sounded like the devil himself – oh, God save us!'

'I'm sure He will,' Simon said soothingly, although he was unpleasantly aware of his own superstitious dislike of the dark. 'Where did it come from?'

Before Constance could answer, he heard a door open and the prioress appeared in the doorway. 'The noise came from outside the cloister, Bailiff – from this side of the church.' Her face was very pale and she suddenly looked ancient.

Simon nodded, pulled his swordbelt around his belly and tied the thongs together. 'Hugh, you stay here to protect Baldwin and the others. I'll go and check.'

'I shall join you,' the prioress said.

'I think you should . . .' Simon began uncertainly.

'Do not waste your breath, young man,' she snapped.

Simon saw argument was useless. Slapping his open palm against his sword-hilt, he nodded, then hurried past the prioress and out, down the stairs to the cloister.

'Through the frater,' Lady Elizabeth called from behind him.

At the doorway Simon peered in. The hall was empty. Lady Elizabeth pointed the way once more, and Simon went to the screens, where he saw the door.

The blood was tingling in his veins now, pounding at his temples. He gripped his sword-hilt and pulled the metal free of its scabbard; the weapon gleamed wickedly where the sharpened edge caught the candlelight. Taking a deep breath Simon darted through.

He came out into a small cobbled yard, smelling of farm animals' dung. A sow grunted at him from a quiet corner. A door was open to a shed-like structure, and Simon made for it obliquely, avoiding the light that streamed out. He went right up to the wall at the side of the door, and then slowly, with every nerve awake for a sound from within, he pressed his free hand to the wood of the door and pushed, sword held out at belly height, ready to slash or stab.

The sight that met him presented no threat. A horrified expression on his face, the smith Elias was kneeling and cradling Agnes's head in his lap, while the blood dripped slowly from her slackly open mouth on to his stained robe.

Luke shrank back against the stonework of the wall as Simon and the prioress dashed past, and only when they had gone did he lick his dry lips and try to clear his head. He was near the door to the frater, but he could hear a chattering gaggle of nuns approaching nervously through it, so he couldn't escape that way. The route to the outer wall of the precinct meant passing by the open doorway where Simon and the prioress no doubt stood staring in horror at Elias and the dead woman. Luke's only chance of escape lay in making his way outside the cloister along the outer, western range of buildings towards the church. Then he could get to the alley that led along the church's wall, and thence to the church itself.

'Why?' Luke heard the prioress demand. Her voice was high-pitched, as if about to break. 'What has this girl ever done to you?'

'Lady Elizabeth, I didn't hurt her! There was a scream – I came here to make sure she was all right. I didn't kill her.'

'Stay where you are!' Simon rasped as Elias tried to get to his feet. 'My Lady?'

'We shall have to put him somewhere safe until morning,' she said. 'If you heard her and came running to protect her, how did you get through the door in the church?'

'It was open, my Lady. I followed Luke.'

'Luke was here?' Simon demanded.

'He bribed Sister Denise to let him in, so that he could see this novice. I heard him arrange it, and followed when he came through.'

'And you?' Lady Elizabeth asked. 'What were you doing here?'

'I came to see Constance one last time, my Lady. I had no interest in this girl – I love Constance.'

'Where is Luke, then?'

'He went straight from the church out to the cloister, and he stopped there, just as I did, because someone came past – Denise. She went into the church, then returned to the cloister. Luke went off towards the garden, and seeing that, I had decided to go round and throw stones up at Constance's shutter, when I heard the cry.'

'What then?'

'I hesitated – I didn't want to be found here, but the cry sounded so full of fear I had to come. I ran through the frater and saw the light. I immediately came in, and found Agnes like this. I held her head to help her soul pass on.'

'When was this?'

'Only a short time ago, my Lady.'

Simon snorted with derision. 'You expect us to believe this?'

'Get Denise here, ask *her*!'

After a moment, Luke heard Lady Elizabeth call for a novice then send her away to fetch Denise.

Here was an opportunity to make good his escape: the nuns and novices, all fascinated by the drama being acted out in the little chamber, had drifted forward so that they could listen better, and their gradual movement had left a space near the door to the

screens of the frater. Cautiously, hardly daring to breathe, Luke
sidled along the wall, away from that hideous light and the scene
within the room. Slipping along slowly, with infinite care to
avoid making a sound, he reached the corner of the buildings and
ducked around into the small garden.

At last he began to feel a little safer. It was only a few yards to
the church. He rushed along on tiptoes, fearful lest he should kick
a stone and waken the nuns to his presence, but he managed to
cover the distance without alarming anyone and soon was at the
alley by the church's wall. Peering into the cloister, he saw nothing.
He paused, trying to still his pounding heart, and moved con-
fidently towards the church's door. Reaching it, he closed it behind
him with a gasp of absolute relief. He had to pause, panting,
suddenly exhausted. But there wasn't time, he could take a rest
when he was back in his bed. He rushed over the floor to the
communicating door.

His heart was thudding less painfully now, with a more steady
rhythm. Thank God he had survived. He cast a smile at the altar,
acknowledging it with a tilt of his head. A genuflection after this
day's work would be an insult, he reflected, and he pressed the
latch to open the door.

But the door wouldn't open. His hand still on the latch, he
tugged at it, pursed his lips and pulled again, then set both hands
upon the handle, his foot to the wall, and heaved until the corded
muscles stood out on his neck, tears of frustration pouring from
his eyes, but the locked door wouldn't budge.

As he sagged, ready to weep, resting his forehead against the
wood, he heard a noise. Spinning, he found himself face-to-face
with Margherita. She stood in a choir stall, watching him with a
small smile of contempt.

'So, Father Luke, you decided to come and adulterate one of
the Brides of Christ yet again, did you?' she asked quietly. 'And
what now, Father? Will you await your fate here?'

He made as if to step towards her, but she shook her head, and
with a speed that surprised him, she moved around behind the
stalls, watching him with a raised eyebrow. 'I would prefer to

keep my distance, Father, especially with all these dead women about the place. It would be a shame to add to their number, don't you think? Not to mention defiling the church with blood.'

'How did you know about her? You saw her there, didn't you!' he accused. Then his frown of incomprehension faded. 'Then you were there before me. *You* must have killed Agnes!'

'Don't talk bollocks like that to me,' she said, but retreated as he stalked towards her, his face white. 'After the scream I saw poor little Agnes there, dead, and I realised immediately it had to be you.'

'It was *me* who screamed – when I found her body,' he protested.

'Only a man could slaughter a nun like that – and who else but the very one who enjoyed corrupting the young wenches in here? Only one man had an opportunity to get in here and chat to the novices regularly, didn't he? *You*, Father. You enjoyed all three of the dead girls, didn't you?'

'No, I didn't!' he shouted.

'Oh, I suppose that righteous little madam Moll refused your advances, and that was why you decided to kill her, so that she couldn't let on. And Katerine – why did you do away with her? Was it that she was annoyed when you transferred your affections to Agnes?'

Luke gawped, standing still. 'Why should I hurt them? I couldn't hurt them.'

Margherita was relentless. 'You had Agnes help you, didn't you? You had her drop extra dwale into Moll's cup, and then you killed the girl. Katerine was easy – you knocked her out down here and then tossed her from the roof like a sack of grain. And Agnes knew all about Moll, so as soon as you realised you couldn't ensure her silence by using her as your concubine, you decided to murder her as well!'

'You're talking nonsense! This is a pack of lies, all lies, to hide your guilt, you murderous bitch!'

'Me?' she squawked.

'Yes, you! Moll found out about your little game with the money, didn't she? You never knew before, that your assistant could read and add up. Your precious Lady Elizabeth can't, but a poor novice saw through your schemes and ruined your plans, so you killed her. Murdered her to cover up your own guilt! But you never realised Moll had shared the story with other novices, did you? That never occurred to you, oh no! And I guess that Katerine came to you with a demand for money and that was when you murdered her.'

'Please enlighten me,' Margherita said coldly. 'What moronic reasoning can you use to explain my murdering little Agnes?'

'Yes, please continue.'

Luke felt the ice enter his bones at that voice; in the doorway stood Lady Elizabeth, the bailiff at her side, sword sheathed now, his hand on Elias's shoulder, and all the novices and nuns filling the space behind. It was a sight to freeze the blood of a saint, and Luke felt the resolution fade from him at the expression on Lady Elizabeth's face. A sob caught at his breast, making his shoulders jerk. He threw a look at the jewel-encrusted cross on the altar, feeling a desperate desire for a moment's calm in which to pray and make his peace.

Turning to the prioress, he tried to hold his head up, but couldn't meet the steely contempt in her eyes. 'Ask her where she was, my Lady,' he said hoarsely.

'Lady Elizabeth, I was walking in the orchard when I heard the scream. I immediately rushed back and saw Agnes's body. At once I realised that I must see whether someone could have entered from the men's cloister and came here. I found the door locked, but a moment or two later this man appeared and tried to escape.'

Luke protested, 'Lady Elizabeth, I had found Agnes's body and didn't want to be thought of as her murderer so I fled.'

'And it took you so long to get here that Margherita had time to find Agnes's body and get to the church?' Simon said disbelievingly.

'Yes, Bailiff. As soon as I screamed I . . .'

'It was *you* who screamed?' Simon pressed.

'Yes. It was horrible to find her like that. I wanted to get away, but there were feet coming from every direction.'

'Margherita, you mean? Everyone else was asleep.'

'Someone was coming through the frater, there was someone from the orchard –' he threw a baleful look at Margherita as he realised he had confirmed her story – 'and someone else coming the way I had, from the church.'

'Who was that?'

Luke went blank. 'I don't know. They never appeared.'

Simon eyed him. 'Could the steps have been running *away*?'

'They might have been – I don't know.'

'Tell us all that happened,' Simon said.

'I admit I came to see Agnes; I had just got to the cloister when I heard steps and saw Denise. She was drunk, so I left her, and when she returned to the frater I went up the alley to meet Agnes, but there was a noise behind me. It worried me and I hurried to the chamber and tripped. When I realised . . .' Luke paused, scarcely able to go on, then: 'I screamed and ran out, but I heard people coming. I didn't know what to do! I went to the frater's wall and hid behind a buttress. When you sent to question Denise I slipped away.' He faced the prioress. 'Lady Elizabeth, Moll had told Katerine about Margherita embezzling priory funds. That was why Margherita killed them both. Agnes found out too.'

'She told you this?' Margherita demanded. 'It is not true!'

'Prove it! Swear it before God, on the gospels, on His cross.'

Margherita stepped to the altar and rested her hand on the book. Meeting Luke's gaze, she declaimed loudly so all could hear: 'I had nothing to do with the death of the novice Moll, the novice Katerine or the novice Agnes. I had no part as an accomplice, nor as the instigator of any one or all of their deaths.'

'Bitch!' he swore, making the sign of the cross. 'You dare lie on God's own book?'

'Enough!' Lady Elizabeth snapped.

Simon had remained silent, surveying the pallid priest. Now he nodded towards Luke. 'Do you dare declare your innocence in the same way?'

Luke immediately stepped up to the altar. As he did so, Margherita moved quickly out of his reach. So that there could be no doubt of his conviction, Luke picked up the book reverently and kissed the symbol of the cross on its calfskin cover, then rested it on his left palm, his right hand flat over the top. 'I declare my innocence of the killing of any of these novices. I affirm my innocence in the sight of this congregation and in the sight of God, and if I am guilty in any way of any of these deaths, if I knowingly or unknowingly took any active part in them, if I persuaded or incited or aided or abetted any person in these murders, may God strike me dead here and now. As I believe in the resurrection and the life to come, I had nothing to do with these deaths.'

'And that,' Simon observed grimly, 'leaves us much better informed, doesn't it?'

Chapter Twenty-Four

Bertrand was called to the cloister as soon as the convent had finished Prime. Simon left him closeted with the prioress, and strode off to the infirmary to allow Hugh, who was nodding with the effort of standing guard, to take his own rest. Simon was happier spending his time mulling over the events of the evening while sitting next to Baldwin. For some strange reason, Simon was sure his friend was in danger. Intuition told him so.

Meanwhile, he could come to no logical conclusion about the trio of murders. No matter how he reviewed the affair he could see no connection between the dead girls that made any sense. Moll was ultra-religious, a bit of a pain, by all accounts, who took everyone else's guilt on her own shoulders and informed them of their offences to make them confess and gain forgiveness; Katerine was nosy, pushy, keen to get on, and unscrupulous, prepared to use blackmail to achieve her ends; Agnes appeared unconcerned by the priory and the people within it, she was simply a child who probably shouldn't have been put there in the first place. Certainly she wasn't religiously driven.

Simon had heard one thing the previous night that had intrigued him: the wild allegation made by Luke to the effect that Margherita had been creaming off the income and profits from the priory. It was hard to credit that a nun would do such a thing, but looking at the state of the place it was all too easy to believe that someone had been fleecing it.

Margherita had always appeared coldly contemplative, a very genuine Christian, yet he realised that although the treasurer had denied any part in the murders, she had *not* denied the charge of embezzlement. If his reasoning was correct, and she wouldn't swear before God to innocence of theft, clearly the fact that she was happy to do so regarding the murders meant she was telling the truth about them.

So he was no further forward, he thought with a heavy sigh.

Baldwin groaned, and Simon leaned forward. 'How are you feeling?'

'As if someone's trying to cut through my skull with a rusty saw,' Baldwin said with his eyes tight shut.

Simon chuckled and passed Baldwin the pot of wine, which the knight soon emptied.

'I doubt it'll stay down,' the knight said, resettling himself on his side. 'I feel like you do after a night drinking all my wine and ale.'

'At least the wound's healing,' Simon said, his tone gentle.

'I can assure you that from my perspective it appears to be getting *worse*,' Baldwin said drily. 'How does your enquiry progress?'

Simon gave him a doubtful look. 'Constance said you should rest.'

'Don't be a fool. I need something to take my mind off this!' Baldwin hissed painfully.

'All right. Well – there was another murder last night.'

'God's teeth!'

Simon told all he had learned the previous day, finishing with the discovery of Agnes's body. 'The prioress has locked up Luke and Elias, thinking that a man who dares enter the convent against God's laws would be capable of murder,' he said.

Baldwin snorted feebly. 'By the same token she should arrest herself! She too must be suspect for she once had an affair and got pregnant. No, that is rubbish. And of course we can assume that Elias was innocent.'

Their voices had woken Hugh. 'But he was found there!' the servant objected sleepily.

'Precisely. Whoever killed the girl would have run. No one would have stood about waiting to be discovered. Luke is a different matter, of course.'

'Except,' Simon interrupted, 'Luke had no dagger on him.

Come to that, neither did Elias. So where was the murder weapon?'

'What of Margherita?' Baldwin enquired.

'She wasn't searched,' Simon admitted shamefacedly.

'Wonderful!' Baldwin muttered. He remained staring up at the beams of the roof for a few minutes. 'All this makes little sense, especially if we take my own wound into account. Three girls, all very different, and me as well. There must be some kind of pattern to all four attacks; something that ties us together.'

Simon gave his friend a smile of sympathy. 'The last thing you need right now is to fret about something like this, and I need to get on as well.'

'Why? What are you going to do?'

'I'm going to ask Margherita what she saw last night.'

Simon left Hugh once more guarding Baldwin. Already, before Simon left the infirmary, Baldwin was sleeping again, and as the bailiff opened the door to the landing, Constance appeared at the top of the stairs.

'Sister, could you tell me where the treasurer is likely to be?' he asked, and she told him to look in the cloister.

Her eyes were red and raw from weeping, and even as he studied her, he saw her blink to keep the tears at bay.

It was this sign of her distress that made him touch her shoulder. She took a quick pace back on feeling his hand, and stared at him with alarm, but he smiled. 'Sister, don't fear. I am sure Agnes died quickly.'

'It wasn't her I was thinking of,' Constance said. She sadly let her head drop forward, feeling ridiculously feeble. It was mere mawkishness to pine for him. 'It was Elias . . . Oh, Bailiff – do *you* think he could have killed them?'

Simon gazed at her blankly. 'Elias? No, not really. Why do you ask that?'

'I gave him dwale to keep the prioress's dog silent when he came to visit me,' she said, colouring. 'I thought he could have dropped some into Moll's drink, and then he could have thrown Katerine from the roof, and last night . . . last night . . .'

Simon patted her shoulder as she began to sob. 'The dwale didn't kill Moll,' he said.

'But I'd already given her some! I gave it to Joan and Cecily as well so Elias and I wouldn't be interrupted. If he gave them more, it could have poisoned them.'

'It didn't, though, did it? The killer smothered Moll, then cut her, so my friend thinks, and I've never known him to be wrong. As for last night, I don't think Elias is guilty – but you might be able to help me with some other thoughts.'

'Anything, if it will help you to discover who is doing all this!'

'Show me where Margherita would normally sleep.'

She turned and led the way to the dorter, stopping at a bed only a short way inside.

It was far from the hole in the roof, but close to the door. Simon pointed to the single bed between Margherita's and the prioress's chamber. 'Who sleeps there?'

'That's Joan's.'

Beside the treasurer's bed was a large chest, which Constance said was Margherita's. It was of heavy wood and bound with iron. Simon idly tried to lift the lid. It was locked.

Seeing Simon's questioning glance moving over the rest of the beds, Constance gave the names of the occupants. 'At the far side, that is Denise's, and that one, nearer the stairs, is Ela's, the kitcheness's.'

'So Ela could have risen last night without waking anyone.'

Constance pulled a face. Simon could see her nose wrinkling above her veil. 'She wouldn't have woken anyone anyway. Margherita often walks around late at night. Especially recently, with these murders and the pressure of the election. And Denise is usually downstairs with a pot of wine until very late. If Ela rose, I doubt anyone would have been here to stir.'

Godfrey's anxious face appeared at the top of the stairs. 'Constance? Oh, there you are. You have a patient who needs my help?'

Constance apologised to Simon and led the canon to the infirmary. They left the door wide open behind them, and Simon saw them march straight to Cecily's bed. While he watched, he saw Godfrey begin to unwrap the dressing on the girl's arm; the canon winced with distaste at the smell, while Cecily suddenly gave a great cry of agony.

Simon could stand most things, but not surgery. Such slicing of flesh and sawing of bone reminded him too forcibly of his own physical frailty. He turned and walked down the stairs while behind him Cecily's voice rose to an insane shriek.

In the cloister he found Margherita sitting with Joan. Joan rose, giving Simon a deeply disapproving look. For her part, Margherita stared white-faced up at the infirmary's window. In her left hand she gripped her string of prayer beads, which she paid out through her right.

Joan appeared enraged. 'So, Master Bailiff, you consider that Margherita is a murderer?'

'I have said no such thing,' he replied. 'But others have, and I must question her.'

'Ridiculous! A woman more dedicated to the priory you'll never meet!' Joan looked at Margherita as if expecting a word from her, but the treasurer sat silently. After a moment Joan gave an exasperated 'Oh!' and left them.

Margherita shivered as a fresh shriek came from the window. 'How is she?'

'I don't know. If Godfrey's as good as some of you think, then Cecily may survive.' There was no need to stress the point: both knew even a young, healthy person could fade astonishingly quickly when gangrene set in. If the infected part was hacked off, the patient often died from shock. 'May I have a few words with you?'

She looked him up and down. 'After last night, I suppose I have little choice. The alternative would be to leave you still more suspicious of me.' She led Simon to a bench at the northernmost wall of the cloister. 'I didn't kill any of them, you know.'

'But you have stolen money from the priory.'

'*No!*' she declared, her eyes flashing as she spun to face him. 'I would *never* take money from this place. I saved it so it could be used to serve the community better.'

As she spoke she turned away from Simon and glowered over the garth towards the church. 'Look at it, just look! Roof falling in, tiles smashed – it's a miracle only one man's been hit by falling slates.'

'If you'd not embezzled the funds, the prioress could have repaired them.'

'Oh, the *prioress*!'

Simon snapped. 'If you hadn't concealed the true state of the accounts, maybe she could have repaired the roofs and wouldn't have been forced to resort to begging a local knight to give her more money – and don't tell me you were acting in the priory's interests! You were hiding it so you could produce it later, when you had won the prioress's job, in order to make yourself look better in the other sisters' eyes.'

As Margherita turned to face Simon, there came a terrible scream from the infirmary, which faded slowly to a whimpering sob. '*Benedicite!*' she said in horror.

'They're taking her arm off,' Simon said relentlessly. 'Because she slipped on the laundry stairs and broke her wrist. You said the stairs were rotten – don't you feel guilt for what you've done?'

'No. I did it for God and for this community!' she gasped. 'I have done nothing for my own benefit, only for that of the people about me.'

'Would that include killing the girls?' Simon pressed. 'Were they enough of a threat to your community for you to seek to destroy them all?'

'You imagine that I could . . .' She stared at him once more, her attention drifting from his stern brown eyes to his forehead, then his mouth and chin, as if seeking confirmation of his seriousness. Sinking back against the wall, she looked drained of all energy. Silently she reached inside her tunic and flung a key at him. 'Take it! It's all in my chest, and on top you'll find a parchment with the amounts scribbled down so that everyone can witness nothing is stolen.'

Simon picked up the key from where it had fallen. Margherita sat like someone shrivelled, as if she had lost much of her substance; her head bowed, shoulders hunched. She didn't meet his gaze. Very slowly she lifted both hands to her face and covered it as she began to sob.

He was about to make his way to the dorter to fetch the hidden money when he heard the brazen call of a trumpet. Surprised, he spun around, but here in the cloister he could see nothing beyond the surrounding walls. Filled with uneasiness, he strode towards the communicating door in the church.

Bishop Stapledon looked at the main gate to St Mary's, Belstone with a significant seriousness in his expression. It didn't go unnoticed by Jonathan when he pulled the little side door open and gaped at the cavalcade before him.

'Open the gate in the name of your bishop,' ordered Stapledon's ecclesiastical staff-bearer, his crosier, who sat before his master near the gate, his trumpet resting on his thigh.

Jonathan swivelled slowly to stare. 'Which?' he squeaked.

Stapledon kicked his horse forward until its head was pushing Jonathan backwards. 'This one, Canon. *I* am your bishop. *Now open that damned gate!*'

As he spurred his mount, Stapledon took in the state of the precinct, squinting shortsightedly. His eyes had been failing him regularly for some time now, and he felt the need for his spectacles, but even without them the sight was not one to please the eye.

For Bishop Stapledon, a man used to residing with the King in the best abbeys and halls, it was shocking to see a place so derelict. The entire area appeared so rundown as to be ready for demolition. Still worse was the attitude of the workers. Those who should have been in the fields stood gaping at the sight of his entourage; those who should have been indoors seeing to the horses, working in the dairy, or producing the ale upon which the whole priory depended, thronged the lane to the stables.

Stapledon clenched his jaw and carefully lifted himself from his saddle, his eyes squeezed tight shut, standing in the stirrups with a small shiver of exquisite pain, holding his breath. Then, giving a little sigh of pure relief, he opened his eyes and permitted himself a faint smile as he leaned forward and swung his leg over the horse's rump to dismount.

It was something that he had tried to think of as a minor cross to bear in this vale of adversity, but most of all he thought of it as a damned irritating affliction. Piles! he thought to himself as he stood a moment, feeling for a second's sheer bliss, the lack of the agony that was so like a dagger thrust between his buttocks.

'Bishop!'

Stapledon turned and smiled gently as Simon bent to kiss his ring. 'Ah, Bailiff Puttock. Good of you to come and welcome me.'

'I had no idea you were to be visiting, my Lord.'

'Neither had I until a short while ago. Sir Baldwin's wife sends him her love . . . but where is he?'

'I fear Sir Baldwin is in the infirmary. He was struck by a falling slate.'

'Good God!' Stapledon surveyed the buildings about him. 'The Lady Elizabeth has a great deal to explain.'

'It wasn't *her* fault,' Simon muttered, and explained about the three deaths while he led the bishop through to the canons' cloister. Stapledon's expression hardly altered as Simon told him of the catalogue of disasters since their arrival here with Bertrand. He only showed emotion when Simon mentioned the stabbing of Agnes.

'She is also dead?'

'I am afraid so, Bishop.'

'Dear God!' Stapledon shook his head, standing still for a full minute. He remembered Agnes: a cheerful young girl. That was at least seven years ago now, when he had last seen Sir Rodney. He could picture her in his mind's eye, a young slip of a thing, fragile as a flower, pretty with her tip-tilted nose and freckles, and with an engaging smile. She had captured Sir Rodney's heart too.

It was difficult to believe that the young woman was dead. Stapledon knew that her death could have an impact on the future of the convent, that Sir Rodney might change his mind and bestow his money and church on a different institution, but that was unimportant to Stapledon. The Bishop had plenty of money himself; he could make good any financial losses from Agnes's death, but he could do nothing to bring her back from the dead. He murmured softly, 'Godspeed, Agnes. Go with God.'

But a moment later the bishop shook off his mood. 'Right, Bailiff. However Sir Rodney feels about this girl's death, we have work to do. Take me to see the Lady Elizabeth. And tell me what else has happened here. How has that fool Bishop Bertrand been behaving himself?'

Simon filled him in on the letter from Margherita, but also mentioned the missing money and pressed the key into the bishop's hand.

Stapledon looked at it, his lip twisted. 'She took the money to make the place appear in the worst possible light, solely in order to justify her own claim to the leadership; at the same time as harming the reputation of the prioress. Such corruption! Somehow it feels worse to be confronted with deceit and betrayal here in a convent, although I should be used to it after the dishonest and thieving politicians who surround the King. Bastards! Crosier, come with me and the bailiff. The rest of you, see to the horses.'

And with these words he swept forward, the episcopal staff-bearer and Simon trotting along in his wake.

Hugh watched as Constance and Godfrey washed the stump of Cecily's arm, wiping the blood away. Blood still seeped from the arm even with the tight tourniquet. Godfrey stood with a worried expression, and then reached for the large iron which sat in a charcoal brazier. Taking a deep breath, he grabbed its handle and thrust it on the stump. There was a hissing; steam rose. The slight figure of the lay sister leaped upwards, her whole body curving like a drawn bow in her agony, before slumping into unconsciousness. Godfrey closed his eyes, shuddered, and dropped the iron back in the brazier, while Constance resolutely swallowed before painting her poultice onto the ruined flesh.

Like most countrymen Hugh had witnessed enough suffering in his time to loathe seeing any creature in pain, but he had also seen many people die because of gangrene. Although he hated to see Cecily in such agony, he recognised and mentally saluted the kindness of Godfrey and Constance. If anything, it was those two who were the most affected in the room.

'An excellent job, I should say,' Hugh heard Baldwin say.

The knight had been unable to sleep through the hideous shrieks that the girl gave until she had been anaesthetised with a strong mixture of dwale in a pot of wine. While they waited for her to succumb to the stupefactives, Godfrey held up a glass jar of the girl's urine to the light, trying to convince himself that he was doing the best for her.

'Thank you, Sir Baldwin, but . . .' Godfrey held out his hands in a gesture of distress. 'Whether she will recover after such an experience is anybody's guess.'

'You were swift to put her to the knife and saw, and swift to seal the raw flesh. Now all we can do is hope that she has enough faith. You have done your best.'

Godfrey gratefully took the pot that Constance proffered and walked to Baldwin's side, letting himself slide to the floor, his back to the wall. 'There are many who would look at such a wound and refuse to operate.'

'Especially clerks in major orders.'

'Balls to that! I can't accept it's wrong to do what I know to be right for the sick, no matter what the Pope may say.'

Baldwin rose to his elbow, and Hugh could see he was intrigued. 'You were a trained surgeon, I seem to remember Bertrand saying. Weren't you at university with him?'

'For a while, yes. I learned my craft before meeting him. We were both called to the cloth late in life. I learned my skills, such as they are, in the old King's wars. I was with a set of London men. While we were in France I met a foreigner, and he showed me how to remove a limb. I know it can save lives when the gangrene has set in.'

'So you were a fighter?'

'Till I learned that peace was better than war,' he agreed and knocked back his wine. Constance refilled it from her jug.

Seeing her sway, Hugh rose and took the jug from her, setting it at Godfrey's side, and helped the nun to sit on a chest. On the floor, leaking blood, was Cecily's arm, and Constance shivered at the sight, turning from it. Hugh brought her a cup of wine, then shrugged and poured another for himself, shoving the putrefying limb away under the bed. Joan walked in a few minutes later, a pot in her hand, which she set on Costance's table, but then she caught sight of the arm. Tutting to herself, she picked it up, wrapped it carelessly in a large scrap of linen from the table, and took it out.

Baldwin saw her burden as she passed. Blood was staining the end of the cloth and the sight made him shoot a glance at Cecily. She was as pale as the bleached linen she lay upon, a fine sheen of sweat dampening her brow and features. Every few minutes a shiver would rack her frame. Fleetingly Baldwin wondered what would happen to the arm. If it had been that of a peasant, it might have been thrown to the pigs – or in a town, tossed into the street, which came to the same thing in the end. He preferred not to think about it.

He faced Godfrey again, speaking gently. 'I have seen the Moorish doctors at work, and Byzantines, and I congratulate your efforts.'

'How could I leave her looking like that?' Godfrey muttered, then hurled his cup from him. It struck the wall, shattering and splashing red wine over the plaster. 'She's the same age as my daughter.'

Baldwin saw Hugh leap into view in the doorway, his hand on his knife. Waving him away, Baldwin peered at Godfrey. 'Your daughter?'

'It was many years ago. I don't think we realised that what we did would become a lifetime's commitment. But it has. Lady Elizabeth was already three-and-thirty years old, and I was five-and-thirty. Gracious heaven, how long ago it feels now!'

He wore a look of bemusement, as if there was truly little that could upset him now. Baldwin was sure that mostly this was a sign of his tiredness after the operation – the amputation had taken all of his nervous energy – but there seemed something else at the back of it. He maintained a steady silence, waiting for Godfrey to fill the emptiness.

'In those days, I suppose she was less certain of her vocation. She and I used to meet when I went to help the infirmarer. I found her kind, sweet, and gentle. I thought so then, and I still do now. She truly believes in what she does.

'Our Rose was a beautiful child. We should never have kept her, we should have sent her away to a wetnurse and ensured that she was given a Christian upbringing in another convent, but neither of us could face sending her away like a pet for which we had no further use. So we kept her here, although we didn't tell her who her parents were.'

'No, it took an especially vindictive woman to do that,' said Baldwin, recalling what Simon had told him of Rose's words.

'Margherita,' Godfrey agreed. 'The bitch has ice in her veins, I swear. Rose went bad from that moment. She wouldn't listen to her mother, wouldn't treat any of her duties seriously, simply ran riot. She thought that if her prioress could fail in *her* oaths, why should she even bother to try? I saw her sometimes, when I came here to help with the sick, and used to feel my heart break within me to see how she was tearing herself and her mother apart. And then she ran away – but not, thank God, too far away, and she still kept coming to see me. Jesus save me, but she offered herself to me once, in gratitude for listening to her, and when I refused, she wept on her knees at my feet, saying that at least I was honourable, and if only she could have copied my example instead of being a jade like her mother. Oh, God! Her words tore at me, showing me how I had sinned – and my penance was the worst of all, not even being able to confess to her that I was her father, for fear that she would turn against me as she had her mother, that she would run away, this time to become a whore in Exeter or London, somewhere where I couldn't help or protect her.'

Baldwin averted his gaze while the cleric sniffed and wiped his eyes on his sleeve. 'I think, Godfrey, you are lucky to have been able to know your daughter while she grew.'

Godfrey looked up and met Baldwin's eyes sadly.

'If only she could have known *me*!'

Chapter Twenty-Five

Hugh returned to his seat, but when he saw that Constance's pot was empty, he poured another measure for her.

She accepted his ministrations with gratitude. The operation had been hideous, and Constance was not convinced of its efficacity. Merely removing the limb without seeing to the inner body's humoural balance seemed wrong to her, and after seeing the bloody object lying on the floor, the shards of bone mingled with the sliced flesh, Constance could understand why people looked upon surgeons as no more than butchers.

'Drink it up and have some more,' Hugh suggested.

Constance shook her head weakly. She had the services to attend, the daily round of work to get on with, she couldn't just sit here and drink the day away. Looking up at Hugh she saw the kindness in his eyes.

It was so like Elias's expression when they had first met, she thought, and with that, to Hugh's consternation, she began to sob.

Simon and the Bishop arrived at the door to the nuns' cloister. Here Jonathan smiled nervously and proposed that they should wait while he went to warn his prioress, so that she could welcome Stapledon in a proper manner.

'You can go and tell her, yes,' Stapledon stated coldly, 'but I shall be two paces behind you.'

'My Lord, wouldn't you prefer that . . .' Jonathan began, but Stapledon waved him aside.

'You have the choice, Canon, of being there before me or after me, but do not again presume to try to alter my mind. Open this door!'

Shaking, Jonathan inserted his key and Stapledon sailed

through, Jonathan skittering after him.

Simon, grinning, watched the bishop cross the nave of the church and stand at the door to the nuns' cloister, tapping his foot until Jonathan realised that the bishop was waiting for him. Darting forward, muttering his apologies, Jonathan tugged the door wide. Stapledon and his staff-bearer instantly passed through, and Simon went after them, while Jonathan leaned against the opened door like a man who has seen a demon.

'My Lord Bishop! It is an honour, and what a relief to see you once more at our humble convent.'

As the Lady Elizabeth crouched before him, kissing his ring, Stapledon peered shortsightedly around the garth, sketching a cross over her head. 'Take me to your chapterhouse, Lady Elizabeth. We need to speak.'

Simon was about to follow, but he knew that the chapterhouse was one place he would not be welcome. It was the hall where any important matters for the community would be discussed, and such things were best hidden from laymen. Instead he set off for the dorter, thinking to see his friend, but as he approached the door, he recalled the screams which had issued from the infirmary. The idea of seeing Cecily's mangled body was not appealing, and unconsciously Simon bent his steps towards the frater.

Denise sat inside, alone apart from her regular companion, the jug of wine. She raised her pot to him, but then returned to her grim contemplation of the far wall. 'Right there,' she said. 'That's where I saw Agnes's shadow, there on that wall; just like Margherita's before.'

'Was anyone with her?' Simon asked.

'No, she was all alone. And then there was that scream!' Her eyes closed in apparent revulsion at the memory.

'Where were you when Elias ran through here?'

She put a hand to her mouth as she burped. 'In the buttery. Getting more wine.'

He himself wished to go to the buttery for an ale; turning on his heel, he went outside into the yard. Something made him cross the yard to the room where Agnes's body had been found. It already felt like days ago.

The room was open. A sow was snuffling at the thick gouts of clotted blood on the straw of the floor where Agnes had lain. Simon angrily kicked the big animal out. It was incredible that so many deaths could have occurred one after the other. In a town like Crediton there would not have been so many in so short a space. And now Cecily would likely die as well.

Simon turned to go back to the buttery, when his eye caught a glimpse of something. Crouching, he picked at a thread lying on the ground. It was snapped, but Simon could see that each end was securely tied, one to a hinge, the other to a protruding nail in the doorframe, both a little over a foot above the threshold. At just the height to trip someone, he realised.

Deep in thought he made his way back to the frater and fetched a cup and jug of ale. He was alone now – Denise had gone. Thank God, he thought fervently. The last thing he wanted was her chatter.

Pouring, he drank deeply, staring across at the wall opposite, where Denise had seen Margherita when Moll died – and Agnes last night.

At first Simon thought it odd that Denise hadn't seen Agnes being followed. Surely the same light which had illuminated the novice's form should likewise have lit up her attacker? Then he shrugged. Agnes's attacker was already in the room and had stabbed her without Denise seeing. The tripwire showed that: surely the killer had been hiding in the room, and when his victim tripped the killer stabbed.

Could it have been Luke? Elias confirmed that he had taken the alley along the church's wall towards the garden. From there he would have circled around the claustral buildings and come to the yard. He could have stabbed Agnes and withdrawn, but if he had, he would have been able to get to the church before the alarm was raised, and finding the communicating door closed, would have gone elsewhere to hide, surely?

Luke said it was his own cry that had alerted the nunnery, and Simon was inclined to believe him.

What about Margherita? It was easy to suspect her. Except she had denied the murders on the Bible.

Elias was a possibility: what if he had lied? Couldn't he have gone through and stabbed Agnes, then returned later? If he had, it meant he must have set the tripwire when he was last in the convent, and there was nothing to suggest he had been earlier, nor that he knew about the chamber. Who did?

Thoughtfully Simon went back to the yard. The alleyway beckoned, and he walked out along it. At the far side it gave out to a new yard, next to which was the herb garden beneath the infirmary's window, where Elias had said he would throw pebbles to waken Constance. Simon studied the ground, seeking the knife which had been used to murder Agnes, but could see no sign of it; if the killer had been here, the easiest means of concealing it was the wall – anyone could have thrown it over into the farmyard beyond. Simon retraced his steps and stood once more outside the room in which Agnes had died.

He couldn't help but keep returning to the same negative thoughts: there was no reason for Elias to have hurt Agnes so far as he knew. The man had no motive – if he'd stabbed in hot blood or fear, thinking she might report finding him there, he would not have remained with her body to ease her soul's passage. And then there was the cord: how could Elias have known Agnes would enter that room?

Luke had no reason to hurt her; what reason could he have for murdering his lover?

That left Denise, a woman prone to sitting up late in the frater.

Elias and Luke had seen Denise in the cloister. Both had said that she was there when they came out from the church. And Luke was in the cloister before Elias. Could Denise have hurried from the cloister to the yard, killed the girl, and then dashed back to the frater in the time it took Elias . . . Simon's brow furrowed. Elias had said he ran through the frater when he heard Agnes cry out. Surely, if Denise had been there, he would have said? Yet where else could the sacrist have been?

Simon recalled the very first time he had met Denise. When

Baldwin had been questioning her about the first murder, the death of Moll, hadn't she expressed her disgust with the novices for their unholy attitudes and lack of commitment?

When Katerine had died, Denise had been in the frater, so she claimed. But she had said that while she had a novice with her, sitting beside her – Agnes, the last novice to have died. What if Agnes knew something about Katerine's death – that Denise had left the hall, for example? Could Agnes have kept quiet about something incriminating?

What could have made Denise want to kill the three girls? Simon's mind kept returning to the expression of disgust on the sacrist's face when she had spoken of the novices after they had inspected Moll's body. Denise had said that they had only an outward show of piety, that she would have had them thrashed; she implied that Moll was almost deserving of her end.

Denise disliked Moll because the girl had made comments about her drinking. Simon wasn't sure that a woman like Denise could have such deep beliefs that she might feel justified in killing – but perhaps she did. Then another idea struck him. Rose had said that Constance and Elias were having an affair; that they were behaving indecorously.

That brought dishonour to the convent as well, he thought. Their affair could be looked upon as a grievous insult to God.

Hugh was in the infirmary when Denise entered. She went over to the sleeping Baldwin and glanced at Hugh. 'How is he?'

When Denise turned to peer at the knight, Hugh stood conspicuously and brought his stool nearer.

Baldwin had started dozing as soon as Godfrey had left the room, and Hugh and Constance had helped him to lie down, pulling the blankets up to his chin. Now he lay as one dead, his face pale and contrasting strangely with his dark beard.

'I mean him no harm!' Denise said when she noticed Hugh's sudden approach.

Hugh studied her abstractly. Her face was flushed: the colour could have been caused by his perceived insult, but then it could also have been caused by drink – and wine or ale could remove a man or woman's fear of retribution, Hugh knew. He said nothing, but stared fixedly as she stepped away from Baldwin, her features darkening with anger.

'Why should I want to hurt him? He was only trying to find the murderer!'

'Yes,' Hugh agreed.

'Do you suggest that I am a killer?'

Hugh shrugged. As he opened his mouth to respond, Constance came from her chamber.

'Denise? What is it?'

'I came to see how this knight was, but this rude little serf accused me of trying to kill him.'

'I said nothing,' said Hugh comfortably.

Constance smiled wearily. She had slept badly the night before with all the excitement, and now this daft old alcoholic was trying to pick a fight so she must be drunk again. All Constance wanted was peace and quiet to reflect on Elias, and the inebriated sacrist was preventing her.

Still more annoying was the fact that Constance did not want Denise shouting in the room and waking the other two invalids. Adopting a tone of gentle persuasion, she suggested, 'Denise, why don't we go to the frater and talk? I could do with getting out of here for a while.'

'I've spent most of the morning in the frater,' Denise muttered, confirming both Hugh's and Constance's impressions.

'Why don't we walk in the garden, then? Some fresh air would do me good.'

Denise nodded. To Hugh's eye she looked almost ridiculously eager to take Constance away. 'Yes, out to the garden. It's nice and quiet out there.'

Bertrand was still panting slightly, an oily sheen of sweat breaking out upon his brow as he appeared before the Bishop of Exeter. 'My Lord, I am delighted to see you,' he declared, and bent to kiss the proffered ring. 'I trust your journey was not too strenuous?'

'Strenuous? No, not overmuch. Yet I would have preferred to travel straight to Exeter and see how things were rather than having to be diverted all the way here.'

'I know, my Lord. It is a disgraceful state of affairs,' Bertrand agreed unctuously.

'Certainly it is,' Stapledon said, peering around at the prioress who stood at his side. 'Three murders and the attempt to kill my friend Sir Baldwin de Furnshill. And then,' he added, 'a fool tries to suggest that my good friend and sister in Christ, Lady Elizabeth, was herself guilty of murder.'

'I was called here by—'

'A woman who wished to remove my Lady to gain power for herself,' Stapledon stated relentlessly. 'And I suspect you foresaw your own enhancement in the matter. You thought you might more speedily gain preferment.'

'Oh, my Lord, no! I was acting for the best interests of the convent.'

'Then who was the murderer of the three?' Stapledon asked silkily.

'I fear I do not know, but I am sure that . . .'

Stapledon eyed him with chill severity. Then he raised a hand and beckoned. Elias had been standing, unknown to Bertrand, just behind him, and the suffragan felt a sinking feeling as he recognised the canon.

'Elias, you shall go with the prioress to the dorter. The prioress will show you where to go. The treasurer has a large chest. You will bring it here.'

Simon rushed from the frater and went to the entrance to the dorter, pounding up the stairs to the infirmary.

'Sir?' Hugh asked.

Simon went to Baldwin and peered down at him. 'Has Denise been in here?'

'Yes, sir. She came in to ask about the knight, but then went out.'

'Which way did she go?'

'Constance suggested the orchard.'

Simon paused. 'Constance is with her?'

'Yes, sir. Said she wanted the fresh air.'

'Shit!'

The noise had woken Baldwin, although Cecily remained deep in her drugged sleep. Baldwin himself felt groggy, woken too soon from a deep slumber. He yawned and stretched, wincing at the quick pain in his head. 'What is it, Simon?'

'I think Denise is the killer, and now she's gone out with Constance.'

'Then go and find them!' Baldwin commanded. 'Leave me and go!'

'Stay here, Hugh,' Simon said and hurried out. On the stairs he came across the prioress and Elias. 'Prioress, I think Denise is the murderer, and she's gone out with Constance to the orchard. Constance might be in danger – where is the orchard?'

Astonished, she gave him directions, and Simon sped away. Elias hesitated, eyes as wide as a startled deer, staring at the prioress.

'My child, I don't know if this is a good idea or not, but Godspeed! Go and guard Constance,' she said, and Elias darted down the stairs after the bailiff.

The orchard was a clear space at the northernmost edge of the precinct. Although sheep and lambs wandered among the apple and pear trees, mumbling at the shin-high grasses, Simon could see no sign of the two women as he rushed along the wall. He was aware of Elias pounding along behind him, but the bailiff's attention was fixed upon the small pasturage, staring about, trying to catch sight of either nun.

He came to a gate, and leaped over, landing solidly and gazed about him wildly. Elias appeared at his side, his head slowly traversing from left to right. It was hard to see anything, the area was so overgrown. Trees stood with their branches unpruned, each looking like a small thicket in its own right, and while the two men should have been able to peer underneath the lowest branches, so many trees had toppled over and the grass itself was so long, that it was impossible to see anything.

Simon pointed. 'You go that way, halfway from here to the far wall, and wait for me. I'll go a similar distance to the right here, and then we'll go in. One of us must see them wherever they are.'

Elias nodded and ran off while Simon made his way further up. Turning, Simon made sure that Elias was in his place, then dived between the ranks of sturdy boughs.

He had to climb over a trunk within a few paces, and then he slipped and almost fell in a pile of sheep's dung, but he kept his head moving, peering intently between the trees, to his left, before him, and to his right, his head swinging regularly as he sought the women. At one point he thought he had found them, seeing a dark movement on his right, but even as he stopped and prepared to launch himself in that direction, he saw that it was a sheep covered in mud. Cursing to himself, he carried on.

The farther wall was in view now, and there was still no sign of them. Simon walked to it, filled with anxious dismay. There were already three deaths, and he felt panic clutch at his throat at the thought that he might be about to find another body.

Then he heard a shout from Elias.

When he looked, he could see no sign of the monk, but he felt sure that Elias needed him. He gave bellow and set off immediately.

'What was that?' Joan demanded, looking up.

Hugh sat still, poised on the edge of his seat. He hated sitting here while his master could be in danger, even if only from one mad nun, but he had been given his order.

Joan ran to the window. 'A call – a call from your master, Hugh.'

He stood, looked down at Baldwin, then over to the window, undecided. 'I can't hear anything,' he said wretchedly.

'I could swear it was the bailiff, and he was in pain,' Joan said, her expression anguished.

'He told me to stay here,' Hugh said, glancing back at the knight.

Baldwin shifted a little on his bed, groaned as his wound pulled. 'Hugh, if Simon is in danger, you should go to him,' he said painfully. 'I order you: go! I could never forgive myself if anything were to happen to him.'

Chapter Twenty-Six

Simon vaulted over a fallen trunk, ducked beneath a low branch, running along the line of the wall and staring between the trees until he saw the movement of a robe. Turning away from the wall, he soon came to the canon.

Elias was standing with his arms around Constance, and at her side, blearily glancing from Simon to Elias, was a befuddled-looking Denise.

Simon was so relieved, he almost sank to his knees in thanksgiving. Nodding to Elias, he said, 'Is she all right?' There was no need for Elias to answer. Simon smiled. 'You take her back. I'll bring Denise.'

Elias and Constance needed no second prompting. They walked back to the convent, he with his arm around her shoulders while she gripped his other hand in both her own. Although her eyes were cast demurely downwards, Simon was sure he saw a tear fall down beneath her veil.

'Come on, Denise.'

'Why? What's going on?' she demanded petulantly. 'I wanted to come out for a walk with Constance, and now you want us to return. What right do you have to order me around, eh?' She was drunk, very drunk, from the look of her, and couldn't help but slur her words a little, even when she spoke with care, enunciating slowly.

'It's no good, Denise,' he said. 'We know the truth. Why did the girls have to die?'

'How should I know?'

'Where were you last night when Elias ran through the frater?'

'I told you: out in the buttery. I heard him running, but I only caught a glimpse of him. I was filling my jug.'

'Why should Katerine and Agnes have died, Denise?'

'Katerine was a nasty little wench who sought power over others. She even tried to blackmail *me*, you know. Said I was drunk before a service, the sow! Asked me for money to keep hush. And Agnes . . . well, she never hid the fact that she liked men. Especially,' she gave a soft belch, 'that fair-haired, fair-skinned, fair-featured . . .' she looked about her blankly for a moment, seeking inspiration, then apparently gave up. '*Priest!* Nasty little man.'

'If all that were true, it was no reason to kill them!' Simon said heavily.

'I never said it was,' Denise agreed.

'So why did they die, then?'

'You'll need to ask the killer,' she said unperturbably.

Before Simon could speak further, he saw Hugh ahead, waiting at the gate. 'What are *you* doing here?' the bailiff asked.

'Well, we heard you shout and thought you might need help.'

'No, no. That was just because Elias had found Constance and Denise. Did you leave someone with Baldwin?'

'Joan's there.'

Joan stood over Cecily, tut-tutting in sympathy. The girl's features were drawn and appeared almost waxen, as if she would melt in direct sunlight or close to a warm fire.

It was strange to look down at her and see that abbreviated, mutilated stump where her arm should have been, and Joan crossed herself, thinking how curious it was that the one woman in the priory who was committed to helping the ill and bringing them back to full health had been the agent of God's will in destroying Cecily. It was not the outcome Joan had anticipated when Cecily had gone sprawling over her leg in the laundry.

Not that it was truly intentional. It wasn't from malice that Joan had made Cecily fall. It was God's will; He had made her grab Cecily's foot in that way so that He could punish Cecily for her foul language.

Joan shook her head slowly. God was kind. Perhaps He had

decided to allow Cecily to survive, even though she would always carry this wound marring her looks and potential – but maybe He would let a new arm grow from the stump! That, Joan thought, would be a miracle to rank with the best.

She left the lay sister's side and went over to Baldwin. Sitting at Hugh's stool, she beamed kindly at him. 'How is your head, Sir Knight?'

'It has been better,' he admitted.

'I am truly sorry it has given you such pain.'

Baldwin was half-asleep, groggy and feeble, and he only listened with a part of his attention, but he managed a smile. 'It was hardly your fault, Sister.'

'No. It was God's will,' she agreed seriously. 'And when He decides to act, there is little ordinary people can do.'

Baldwin said. 'It wasn't God Who attacked me.'

'Anyone is only a source of good, acting as He tells us, or bad, ignoring His instructions,' she explained gently.

'Whoever dropped the slate on me was not acting for God,' Baldwin said, closing his eyes. 'That person murdered a young novice, which was a blasphemy.'

'No, for God had ordained it. And she was of little importance, anyway. Just another of the young sluts that populate the world now. She would never have made a nun.'

'Of course she was important,' Baldwin said. 'She was only a youngster, a girl.'

'You can't understand, Sir Baldwin. I think God chose to protect the convent in the only way left to Him. He couldn't help but retaliate when these girls misbehaved so obviously.'

Baldwin looked at her, puzzled.

Joan went on carefully, as if trying to help him comprehend something terribly important: 'You see, Lady Elizabeth has ruined the place, and that goes against the Rule created to save souls. It's far too important for a philandering woman like her. She has disgraced her cloth.'

'Who should be in charge?'

'That's down to God, but Margherita's a good nun, and would

make an excellent prioress. She is reliable and pious. I've known her all her life. Ever since poor Bridget gave birth to her.'

Baldwin frowned. His head hurt abominably, but he knew it was crucial to keep concentrating. 'That was the nun who ran away?'

'She did.' Joan gave a thin smile. 'And came back with a child – Margherita.'

'But she ran away again, didn't she?'

'No, she didn't. You see, God was angry that she had disgraced her cloth. He told me to punish her.'

Baldwin suddenly felt calm. He was sure Joan was mad, and he listened carefully as she spoke.

'It was because of her affair with Sir Rodney. He was a very good-looking man, you know. He fell from his horse not far from here and was brought in to be nursed. Bridget was the infirmarer in those days, and she took care of him. When I realised what she was about, I remonstrated with her, but she wouldn't listen, and then she ran away. The bishop himself was involved in fetching her back. The shame she brought upon the convent! God demanded that she be punished, and put a hammer in my hand. I walked with her to a shed near the main gate one night, and inside it I struck her down. Then I buried her beneath the floor and burned it down. God told me to.'

Her features radiated calmness and reverence. Baldwin found it hard to keep his voice steady as he absorbed her story. 'So you would prefer to see Margherita in place?'

'Yes. I have looked after her since poor Bridget had to die, and God believes she would be the best woman for the convent. She would steer us out of the dreadful state we have got into.'

'Why did the novices have to die?'

'Those girls?' For an instant her face altered. An angry frown marred her serenity. 'Moll was nasty. I heard her speaking most sharply to Margherita, very disrespectful. And she spread rumours.'

'How?'

'She came to me and told me that Margherita was stealing

from the priory. Silly. God didn't want her to tell lies. He had to silence her.'

'You killed her?'

'No. God did – to protect Margherita. Katerine was no better: a nasty child, I am afraid, keen to use information about other people to bend them to her will. She had heard about Constance and was going to tell the world about her with her man. Terrible! Think how that would reflect upon the convent.'

Baldwin nodded seriously. 'And Agnes?'

'Ah, yes. Agnes,' Joan said primly. 'Well, she was a demon in human guise. She seduced that poor priest and bedded him many times. In the convent's precinct here, if you would credit it! Within the cloisters, often in that room where she died. Denise saw her only yesterday, out in the garden copulating like a wild beast! Disgusting!'

'And me?'

'I am sorry about the tile, but it was intended to kill you, not to cause a painful injury. I thought you saw me on the roof – and now God wouldn't want you to continue with your investigations. News would spread and if you finished your enquiry, the convent might be closed. And that would be displeasing to Him.'

'So it is best that I should be silenced?' Baldwin asked. He gave a small smile when she nodded. 'And then the bailiff? And after him the bishop?'

'Oh no. It's only the secular folk whose mouths must be stilled. I only have to dispose of your friend the bailiff and his servant.' She stopped, her head on one side as if listening. 'Oh yes, and Rose, of course. The prioress's bastard, the whore from the vill. She must die for her sins.'

'What of the prioress herself? She gave birth to Rose, after all.'

'She confessed and was given absolution,' Joan pointed out in a surprised tone. 'She has been pardoned by God.'

'Ah, I see.'

'I'm very sorry,' she repeated. As she spoke she reached into her robe and pulled forth a pair of small bottles. 'Dwale from Constance's stores,' she said, holding up one. 'And a bottle of pure hemlock juice. Her dwale contains some, you know, but there is enough in here to kill.'

She emptied the dwale into his cup, and held it out to him.

Baldwin shook his head slowly. 'I fear I cannot drink it, Sister. I choose not to submit to my murder.'

Joan sighed and set the pot back down on the table. Then, faster than Baldwin would have expected, she leaped on to him, straddling his chest. Picking up the cup again, she held it beneath his nose so that he could inhale the rich aroma of spiced wine. 'Come along, Sir Baldwin. If you drink this, you'll know nothing about the hemlock, I promise you. There's enough poppy syrup in this to make you forget everything and sleep. Otherwise I'll have to force you to drink the hemlock neat, and that wouldn't be pleasant.'

Baldwin was surprised at his defencelessness. Joan could only weigh a few stones, and yet he was suddenly aware that with her seated on his chest, her knees pressing on his upper arms, in his weakened state he was almost incapable of protecting himself. She pressed the rim of the cup to his lips, trying to force him to open his mouth, pushing harder and harder, until he became anxious that she might break his teeth. He opened his mouth and took a long draught, but as she smiled down at him, he spat it full in her face.

While she gasped with disgust, wiping her cheek ineffectually with her sleeve, he lifted his legs and rolled to one side, using the leverage of his whole body. She was tipped a little off-balance, enough for him to be able to free an arm, and he shoved at her hard. With a short squawk she fell.

Quickly he stood, but almost immediately reeled. Rising after the burst of energy disorientated him, and he toppled backwards, raising a hand to his head. It felt as though someone had slammed a sledgehammer at the back of his skull, and he retched with a sudden sickness that seemed to come up from the soles of his feet while the room span about him.

He became aware that Joan was up again. She glowered at him as she might at a recalcitrant novice, one who was resolutely incompetent at repeating the *dies irae*. Muttering under her breath, she retrieved her little bottle, and approached again. 'I'm sorry about this, it's bitter, but the dwale has gone so you'll have to take the hemlock neat.'

'I think I prefer not to,' Baldwin said. He was suddenly struck with the impression that this was a weird dream. It must surely end soon.

'It's God's will,' she said relentlessly. 'Do you want to oppose Him?'

Baldwin retreated. He had no wish to fight with her; she had a wiry strength in her body, and in his present enfeebled state he wasn't sure he could protect himself. 'I only oppose you, Sister Joan. I think you have mistaken His will.'

He saw her shake her head in irritation, and then her eyes lit upon the table. On it was Godfrey's toolbag. His blood-stained saw and razor lay near. Baldwin was about to try to jump forward and knock them from her when she pounced and snatched up the razor. Turning to him, she held it out. 'See? God puts everything in my hands.'

Baldwin could think of nothing to say. His head was swimming, his legs felt like putty, and his vision was slipping out of focus even as the pain in his head appeared to grow. He tried to move back further, but stumbled, and felt himself going over backwards. He was close to the wall, and although he flung an arm behind him to break his fall, his head caught the wall before his hand touched the floor, and agony thundered in his head – a sickening, throbbing spasm that made his belly clench and vomit up all its contents.

Baldwin could make out Joan's feet approaching him even as he felt himself slide away from consciousness and into a deep sleep.

'Joan?' Simon repeated. 'You left him in *her* care?'

'She's all right, isn't she?'

'If I'd been wrong and someone else was the murderer, Joan'd hardly be strong enough to protect Baldwin, would she?' Simon pointed out.

'Have you caught the murderer, then?' Denise asked innocently.

'*You*,' Hugh said sternly. 'We know you did it.'

Denise stopped dead in her tracks, her face a picture of shocked denial. '*Me!*' she squeaked.

Simon said, 'You were all alone on the night Moll died . . .'

'So were others!'

'And no one saw you when Katerine was killed.'

'I was in the frater.'

'And when Agnes was murdered, you were alone again.'

'I was in the buttery getting a drink!'

Simon looked her up and down, sceptically. 'Conveniently alone yet again.'

'So was Margherita, and the prioress, and Joan . . .'

'Certainly,' said Simon grimly.

Hugh frowned. 'You say you saw Joan last night?'

'Yes.'

'Where?'

'In the cloisters. I saw her walking about in the moonlight before I went to the frater. She's often there while the others sleep.'

Simon made his way at full speed to the gate, then along the wall, back to the cloisters. All the way he cursed his stupidity, his inane foolishness at following his gut feelings instead of staying with his friend.

He got to the garth and skidded on the flags, almost falling, but managed to recover his balance and pelted off along the corridor towards the door to the dorter, and all the way he recalled the happiness on Baldwin's face when he was married only a few weeks before. Jeanne, too, had been radiant on her wedding day.

Simon reached the door and pressed the latch, panting a moment, then lurched up the stairs. Jeanne would never forgive him if anything had happened to her husband.

Simon would never forgive himself.

Lady Elizabeth stood in horror, automatically stroking Princess.

Joan's words carried clearly out here to the prioress's chamber, and yet Lady Elizabeth was so stunned at what she had heard that she was almost convinced she had misheard the whole story.

Carefully she set the dog on the bed and walked to the door. Her duty was clear: she must protect Sir Baldwin, the invalid who had relied on her infirmary for his protection and recovery. As her hand touched the door, she heard the loud crash as Joan fell from Baldwin to the floor, and the sound made the Prioress think again. She went to her chest, threw open the lid, and withdrew a large dagger. Pulling it from its sheath, she went to her door.

She heard the clattering of feet on the bare boards, and Joan's exultant cry, 'See? God puts everything in my hands.'

The prioress thrust the door open. Baldwin lay on his side, a pool of vomit on the floor by his mouth. Joan was standing before him, a razor in her hand. She lifted it as the prioress came in and, with a snarl, launched herself at the startled Lady Elizabeth. The prioress thrust out her arm defensively – the dagger in her hand. Joan sprang forward and ran straight on to the blade, impaling herself. Lady Elizabeth felt it jerk and thrash as Joan screeched, slashing wildly in a futile attempt to cut Lady Elizabeth's face or stab her throat. As she watched in horror, Joan's shrieking subsided, and a curious confused expression came into her eyes. Then Lady Elizabeth's arm was dragged down as the older nun gradually slumped, her body unable to muster the energy to continue. Beneath her robe, the thick blood pooled on the infirmary floor.

When Lady Elizabeth looked down at her, Joan was still alive. She stared up at the prioress with a fierce loathing. Only then did Lady Elizabeth realise that her own arm had been slashed, that the whole upper part was criss-crossed with thin cuts. And only then was she grateful for the length of her arms, and the fact that Joan's were shorter.

Chapter Twenty-Seven

The staircase was steep, and Simon reached the top with his lungs tingling. He wanted to fall to his knees, to gasp, but he forced himself on, lurching to the door.

In the infirmary he found the prioress tending to his friend, who lay on the floor. The acrid stench of vomit filled the room, and Simon saw that Baldwin had been sick, but Lady Elizabeth was dabbing at Baldwin's face with rosewater.

She looked up as he entered. Simon fell to his knees beside Baldwin and stared. 'Is he all right?'

'Yes, though if I had been a few moments longer he wouldn't have been.' She stood. 'I fear Joan has died.'

Following the direction of her gaze Simon saw a slumped body near the door. 'What on earth has happened?'

'I heard them talking. She admitted to the murders,' the prioress said in an exhausted tone. She moistened Baldwin's brow. 'She wanted to protect the priory from any stain on its reputation. She thought the three girls were evil, and thus deserved death. She was going to kill you as well, if she could. Purely because she had to stop the spread of rumours about the place. Didn't want Sir Baldwin or you or other outsiders talking about what you might have seen here.'

She started to her feet, but tottered, and Simon had to go to her side and grip her elbow. Giving him a weak smile, she insisted that he should leave her, and that he and she should lift Baldwin on to a bed, but Simon led her to a chair. She had just sunk down into it when Hugh appeared in the doorway. Denise, behind him, was immediately despatched to let the waiting bishop know what had happened and as she scampered away, Hugh helped Simon lift the knight back to his bed.

Once Baldwin was settled, Simon bent to the figure of Joan. She lay like a crumpled parchment, and there was a stain spreading over the floor. Simon glanced up at the prioress.

'I had no choice,' she said simply. 'And now, could you call Godfrey? Your friend needs his help.' And so do I, she added to herself as she felt the sharp tingling of the razor-sliced flesh beneath her tattered habit.

Simon remained at Baldwin's side in the infirmary, a grim, anxious temper overwhelming him. His friend had taken on a deathly pallor, almost blue-white, his lips grey, his breath coming in stuttering bursts. While Godfrey carefully treated Lady Elizabeth, using a styptic on her wounded flesh and cauterising the worst slashes, Simon watched over Baldwin, miserably convinced that his friend was dying. He had seen so many men die, some from stabbing, others from illness, that the signs before him appeared unequivocal.

Godfrey left Lady Elizabeth to Constance, who set about gently wrapping her wounds. He walked to Simon's side and took Baldwin's hand, studying the knight's face.

Simon wanted to ask whether his friend would survive, whether Baldwin would ever open his eyes again, and he was about to question the canon, when Godfrey walked out to Constance's room. He soon returned with a small oil lamp and a handful of feathers. These he dropped unceremoniously on Baldwin's chest. Taking two or three, he held them under Baldwin's nose while he singed them with the flame.

Baldwin coughed, groaned, his eyelids fluttered, and he winced, before retching and bringing up a small gobbet of vomit.

It was then that Godfrey shrugged. 'He'll be fine.'

The relief made Simon sag on his stool. Suddenly he realised how exhausting the last hours had been. He managed a grin and stood. 'I'll leave him in your care.'

Outside the sun had decided to escape its confinement behind the clouds. The garth was filled with a renewing warmth. Simon stood, eyes closed, soaking in the energy.

'Perhaps you should yourself be resting.'

'Constance, I think I shall have to.'

She walked over to a stone bench, sat and folded her hands in her lap. 'Why don't you sit?'

He took his place at her side, sitting down heavily. 'It's lucky Joan confessed,' he said quietly.

'Yes. Otherwise we might never have known who was responsible.'

'Except she couldn't have killed Moll.'

Constance shot him a look. 'What do you mean?'

'I know little about dwale, but I do know this: the older the person, the faster it will act. And you told us that Joan had taken her dwale.'

'I can't have given her enough.'

'You think so?' he asked. 'You don't really, do you?'

'The prioress said Joan confessed to the murders. Why should she lie?'

'Simple. To protect someone else. Someone she wanted to protect.'

Constance blanched and gazed at him fearfully. 'I swear I had nothing to do . . .'

'I didn't mean you, Constance. Joan believed someone else had killed Moll: Margherita.'

'But why should Joan want to protect *her*?'

'Guilt, perhaps? She had killed Margherita's mother Bridget, after all. Forever after she was Margherita's closest ally. She certainly seemed to want her to win the prioressy.'

'Why did she kill the other girls?'

'I think it's easy to speculate. Moll could read and add, and she saw Margherita embezzling funds. Margherita was a powerful lady here, and Moll wouldn't have dared to confront her directly. Instead, she went to a woman she trusted – Joan. You all used to go to her with little problems, didn't you? Or perhaps Moll did dare – yes, that's it! She told Margherita what she knew, and Margherita refused to confess in chapter; that was when Moll spoke to Joan.'

'So Joan *did* murder her?'

'No. But when Moll died, Joan was convinced it was Margherita. And when she heard Katerine telling the same story, spreading it among the novices, Joan decided to protect her candidate for the prioressy by killing off the story at its source.'

'What about Agnes?'

'I think Joan was mad. She couldn't bear to see her priory being ruined, and she thought that the place was falling about her ears; she wanted Margherita to take over Lady Elizabeth's job. That way, she thought, Belstone would be protected. But Agnes was a threat. If news of her behaviour with Luke should get out, Sir Rodney wouldn't dream of supporting the place.'

'Surely Sir Rodney would take a more pragmatic attitude? He wanted a place for his bones, and at least St Mary's is near his home.'

'He would be very pragmatic, I think. He'd think only the priest can hold Mass over his chapel; Luke, a man who has been subverting novices and enjoying their bodies. Surely the least desirable priest in the country.'

'So Joan thought she should kill Katerine and Agnes to protect the convent?'

'And to protect the woman she loved.'

Constance shook her head in slow disbelief. 'So you think Margherita . . .'

'No!' Simon said. 'She was innocent; she swore that on the Bible, although she wouldn't swear a lie about taking the money.'

'Then who?'

'What happened on the night Moll died?'

'I gave out dwale before Compline.'

'To all your patients? Did you do that every night?'

'Not usually. But Elias was coming to see me.'

'Was it the same mixture you gave to all?'

'All of my patients had the same.'

'What then?'

'Elias arrived some time after, and when I went to the door, he made a sign to be silent. He had heard Margherita behind him.

Soon she was there, but she stood on the landing for some time before knocking at my door.'

'She'd have been listening to see if the man was in with Lady Elizabeth.'

'After a while she came and banged on my door. She was so noisy.'

Simon drew in a breath. 'Where was Elias?'

'In my chamber.'

'Margherita didn't see him?'

'I blocked the door and pushed her out, talking to her on the landing.'

'And then?'

'I told her not to be so silly and went back to Elias,' she said, avoiding his gaze. 'I had to tell him about our child, and he hugged me and began planning our departure from the convent.'

'Did he leave you then?'

'No. We were together all the time. I didn't sleep,' she asserted with a maidenly blush. 'When it was near the time for the bell we rose and went down to the cloister; he needed time to get back to the canonical cloister, and I had to wash.'

'Moll was alive then? So you left him when you went to the laver?'

'Yes, but I'd seen him go to the church already.'

'What would have stopped him turning and returning to the infirmary?'

'There was no need!'

Simon looked away. 'What if Margherita's noise had woken Moll, for example, and she saw Elias there?'

Elias sat alone on a bench near the frater. Simon saw him from the church's door and crossed the grass to him.

'Elias, Joan is dead. She confessed to the killing of Katerine and Agnes.'

'I had heard. News like that gets around quickly.'

'I thought you could help me with Moll's death.'

'Me?' Elias attempted a surprised note, but only succeeded in sounding peevish and fearful. 'Why me?'

Simon stared at his boot. 'Because you were in the room with Constance. Joan was asleep – the dwale – and Margherita knocked on the door but was turned away by Constance. But Margherita made a lot of noise. I think Moll woke and saw you.'

Elias closed his eyes and let his head fall into his hands. When he looked up it was with a kind of resolution. 'I saw her eyes widen. You don't know what she was like! She stored up anything to threaten other people. Any sort of information; it didn't matter what, so long as it served to make her look holy.

'Margherita banged on the door and Constance kept her from entering. I think Margherita was pleased Constance was alone because it confirmed her thoughts about the prioress. When she'd gone, that was when Constance came back and told me about our child. That was when I realised how much of a threat Moll was. If she was to tell the prioress, we'd be separated for ever. Constance would be sent away to another convent, and I'd be shipped to a strict monastery in Scotland or Ireland. I'd never see my own child.

'The only thing in my mind was that Moll could ruin everything. It kept going round and round in my head, that I was to have a child, and that Constance and I should try to run away and escape. And that Moll threatened us both, and our child.'

'How did you kill her?'

Elias swallowed hard. 'I sat on her chest and held a pillow to her face until she stopped breathing. Then I slit her artery.'

'And this was while the church service went on? You were alone in there?'

'Before the church service. Constance and I went down, and I walked off towards the church, but it was as if I was *pulled back* to silence Moll. I didn't want to, but she threatened our future lives.'

Simon nodded and stood.

Elias gripped his robe. 'You don't have to tell anyone, Bailiff. Leave it to me to confess. I shall, I swear, just as soon as I—'

Simon shrugged himself free. 'I was sent here to investigate a murder. Do you expect me to keep the truth from the bishop?'

It was two days later that Bishop Stapledon stood in the chapter-house and eyed the nuns with a scowl.

'You have heard the story, God help us all. Does anyone have any further comments?' he rumbled.

Margherita stepped forward. Her head was lowered, as it had been for the previous days, and her voice was muted. 'I beg forgiveness from my sisters. I have behaved appallingly, and don't deserve to be forgiven, but I have confessed my sins and the good bishop has given me my penances.'

'Sister Margherita has insulted the whole convent,' Stapledon said. 'She has shown herself to be contemptible and cannot continue as treasurer. As well as her personal penances, she must demonstrate her absolute humility. I have decided that for the next year she must lie at the door to your church at every service. You will all step over her on your way inside.'

'I have returned all the money I took,' Margherita said, and her voice trembled. 'And I have thrown away my chest.'

'As will the rest of you,' Stapledon growled. 'This is a convent. Your Rule forbids private possessions. Likewise, when the roof has been mended, any partitions will be taken down. You are all equal here, and all will have the same space, the same belongings . . .'

Lady Elizabeth could not help her mind wandering as he continued. Would there be mention of her dog? Ah yes.

'And no more dogs! The only pets suitable for you are cats, because at least they perform a useful function. But you won't have them in the church during services or at any other time.'

Lady Elizabeth winced, but wasn't overly concerned. Princess was not going to be thrown from the convent. She would remain with the prioress, no matter what the bishop said.

Stapledon moved on. In this speech he covered every aspect of their Rule, and when he was sure they understood, he turned to watch Bertrand while he wrote furiously confirming the bishop's commands. Bertrand did not look happy, Lady Elizabeth noted with pleasure.

Neither did some of her nuns. Denise had not recovered from the bailiff's accusation that she might be a murderer, and she stood glowering bitterly at her place. Constance was unhappy too. The nun stood with her face cast down, like a young novice accepting a severe sentence after misbehaviour. Lady Elizabeth shook her head slowly. So young to be so unhappy, but she had taken the vows. The prioress frowned, but was drawn away from dangerous thoughts by the Bishop's raised voice:

'. . . And in future you will not be drinking until all hours after Compline. This kind of behaviour leads to shame – for you here among your servants, but also abroad, for news of your behaviour will spread to the outside world. It will also lead to oversleeping when you should be at services,' he said glancing meaningfully at Denise, 'and that means you miss your duties. This will stop. In future you will *all* attend *all* services unless there are excellent reasons why you should not.'

'Thank you, Bishop,' Lady Elizabeth said soothingly. 'We understand your anger and we shall of course do all within our power to atone for our past sins.'

'There is one last detail. Sister Margherita wrote to my suffragan suggesting that the prioress here had embezzled funds. That was untrue. She alleged that your prioress was guilty of murder. That was untrue. I find there is reason for censure of Lady Elizabeth, but not sufficient cause to remove her from office. I expect you to support her in her difficult role. I would have removed Margherita and sent her to a more strict convent, but the prioress herself begged for compassion. Because of her pleas I have decided she may remain here.'

Lady Elizabeth smiled graciously. 'Now, is there anything else to be discussed?'

In a few minutes the meeting had closed and the nuns were all on their way to their work.

Constance had listened with quiet sadness, and now turned

slowly and with a sigh to go to her place of work. There was much to be done now: Cecily was beginning to recover, and Sir Baldwin was healing nicely after his ordeal. She was in the cloister and making her way to the infirmary when the bishop and Bertrand overtook her. They reached the door before her and disappeared. She was about to enter herself when she felt a finger touch her shoulder.

'Prioress?'

'Constance, you looked so tired in there.'

'No, I am fine, my Lady. Just . . . well, you know. I miss him.'

'Hardly thoughts a young nun should entertain,' the prioress said primly. 'Your mind should be set upon higher things, not men like a lovesick novice. How old are you?'

Constance reddened under Lady Elizabeth's attack and said coldly, 'One-and-thirty, my Lady.'

'After so many years you should know your duties. How long have you been a nun?'

'Nine years.'

'My word, really?' the prioress exclaimed.

Constance heard an edge to her tone. She shot the prioress a look. Lady Elizabeth was studying a novice at the far side of the cloister. 'Look at that child. She wants to be a nun, but she can hardly set her wimple straight on her head. Three-and-twenty is too young to take the vows. How can a girl tell her vocation at such an age?'

'Some of us know our vocation!' Constance declared with feeling. She was silent as the prioress cast her a sly look.

'Really? And look how they show it!'

'That is unfair. I struggled and was found wanting, but I will not fail again,' Constance said, feeling the tears start. She sniffed and wiped them away.

Lady Elizabeth turned away. The novice was seated at a stone bench set into the wall. 'So young . . . well, no matter. Until she is four-and-twenty, her oaths would be invalid. No woman can become a nun until then.'

So saying she entered the frater, and she smiled as she heard

Constance give a short gasp of comprehension even as Elizabeth set her foot upon the first of the stairs.

Chapter Twenty-Eight

'So! Sir Baldwin, I see you are quite the warrior when it comes to fighting old women.'

The knight eyed the bishop with a bitter grimace. His head was not better for his exertions. 'Put it down to chivalry, my Lord Bishop. I wouldn't wish to hurt a poor woman of her advanced years.'

Stapledon laughed. 'I'm glad to see you are well enough to banter. How is it?'

Simon stepped forward. 'Godfrey says he needs to rest. Later Godfrey will bleed him to remove some of the evil humours.'

'You say that a surgeon will be called, Bailiff?' Stapledon said pointedly.

'Yes,' Simon grinned. 'A surgeon from afar.'

'Good. A clerk in major orders couldn't undertake such a duty.'

'Do we know what led to all these murders?' Bertrand asked. He stood nervously behind the bishop, reed and ink ready to note any details.

Stapledon glanced at him, considering, but when he faced Simon and Baldwin he nodded. 'It should be recorded.'

Simon took his seat upon a stool. 'The reasons *why* are quite straightforward: for reputations. It all started years ago with Sister Bridget, who ran away and became pregnant, giving birth to Margherita. Bridget returned to the convent, although whether she was caught or voluntarily returned . . .'

'She was caught,' said Lady Elizabeth, who entered at this moment. 'But you never heard the beginning. Sir Rodney came here one day because he had fallen from his horse. Bridget was the infirmarer at the time, and the two fell in love while she nursed him. Shortly after he went home she ran away to follow him. I was a young novice at the time, but I remember it well. The bishop had her sought and returned to us, but she carried the proof of her unchaste behaviour: Margherita. Bridget was here for only a few weeks, and then disappeared again. Joan said that Bridget had been despondent and hinted that she had run off again. When she disappeared, we all thought that was what had happened.'

Baldwin spoke softly. 'Even then Joan was unhinged. She murdered Bridget and buried her – she said in the floor of a shed near the gates – and then burned it to the ground.'

'I remember it!' Lady Elizabeth said. 'We thought that the fire was started to distract us from her escape – that Bridget herself had started it.'

'The fire was designed to conceal her murder,' Baldwin said. He threw a look to Simon, who stirred.

'So we come to the more recent deaths. Joan heard that Moll thought Margherita had stolen from the priory's funds.'

Again Lady Elizabeth was able to help. 'Joan was the oldest nun. Many novices would tell her secrets they wouldn't share with their closest friends.'

'That must have been it,' Simon agreed. 'Moll saw what the treasurer was doing and didn't know what to do with the information.'

'Usually she would speak to whoever was guilty of breaking the Rule in some way,' said Lady Elizabeth. 'But I think she was awed by the size of the crime and by Margherita's position. Maybe she sought advice from Joan. Joan was old and Moll probably thought she would know how best to deal with such a thorny problem.'

Stapledon frowned. 'How would a novice have learned such a thing?'

'Moll could read and add,' Simon said simply. 'It was her misfortune. If she was like the other girls, she would have had no idea what was happening. Although I still don't know how she realised that Margherita was taking the money.'

Bertrand looked up from his paper. 'I can explain that,' he said.

'I saw the discrepancy myself on the rolls when I looked at the figures given to the priory; I was present at one meeting when money was handed over, and so was Moll. Perhaps she saw the numbers put in the ledger and asked Margherita why they didn't match.'

'And Joan,' said Simon, 'was convinced that when Moll died, Margherita must have done it. Joan never realised Elias killed Moll to conceal his affair with Constance.'

Baldwin agreed. 'Joan was intensely protective of Margherita. Perhaps even in her madness Joan felt her guilt of making Margherita an orphan.'

'Which leads us to the other two,' the bishop observed.

Simon took up the story again. 'Katerine was sly; she sought out secrets and used them for her own advantage. I think Katerine had learned about Margherita's theft. Anyway, for whatever reason, Joan decided that she had to be silenced. Joan must have tricked her into going with her to the church then she bludgeoned her skull. Perhaps with a candle-holder. Denise has mislaid one recently. Joan must have carried Katerine's body up to the roof. There she saw Baldwin walking about the cloister and thought he must have recognised her.'

'I didn't,' Baldwin said ruefully. 'I had an eyeful of snow at the time.'

'Joan hurled a slate at him before tumbling Katerine's body over the parapet.'

'*Carried* her to the roof, did you say?' Stapledon demanded. 'A woman her age?'

Baldwin gave a faint smile. 'She had been the priory's cellarer for twenty or more years, Bishop. She could have picked *you* up and taken you up those stairs, I daresay!'

'Good God!'

'And lastly there was Agnes,' said Simon. 'Agnes was carrying on an affair with the priest: Joan decided to end their fun. She knew where Luke and Agnes were to meet – Rose told Simon that Agnes and other nuns used that room on occasion – and she set a tripwire at the doorway, hoping to catch them like beasts in a trap. As soon as Agnes came in, she fell and Joan was on her. The novice didn't stand a chance. If Luke had arrived first, he would probably be dead now, too.'

'Did no one see her about her murderous business?' Stapledon asked.

Simon said, 'Nobody saw Katerine or Joan going to the church: everyone else was at work. As for Agnes, Joan managed to get downstairs while the convent slept. Agnes would have passed her empty bed, but probably thought Joan was still in the infirmary and didn't realise the woman was to be her nemesis.'

'This is all very well, but I don't see how she could have thought she could cover up so many deaths. You say she had the interests of the convent at heart, yet if news of these murders gets out, the place will be ruined.'

Baldwin winced as he cocked his head. 'It is not easy to understand how a madwoman's mind works, but I think that the convent and Margherita came together in Joan's mind. She thought that she must protect the child whose mother she had killed, and that meant seeing Margherita taking Lady Elizabeth's job; but she also wanted to see that the convent was safe for the future. The two became one in her mind: Margherita, she thought, needed help and Joan must set her in charge of the priory; the convent needed protection because of the way it was falling apart, and the prioress must be replaced because Joan blamed her. Margherita must lead the nuns back to piety.'

'And all Joan managed,' Lady Elizabeth said sadly, 'was to wreck our future.'

'Not necessarily,' said Stapledon. He stood. 'I shall remove your present vicar, my Lady. I am not sure how he arrived here in the first place, since I personally instructed Bertrand here to send him to a parish in the far west of Cornwall.' Bertrand squirmed shiftily as the bishop continued, 'But I shall find out the reasons. For now, I propose to visit Sir Rodney and ask him to continue with his generous offer.'

Lady Elizabeth smiled sadly. 'I fear he would prefer a monastery to be the recipient of his largesse.'

'Well, I shall have to try. He has responsibilities here. Such as his daughter.'

'That,' said Lady Elizabeth, 'is the problem. Agnes is dead.'

'I meant Margherita. I shall point out to him his opportunity of seeing his soul honoured by those he has most wounded in his life,' Stapledon said with an unpleasant smile, 'and if he doesn't listen, I'll put the fear of God into him!'

Luke was at the altar of the canonical church, praying, when the three came through the communicating door. Hearing them, he started and clambered to his feet. 'My Lord Bishop, I am so happy to see you once more and—'

'I doubt it,' Stapledon said drily. 'How did you get to come here?'

'To pray today?'

'No. *Here* in charge of the souls of a convent of nuns.'

'Your orders, Bishop.'

'*My* orders?'

Luke nodded disingenuously. 'Of course, sir.'

Bertrand felt the eyes of the bishop light upon him. 'I only obeyed your orders, Bishop. I wouldn't have sent Luke here if you hadn't told me to.'

'I think we shall find that my records show you are wrong,' Stapledon said smoothly. 'No matter. Luke, prepare to leave this place. I have a pleasant new post for you.'

'You wish me to be vicar of a little parish?' Luke asked hopefully.

Stapledon looked at him. 'I think I can do better than that.'

Hugh entered the infirmary as soon as the bishop and the others walked out. Simon was at the window, chatting to Baldwin and he scarcely appeared to notice Hugh. There appeared little point in remaining, not with Simon entertaining the knight, so Hugh accepted Constance's offer of a cup of wine and followed her down the stairs to the frater.

The nuns were so well-used to the sight of men in their cloister by now that they scarcely glanced in his direction, but Hugh felt out of place nonetheless. He wasn't used to the presence of so many women in religious garb.

Constance was quiet, sipping slowly at her drink. Hugh was confused when he watched her. The infirmarer was sad, and every so often she glanced about her at the other nuns, all of whom appeared keen to avoid meeting her eye.

'I'm sorry Elias has been sent away,' Hugh said kindly.

She toyed miserably with her cup. 'It's as if there's a hole in my life. Everything I had planned, expected, aimed for – has gone. I was happy as a nun, dedicating my life to God seemed better than some of the alternatives, but when Elias touched me, it was as if I'd been hit by a thunderbolt, and all my life changed. Especially when I found I was pregnant,' she said thoughtfully, looking down at her belly.

'What'll you do now?'

'Leave.'

Hugh blinked. 'But you can't, can you? You're here for life now you've made your oaths.'

'I made my oaths before I was old enough. The prioress has told me I can leave whenever I want.'

Unaccountably, her eyes filled with tears. Hugh glowered at the table as she snuffled and wiped them with her sleeve. 'I'm sorry,' she said. 'It's just that last week I had a lover and now I am carrying a murderer's child.'

'Better than carrying a murderer.'

'I suppose.'

'Or someone like Bishop Bertrand.'

She laughed at that, chuckling drily at first, but then, when Hugh joined her, laughing with sheer pleasure for the first time since Moll's death.

Chapter Twenty-Nine

It was a month since the bishop had left the convent, but Luke felt no comfort. He couldn't remember such irrelevant matters, not when his stomach was close to rebelling again. As the distant horizon rose, circled, swooped and suddenly dived before him, he closed his eyes in anguish. As if in sympathy, the contents of his belly rose and he leaned over the rail to retch.

The master of the boat strolled along to him with a blankly surprised expression on his face. 'You all right?'

'When will this storm abate?'

The master eyed him dubiously, then cast a look at the mild swell. 'Don't rightly know, Father,' he answered diplomatically. 'But we'm soon in port and safe there.'

Luke gave one more heave and collapsed on the bare boards, wincing from the bile. His mouth was sour, his teeth roughened by acid, and his only desire was to leave this miserable cog before it was wrecked. Death was attractive.

'Damn the bishop!' he groaned, then returned to the side of the ship.

It was all Stapledon's fault he was here. A new place, he'd said. Somewhere Luke would be safe from fleshly temptations.

In Ireland.

Luke made his way to the barrel of fresh water and rinsed his mouth. He dared not swallow any, for fear of more sickness, but swilling and spitting it out made him feel a little refreshed.

'Will this gale never cease?'

Luke felt another spasm threaten. 'Only when we arrive in port,' he grunted.

'Where is this Trim, anyway?'

'Bertrand, if you don't know where, that's your trouble.'

Bishop Bertrand sank weakly to the deck. 'Stapledon has sent us to our graves,' he lamented.

Luke spat again. The gobbet was caught by a gust, flew along and landed on Bertrand's shoulder.

This was Stapledon's sense of humour, Luke knew. Bertrand wanted promotion, and Luke had to be found a place where he would find it difficult to molest women; the answer was to send both to the wild lands of Ireland. Together. Luke would be the vicar to the de Greville family at their castle at Trim, and Bertrand would serve the bishop. Bertrand would have no opportunity for politicking in a new place where he knew no one, and where all his colleagues would distrust him as a foreigner – worse, an Englishman.

And matters would be as bad for Luke. Set down on this grim and forbidding island to see to the miserable garrison of the castle, there would be little opportunity to seek out interesting companions to relieve the monotony.

Although at present, Luke thought, rolling forward to rest his slackly open mouth against the gunwale, a little monotony would be infinitely preferable to this terrible wretchedness.

Baldwin and Simon arrived back at Baldwin's house just as a carter was setting off. Baldwin gave it an anxious look before glancing suspiciously at his house.

'More furniture?' Simon asked, laughing at his friend's expression.

'I could swear that was William Lodestone,' Baldwin agreed. 'He makes chests. We have enough chests. Why should a chest-maker be here?'

'Perhaps your lady doesn't think you have enough.'

'Possibly not.'

Simon watched as Baldwin swung his leg over his horse and dismounted carefully. Baldwin was not happy to be helped. 'Makes me feel like an old man. Get your hands off,' were his most common comments, but Simon was nervous to see how he was pushing himself.

With his stubbled hair where Godfrey had shaved his scalp and the wicked scar that reached from the top of his scalp to behind his ear and down almost to his shoulder, Baldwin looked like a man who had returned from a vicious battle.

Grooms took their mounts and a falconer took their birds.

'When will he be back?' Baldwin asked.

'I told him he could stay away as long as he wanted, but I don't think he'll be very long.'

'He hasn't left permanently?'

'I don't think so. Hugh's a miserable bugger at the best of times. Never really talks much, as you know. But I think he likes the family too much to stay away for long. He's helping her, that's all. He won't marry her.'

Baldwin glanced at his friend. He was about to speak when Edgar appeared in the doorway. Edgar took the heavy satchel of game from Simon before leading the way inside.

At the sight of his wife, Baldwin grinned. Jeanne was sitting innocently at the fire, her hands decorously clasped as if she had never met a carpenter or joiner in her life and never opened his purse to one.

'Husband, I thought you would be out for longer.'

'Aha! I know that well enough. What is it? A new chest, or maybe a table?'

For all his banter she could see he was exhausted. There were dark rings beneath both eyes and although he didn't teeter, he gave every indication of being close to falling. Yet she knew he hated to be cosseted, or to admit to needing assistance. The nearest he had ever come to losing his temper with her was when she had tried to help him across the hall when he and Simon had first arrived back from Belstone.

Jeanne was not devious, but she was worried for her husband. That was why she was glad to be able to give him something useful. She stood and motioned to Edgar. 'Bring it now, please.'

With Wat helping him, Edgar brought in the new chair and set it near the fire.

Baldwin walked over to it. It was a solid throne of fresh, light-coloured oak, carved ingeniously to incorporate his arms. 'It is lovely,' he breathed.

'Then sit in it, husband, and make sure it is comfortable,' she said lightly. She took the tray from the girl who had brought the wine and poured for Simon and her man, and as she leaned over Baldwin to give him his cup, she whispered, 'And may it persuade you never to leave me again.'

'To go somewhere and leave you to destroy all my chairs?' he asked and lifted an eyebrow sardonically. 'To be frank, if I never see Belstone again, I would be delighted.'

He sat and felt the muscles ease in his legs, the tiredness washing over him. He knew that matters would get worse. The reports from the Marches hinted at men-at-arms preparing to fight the King's army. Once more the barons of England were being forced to wage war because of the King's favourites; his patronage.

But at this minute, Baldwin only knew that the chair fitted him like a glove. War could wait.

The bell rang and the cloisters echoed to the slap of monks' sandals pattering along the pavings towards the church.

Here the air was chill. Their breath froze, forming plumes before them in the nave as they shuffled uncomfortably into their pew stalls, leaning back against the tiny shelves designed to save their legs during the long hours of standing and singing or praying.

The candles guttered, the cheap tallow forming a noisome barrier to all thoughts of beauty. Swinging and delivering its perfumed cloud, the censer failed to overcome the other stenches: unwashed bodies from the lay brothers' stalls, damp woollen clothing, badly tanned leather.

At the signal the monks opened their mouths and began the first service.

Elias huddled miserably. He tried to keep up with the singing, but found it hard to concentrate. It was impossible with his workload and lack of sleep. There were no nuns here, so he was saved from temptation, but for all that his thoughts were constantly with Constance. He remembered her brow, her wide-spaced eyes, her lips, her breasts, her flanks, her belly.

When Stapledon had ordered that Elias be sent here to the wastes of Yorkshire, the bishop had thought he was setting Elias somewhere he could forget Constance and could live as a penitent, his faith saving him from depression.

Instead Stapledon had managed to ensure that Elias could never forget her.

Lady Elizabeth stood alone for a few moments as the others filed away. Head bowed, she offered another short prayer.

It seemed only right that she should do so. The only thoughts anyone had held about the woman had been sour, vindictive and bitter: she had shown her disloyalty by running away – and yet she was innocent of that.

The grave was a black, peaty scar in the grass. No stone was erected, only a little leaden cross.

'I thank you for having her buried.'

Lady Elizabeth turned and smiled at Margherita. 'It was the least we could do after suspecting her of apostasy for so many years.'

'She died without confessing.'

'So do many, but God will know her.'

Margherita nodded, but was silent, her head bowed. As the prioress watched her, Margherita's gaze went again to the three other graves. To Lady Elizabeth's knowledge Margherita had visited Agnes's every day since the girl's death. She had never known that she had a sister – even if only a half-sister. Dark patches appeared on Margherita's veil where tears marked the thin cloth.

Silently Lady Elizabeth moved away and walked back to the precinct.

There was much to do. Sir Rodney had agreed the final sums to be paid: workmen were already congregating ready to enlarge the church, expand the cloisters and, with Walter

Stapledon's assistance, destroy the dorter and frater and build new ones half as large again. As she approached the site, the prioress's face lit up. The scaffolding was lashed in place, stones from the quarry were arriving and being cut and dressed, and there was a wholesome bustle. Then her eye fell upon a familiar figure.

She hurried to the novice and interposed herself between the workman fingering his purse and the girl. 'Begone!' she roared at the man, who grinned sheepishly and walked off.

'Remember your place,' she hissed sternly. 'You're here to dedicate yourself to God!'

'Yes, Mother,' said Rose meekly, hitching up her veil to a more becoming level. 'I'll try to remember.'

Constance stood in her little garden, a frown of pain creasing her brow as she straightened. No matter how few hours she spent tending her plants, her back always ached: always had, ever since she'd been a novice.

Standing, she looked over at the view. Dartmoor was a hulking mass southwards, blue and grey with the distance in this dim light. Looking back from here, she could almost dream she could see the priory's sheep on the hills.

At least now, with summer fast approaching, the weather was improving. Today the sun had shone weakly almost from dawn, without even a drizzle of rain.

A movement in her belly made her smile with self-satisfaction, thinking that their child was as delighted as she herself. But her child would never know how lucky it was. For he would be born outside the cloister, and far from Belstone. He may never have a father, but her son would not feel the lack. And when he was old enough to learn, Lady Elizabeth had promised a place within the priory for the lad.

Constance pulled up a weed and considered her patch. There were most of the medicinal herbs here and she was sure that by the end of the summer she would be able to produce almost all the draughts she would be likely to need. There was a sense of comfortable fulfilment about her. Constance was happier than she had ever thought possible.

It had surprised her how the prioress had pointed out that Constance had not made her vows legally; it wasn't something that had occurred to her before, but it was true. Constance had made her vows when she was only two-and-twenty: too young for her consecration, although she had a niggling doubt at the back of her mind that refused to go away. All novices made their profession from the age of sixteen, as she had. The consecration was surely merely an affirmation of their oaths – but Lady Elizabeth had made her comfortable and insisted that she need not consider herself bound. If she were to leave, Lady Elizabeth would not try to have her recaptured.

The Lady had suggested that the priory's village at Iddesleigh would be grateful for a woman trained in leechcraft. She had even provided Constance with a carter to take her so she wouldn't get lost, and Rose as a chaperone. And a purse for the child.

At the time Constance had felt that the woman was trying to remove an embarrassing reminder of the horrible events when so many had died, but now she thought Lady Elizabeth had a different motive.

It was something the Lady had let slip while they spoke quietly one morning. 'I was always so grateful God had given me a daughter. It meant I could see her grow and spend much time with her. If He had given me a boy . . .'

She had leaned across and patted Constance's hand, and in that moment Constance understood. It was then that she decided she must leave the convent. She would never be able to leave her child with some unknown wetnurse outside the cloister.

And she was sure it would be a boy. Shyly she looked down at her belly. She knew who she would name him after.

There was a cracking, ripping, rustling roar from behind her, and she turned to see the elm toppling. It shuddered, then gradually accelerated towards the ground.

He was behind it, face still fixed in its morose glower, leaning on his axe. When he saw her, his features eased slightly.

'Hugh, do want some ale?'

And her son's namesake dropped his tool and joined her.

The Merchant's Partner

Michael Jecks

Fourteenth-century Devon . . .

Midwife and healer Agatha Kyteler is regarded as a witch by superstitious villagers of Wefford, yet she has no shortage of callers, from the humblest villein to the most elegant and wealthy in the area. But when Agatha's body is found frozen and mutilated in a hedge one wintry morning, there seem to be no clues as to who could be responsible. Not until a local youth runs away and a hue and cry is raised.

Sir Baldwin Furnshill, Keeper of the King's Peace, is not convinced of the youth's guilt and soon manages to persuade a close friend, Simon Puttock, bailiff of Lydford Castle, to help him continue with the investigation. As they endeavour to find the true culprit, the darker side of the village, with its undercurrents of suspicion, jealousy and disloyalty, emerges. And what is driving the young foreigner, son of a nobleman, who has visited the normally sleepy area only to disappear down towards the moors?

0 7472 5070 7

HEADLINE

The Demon Archer

Paul Doherty

The death of Lord Henry Fitzalan on the feast of St Matthew 1303 is a matter widely reported but little mourned. Infamous for his lecherous tendencies, his midnight trysts with a coven of witches and his boundless self-interest, he was a man of few friends. So when Hugh Corbett is asked to bring his murderer to justice it is not a matter of finding a suspect but of choosing between them.

Immediate suspicion falls on Lord Henry's chief verderer, Robert Verlian. His daughter had been the focus of Lord Henry's roving eye in the weeks before his death and he was not a man to take no for an answer. But the culprit could just as easily be Sir William, the dead man's younger brother. It is no secret that Sir William covets the Fitzalan estate – but would he kill to inherit it? The possibilities are endless, but the truth is more terrible than anyone could have imagined . . .

'The best of its kind since the death of Ellis Peters' *Time Out*

'Supremely evocative, scrupulously researched portrait . . . vivid, intricately crafted whodunnit' *Publishers Weekly*

'Wholly excellent' *Prima*

0 7472 6074 5

HEADLINE

Now you can buy any of these other bestselling books by **Michael Jecks** from your bookshop or *direct from his publisher*.

FREE P&P AND UK DELIVERY
(Overseas and Ireland £3.50 per book)

The Traitor of St Giles	£5.99
The Boy-Bishop's Glovemaker	£5.99
Belladonna at Belstone	£5.99
Squire Throwleigh's Heir	£6.99
The Leper's Return	£5.99
The Abbot's Gibbet	£5.99
The Crediton Killings	£6.99
A Moorland Hanging	£5.99
The Merchant's Partner	£6.99
The Last Templar	£5.99

TO ORDER SIMPLY CALL THIS NUMBER

01235 400 414

or e-mail <u>orders@bookpoint.co.uk</u>

Prices and availability subject to change without notice.